A CAPTIVATING CAPER

A Scandalous Spinsters Novel

MICHELLE HELLIWELL

ISBN: 978-1-9994965-8-6 (ebook)

Cover Design: Selena Blake

Editor: Donna Alward

Also by Michelle Helliwell

The Scandalous Spinsters
A Dangerous Diversion

Enchanted Tales
No Place for a Lady (novella)
Not Your Average Beauty
No Prince Charming
Never Trust a Rogue in Wolf's Clothing
Nothing Magical About Midnight

Praise for Michelle Helliwell

Strong, smart, and scandalous...a brilliant beginning to Helliwell's new series!

— DONNA ALWARD, NEW YORK TIMES
BESTSELLING AUTHOR

I'm a huge fan of Michelle Helliwell who writes a very special kind of love story.

— JULIANNE MACLEAN, NEW YORK TIMES BEST
SELLING AUTHOR

Michelle Helliwell is a master at pulling the reader in with her stories and not letting go until the end!!

— GOODREADS REVIEW

Michelle Helliwell is truly a gifted writer. She pens page turning books with clever, memorable characters that stay with you, unique plots with heart melting endings, and gorgeous, historical settings filled with beauty, charm and warmth. Be prepared to stay up past your bedtime!"

— - CATHRYN FOX, NEW YORK TIMES BEST
SELLING AUTHOR

For Rob

Acknowledgments

This story would not be in your hands if it was not for the multitude of people who supported me to bring it to you. A huge thanks to Donna Alward, my editor who understands my strengths and gently (but firmly) guides me over the rough patches and miraculously makes it look like I knew what I was doing all along. And to Selena Blake, who gave me a cover that once again makes me feel like a 'real author'.

I cannot express how much appreciation I have for Sue Slade and that fabulous community of readers at the Dartmouth Book Exchange, who support local authors with such devotion, and local romance authors in particular. They have been tireless in their support of my work, and the work of my fellow local authors, and I can't say enough about how lucky I am to have them in my corner. Thank you.

To Margrete, Chris, and the other hard working interpreters at Prescott House Museum, thanks for allowing me to use that precious space as a blueprint for Everwell Manor. Our museums are vital links to the past, and as we have important conversations about the impact of legacy on current social issues, they are more important than ever. They have been so inviting to me, inspiring me, and help bring Everwell to life for all of us. Everwell would be no where without you.

As always, I want to thank my husband Rob for his unflinching support, enduring bouts of loud sighs and grumbling about plot holes, and reminding me that it's all going to work out in the end. He smothers my doubts with his belief in me, and for that, and a million other reasons, will always be the hottest guy in the room, regardless of who else is in there with him. (My apologies to Henry Cavill).

Lastly, to my writer's group, the Romance Writers of Atlantic Canada, especially Cathryn Fox, Tim Covell, Kelly Boyce; and my writing colleagues beyond in Ottawa and Toronto, thank you for the community even through lock downs and cyberspace. In particular I want to thank Jacqueline Kennedy, Jacquelyn Middleton, Jenn Burke, Milly Bellegris, Hudson Lin and Roseanne Leo for all the likes, comments and little hellos on the socials. They keep a writer going and help create community which I so dearly appreciate. Thank you so very much for being part of such a vital Canadian romance community.

A note for the reader

The Scandalous Spinsters series is set in Kjipuktuk/Halifax, Canada.

This is a work of historical romance, maybe even historical fantasy. For those of you who know the city, this means some of places, the streets, and aspects of the city are based in what was actually so.

But it also means that some of it is entirely my own imagination—mostly in the realm of characters, but also some places and institutions that place a central role in this story.

For my readers from the U.S., and other parts of the world, this is also a signal that I'm writing in 'Canadian English' which means you will see some spelling differences throughout the text. They are intentional—just my actual 'voice'. I trust that you'll navigate them easily enough :) .

All the best,

Michelle

Chapter One

SEPTEMBER 22, 1875

The most satisfying part of thievery was not, in fact, the theft. It was the thrill.

The actual theft was inconsequential—except as part of a larger plan hatched by the Scandalous Spinsters to help women that neither polite society nor official channels saw fit to assist. Indeed, half the time Gemma had been tasked in one the Everwell Society's special projects, the only thing to steal was a secret.

It wasn't what was in the pockets Gemma picked effortlessly on a busy Halifax street that gave her satisfaction. The thrill that came with knowing that, at any moment, she could be caught. And Gemma Kurt loved it.

It reminded her of her days before the Scandalous Spinsters— when she was part of *The Flying Fabrizis*, her family's acrobatic troupe. Picking a pocket or slipping unnoticed into a place she didn't belong required quick reflexes and a light touch, and Gemma was gifted with both. The dark, the shadows, and a well laid-out plan formed the safety net. And then there was the rush of knowing that it could all fall apart.

For this job, she had expected no such thrill—simply recover a packet of papers that had been hidden by the former owner of a now unoccupied house on Barrington Street. The hardest part of the entire affair was supposed to be gaining entry to the place, which for Gemma wasn't particularly difficult. Pick the lock on the rear entrance, move through the kitchen, up to the first floor, to the butler's pantry behind the dining room, find the dumb-waiter shaft, pull out the envelope that was supposed to be shoved in the inside, and then leave the same way she came in. Simple enough.

And the first part had gone swimmingly. With a heavy morning fog rolling in off the harbour, the business of being unseen had been rather straightforward. Her fellow Scandalous Spinsters, Madeline Murray and Rimple Jones, were a block away waiting in their horse and buggy. They'd expected to have the early morning job done and be home at Everwell Manor by now, sipping on strong tea and getting ready for the day.

The elegant three-storey Georgian home had been unoccupied since its eccentric builder and owner, a Mr. Edgar Dalrymple, died a year ago. According to the papers, there had been no will, leaving his modest but still rather respectable fortune entirely to his relations, a Mr. and Mrs. Hatchett of Toronto. According to the Everwell Society's latest client, the papers had been misinformed, Mr. Dalrymple had indeed written down his final wishes. It was this document Gemma had been sent to retrieve.

Mr. Dalrymple's relations had already leased the property, but the tenant was not due to arrive until the end of the month. This generous window of opportunity gave Gemma plenty of time to complete her task, and with no one about, the need for stealth was minimal. Even the heavy curtains on the windows had been drawn, allowing her to light her small Davy lamp and move through the house without being noticed by the growing number of delivery drivers already on their way to the centre of the commercial district.

The Scandalous Spinsters's latest client was the niece of Mrs. Anne Lynde, Mr. Dalrymple's housekeeper. She'd disclosed the likely location of the will was the dumbwaiter in a small pantry off the dining room, where Gemma now stood. The low lamplight spread over the beautifully polished floors, revealing a large dining table that might easily sit a dozen guests. The scent of lemon oil filled the air as she tiptoed along on her soft-soled shoes, taking a moment to linger as she marvelled at the elegant marble fireplace that appeared like a ghostly form out of the shadows. She ran her fingers along the smooth, elegantly carved curlicues, and continued on to the small butler's pantry at the back of the room.

Gemma carefully set the Davy lamp down on a nearby shelf, its light gleaming off the glassware that had been carefully placed on sturdy wooden shelves. Should that glassware be...gleaming?

She pushed that thought aside, ignoring the niggle in the back of her mind as she turned toward the dumbwaiter door and eased it open. Reaching into the darkness, she bit back a moment of disquiet at the thought of running into an errant spider as she put her hand into the shaft. She stretched her fingers over the wood surface, feeling for any crevices where might hide an envelope containing the last will and testament of Hasting House's previous owner. Nothing. Undeterred, she leaned over, poking her lamp into the blackness of the shaft, then stuck her head in, peering up and down. Still nothing.

She closed the door, swallowing her disappointment. This wasn't the first time a job had not gone to plan. Even their client had cautioned that her aunt's notoriously eccentric former employer had hiding places all over the house and before his demise, may have moved the will to any of them. Perhaps it would be better to bring all the Spinsters in and do a methodical search of the house. According to Phillipa Hartley, Everwell's mastermind, the new tenants would not be in the house for another week.

The clicking of keys in locks commanded her attention. Gemma straightened, her heart pounding a little faster as the sound of heavy booted steps echoed from down the hall. Extinguishing her lamp, she sized up the dumbwaiter shaft—it would be tight, but not impossible to hide in—but decided against it, in favour of a servant's stairwell that led down to the kitchen and up to the second floor. With movement coming from not only the main floor, but now from below her, it was her only option. With just enough light from windows at the back of the house, she deftly climbed the stairs, reaching the second floor, exiting out a small door that opened to the hall. Leaning over a railing, she peered to the floor below. A host of strong-backed soldiers carrying trunks and crates and all manner of things moved through the main floor of the house with astonishing efficiency. She'd barely formed the thought when she realized the creeping light from lanterns was crawling up the walls.

They were coming her way.

She dashed ahead of them to the third floor, because they kept coming, marching up and down stairs as if on parade. Gingerly she twisted the knob on a door near the top of a stairwell, uttering a silent prayer of thanks that the hinges did not betray her presence.

Gemma slipped inside and let out a breath. Surely to heaven she'd be safe here until she figured out her means of escape. The room was narrow but long, taking up nearly the entire length of the house, with two windows facing north, and two to the south, allowing her to get some sense of the room. She treaded lightly across the broad planked floors in her leather slippers, the ghostly grey light attempting to reach into the darkness.

She didn't fear the dark like many people did. She'd grown up with monsters and creatures and people that some saw as scary and strange. At the Everwell School, where she was not only the Scandalous Spinsters' talented thief but a teacher as well, it often fell to Gemma to quell the fears of the new students who were coming to stay for the first time.

Gemma positioned herself to one side of the windows that looked over the street. Below, she could make out a series of carts brimming with belongings being unloaded and moved inside by at least a dozen red-coated soldiers. Directing it all was an officer of some sort. Every time a piece was unloaded, the men would pause for a few seconds as he spoke, perhaps giving orders as to where which box or crate or chair would have to be placed.

Who on earth started such an operation at the crack of dawn?

The lamps outside the house had been lit, their warm light bathing the front step and the officer in its glow. There was something about him that, even at this distance, twigged in Gemma's memory. Then again, maybe she was just captivated by the breadth of his shoulders, or his decisive bearing. Like a ringmaster, he kept everything moving, making order out of what, under a lesser person, could have been chaos.

And while she was standing there, somehow temporarily lost in her own thoughts about soldiers and red coats and how in the blazes she was going to get out of here, he looked up.

He did more look up, actually. He stopped what he was doing, tilting his head just so, as if trying to decide what he was seeing.

Gemma on the other hand knew exactly who she was seeing. A well-built, impossibly square shouldered man in a red coat.

Oh dear.

She froze like a deer in the wood, avoiding quick movements that would make her presence more obvious to his eye. In the dim light of the morning, with the glow from the light lamplights outside, she would be difficult to see. She was clothed in black— her uniform for such occasions. Only her face would be visible— her gloved hands were also hidden. She might be mistaken for an apparition, or a trick of the light.

But there was no mistaking him.

Red-coated soldiers were hardly an anomaly on the streets of Halifax. The British laid claim to the lands more than a hundred years ago, pushing off the Mikmaki and taking advantage of the land's position and the deep ice-free harbour to reinforce their hold on the North Atlantic. Even with Confederation, the British remained garrisoned in the city—so a man in a British military uniform was hardly something to note. Except this one. No man, she was sure, filled a red coat quite as perfectly as this one did. And they had met once before.

She hadn't caught his name, and even if she had, it would have hardly mattered. She'd been in disguise as a servant at a private party, assisting her fellow Scandalous Spinsters in their last job, which involve stealing—or, rather, reclaiming—an expensive vase in the middle of a dinner party from one of Halifax's fanciest addresses. She'd only seen this miraculous man in a doorway, but he'd captured her attention with his towering presence, his fair skin, intense grey eyes, Roman nose, and the hint of lingering melancholy that reached right into her insides and squeezed at her heart.

Thankfully, his attention was now pulled away by four soldiers walking past him with a ridiculously large desk, which despite their brawn, clearly strained them. He turned away, helping to direct their movements and only then did Gemma release her breath.

She ducked out of the window, heart pounding. From below, the sounds of movement had gotten louder, and though the activity seemed to be contained to the lower quarters of the house, eventually those empty crates and boxes would have to move their way up to the attic. She needed to get to the back of the house where she had the best chance of escape.

Gemma kept her steps light, taking advantage of the noise below to disguise her movement as she moved toward the windows at the back of the house. They looked down over a tiny courtyard and servant's entrance which had some occasional traffic, but was far less busy than the commotion at the front of the house. The sun was now rising, its growing strength cutting through the morning mists and pulling back another layer for her to hide behind.

A quick scan of her surroundings revealed a drain pipe leading down from the roof. It was a chance, but she'd take it. The servants were preoccupied with their own tasks, and with the heavy shade from the building to the rear, her chances of being detected were slim, if she was careful. And she was always careful.

She opened the latch and gently pushed open one of the windows, the fresh morning air kissing her nose and reviving her confidence. Once upon a time she'd swung from the trapeze and climbed up poles and flew through the air like a bird in flight. She'd been capable of things that others thought magical. She still was, she reminded herself, as long as she was invisible. Being invisible had become her greatest trick.

Gemma took off her gloves and shoved them into a pocket, then reached into a small pouch at her waist and applied a fresh coat of chalk to her hands. Carefully, she slid out the window, her hands gripping the top of the stone edge, her feet on the ledge, easing the window shut. Closing her eyes, she let out a low breath, calming the rush of blood in her ears. Centering her body, she reached for the gutter pipe to her left with her leg, wrapping it as tightly as possible around the pipe before pulling herself over. She stilled again, listening for any signs of alarm, and smiling inwardly at her success, looked down.

The sound of movement from the other side of the window caught her attention. A young girl was staring back at her with undisguised curiosity, then tore off, her cries threatening to bring attention to Gemma's location. *Merda.*

With cat-like efficiency, Gemma climbed down the pipe, where, thank the gods, no one at the bottom saw her. She slid into the narrow space between this house and the neighbouring building, heart pounding, only daring to peek out to see the parade of servants had abated. She looked up one last time to the window, but the child had retreated inside, leaving Gemma to do what she did best.

Disappear.

"Papa!"

Jeremy Webber betrayed only the slightest hint of exasperation as the excited cry of his ten-year-old daughter Ivy rose over the commotion of a dozen heavy-footed soldiers moving furniture. Jeremy was certain that had Ivy been born a boy, her lungs alone would have earned her a post as a sergeant major.

A flurry of small but determined footsteps rushed toward him. Ivy had only arrived three days ago, the next-to-final step in his plan to make a new life for himself and his daughter after far too long apart. It had not been lightly undertaken. Although crossings were commonplace, disaster was not out of the question, and indeed, not twenty-five miles from where he stood, over five hundred souls had been lost only eighteen months ago. Jeremy had already lost a wife. Losing Ivy would have finished him entirely. He'd conferred over countless telegrams with his brother to oversee the arrangements for Ivy's travel. This included having her travel under the watchful eye of a woman of apparently impeccable references that Jeremy's brother Alexander had personally hired to be Ivy's chaperone and governess. But from the moment the ship set sail, Jermey hadn't breathed until Ivy had had her feet on solid ground in front of him in Halifax.

It had shocked him to see how much his daughter had grown since the last time they'd seen each other. Since Isla passed, he'd left Ivy in the dutiful care of his brother, who, having the resources of an influential Viscount-ship at his disposal, gave Ivy only the best tutors and governesses. Considering he'd sent such a governess, who'd quit her post the moment she and Ivy landed on the pier in Halifax, made Jeremy wonder about his brother's so-called impeccable standards. It had also left Jeremy scrambling to find a replacement.

But his daughter was here now, and Jeremy had hoped that his post as Private Secretary and Aide de Camp to Nova Scotia's Lieutenant Governor, which had taken him away from the warm, arid climate of the Suez to the cool, misty shores of Canada, would allow them to be a family in more than name once more.

Ivy weaved her way through the activity with the ease of a

vervet monkey he'd once seen winding its way through a spice market in Cairo, her tawny curls bouncing with every step.

"Papa!" she exclaimed, nearly breathless, only coming to a stop once she'd thrown her hands around his waist. "You have to come straight away!"

Jeremy put a hand on her back, about to answer her when his soldier-valet Harold Babcock approached. Babcock had been at Jeremy's side from almost the moment he'd gotten his commission, and over the years had become something of a surrogate parent to Ivy.

"Sorry sir," he said, motioning to Ivy. "I tried to keep her occupied, but the lads needed help."

"Not a worry," Jeremy said. "None of us were blessed with six arms or an extra set of eyes in the back of our heads. I'll deal with this."

"I saw a man climbing down the side of our house," Ivy burst out.

Jeremy flicked a gaze toward Babcock, then bent down to look Ivy in the eye, all the time struck that she was probably a foot taller than she'd been last time they'd truly been together.

"A man?" he asked, trying to be patient. "Where?"

She looked over his shoulder and pointed toward the southeast corner of the house.

"Are you certain that it wasn't a raccoon?" he asked.

Ivy gave him that look—a half-cocked eyebrow, a subtle tilt of the head, lips pressed together. Jeremy's heart squeezed at the sight. Isla had also blessed him with that expression, usually when Jeremy had said something that she'd clearly thought was half mad.

"No, Papa," she said, and Jeremy could have sworn he'd just been humoured—humoured!!!—by a ten-year-old girl. If any of his men spoke to him like that, the sergeant major would have them doing extra drills for weeks. She clamped her hands around his, determined to show him whatever beast had dared scale the stone walls of Hastings House, no doubt scared witless from its hiding place by the early morning arrival of its new occupants.

Jeremy stifled a groan, then allowed Ivy to lead him up to the top floor, to the room at the back of the house.

"Was this where you saw it?" he asked, gesturing to the window that gave an excellent view of the harbour. It was slightly open.

"It wasn't an *it*, Papa" Ivy protested, clearly not pleased at his insistence that it might be anything other than a man. "They had arms and legs like a person. I saw their eyes."

"And what did their eyes look like?"

She paused, considering his question, before looking up at him.

"Like they were fretting."

Jeremy stifled a laugh.

"Fretting?" He examined the gutter pipe. If he had to crawl down it that questionable piece of metal, he'd be fretting too. The pipe was at least five feet from the edge of the window, and a fall would make a quick end to anyone who'd lost their grip. It had to be something else.

"Well, he's gone now," he said, eager to get on with the considerable work at hand. He had secured the lease to this house through a mutual acquaintance eager to have a trusted tenant occupy the house as soon as possible. With its proximity to Government House, no more than two hundred paces away, it was a perfect location for he and Ivy to make a new start. "I hope you will like it here. And my work is right next door, so I shan't be far."

She gifted him with a smile that bolstered his spirits and chased away, temporarily at least, any doubts he'd had about raising his daughter alone.

"Now, why don't you go to your new room, to make sure things are just as you like them?" he said.

Satisfied for the moment, she skipped away, leaving Jeremy to survey the upper floor. Here would be the nursery, and a large room that would be perfect he decided, for his painting. He walked to one of two front windows that overlooked the street, where the soldiers were making quick work of emptying the carts. Only a few moments ago he'd been down there, looking up, his attention caught by something in this window. A person? A presence?

He'd brushed off the idea almost immediately—mostly because he didn't believe in ghosts. Memories haunted him of course—of the woman he loved and how he'd been thousands of miles away, ignorant of her illness until it was too late. They were supposed to go to Egypt together. That had been the plan. But at the last moment, she'd changed the plan, insisting he go ahead of her. She would follow, with Ivy.

It never happened.

The sound of Ivy's voice wafting up the stairs from below, along with the sound of what might have been a chest being dropped pulled Jeremy away from his woolgathering and back to his lists. There was far too much to be done here today to be daydreaming about what might have been. He turned away from the window and started down the stairs, his mind turning to the multitude of tasks he had neatly stacked in his head. Though Babcock and Mrs. Whitehouse, his new housekeeper, would assist in getting the furniture placed and the house to rights, Jeremy wanted to ensure that things were the way they were supposed to be. The placement of the desk in his study would be the way he liked it, and his books on the shelves in his preferred order. Order gave Jeremy a sense of calm in a chaotic world. A world that could unravel and leave a man adrift. And there was no better anchor than a well thought-out plan. An agenda, checked and double-checked. Lists neatly ticked off. And he had created dozens of them just for this very day.

And on the top of his was finding a new governess.

Chapter Two

GEMMA SIPPED ON HER TEA, watching the sun set as she sat in her favourite corner in Everwell's front parlour. A riot of red and orange spilled over the gardens, skimming the tips of the trees, which had started to turn to match the colour of the setting sun. Her tea was cold, mostly because she'd found herself preoccupied with stabbing a piece of fabric with a needle in an effort to distract herself from the stinging sensation of failure that had been nagging her since her exit from Hastings House that morning.

"Gemma, stop torturing that poor piece of linen."

The light Welsh accent of Rimple Jones, Everwell's resident scientist and general ray of sunshine, broke through Gemma's cloud of self-doubt and painful self-examination. She looked up from her corner in the front parlour to where the others sat, deep in conversation. Rimple's movements were animated. Her bright expression, dark hair, and golden-brown skin were the perfect counterpoint to Madeline Murray, who in Gemma's eyes was a red-haired, fair-skinned giantess who loved books and despised frivolous conversation of any kind. Also with them was Phillipa Hartley, the eldest of the five teachers. Phillipa's light brown hair, shot through with silver strands, seemed a point of calm amongst all the quirks of the group of women who were at the heart of the

Everwell Society for the Benefit of Sorrowful Spinsters and Woeful Widows, as the charity was officially called. Missing from amongst their small band was Elouise Charming, who'd accompanied her fiancé on some business matters and was expected to be by later this evening.

Gemma looked down at her handiwork, swallowing the urge not to hurl it into the fire. It was agreed that amongst the Spinsters, Elouise was the least skilled with the needle. But now that she'd been actively courted by her fiancé, Dominic Ashe, she spent less time at Everwell Manor. And while Gemma was extraordinarily happy for her friend, it meant that on the pecking order of those skilled in the matter of so-called feminine needle arts, Gemma had moved quite dramatically to the bottom.

"I wasn't torturing it," she'd said, holding it up for inspection.

Maddy, never one to spare a word when an expression would do, cocked an eyebrow.

"Gemma dear, you should stop punishing yourself about what happened," Phillipa said. "We clearly had some misinformation about the location of the will. Given the challenges with Mrs. Lynde's situation, as well as her former employer's reputation, we should have expected this."

According to Mrs. Lynde, Mr. Dalrymple's lawyer had written the will, and she had witnessed it. Mr. Dalrymple, who had a distinct lack of trust in the business establishment and his own family, then stored the document, 'for safe keeping', somewhere in the walls of Hastings House. That decision—and the inability for anyone to produce the document since—had paved the way for his next living relations to do the very thing he'd not wanted, which was to claim everything as theirs. Without proof, it was the word of a powerful, well-to-do family against that of a forty-two-year-old servant.

Mr. Jennings, Mr. Dalrymple's lawyer, had left his best pair of socks. To Mrs. Lynde, he'd left two year's salary and a tract of land near Parrsboro, a small town a day's travel north of Halifax.

The ladies of Everwell—known to a select few as the Scandalous Spinsters and Wayward Women—had been approached by Mrs. Lynde's niece, who'd advised them of aunt's perilous situation.

"Do we know the will is actually in the house?" Rimple asked, her eyebrow cocked as she expertly threaded her needle with a fine gold thread. "It's possible it was removed, or even destroyed. Jennings has been wrong before. You remember the Beanstalk job? He forgot to mention that ridiculous goose. If it wasn't for Gemma's quick thinking, we would have been caught."

"Jennings isn't the brightest of men, but he has a good memory," Phillipa answered. "If Dalrymple told him the location, he would be certain of it."

"Perhaps it fell down the dumbwaiter shaft," Gemma said, then tucked away the sampler in the basket by her chair, picked up her tea and joined the others.

"Both Tilda and Lady Em are convinced Jennings is correct," Phillipa said, referring to Mrs. Clotilda Gilman and Miss Emmaline Everwell, Everwell's founding matriarchs.

Phillipa's proclamation instantly quieted the Spinsters. Tilda and Lady Em did not give their opinions lightly, particularly on matters related to the occasionally extra-legal activities of the Scandalous Spinsters or the people who'd come to them for their particular brand of assistance. And if Lady Em and Tilda had declared that the Holy Grail and the Crown Jewels were somehow stuck in a dumbwaiter shaft in Hastings House, the Spinsters would have counted on finding them there.

As it was, it was neither the Crown Jewels or the Holy Grail, but to Mrs. Lynde, something just as precious—the deed to a plum piece of farmland that would provide the opportunity for a steady income and for the family for generations.

So the hunt was on.

"Maybe it fell down the shaft," Gemma offered. "Or maybe it's just elsewhere in the house. If I only had more time, I could have looked. As it was, I'd barely found the dumbwaiter before an army of soldiers started marching in with furniture. I thought the house was supposed to be unoccupied for at least another week."

Phillipa pressed her lips together.

"That was my understanding," Phillipa said, then shrugged. "Apparently the new tenant had the gall to change his plans without notifying us."

"Counting on men to be helpful is like counting on April to be dependable picnic weather," Maddy said, her nose in her book, where it normally was. "Generally ill advised."

"Come now Maddy," Rimple interjected, "Even you have to admit that Dominic has been very helpful. And he's a man."

Dominic Ashe was a former client who'd hired them to assist in retrieving a priceless piece of Chinese art in exchange for funds to help fix Everwell's leaking roof. He also happened to be the fiancé of Elouise Charming, one of their fellow Scandalous Spinsters.

Maddy, as always, merely shrugged.

"I've seen him before—the new tenant," Gemma said, reaching back into her memory to earlier this summer, when she and Maddy were helping Elouise and Dominic retrieve a vase in the middle of a dinner party. He'd been there as well, she recalled. Though she hadn't gotten a good look at the officer this morning, she knew instantly it was the same man. His imposing form and chiselled features were impossible to forget. "At the Coughlins'. His timing has something to be desired."

"His daughter has recently arrived from Britain, where she was staying with family," Phillipa continued. "His name is Colonel Jeremy Webber, the Lieutenant Governor's Aide de Camp and now his private secretary. Clearly he's made arrangements to get into the house earlier than he intended...unless our information was wrong."

Gemma almost let out a snort. Phillipa, wrong? Phillipa had eyes and ears all over the place.

"He's a colonel. He may have woken up yesterday and decided he didn't want to wait any longer, and started barking orders," Gemma said. "Men like that don't wait to get what they need."

"What do we tell Mrs. Lynde and her family?" Rimple asked. "Those odious relations of Dalrymple's mean to displace her if they can. That will is the only proof they have that the Parrsboro property isn't theirs."

Though Rimple hadn't meant it, her comment pricked Gemma's conscience. It wouldn't be the first time someone paid a heavy price for her mistake. Would a woman be homeless because she'd failed?

"Nothing yet," Phillipa said, shooting them all a look of confidence. "When have we ever given up on anyone after one attempt? You all know these things rarely work out as planned the first time."

"What doesn't work out?"

Gemma looked up to see the missing Scandalous Spinster, Elouise Charming and her fiancé, Dominic Ashe, walking into the room.

"Case in point," Maddy said, looking over at Gemma with a wry expression.

"Dominic, I am thrilled you fixed the squeak on the kitchen screen door but I am going to insist that you unfix it," Phillipa said, flashing him a warm smile. "It was my early warning system."

"Is this how you know about everything going on in the city? The ears of a cat and a series of squeaking hinges?" Dominic replied playfully, as he offered a chair to Elouise before taking one beside her.

"I'll never tell," Phillipa said. "But at this point in my life I've come to realize that it's the quirks and imperfections can be more valuable qualities."

"I was seen leaving Hastings House this morning," Gemma blurted out. "I didn't have a chance to get the will."

Silence fell on the small parlour and Gemma wanted to crawl

inside of herself, if that was possible, and disappear. Wordlessly, Rimple reached over and squeezed Gemma's hand.

"It seems the new owner of Hastings House decided to take up residence a week ahead of schedule," Phillipa said, "and we haven't been able to get Gemma to excuse herself for the sin."

"You were in your darks, weren't you?" Elouise asked. "Was it one of the staff?"

Gemma shook her head. At least she'd had the presence of mind to pull the mask over her head before she climbed out the window.

"It was a child," she replied.

"The Colonel's daughter, we believe," Phillipa said. "Hardly the end of the world."

It felt like the end of the world. Since that horrible performance under the big top with Penny, Gemma had never been able to fully regain her confidence. The sense that at any moment, something she might do would cause someone else harm stayed with her like a shadow. Sometimes that shadow seemed to swallow her completely. But with her friends around her, she was sometimes able to shake off this inexplicable feeling of dread clawing at her.

"I didn't speak with Webber for long, but he seemed like a reasonable man," Dominic offered. The two had met briefly at the last job the Spinsters had completed, along with Dominic, who'd posed as a businessman from his native Boston. "Why don't you simply ask him if you can search the house? He has nothing to gain."

"The matter is somewhat delicate," Phillipa said, pausing to take a sip of tea. "I still have some checking to do, but there is apparently some connection between the colonel and the Hatchetts. He may not allow a search for a document that would forfeit their supposed inheritance."

"I see. So sneaking it is," Dominic said.

"We need more time," Gemma said. "I couldn't truly verify the document wasn't in the exact space Mrs. Lynde claimed it to be, and it's possible Mr. Dalrymple moved it. Searching the entire house would take days. Maybe longer, if there are hidden compartments."

"Clearly we need a new plan," Phillipa answered. "I'll come up with something."

Gemma stared down into her cup, going over this morning's events in her mind. Her quick escape. The sound of the girl's cries, summoning her father as Gemma scurried down the pipe. A busy father. A young girl in need of a governess. Satisfaction at this glimmer of an idea, a hint of plan, uncoiled in Gemma's belly as she sat up, as if buoyed by an idea. A good idea.

"Elouise," she blurted out, excited by the idea forming inside, "perhaps you could do it. Posing as a nanny, or governess, or something. He has a daughter, I believe. And in between lessons, you could take a look through the house?"

"That's a brilliant idea," Phillipa said, a smile spreading across her lips that made Gemma ready to collapse with relief until it stalled. "Except—"

Phillipa glance passed between Elouise, Dominic and the others, before landing at last on Gemma. "Elouise isn't the right person for this."

Elouise exchanged a look with Phillipa before turning to Gemma, nodding apologetically. "I spent far too much time in the colonel's company not that long ago."

"It was four months ago." Gemma protested. "And you looked very different then. He wouldn't recognize you after all that time."

Elouise had been masquerading as the flamboyant Boston socialite Elouise Walker, her short dark blond hair hidden underneath a bright blond wig, her manners and her speech altered to suite the character. It never failed to amaze Gemma how Elouise could inhabit one disguise or another effortlessly. Of course, it wasn't effortless, but Elouise was gifted at diversion. Not like Gemma.

"Elouise isn't the right person for this job," Phillipa said.

"She isn't?" Gemma asked, then looked to Rimple. "Rimple then?"

That would make sense. Rimple Jones' keen mind was matched only by her natural warmth; the children at Everwell School all loved her. Her mixed descent might prove a challenge, as unfortunately her beautiful, warm brown skin and clear Indian heritage was often viewed as a less than desirable trait amongst the white protestant elite of the city. But her lovely middle class Welsh accent and upbringing in a British household would make her an instant favourite with someone of Webber's apparent pedigree. And with a house rumoured to be full of Dalrymple's engineering eccentricities, Rimple's scientific brain would love the puzzle.

Yes, Gemma thought with a wave of relief. Clearly Rimple was the perfect person for this job.

"No dear," Phillipa answered, clearly indicating to Gemma that she had lost her mind. Because it couldn't be Maddy. Madeline Murray was Everwell's librarian, and while she was a very capable teacher, her no-nonsense approach to everything and general dislike of people in general wasn't the reason she'd be the wrong choice. Indeed, some of Maddy's outwardly bristle-like qualities would, in the eyes of many, make her an excellent governess. But Maddy also had a very heavy foot. Sneaking was not her forte.

"And it's not Maddy either," Phillipa added, as if she was reading Gemma's mind.

"You're going to do it?" Gemma asked, knowing full well that was a ridiculous question but somehow, that was the only other conclusion she could arrive at.

Maddy snickered in the corner, which could not have been good. Because Maddy never laughed. Heck, she rarely smiled.

"Gemma, this job still needs someone who can be discreet," Phillipa said, her voice gentle and quiet. "No one can slide into a hallway or a room without being noticed as well as you can."

Realization prickled at the back of her neck as a pit opened up in Gemma's stomach. She looked to Phillipa, who was smiling in that way of hers that, when it was directed at other people she was enticing to do things they didn't think they could do, always seemed warm and encouraging. Until it was directed at her. Without realizing it, Gemma had gripped Rimple's hand. Hard.

"Phillipa's right," Rimple said, taking her other hand and resting on top of Gemma's. Blood pounded in Gemma's ears as she felt the urge to run or yell or do anything other than agree to be on display in the middle of a job. It was impossible. She'd already had one misstep on an earlier job that caused her to fumble and sprain her ankle—all because she'd gotten nervous simply walking through a crowd of people. And the last time she'd been the main event, she'd caused a disaster.

"Phillipa," she heard Rimple say above the sound of blood pulsing in her ears, "let's give Gemma some time to think about it, shall we? And in the meantime perhaps we can try to get some plans of the house if they exist."

Gemma didn't stay to hear Phillipa's answer. It was as if someone else had inhabited her body, forcing her from the threat lurking nearby.

"Gemma?"

She stood abruptly, vaguely aware that someone was calling her name. Her chest was tight, inexplicable rage building in her chest which made absolutely no sense, but it was there, under the surface.

"I need a moment," she said, and sprang from the room, brushing past Phillipa, and out the front door into the fresh air. The early autumn breeze was crisp. She jumped off the step and walked in the direction of the water, where the sun was starting its slow descent. Her skirt brushed some of the herbs in the kitchen garden, releasing sage, thyme, and mint into the air. She breathed them in, allowing them to soothe her as she walked down the path leading toward a large oak tree. A swing hung off one of its branches, an addition Dominic had built this summer. It has quickly become a favourite place for Gemma to sit and think.

Why on earth would Phillipa think Gemma, of all people, would be the right person for this? A job like this would take her days, if not weeks, depending on how many nooks and crannies old Dalrymple had built into it. They were looking for a veritable needle in a haystack.

But that needle would keep a good woman from being left out in the cold.

"Gemma."

Gemma turned to see Phillipa approaching. Her expression was contrite, her smile soft. Embarrassment burned in Gemma's chest.

"Phillipa— "

Phillipa shook her head, then smiled in a way that was somehow motherly even though she was only a dozen years older. Gemma hadn't seen her parents in years—being part of a travelling circus meant never being in one place for very long. In their absence, her fellow Spinsters had become more than friends. They had become family. And she'd already let down family once before, and she would never forgive herself for it.

"Please," Phillipa said, her mouth turning up into smile. "There is nothing to apologize for. In fact, if there is anyone who should be making amends, it's me."

Phillipa took Gemma's hand and Gemma looked up at her friend. Gemma was short; her petite frame made her a natural to do the acrobatics she loved so much. Phillipa, she realized, wasn't much taller, however. Still, amongst them, she was their accepted leader and she seemed much taller than she actually stood.

"I should never have rushed presenting such a plan to you," she continued. "I should have realized it would be troublesome. You do such a remarkable job here with the girls, that I sometimes forget that an assignment like this might be troubling for you."

Gemma, like all the Spinsters, worked at Everwell, which functioned as a small school for disadvantaged children, as well as a society to assist women and families in need. Gemma taught geography and other social studies, as well as Italian, Latin, and

ight—no one could go through that house the way
Gemma could. She'd run away from her family once. She couldn't
let down this family too.

"Phillipa," she called out. "I'll do it."

Chapter Three

JEREMY SAT at his desk in his newly furnished study, the sounds of horse-drawn carts slipping in through the open window as he reviewed correspondence in preparation for a meeting with his superior, Lieutenant Governor George Tupper. Even after months in his position, George Tupper still managed to keep Jeremy on his toes. They were planning for the arrival of a new American Counsel General, and Jeremy needed to be sharp. Along with a steaming pot of Sergeant Babcock's strongest coffee, Jeremy held out some faint hope the fresh air would revive him after a series of sleepless nights.

Sleepless nights were not a new phenomenon—he was a soldier after all—and even for the comfort of an officer, it meant late night duties and early morning battles. After his beloved Isla died, he hadn't slept for weeks. Even now, the memory of holding his brother's telegram, urging Jeremy to return to London at once, brought a rush of unholy emotion that clawed at his chest. Grief. Anger. Regret.

When he'd arrived in Halifax in the spring Jeremy found a potent remedy for anger in a new setting with new faces and personalities to learn, including the idiosyncrasies of his employer. Grief was a constant companion, but he'd managed to stretch his workday into the wee hours of the night, leaving him too tired and busy for much of it.

Regret was another matter. His failure to do the right thing when it mattered most was emblazoned on his heart like a tattoo on an old sailor's arm—faded and misshapen perhaps, but under his skin nonetheless. Before he'd left for Cairo, taking his family with him had been part of the plan. He'd found the perfect little set of apartments, and made the right connections so Isla would find companionship while he was working. It would be their latest adventure.

But Isla changed the plan. And instead of insisting on doing things his way, the way it was meant to be, he went on without her, coming back only when it was too late to say goodbye.

There would be no way to rid himself of it completely, but every day he was alone here, without his family, was a reminder of that horrible decision. The one he couldn't take back. So he'd made the plans, double and triple checked for every eventuality, and sent for Ivy. They both needed a new start. Someplace safe. The rationale for leasing Hastings House was its proximity to his daily duties. He would never be more than five minutes from his daughter. There would be no more regret.

Ivy's arrival had brought with it expectation and anxiety. They'd been separated for eighteen months, and the cherub-faced eight-year-old he'd left in Sussex was now ten, somehow nearly a foot taller, her blond hair a shade or two darker than it used to be. They were strangers becoming reacquainted, and the reunion had been joyous but not easy. Particularly when Ivy's governess deposited Ivy on the dock, then quite unceremoniously climbed aboard another ship bound for Boston.

He brushed off the predicament initially. How hard could it be, he reasoned, to find a governess? Ivy was grown in all the ways that mattered--there were no nappies to change or feeding to do. She'd barely been in town for half a day before the New Women's League, a local women's group helmed by some of the most respectable families in the city, offered its assistance. Indeed, his new housekeeper was a member and spoke very highly of their credentials. They had taken a particular interest in his situation and produced a list of potential candidates with an efficiency Jeremy had felt could only bode well for his situation. With their help, Mrs. Whitehead had assured him, he'd have a suitable governess before the end of the week.

The week had nearly come and gone.

His attention trailed to a stack of letters on his desk, each extolling the virtues of the latest candidates for Ivy's governess, but none had made the grade thus far. They were either too harsh, not harsh enough, or seemed unable to manage a ten-year-old girl who would rather explore the nooks and crannies of a graveyard than sit quietly and practice her letters. He'd dismissed one after a day and a half, and a second had dismissed herself after discovering Ivy's propensity for mischief.

"Colonel Webber."

Jeremy looked up to see Mrs. Whitehead in the door, stiff and starched like all good orderly people were, though the corners of her eyes were already strained with the rampant disorder that his daughter had brought. Mrs. Whitehead's service came as part of the lease agreement with the Hatchetts. Since he'd arrived, she had brought the novice but small staff up to expectations.

"Yes, Mrs. Whitehead?"

"There is a woman at the door about the position."

A woman? Thus far the candidates presented to Hasting House had been fresh-faced girls, often no more than twenty. Mrs. Whitehead had never referred to any of them as 'a woman'.

"Mrs. Coughlin works very quickly," he said, referring to one of the NWL's founding members who'd taken it upon herself to search out a new governess. He held out his hand and waited for Mrs. Whitehead to present him with the prerequisite letter of recommendation. "Let's see it."

"Mrs. Coughlin did not send her, Colonel," Mrs. Whitehead answered, her lips pulling into a tight line. "And the lady insisted upon speaking to you directly."

Insisted, did she? Instantly an image formed in his head of a no-nonsense school marm who might be a little overbearing in the short term, but perhaps exactly the firm hand Ivy needed. Still, he had a process for these things, and the fact this person was showing up on his doorstep unannounced was not exactly a check in this person's favour.

Jeremy cast a glance back at the stack of applications and reminded himself that he had a meeting with the Lieutenant Governor in less than an hour. There was being a stickler for process, and then there was being pragmatic, and after nearly twenty years in the army, Jeremy wanted to believe he knew when the latter was more important.

"Show her in."

Mrs. Whitehead disappeared and returned a moment later, followed by the woman in question. Whatever impressions Jeremy assumed he would make were utterly torn to pieces as she came to a stop a foot from the other side of the desk. She stood ramrod straight two feet in front on the desk, clad in a simple, dark cotton dress that might have been drab on another woman, but brought out the warmth in her olive-toned skin. She was clutching a small bag so tightly Jeremy was certain he could see the white of her knuckles under her gloved hands. Her features were uncommonly fine and petite, and at first glance she appeared much younger. He didn't know what to expect of course, but he hadn't expected to have the breath nearly sucked from his chest.

And yet, there was something about her that felt...familiar.

"Miss Gemma Kurt," Mrs. Whitehead said, then nodded and took her leave.

For his part, Jeremy brushed off the sensation, chalking it up to the fact he'd been living in a city that by any reasonable measure would have qualified as a town. He could have easily seen her on his daily walks from his former accommodations down to Government House, or in a shop. Still, Jeremy was quite certain he would have remembered the impossible depths of her brown eyes, or the hint of the delicate skin where the edge of her glove didn't quite meet the edge of her sleeve.

"Good morning, Colonel Webber sir," she said, her voice clear, though Jeremy detected a hint of forced pleasantry.

"Good morning Miss Kurt," he said, shaking off whatever madness had temporarily robbed him of his ability to speak. "I understand you are here about the position as governess."

"I am."

"Do you have a letter of recommendation?" he said, taking her in. Her posture was excellent, her shoulders square, though he detected more than a hint of nerves.

She produced a letter and handed it to him.

He opened the note, which was penned by a Miss P. Hartley of the Everwell Society, extolling the virtues of Miss Kurt, including her considerable experience in the instruction of young girls.

"Everwell?" The name twigged his memory, though he couldn't recall its significance at the moment.

"The Everwell Society for the Benefit of Sorrowful Spinsters and Woeful Widows," she said. "It is a charitable organization that supports women and young girls in distress to find meaningful employment."

"You are a sorrowful spinster then?"

The question somehow slipped out of his mouth, hanging in the air. To distract himself from his own idiocy, Jeremy looked down at the letter she'd provided, but found his attention being drawn to her hands, which were of course gloved, but the need to search for a ring on her finger seemed to trump all possible reason.

She responded with a tilt of her head to the side, her eyes narrowing, lips pursed, as if she was choosing her words very carefully. The gesture was artless, but its effect on Jeremy was immediate and utterly disorientating. He sat, dumbstruck, all thoughts of schedules and agendas and governesses tossed aside by this creature standing before him.

"I am a spinster, yes," she said at last. "But I cannot say I'm sorrowful about it."

Indeed. How on earth this woman had remained unmarried was remarkable. She was singular in her beauty--her dark brown eyes were striking, her cheeks well defined. And yet there was this nervous energy about her that was just below the surface. He could feel it somehow. Or maybe the energy was his. Somehow every ounce of him was tuned to this diminutive woman standing before him.

He cleared his throat and forced himself to pay attention to the matter at hand, which was not that slender bit of wrist peeking out from the edge of her grey gloves.

"And this Everwell Society is a respectable local charity, is it?" he asked.

"Everwell supports women of good character that other, more fashionable charities for one reason or another may overlook," she continued.

"I see," he said. "And you have been employed at the school for some time. Did your regular work not appeal to you?"

"Oh heavens, it appeals to me a great deal," she said, brightening as she spoke. She had quite a captivating smile—not that he should have noticed. But it was kind and warm, and might be exactly what Ivy needed...along with a firm hand. Whether or not Miss Kurt could provide that was another matter. Though it seemed...unlikely. He could tell by the subtle movement that she was rolling back and forth on the tips of her toes. "In fact, it was the headmistress at Everwell who sent me here. We've come to understand that this position has been particularly challenging to fill."

Jeremy started at her admission. "You have, have you?"

"Halifax is a small place," she said with an apologetic smile. "Word does travel."

He could only imagine what she'd heard. Since arriving, his status as a widower had made the society rounds faster than a cheetah racing across the African plains, and the fact his family belonged to the aristocracy made hunt even more intense. The good ladies of the city had made numerous overtures about addressing his marital status. But they didn't know how much Isla's death devastated him. And how resolute he was not to have a second marriage in his plans.

He sat back in his chair, folding his hands in front of him.

"And what word has reached you?"

"Well," she began, pausing when the clock struck half past the hour. He had twenty-five minutes to end this before he needed to dash out the door. He needed to hurry this along or he'd have more than one temperamental charge to worry about.

"Miss Kurt," he said, impatience edging into his tone, "you need to command the room if you are going to be the governess for my daughter."

She let out a laugh.

"Just because I don't speak with a booming voice doesn't mean I don't know how to work with your daughter," she replied. "Being loud isn't a quality unless you are summoning help from the bottom of a well."

Well now. Jeremy stifled his urge to smile at this flash of emotion from Miss Kurt, who had gone from being a pretty face to something irresistible in the blink of an eye. Her grip had relaxed. The teetering on her toes had paused.

"The Everwell Society believes in assisting people with overcoming their challenges, not martyrdom," she continued, her dark eyes flashing. "I understand you have an exuberant ten-year-old who is in a new place with no friends and may feel ill at ease. I have plenty of experience in that department, as you can see from my letter."

He unfolded the missive, which was written in a very tight but elegant hand.

"You have been teaching at Everwell for four years," he said, reviewing the contents. "You've begun your teaching career quite late."

She raised her chin, adopting almost a regal stance, and cocked one eyebrow, which should absolutely not have been as perfectly enticing as it was.

"Are you saying I am old, Colonel Webber?" she asked.

Old? Hardly. Certainly, Miss Kurt was no young miss. She looked to be thirty, or close to it with fine features that reminding him of Cypriot women he'd met in the markets there.

"You teach geography and history," he said, pointedly ignoring that question that came out as a dare.

"I do."

"And" —Jeremy paused, intrigued— "—and languages? French, I presume?"

"Italian, actually, and Latin. Some Turkish. Enough French to get by," she said. "I am learning a few Mi'kmaq phrases from a gentleman we buy supplies from."

"Excellent."

"I can also swear in Mandarin, Greek, Spanish and Norwegian," she continued, "though I will be sure not to share those words with your daughter."

"I trust not," he continued, wondering how one might pick up such a smattering of languages as he continued to read the letter, looking over her accomplishments, when he paused again when he saw the phrase *Young & Chesterman's Travelling Circus*.

He paused, and read that again, just to make sure he'd read it correctly. Circus?

"You worked…in a circus?"

She nodded, as if she was actually proud of such a fact.

"With lions, and elephants and clowns?"

"Only one elephant," she replied. "And an ostrich."

"An ostrich," he parroted, trying to imagine this mouse of a woman in amongst lions and tigers and strong men.

"I was raised in one actually," she said. "That's how I learned so many languages."

"Raised in one?" Jeremy sat back in his chair. He'd been to a circus—and while they were a fanciful distraction, they were exactly that. Barely contained chaos with animals and acts meant to be fantastical and deliberately outlandish. Neither of those things were what Ivy needed. She needed structure. Security. Order.

"Miss Kurt, my household is an orderly one," he said, not bothering to hide his incredulousness. "Where no one is flying through the air in feathers. And no wild animals to be found."

His assertion was met with slight fluttering of her dark lashes and a flush of pink to her cheeks.

"With respect Colonel," she said, her tone far more even than his own had just been, "have you been to a circus?"

"I do not have the time for such frivolity."

"Well then, perhaps you are ill-informed," she said. "While there are always exceptions of course, a well-run circus is as orderly as a military encampment. For a production involving so many different people, equipment, and animals that move from place to place on a schedule to operate safely, there are rules to be followed, and orders to be given and heeded. Equipment must be raised, roped, tied, and checked. Lives are at stake. Everyone has a job. Everyone contributes, in order for it to work."

"It looks like controlled chaos."

She shrugged and let go an incredulous laugh. "And a battlefield does not?"

Jeremy stilled. The vixen had a point.

"And what was your job?" he continued, brushing aside that point. "Or did you have one?"

"My family are acrobats," she replied.

"And you?"

"I am not. Not any longer."

She swallowed then, her smile fading and damn it if he didn't want to kick himself for that. But there was nothing for it. He couldn't have an acrobat in the house. Even a former one.

He closed his notebook.

"I'm afraid, Miss Kurt, that you would not be suitable for the position."

"Colonel Webber, I am an excellent teacher," she said taking a step toward the desk. "Allow me the chance to prove it to you. You are a man of the world. I would not think you would shrink from a woman simply because she has experienced life outside the confines of the kitchen, would you?"

If he didn't know better, he would have thought she'd just dared him to hire her.

"I will never take bets with my child's wellbeing."

She opened her mouth as if to say something, then closed it, as if she'd thought the better of it.

"Very well," she said, giving him a curt nod. "I wish you the best of luck finding your perfect woman."

Jeremy watched as she completed a sharp about-face and marched out the door with all the efficiency of a master drill sergeant. There was something about her movement that was absolutely captivating—fluid, yet precise. Miss Gemma Kurt moved with absolute purpose and Jeremy found himself transfixed, still staring at the door long after she'd moved past it and out of his sight.

He let out a breath trying to brush off this inexplicable sense of absence that lingered after her departure, then turned back to the stack of applications. He had another quarter hour before he needed to meet with the Lieutenant Governor and he wasn't going to waste another moment of it.

Unfortunately, his household didn't share his sense of urgency. A quick knock at his study door interrupted Jeremy a second time. He looked up to see Babcock standing in the door frame, wearing a stance that drew Jeremy to his feet and dropped a stone in his gut.

"Ivy?"

Babcock nodded. "She's gone."

Chapter Four

Gemma practically flew down the stone steps of Hastings House, congratulating herself on keeping her temper in check until she reached the sidewalk. And she deserved it too, considering she hadn't realized until a few moments ago that she had one.

She should have been satisfied. Smug, even. For once, Phillipa and others were wrong. Elouise should have been the one to go and charm her way into the position in Colonel Webber's household. She was, by common vote, the prettiest of them all, even when she wasn't trying to be, and her ability to read people's emotions and use them to her advantage bordered on the supernatural. Which was why on most jobs, they made an excellent pair —Gemma stayed in the shadows, deliberately overlooked, on the hunt for whatever object she was required to steal, or even occasionally, plant, while Elouise was front and centre, providing the diversion.

Thankfully, the colonel hadn't recognized her from their chance meeting during the Scandalous Spinster's last job. She'd remembered him, of course. He had a face that looked like it had been freed from a hunk of Italian marble by a Renaissance master. At the time, she'd pretended it was his red coat that had caught her attention, brushing aside the very inconvenient thought that Halifax was still home to a British garrison, and men in red coats were a dime a dozen. Even more inconvenient was the way Colonel Webber filled out that red coat and made those regimentals absolutely sinful.

The day was pleasant, and eager to drive off her cloudy mood, she crossed the street, not bothering to look back. Disappointment niggled at her. She hadn't been thrilled about having to take the position, but his rejection stung nonetheless—a reminder that her ego was alive and well. Her brief interaction with Colonel Webber was yielding all kinds of self-discovery of a most uncomfortable nature.

Better for her, then, that it was behind her.

A breeze brushed through the trees along St. Paul's Cemetery, which provided a lovely canopy to the souls that rested beneath. Dominating the entrance was a massive lion—a memorial to those who'd gone to the Crimea. Indeed, Lady Em had donated to its completion. Both she and Tilda had been there, Tilda working with Mary Seacole in her hospital, Lady Em not far away. Gemma paused, taking in the large stone creature standing in silent command at its post.

She was about to continue on her way when a flash of pink caught her eye. She straightened to see a young girl pulling herself into a tree twenty yards away.

Gemma bit back a smile as she watched, all the while waiting for an anxious parent or caregiver to run up to the child to either coax her down or scold her for even making the attempt. But there was none forthcoming. Indeed, as Gemma did a quick survey of the cemetery, she quickly concluded that the child was very much alone.

She frowned, her natural instincts on alert. Taking a few cautious steps forward, she rounded the monument and stopped again. From this distance, snippets of conversation coming from the tree caught Gemma's attention. Who was the child talking to? Perhaps Gemma had missed an indulgent caregiver nearby, perhaps resting against the tree the girl was determined to scale. But there was no one. She was merrily carrying on a fulsome conversation with herself. It both amused Gemma and sent a small twinge into her heart.

Was the girl lost? If so, she didn't appear to be in distress. Even from this distance, it was clear that the child was well nourished and cared for. The dress looked new and of expensive materials.

Gemma approached, careful not to startle the child and cause her to lose her balance. Keeping herself several arm lengths away, she spied a rather fine, if weather-worn doll at the base of the tree. This was the object of the girl's conversation.

"The enemy is just beyond the ridge," the girl said, calling down to the doll in a rather crisp, upper class British accent. "If I can get a little higher, I may be be able to see how many."

Higher? Gemma winced. The girl was a natural climber, but she was high enough now that serious injury would result from her fall.

"Good afternoon," Gemma called up.

"It's not a good afternoon," the girl called down. "We're going to be attacked."

The accent. The cool indignation at being interrupted. Gemma looked across the road, where Hastings House stood. Did the colonel know his beloved daughter was swinging in the trees like some kind of monkey?

"Dear heavens," Gemma said. "Who is it now?"

"The Swedes," the girl replied.

Gemma nodded, wondering why the Vikings would pick a perfectly sunny day to attack, and how to bribe the girl down.

"I had no idea we were at war with the Swedish," she replied.

The girl looked at Gemma as if she had two heads—a look so similar to what she'd just experienced in Hastings House that if she'd had any doubts about the girl's parentage, they'd just been satisfied.

"Shouldn't we alert someone?" Gemma asked. "Perhaps send a runner to the Citadel?"

MICHELLE HELLIWELL

The Citadel was a star-shaped fort only three miles from where they stood. It had provided, along with a natural harbour and other fortifications, a strong hold for the British Army to keep out the French, the Americans, and other invaders over the years.

"Hilda can go," the girl replied.

"Hilda?" Gemma looked around. Perhaps there was a servant or someone watching. When no adult was to be seen, she turned her attention back to the girl. "I don't—"

The girl pointed to the base of the tree, where the doll sat.

Of course. When Gemma was young, she'd been surrounded by adults. Her mama had made her a stuffed dog she'd called Tali.

"I think Hilda is concerned you might fall," Gemma said. "Are you here alone?"

"I'm with my Papa," she answered.

"Do you mean Colonel Webber?" Gemma asked.

The girl nodded. Did Colonel Webber even know his child was missing? She doubted it.

"Perhaps he would know what to do about the Swedes."

The girl paused, as if she were considering the idea, while Gemma turned her attention to Hastings House. As if on cue, the older woman who'd answered the door for her came out of the house and stood on the step, looking up and down the street. Behind her, looking wild-eyed, was one Colonel Webber.

Gemma wasn't prone to scheming in the same way Phillipa was. But she knew an opportunity when she saw it.

"May I ask your name?" she said, returning her attention to the girl. "I am Miss Kurt."

"And I am Miss Webber," the girl answered. Gemma bit back a grin at the formality of it.

"Miss Webber, as you are new to the city, you may be unaware of the Code."

"The Code?"

"Halifax is a port city, and very strategic to the British," Gemma continued. "If you see invaders, all Haligonians have a sworn duty to report to the Lieutenant Governor."

36

"What's a Haligonian?" the girl asked, a deep frown line across her brow.

"Someone who lives in Halifax."

The frown line deepened. "That doesn't make sense."

Gemma shrugged, unable to disagree. "No, I suppose it doesn't. But the Code remains all the same."

"Papa is the Lieutenant Governor's Secretary!" the girl cried, excited.

"Is he?" Gemma asked, feigning surprise. "Well this is very fortunate! May I help you down, so you might inform him right away?"

"I don't need help," Miss Webber said, and without hesitation, she scrambled down the branches. The edge of her hem caught in a branch, which caused her to slip, but Gemma caught her easily before she fell. The child wiggled out of Gemma's arms, then grabbed her doll.

"Let's go see your father, shall we? I believe I see him approaching."

On instinct, she held out her hand to the girl, who shocked Gemma by talking it.

Jeremy forced himself to calm down, even as he fought to keep his breathing in check. This was the third time since Ivy had arrived that she'd magically escaped the house under the nose of every adult in the place, including him. One governess had quit as the child ran out, and the second one he'd fired. He could hardly fire himself.

He did up the last button on his coat as his feet hit the bottom step, his gaze moving to the cemetery across the road. The last two times Ivy had run, he'd found her there amongst the verge. The child seemed to thrive out of doors, and the stand of oak and maple trees drew her like a moth to a flame. He darted across the road, fully aware he was not properly attired. He looked past the iron fence to the trees, but caught no sight of her.

"Papa!"

The sound of Ivy's cry rang in his ears. She was in the grave-yard somewhere. Had she fallen out of a tree? Hurt herself? Panic tightened in his chest as his mind raced through dozens of horrible scenarios that ended with Ivy being taken away from him.

"Papa!" came the call again, louder this time. He was getting closer, and somewhere in Jeremy's brain he realized the cry was not fear or pain, but excitement.

As he sprinted to the cemetery entrance, he saw Ivy practically skipping along, accompanied by a woman.

Not just any woman. *Her.*

"Ivy!" he called out, relief washing over the panic and anger. He was furious, but there was no space for that now.

She let go of Miss Kurt's hand and dashed to him, her light brown plaits bouncing off her shoulders. If he'd been worried that she was hurt or in distress in anyway, the utter determination in her stride and smile wicked it away. She reminded him of a runner on the battlefield, coming to him with orders.

"Papa!" she said, practically plowing into legs. "The Swedes are coming."

Jeremy crouched down and quickly examined her. No cuts or scrapes. Nothing seemed amiss, except for a small tear in her hem. Thank God.

"What did I say about you leaving the house alone?" he said.

"It was important, Papa," she said. "The Swedes are coming. I saw them from the tree. Miss Kurt told me about the Code."

"The Code?"

His gaze flicked up to Miss Kurt, who was holding onto Ivy and giving him a conspiratorial look.

"Good morning Colonel," she said, as demurely as if she'd just come from church. And yet there was a tinge of smugness there that he wanted to kiss right off her face.

Good heavens.

"Good morning, Miss Kurt," he said, determined to push that

rather inappropriate thought so deep inside him it could never resurface. "Thank you for retrieving my daughter."

"I didn't retrieve her. She's here on a mission sir," she said. "I told her about the Code."

The code? Jeremy had been here for months, reading over heaps of memos and correspondence and aside from a particular knock at a side door of the Halifax Merchant's Club announcing the arrival of hired companions for some of the Club's most important members, he knew nothing about a code. And he wasn't particularly thrilled to know about that one.

"The Swedes are coming," Ivy continued. "You must tell the Lieutenant Governor straight away."

Jeremy must have looked utterly confused, which he owed to having his day completely discombobulated by two females.

"I am shocked Colonel, that you of all people did not inform Miss Webber about the Code which dictates that all threats to the city must be reported to the Lieutenant Governor immediately," she said. "When she informed me of this very distressing news, I suggested we go inform the Citadel as per normal protocol, but I was happily informed of a superior plan. Miss Webber immediately suggested she report this to you directly."

A curious sensation that might have been awe—or perhaps simple, unabashed surprise—warmed in Jeremy's chest, nearly forcing a smile on his face. Miss Kurt wasn't a cat with a canary. This little plan of hers was pure guile. A fox, perhaps. But a brilliant piece of tactics nonetheless.

He felt a tug on his sleeve, Ivy demanding an answer. "What are we going to do Papa?"

"I shall send a note directly," he said to his daughter.

"You will need details," Miss Kurt said to Ivy. "How many, and their relative position."

What was she doing?

"Miss Webber," she continued, "I suggest you write them down. If your father has some paper and ink he could provide."

"Of course!" she said, then grabbed her father's hand. "Come!"

Jeremy hoped he managed to keep is expression bland even as he was struck by the fact that Miss Kurt had, in the space of less than a moment, performed one, and perhaps two minor miracles. She'd coaxed his daughter to willingly come inside, and to sit down and write.

"A moment my dear," he said to his daughter, before turning to the diminutive Miss Kurt who, somehow, seemed to be standing a little taller. "Miss Kurt, thank you for seeing to Ivy's safety. I am in your debt."

"It wasn't a problem. Being vigilant for stray children is a skill I've honed while working at Everwell School." Miss Kurt held out the doll, which he took, taking much care to ensure that his fingers didn't make contact with hers because even looking at this woman did things to his senses. "Of course, being observant for danger and working with wild animals is something I learned at the circus."

Jeremy paused, searching for some kind of riposte for that jab, and found himself wanting. He took the doll, having no other reply except for a tight smile and the damnable sensation of being schooled in a battle of wits by a wisp of a woman in a faded cotton dress and eyes he could drown in.

"Good luck to you both," she said to Ivy, and then to him. And then, having accomplished the remarkable feat of being somehow indispensable to him on the one hand and the last thing he needed or wanted in his life on the other, she turned in that smart way of hers and started walking away.

Way of hers. He'd thought that like he'd knew her. He knew nothing about Miss Gemma Kurt of the Everwell Society for the Benefit of Sorrowful Spinsters and Woeful Widows. But at the moment he felt like the most important thing he needed to do was learn every detail, no matter how minuscule. Capture every line, every curve of her, commit it to memory, and pour it out on a canvas.

Apparently, the other thing he was doing was losing his damn mind.

She walked past him, her carpet bag held smartly at her side, shoulders square, the hem of her skirt teasing the hint of her boots beneath. More to the point, the woman who'd just singlehandedly managed his daughter without appearing to manage her, was walking away from him. Meanwhile, Jeremy was left to oversee Ivy while she wrote a piece of imaginary battle intelligence, instead of attending to the mountain of duties before his meeting with the Lieutenant Governor in ten minutes. He had no idea how to manage both.

The improbable answer to his quandary was walking away. And because Jeremy had a very healthy ego, he stood and wrestled with the risk of choking on it as he considered running after her.

"Papa," Ivy said, pulling on his hand. "The Code! This is an emergency!"

"Right." He started walking leading her on the street, the sound of a church bell ringing the hour. So much to do. But Ivy needed care. This was an emergency.

He looked up to see Mrs. Whitehead coming toward them. "Go with her and tell her I said to get you some paper and a graphite at once."

Once safely in the housekeeper's care, he turned on his heel and walked in Miss Kurt's direction. If there was one advantage he seemed to have over the Everwell Spinster, it was the length of his legs. He easily caught up to her.

"Miss Kurt," he called out. "A word please."

She paused, then turned. "Yes?"

He chose to ignore the way her eyes suddenly widened, or how the corner of her mouth turned up, teasing a smile she was no doubt trying to hide. A bloody smirk of triumph.

"Thank you for seeing to my daughter," he said. "You have proven yourself most capable."

"Thank you," she replied. "Now I really must go."

She was about to turn around when he reached out and took her by the arm. The movement shocked them both. And the rush of heat that bolted through his body and put it on alert should have been a warning signal that what he was about to do next was perhaps the most ill-thought-through event of his life. But he didn't have much of a choice.

"Miss Kurt. Would you come home with me?"

Her eyes widened. "Excuse me?"

Christ. He put two fingers to his temple in some vain attempt to get his thoughts in order.

"My apologies, Miss Kurt. It has been a taxing morning," he said, ignoring the hint of a smug smile teasing her plum-coloured lips. "I meant, the governess position. I would like to offer it to you if that is acceptable."

She paused, no doubt basking in his desperation, but he decided to sacrifice his pride to the higher purpose. He had a meeting in ten—make that five—minutes.

"And when would I start?" she asked.

"Ten minutes ago."

Chapter Five

NOT TEN MINUTES after she'd left, Gemma returned to Hastings House and was shown to her room on the second floor, opposite her new charge.

"Is that all you have, Miss Kurt?" Mrs. Whitehead asked from the doorway. The housekeeper was a prim, sturdy sort of woman, probably ten years Gemma's senior. Phillipa's age, she considered.

"At present, yes," she said. "I shall send to Everwell for the rest of my things."

She watched the older woman carefully as she said the name Everwell. The Society was a somewhat divisive entity in the city, famous—or infamous, depending on one's point of view—for the insistence on supporting women and girls regardless of their background. Only Lady Em's status as the daughter of lesser British nobility and a local war hero kept them from being ignored completely.

"Miss Webber is in the schoolroom at present, having some refreshments," Mrs. Whitehead said. "If you like, I can take you on a tour of the house before you begin your duties."

"You are not concerned she might bolt again?" Gemma asked.

"This will take but five minutes, and Sergeant Babcock has been deployed as watch," the housekeeper replied.

Gemma pushed aside her concern about the requirement for a full-grown man to act at guard for a ten-year-old girl, but reminded herself that she was also here for a job. The faster it was concluded, the faster she would be back at Everwell. She hadn't been the star of the show, as it were, for a very long time. Resisting the urge to ball her hands into tight fists, she followed Mrs. Whitehead as she was taken through the house.

"I had heard the house was riddled with hidden compartments," Gemma asked, trying to sound natural as she prodded for information. The finishes were elegant and obviously had been built with great care, and if Mrs. Lynde was correct, with plenty of panels that could provide a hiding place for a small packet of papers.

"I have discovered only one, and nothing of consequence in it." Mrs. Whitehead paused, and narrowed her eyes as she turned to Gemma. "But any unexpected findings are to be reported to me directly. I have been instructed by my employer to keep them for their inspection when they arrive."

Gemma started, assuming she'd misheard. "Your employer isn't Colonel Webber?"

"Mr. Lawrence Hatchett is my employer. He inherited this property, as well as other holdings belonging to his late great uncle." she said. "They plan to visit the property themselves with their lawyer to oversee the final execution of Mr. Dalrymple's will."

"I thought the will hadn't been found," Gemma said, the words slipping out before she had the chance to think. She resisted the urge to close her eyes at her own stupidity, trying to push the panic that she'd just somehow ruined the entire job before it had even started. She reached for the next thought, hoping to regain her balance. "I mean—that is to say—I thought I had read it. In the Chronicle."

Why oh why had she volunteered for this?

She smiled, innocently she hoped, and dared herself to look Mrs. Whitehead in the eye. She managed to catch the woman's eyebrow creak up in an arch that had no doubt been perfected after years of practice.

"If it had, it was inaccurately reported," Mrs. Whitehead replied. "Mr. Dalrymple had a will drawn up a decade ago by a lawyer in Toronto, where much of his remaining family still reside. It is clear about the disposition of his estate."

Did Gemma imagine it, or was there a particular edge in the housekeeper's answer?

"And are you here to guard the house until their return?" Gemma asked with a smile, trying to make something of a joke, which judging from the complete lack of amusement Mrs. White-head's face, fell as flat as Gemma's last attempt at baking a cake.

"I am here as a personal favour to the Hatchetts, to ensure that the house is kept to their standards until they arrive, as well as provide Colonel Webber assistance in running the household. Mr. Hatchett and Colonel Webber are old acquaintances, you see. He is a very busy man, and my being here saved him the trial of having to find someone up to his exacting standards," she added, her eyes narrowing before a hint of a smirk pulled at the side of her mouth. "It is unfortunate the same could not be said of Miss Webber's governess."

If any other of the Spinsters were here, they would know exactly what do with Mrs. Whitehead's insult. Elouise would have charmed Mrs. Whitehead so that the sentiment never entered her head, and Maddy would have either glowered so intently as to make Mrs. Whitehead run in the other direction, or simply ignored it altogether. Phillipa, who was probably Mrs. Whitehead's age but seemed somehow twenty years younger, would have silenced her with a smile and the tease of information about her past. Rimple would have laughed it off, then called her on her poor manners in the way only a woman raised by an English aristocrat and a no-nonsense Jamaican doctoress could.

But Gemma just wanted to hide. She wasn't good at being feisty. She'd expended the meager portion she had walking away from Colonel Webber outside the gates of the St. Paul's cemetery.

Feisty required a certain type of energy she didn't have. Elouise was feisty. Rimple was feisty. Gemma was just...exhausted.

She needed to lie down. Lie down and negotiate how she was going to search a house that was under the careful and hawkish eye of one Mrs. Whitehead.

They continued on in silence until they'd reached the top floor. Gemma relived the memory of hiding from the invading army of soldiers bustling about with crates and furniture. The doors she'd used to escape notice and exit the house were now closed.

"The school room is just this way." Mrs. Whitehead said, reaching to close the same door that she'd bolted into in her escape. "This room is off limits to everyone save the colonel."

Curiosity flared, but she had no need to go into the space unless she had to. It was one thing to be on the hunt; it was quite another to invite trouble by being reckless. Besides, she'd already been inside—it was the same place she'd spied the colonel only a few days ago. Instead, she turned her attention to a fusilier standing at attention near a door that was clearly Mrs. White-head's destination.

"Good afternoon," Gemma said to the impeccably dressed soldier—a sergeant, she guessed from the markings on his uniform— standing smartly at attention outside the nursery door. He was a sturdy man with a strong jaw, keen hazel eyes and, if she guessed correctly, a closely shaven head under his white helmet.

"Good afternoon Miss Kurt," he said, his tone unexpectedly warm given his rather solid and somewhat serious intimidating presence. "Sergeant Harold Babcock."

"Sergeant Babcock is the colonel's soldier-valet," Mrs. White-head explained before turning to the man. "Is there something we can do for you, Sergeant?"

"I'm just here waiting for Miss Ivy's report, ma'am," he said, then cast a glance toward the nursery, leaned in toward the ladies, and lowered his voice. His accent was English, but it was clear this man came from far humbler beginnings than Colonel

Webber or his daughter. "And to ensure no further escape attempts."

There was a warmth to Sergeant Babcock that instantly appealed to Gemma. Despite his immaculate uniform and military bearing, she sensed a convivial spirit. He appeared older than the colonel by several years, and she noticed some scarring on his neck that disappeared under the collar of his coat. This man had no doubt survived combat, and yet he seemed genuinely bemused by the military intelligence he was waiting to deliver from the hands of Ivy Webber.

Gemma compared Sergeant Babcock's bearing with his superior officer. Colonel Webber had seen battle as well—Gemma was certain of it. His chiseled features bore the lines around his eyes not only of his age, but his experience. Experiences etched into his face around his sharp grey eyes and the corners of this mouth. On any other man, they might have made him look haggard, but Colonel Webber's looks were only improved by them.

Mrs. Whitehead opened the door, which Gemma noted was well oiled. All the doors had been, in fact, no doubt a product of Colonel Webber's exacting standards. Gemma bit back a smile at the irony he'd made her job that much simpler, and no doubt assisted Ivy in escaping with less resistance than might have been if he'd let the door creak.

Every strength came with a corresponding weakness. Gemma's had been her ease with the trapeze, the confidence that her body could do what she'd wished it to. Confidence that had bubbled over into overconfidence. Into taking risks not only for herself, but for those around her. Unwanted memory intruded her thoughts—Gemma after practicing a new trick with Penny, convincing her friend they were ready. Penny hadn't been sure. Penny had pressed to do the highwire act, which Gemma hated. The triumph of persuading Penny to go through with the trapeze shattered with the memory that would haunt Gemma forever: Penny reaching out for Gemma as they passed each other on their swings, her fingers slipping out of Gemma's grasp.

"Here she is," Sergeant Babcock said, his booming voice pulling Gemma from the well of her thoughts, able to focus on her pupil who was sitting at a small desk.

The nursery was a pleasant room with covered with bright yellow paper and had all the accoutrements of a schoolroom, including a large slate board, and a modest sized desk for Gemma.

"How is your report coming, Miss Webber?" Gemma asked, stopping along side her pupil.

"Nearly there," she said. "And then we can take it to Papa."

"Your papa had gone to work, but Sergeant Babcock is waiting to take your note," Gemma answered. "Can you show me what you have written?"

Ivy pushed the paper over to her. The girl's penmanship was more than adequate for a child of her age, though the formation of some of the letters needed improvement. Still, it was lucid and legible, and Gemma wanted to start her relationship with the child with praise.

"Very good. I believe you have captured the facts of it," Gemma replied. "Why don't you pass it on to the sergeant?"

The girl did as she was told while Gemma turned to peruse a small shelf of books on the wall. There were several readers and a book of manners, but there was a distinct lack of mathematics and science and not a single map was to be had. She made a mental note to speak with the colonel about the materials, even as she wondered why on earth she would do so, since her primary object was to get the will and end this charade as soon as possible.

She was about to shoo the sergeant and Mrs. Whitehead out the door when the housekeeper held out a folio to Gemma. Inside was a piece of paper with what looked to be a schedule. It began at six o'clock in the morning, and continued in thirty-minute increments until eight o'clock in the evening. From dressing to breakfast to when certain lessons were offered, and then prayers and bedtime, it was all there in black and white.

"Colonel Webber has insisted upon providing his daughter

with as much structure as possible," Mrs. Whitehead said. "He puts a great emphasis on punctuality."

And far too little, it seemed, on actual learning, Gemma couldn't help but notice. With the exception of a single lesson on something entitled *'the art of moving in a manner suitable for a young lady'*, there was far too much focus on sedentary activity. If this was Ivy's day, no wonder she'd tried to escape up a tree. Reading this made Gemma want to escape up a tree.

"Is the expectation that I adhere to this schedule?" Gemma asked. "I am thinking on finer days, we could take some lessons out of doors."

Mrs. Whitehead inflicted Gemma with another arched brow.

"The Colonel is very particular about his daughter's education," the housekeeper said, then with an undisguised beat of hesitation, presented Gemma with a key to the nursery door. "Shall I send up a little lunch for you, Miss Kurt?"

"That would be much appreciated," Gemma replied, tucking the key into the pocket of her apron. Later, she would test that key on other locks, as she was more than willing to bet it worked in several, especially after she tinkered with it. She gazed back down at the folio, then stopped to check the watch on the small chatelaine that she wore. Half past noon. According to Colonel Webber's schedule, Ivy had an hour of quiet reading before another hour of practicing arithmetic.

Ivy returned but a moment later, a deep furrow in her brow.

"Mrs. Whitehead, I think we are settled here, thank you," Gemma said, then waited for the housekeeper to leave and the door to close before returning her attention to Ivy, who slumped into her desk, arms crossed. "Is there something amiss, Miss Webber?"

"Sergeant Babcock wouldn't let me go with him to deliver the message."

"You have lessons to attend to," Gemma said. "But I do believe you have fulfilled your duty to the Code."

Ivy let out a huff. "If this was Grenfell Hall, the servants would have to listen to me."

"Would they?" Gemma asked.

"Yes. And I overheard Uncle say that Papa wouldn't know what to do with me because he wouldn't have nearly enough servants to look after me. Because I am too demanding."

"Are you demanding?"

Ivy shrugged, and for the first time, Gemma detected a hint of uncertainty in the girl's expression. "Uncle seemed to think so. And he is a Viscount."

A Viscount? Gemma knew Colonel Webber was from a good English family, but she had no idea his lineage was quite that rarefied.

"Well, you're here now, and your father is the colonel, and Sergeant Babcock follows his orders," Gemma replied, nodding toward Ivy's seat. "There is nothing wrong with asking for what you need. At the same time, there needs to be a consideration of the needs of others. It is a bit of a balancing act. And right now, I need you to be writing out your multiplication tables."

The girl was about to protest, but must have thought the better of it, for she sat down in her chair and turned her attention to her slate.

A few moments later, a tray arrived at the door, delivered by Mrs. Whitehead herself. While Gemma was thankful for the refreshment, she couldn't help but wonder if the delivery by the housekeeper wasn't an excuse for the woman to keep an eye on her. Between the rather atrocious schedule and the sensation that Gemma would rarely be left alone, she was beginning to wonder how she'd find any opportunity to search the house.

She reviewed the itinerary Colonel Webber had created, knowing she needed to speak to him about it. While someone of Ivy's station would have an expectation of deportment put upon her, surely she would benefit from movement and activity that exercised the whole child.

Of course, why did this even matter? Playing at governess was only a means to search the house for Mr. Dalrymple's will. And she was never going to be able to discover it if she was locked away in this room for most of the day. She walked around the small schoolroom, idly running her hand over papered walls, feeling for any irregularities that might reveal a hiding place. She tamped down a bit of panic in her chest. Unless the document was the size of a novel—which was highly unlikely, even for a man as unconventional as Mr. Edgar Dalrymple—it could be stuck underneath some floorboards or wedged in a heating grate. Once upon a time, for another job, she'd recovered a stack of stolen letters in a hollowed-out bed post. She could spend hours doing nothing else but searching this room, and aside from the newly installed water closet, this was the smallest room in the house. She needed to be methodical and map out a plan. And she was not going to be able to get near it with a soldier outside the door.

Gemma slid a glance over to Ivy who was sitting straight backed in her chair, working quietly. While this served Gemma's purpose perfectly well at the moment, she could hardly imagine Ivy sitting in this position for hours. All that energy, that curiosity needed to be harnessed. Which gave Gemma an idea.

If she could convince the colonel that Ivy would learn much better by having the lessons move through the house, it might give Gemma more opportunity to search the house in broad daylight. It would be a juggling act of sorts, she mused. But she knew how to juggle.

Of course, she'd have to speak with Colonel Webber, and she had no idea how a man would take to having his orders questioned. There was something about him that put Gemma off kilter, like the first time she'd walked a tightrope. It was the one trick she'd always hated. There was no sense of flight, no thrill of soaring, no way for her to shut out the fantasy that it was just her. It was Gemma, consumed by the awareness that five hundred sets of eyes were watching her every step, waiting to see if she would fall.

Was he waiting for her to fall? Waiting for an excuse to let her go?

Indecision twisted inside her. Normally Phillipa made decisions like this and Gemma simply acted on them. But the head of the Scandalous Spinsters wasn't here to confer with, nor any the others she'd come to rely upon. Maybe it would have been easier if it was only Gemma's wellbeing that hung in the balance. But the wrong decision could cost Mrs. Lynde the inheritance she was owed and the ability to live with a modicum of dignity—and Gemma didn't know if she could survive hurting someone else by making the wrong choice a second time.

Chapter Six

THE MOMENT JEREMY set foot on the freshly brushed red carpet of Government House, any misgivings about hiring Miss Kurt were pushed aside by a small gathering of harried clerks and other house staff waiting for him. There was correspondence that required his attention, decisions to be made that only he could make or required him to consult with the Lieutenant Governor. The matters ranged from some low-level political delicacy, such as the hosting of the new U.S. Consul General for dinner, to matters of the more mundane, yet potentially troublesome, like the strange sound and worrisome smells emanating from the sink in the kitchen.

Even in this rush of fresh problems, Jeremy was calm. First, they were solvable. Second, they were a reliable distraction from his own. He'd spent the years since Isla died throwing himself into problems and found a curious sort of solace there. And after several days of broken concentration and up-ended schedules in the process of finding a suitable governess for Ivy, he was prepared to dig in at last. By the time he reached his office, a message for a plumber had been dispatched, a strong pot of tea ordered, and a sample menu for an upcoming dinner placed in his hands, which he reviewed and made some adjustments to even before he'd turned the knob on his office door.

Greeting him was his young clerk and a stack of correspondence that had grown considerably since yesterday. Jeremy stifled a groan, knowing it would take several late evenings to go through it. So much for the quiet evenings at home spending time with Ivy, and perhaps finally opening his long-neglected box of paints. One of Jeremy's strengths was understanding what could actually be accomplished in an hour, or six, and how to leave room for the inevitable delays or unexpected happenings.

But Ivy's arrival had tested his abilities in a way he had not yet been able to manage. Of course, there needed to be a settling in period—an adjustment of sorts, for both of them. He had anticipated that. Perhaps what he hadn't counted on was just how much there was to settle. How many emotions and memories would be stirred.

He checked his watch once more as he sat, taking stock of the multiple priorities sitting on his desk. He needed to accomplish something before his meeting with the Lieutenant Governor added to the growing piles on his desk. Keeping up with the Honorable Mr. Tupper's schedule was a quixotic venture at best, especially given his propensity to change the plans Jeremy had painstakingly put together. Of course, part of him loved the challenge, and he was damned good at it. But when his attention was elsewhere—back at Hastings House where his daughter and her unorthodox governess were no doubt staring each other down in a battle of wills that Miss Kurt was no doubt destined to lose—it made an already challenging act more precarious.

Perhaps Miss Kurt could advise him on that—after he dealt with dinner for the U.S Consul General.

"Take a letter please." He cued the clerk, who positioned himself at a smaller desk in the corner. After his unexpected challenges finding a governess, and being forced to hire a woman whose background was so completely unsuitable for the position, he needed his professional life to proceed smoothly.

He cleared his throat, gathered up his thoughts, and started to dictate. "We are looking forward to your visit with great anticipation..."

What should he anticipate when he arrived back home? Perhaps Miss Kurt was already packing her bags, which might have made him feel temporarily better about being right in dismissing her at the outset and yet very wrong at the same time. Shouldn't a woman who worked in an environment with wild animals know how to deal with a ten-year-old girl?

"We trust that this meeting will provide an opportunity to mend strained relations and open new dialogue on matters important to your great nation and ours..."

Did she tame tigers?

"...I am personally looking forward to discussing matters that will be of mutual interest..."

Or did she say she was part of a performing act? And good God, did she wear one of those utterly scandalous costumes that was as close to nudity as a woman could be in public? And Christ Almighty, why was he thinking about Miss Kurt wearing next to nothing?

"Colonel Webber, sir?"

The sound of his name pulled Jeremy's attention away from that tempting if utterly inappropriate image and somehow made him want to blush. *Blush.* Like a school boy who'd just been caught with a stack of pictures he'd bought from Holywell Street.

"Apologies," he said to the young, fresh-faced clerk who was waiting on his next few words. "Where were we?"

"We were confirming the date and time for the soirée with the American Consul General," came the reply.

"Right," Jeremy continued, inwardly cursing his lack of focus. Between the repairs to the plumbing at Government House and his other duties, this wasn't the time to be dwelling on Miss Gemma Kurt's dark eyes, or how she might taste if he kissed her. Relations between the U.S. and Canada were slowly warming after years of tension following the U.S. Civil War and Fenian

Raids, and Jeremy was not eager to inadvertently contribute to a political gaff that would interfere with progress because he was daydreaming about Gemma Kurt's legs.

He cleared his throat and continued to dictate.

"We trust his excellency has had ample opportunity to become settled in his new accommodations, and be able to enjoy the hospitality of Lieutenant Governor Tupper. Yours, etc."

He made a gesture with his hand to indicate he was finished.

"Right," Jeremy said, shifting course. "The Welcome dinner. Were we able to secure the string quartet?"

"Yes sir," his secretary nodded. "And we've put in the order for two cases of brandy and champagne."

"Better make it three," Jeremy added. "And let the chef know that the Counsel General's favourite dish is oyster bouchées."

The secretary scribbled quickly as Jeremy checked his watch. One minute.

"Anything else, Colonel?" the Secretary asked.

"Not at the moment," he replied, already walking toward the door. He hated keeping the Lieutenant Governor waiting. "I'll be back directly."

Jeremy marched at a smart clip down the hall to George Tupper's office and knocked.

"Come in!"

Jeremy stepped inside. Lieutenant George Tupper was a short, burly man with a round face and a set of sideburns that would make Ambrose Burnside envious. George Tupper was a former judge and politician who'd been in his position for nearly two years before Jeremy arrived in Halifax. The two men got on reasonably well despite the fact that Tupper was as unpredictable in his habits as Jeremy was dependable. It was one of the reasons why Jeremy had been the third Aide de Camp appointed during Tupper's tenure as Lieutenant Governor and given the additional responsibility of Private Secretary. Despite their differences, or perhaps because of them, the two men managed to find a comfortable rhythm with each other. Jeremy had learned to read Tupper's moods and anticipate if not all his whims, at least find a way to manage them. So when he entered the Lieutenant Governor's office and was struck by a pungent cloud of George Tupper's favourite pipe tobacco, Jeremy steeled himself. Tupper's pipe smoke was a harbinger of storms—storms of ideas, news, or other external forces that would turn Jeremy's carefully laid-out itineraries inside out.

"I've got something that's right up your alley," he said, pushing a notice across the table at Jeremy and gesturing for him to sit. "We're going to have some aristocratic visitors. Friends of yours, maybe?"

Jeremy picked up the note--a telegram--and scanned the bottom. The name instantly caught his eye.

"Reginald Pembroke, Earl Newport, and his wife Genevieve," Jeremy said.

"Sounds high and mighty enough," the Lieutenant Governor replied, taking a general puff on his pipe.

"You do represent Her Majesty," Jeremy reminded him, unable to hold back a smile. "That technically outranks the second son of a marquess."

Reginald was the eldest son of the 7th Marquess of Barronsfield. They'd met only once, at a Christmas party hosted by Jeremy's parents. According to the telegram, they were enroute to New York, but wanted to stop by Halifax, where Reginald's grandmother's family lived, and where she had resided in her earlier years.

"I'm the son of ship chandler, not a Viscount," Tupper said, pointing his pipe in Jeremy's direction. "They arrive late October."

Jeremy sat back in his chair, thinking about the implications. The schedule was already full to bursting. But it wasn't every day that someone representing the British aristocracy came to town, particularly someone of Reg Pembroke's standing. There would be dinners and gatherings and maybe even a ball.

Christ. He'd wanted to slow down. To get a chance to know

his daughter again. But he also needed to provide her with some stability. To show her that she could depend on her father.

"Have you replied yet?" Jeremy asked.

"That's your job, remember? You are my secretary," Tupper replied with a coy grin, then sat back in his chair.

"I am flattered by your confidence in my abilities sir." Jeremy nodded and rose, having been dismissed with a curt nod. He walked back to his office with a new problem to sort. He supposed he should be grateful for the distraction. Ivy's arrival had been welcome, but it also churned up a host of unwelcome memories and emotions. Her presence was a paradox of comfort and unease. It wasn't just that she reminded him far too much of her mother. It was the fact that Isla had somehow trusted her secret to their young child rather than her husband. That was harder to reconcile.

In some harsh way, in the years since Isla died, nothing had changed. He was at his assigned post, his family was far away, and work had to be done. And that sameness, that routine, that relentless sense of order helped him deal with the incomprehensible pain of his loss. Maybe Newport's arrival would just get him over this last hurdle and provide him enough distraction to allow Ivy to settle in. Then life could get back to normal. Whatever that meant.

৩৯৩

Any modicum of accomplishment Gemma had gained since securing her post had dissipated by supper hour. She and Ivy had eaten together after receiving word that the colonel's schedule would not allow him to dine with his daughter as originally planned. While Gemma felt a sense of relief at the colonel's absence, Ivy's disappointment at her father's absence was palpable.

"I don't like peas," Ivy said, as she idly pushed them around her plate.

"Peas remind me of being a little girl, actually," Gemma said. Her mother often made pasta with fresh peas in the spring, a dish Gemma realized she hadn't eaten in far too long. An unexpected bit of longing caught her as she carefully scooped a small handful of peas onto her fork. "If you don't like peas, try eating them with something you do like. It might help."

"Nothing will help." Ivy pushed aside a pea and took a stab at a carrot. "If Papa was here, I would tell him to tell the cook not to make me peas. Perhaps I should wait up for him so that he knows."

"According to the note, the colonel may be many hours yet, long past both our bed times," Gemma said, stifling a yawn. "But if he's home before bed, you absolutely can tell him. Would you like me to read you a story before bed? Or I could tell you one perhaps."

"What kind of story?"

"I'm sure I could make one up," Gemma said. "Do you like fairytales? I think the princess and the pea might be a good one. I promise there is only one pea to be had and it's not on anyone's plate."

Ivy nodded begrudgingly, if only because having a story or two might allow her to stretch out her bedtime until the colonel had returned. In the end, Gemma had told not only that tale but three others before Ivy finally dropped off to sleep.

Now Gemma sat up in her room, listening for the colonel to return and retire himself so she would have the house to herself. When the clock below chimed ten and he hadn't arrived, she risked returning to the dining room, Davy light in hand, to explore the dumbwaiter shaft a second time. She painstakingly went through every nook and cranny of the butler's pantry, looking for any hint of an envelope, knocking on every panel, listening for a hollow sound where there shouldn't be one. Nothing.

Gemma had been tempted to start a search of the dining room itself when a key jangled in the lock at the front door. It was soon followed by the hurried steps of Mrs. Whitehead, coming up the stairs to greet the colonel and Sergeant Babcock in hushed tones. Gemma quickly extinguished her lamp and waited.

Thankfully, the colonel headed directly to his room. She waited, counting the steps—thirty-five from the bottom of the stairs to his room—when she heard him pause just outside Ivy's door. Something in Gemma softened at the realization he'd gone to check on his daughter. Then, once she heard his door shut, her shoulders relaxed and she silently climbed up the stairs to her room.

Eagerness to finish the job competed with the requirement for patience. Patience to learn the household's habits and the movements of the household staff. Rarely had she even gone into a house to do a job without an excellent sense of the rhythm of a household—when it tended to be quiet, or when a particular room was normally occupied. They often came courtesy of Rimple Jones and her trusty spyglass, supplemented by intelligence gathered by Phillipa, or an intervention in the form of a diversion by Elouise.

This time she was truly on her own. On the highwire.

And then there was the business of Ivy Webber. The disappointment on the girl's face at her father's absence was unmistakable. What would make life easier for Gemma—Colonel Webber's absence—was clearly not what Ivy needed. But there was the business of that well-meaning but horrid curriculum she needed to speak with him about. She just needed to get up the nerve—something she'd lost a long time ago.

Chapter Seven

THE NEXT TWO days were much like Gemma's first at Hastings House.

If Gemma had been looking for an excuse not to talk to Colonel Webber, she didn't need to search for one. He was hardly home. He rose early, had breakfast in his study, went to work, came home late or, if on time, took the smallest amount of time with Ivy before disappearing into his study again.

No wonder Gemma had first discovered her up a tree. The child was clearly starved for adventure and her father's presence.

Gemma shouldn't have been concerned about that. She'd been in the house for two nights thus far and had no luck finding the will—and if Mrs. Whitehead was correct, the Hatchetts had clearly fabricated a second document to aid their claim. But Gemma wasn't only the Scandalous Spinster's best burglar; she'd become a passionate teacher. And Ivy was her student. Just because Gemma was here with an ulterior motive didn't mean she couldn't give the girl the time and attention she so clearly needed.

Today, Gemma and Ivy were back in the schoolroom, the lamplight cutting through the gloom. Rain poured down on the cobblestone streets, the sky above a dull gunmetal shade of grey that pervaded Hastings House. Ivy started the day determined to be in a bad mood, and no amount of Gemma's coaxing could entice the child out of it. The day started with arithmetic, which Gemma enjoyed. But after only a few minutes of quizzing Ivy on multiplication tables and receiving either blank stares or outright ridiculous guesses, Gemma resorted to having Ivy focus on memorization. It was not quite as useful as understanding the concept of multiplication and rapidly adding up sets of numbers, but it was a start, at least. Or she thought it was, until she looked at the girl's slate only to see it filled with little chalk doodles.

Moving on from multiplication tables to history was only a marginal improvement. Gemma read from the text, included a rundown of the unfortunate wives of King Henry the eighth. To Gemma's dismay, though perhaps not her surprise, the grizzly ends of Anne Boleyn and Catherine Howard did perk up her pupil somewhat.

"I don't know why Henry could have a mistress but his wives could not," she said. "It seems very unfair, especially if he was going to murder them for something he could do."

"Henry was a man," Gemma by way of explanation, which felt as unsatisfactory as it was true. "It is the way they hold on to power—by making sure the next king is actually their son. If a woman could inherit the throne, then any man would do."

"Like Uncle Alexander. My cousin James will become Viscount, even though my cousin Margaret is two years older," she said. "It's not fair."

Gemma let out a breath. "No, it isn't. Unfortunately there are lots of things some people get to do because of who they are, and others who can't."

"When I get older, I'm going to have a mistress and inherit a castle," Ivy said with utter certainty.

"Does anyone in your family have a castle?" Gemma asked.

"My mother's uncle has one, in Portugal. It's on the ocean," she said. "And Mama promised me I would inherit it."

It was the first time Ivy had talked about her mother. Gemma knew Colonel Webber was widowed—in fact, his status as a handsome and eligible widower had made him quite the star of the society pages in the Halifax Chronicle. It had all felt very predatory and gave Gemma an inexplicable niggle of dissatisfaction at the idea of matching him up with anyone.

"Intriguing," Gemma said, urgent for some connection. She pulled out a sheet of paper from her desk and set it down in front of Ivy. "Do you think could you draw it?"

"I've never seen it," the girl complained.

"Well someone must have spoken about it with you," she said. "Your mama, perhaps?"

"She said it was on the ocean, and it was tall, but that's all I know," she said.

"Well, start with that, and let your imagination help you. If you were going to inherit a castle on the coast of Portugal, what would it look like?"

Ivy started to draw, while Gemma paced the floor. Sergeant Babcock was at the door again today, no doubt to keep an eye on his employer's charge and Gemma, too. The sergeant was amiable at least.

"I can't do it!" Ivy exclaimed after a few moments, in a fit of frustration.

Gemma looked over to see the paper cast aside, the pencil on the floor and a brow furrowed so deeply Gemma was certain she could use it as a shelf.

Gemma bent down and scooped up the art work. She was not at all gifted in the visual arts, but Ivy's proclamation that she couldn't draw was not supported by the evidence on the page.

"It looks to me like you can," Gemma said. "This is very good."

"It looks better in my head," she cried. "I hate drawing."

"Well, why don't you describe it with words then?" Gemma offered.

"The words in my head go too fast for my hands," Ivy said.

"I could write it for you," she said, "and you could dictate it to me. Like your father composes his letters," she added quickly at the end.

Gemma was about to silently congratulate herself on what was surely an offer that could not be refused...an offer that could, at some level, allow Ivy to be in some kind of alignment with Colonel Webber. However, before she had a chance to even consider it, Ivy huffed out a large sigh, followed by a very dramatic splat across the front of her desk, in an act that would make her worthy of a starring role in one of Elouise's little plays she had the girls put on at Everwell. But as Ivy pulled head back off the desk, her hand knocked the small bottle of ink at her desk, sending the pen inside it flying, causing ink to fly not only over part of the desk, but onto Ivy's and Gemma's skirts as well.

Ivy's face flushed, and the furrow of indignation quickly turned to tears.

"I'm going to be in trouble, aren't I?" she asked.

"Everyone makes mistakes," Gemma said. "It's how we manage them that makes all the difference. So let's begin by doing our very best to clean this up. You start by retrieving your pen."

She smiled at the girl, trying to reassure her, biting back the hypocritical feeling in her gut. Once upon a time she'd made the most horrible mistake possible. They was no way to undo what she'd done, and no chance to apologize.

"I'm sorry," Ivy said, her voice wavering as she picked up the pen off the floor and looked down at her once yellow pinafore that was now covered in ink that Gemma was certain no amount of soaking could fix.

"Well," Gemma said, surveying the damage, which would amount to an evening spent soaking her skirt in vinegar and soap, "I guess I know what we're doing next."

Gemma handed Ivy the cloth she used to wipe down the chalkboard, then went to the door where Sergeant Babcock stood, bless him, at attention.

"Sergeant Babcock," she said, putting on a smile. "We seem to have had a minor incident involving some ink." She gestured to her plum skirt, which bore a flourish of black. "Would you be so good as to fetch us some rags and warm, soapy water?"

He looked at her, clearly uncertain if this was some ploy to remove him from his post while they went exploring somewhere they weren't supposed to. She remedied his doubt by taking him by the hand, into the room itself, where Ivy was trying to dab up the ink with the cloth Gemma used to clean off the chalk board.

"Of course," he said at last. "Back in a moment."

With that, Ivy sat down in her chair.

"Excuse me," Gemma said, "but your work here is not done. You have a cloth in your hand, so you may continue to put it to good use."

"But that's what servants are for," she said. "At Grenfell the servants cleaned all our messes."

"Well, we are at Hastings House now," Gemma said, "And while Sergeant Babcock has many duties, I suspect cleaning up your messes is not one of them."

Within minutes, Sergeant Babcock returned.

"Thank you, Sergeant," Gemma said, relieving him of the bucket. "We shall see to this, won't we Ivy?"

Ivy nodded and started sopping up the ink.

"Do you want a hand?" the sergeant asked. "After all, getting rid of stains is one of my specialties."

Gemma smiled at the idea of this strapping man fussing over the stains in Colonel Webber's shirts. She had no doubt that he would know exactly how to handle an ink stain like this. But working in a school meant Gemma was no stranger to messes like this, either.

"I think we will manage," she said. "Besides, a little exercise will do us both a world of good on this rather dreary day. Sergeant, I appreciate you are here on the colonel's orders, but I think we will both be well here for the time being, won't we Miss Webber?"

"Yes Miss Kurt," she said, smiling sweeter than one of Phillipa Hartley's sticky buns. The girl wasn't foolish—she knew that as dreadful as scrubbing a floor might be, being forced to sit back at her desk for several more hours was far worse.

The two worked diligently for the better part of an hour. Gemma rose from her kneeling position, stretching her back. While she was strong, being in a single position for so long still required a stretch. She tossed the rag in the bucket and wiped her brow with the back of her hand.

"Well," she began, rising to her feet, taking a rag from Ivy and setting the bucket to one side, "I think we are done for now."

Ivy rose to her feet and walked back to her desk, defeat evident in her eyes. It was clear to Gemma that there was little more to be learned in the way of multiplication tables or recitation of bible verses or whatever else had been on the original schedule.

Gemma picked up Ivy's drawing, took Ivy by the hand, and went to their rooms to change. Sergeant Babcock waited to receive the soiled clothing, insistent that he oversee the removal of the stains. Once he'd gone, Gemma looked up the stairs where the schoolroom was waiting.

"I think we've had enough lessons for one day," she said to Ivy. "Don't you think?"

Ivy's face instantly lit up and she nodded, which couldn't help but make Gemma smile.

"Right, this is what we're going to do," Gemma said, rubbing her hands together. "Let's have a picnic."

"A picnic?" the girl asked, her little face scrunching up in confusion as she turned toward the nearest window which was streaked with rain. "But it's raining."

"We'll have it here," she said, surveying the room. "We'll push your desk into the corner, along with the chalk board. I'll gather some food from the kitchen, and perhaps you can find a blanket and some pillows and we can be comfortable with on our freshly scrubbed floor."

Ivy beamed from ear to ear, then scurried off on her quest. Before long, the two of them were sitting in the attic, spread out on a blanket with pillows to rest on, nibbling on molasses cookies and lemonade, listening to the rain drum on the roof. In the lamplight, it was quite cozy. Ivy was free to get up when she pleased, and her mood had improved tenfold over what it had been only an hour before.

"I heard Mrs. Whitehead say you were in a circus," Ivy said between bites of a cookie. "Is that true?"

Gemma frowned, perturbed by the idea of Mrs. Whitehead speaking about her past without her consent. "When did she tell you that?"

"The day after you arrived. She wasn't very happy about it," she said. "I was listening from outside father's study."

"It's not polite to listen in on others," Gemma said. "But you did hear correctly."

Ivy's eyes lit up and she pulled herself up on her knees and leaned forward. "Really? Did you see tigers?"

"Yes," Gemma replied. "And lions. And elephants. Well, one elephant anyway. Her name was Ginger."

"That's an odd name for an elephant."

"Most human names are probably odd for an elephant," Gemma said. "But Ginger was lovely. I used to ride her."

Ivy sat up with rapt attention, and Gemma realized that instead of beginning with Kings and Queens and multiplication tables, she should have started with Ginger.

"Can you juggle?"

Gemma grinned.

"You can!" Ivy burst out, her eyes wide. She picked up a pear and two apples from the small basket Gemma had brought for their picnic and thrust them at her. "Show me."

Gemma held up her hands, unsure.

"I'm not sure your father or Mrs. Whitehead would appreciate me showing you this."

"I won't tell," she replied, practically vibrating with excitement. "Please. I'm good at keeping secrets."

Ivy's strange admission caught Gemma's attention. Why would she have to be?

Gemma had taught countless children at Everwell to juggle. It required concentration and coordination to pull it off. Patience to learn. It also required good posture.

"I can," she said after a moment, and accepted the fruit from Ivy. She pulled herself to her feet. then started tossing them into the air, catching and releasing it again. catching the fruit with just enough dramatic flair to finish the trick. "On two conditions."

"Anything!" The child said, bouncing and clapping her hands.

"One, I will inform your father. And two, that you practice your multiplication tables."

Ivy stilled, and Gemma was certain she could see the war going on in the girl's head. My word, she thought, this child had a stubborn streak. Gemma could see echoes of the girl's father as she performed the analysis of whether the gain was worth the trial. So Gemma decided to sweeten the pot.

"If you get very good, you can do this with torches, you know," Gemma added, careful not to specify that the torches, if any could be procured, would not be lit.

"Yes," Ivy said. "Teach me!"

Gemma handed Ivy a single apple and held one in her own hand. Holding the fruit out, she tossed a single apple into the air, catching it with the same hand.

"I want you to practice this one motion."

"But I want to do three," she complained.

"If you start with three, you'll never learn. Start with this, and when you can throw it up and catch it again while looking straight ahead, then we'll move on. Trust me, it's harder than it looks."

As if to prove her point, Ivy threw the apple up far too high. It dropped to the floor, narrowly missing a full tumbler of lemonade.

"See?" Gemma said. "Just be gentle with it. You don't need to toss it too high…just gently send it into the air, like it's on a string, and allow it to fall back into your hand."

Ivy kept on trying, the apple falling again a couple of times but already, her control was improving.

"Excellent," Gemma said. "I have some bean bags in my valise that I use to practice with. I shall let you have one to work with and we can save the fruit for eating."

"What else do you know how to do?" Ivy asked. "Can you do a somersault?"

Gemma laughed. "Not in this corset, no." She paused, then crossed her arms, struck by another idea. "What if I showed you how to do a handstand?"

"Yes!" she exclaimed, squealing with joy. "What do I have to do to learn that?"

"Verses. I want you to practice your penmanship. For that, you will learn one handstand."

The girl took a bit of her apple. "I can't wait to tell Papa! He'll be so excited!"

Gemma very much doubted that. Indeed, she could hardly imagine him being excited about anything, except for maybe a well-organized shelf.

They continued with the lesson, satisfaction settling on Gemma's shoulders. It was the same sensation, she realized, that enveloped her after the completion of a job. Or even when she'd landed a difficult trick on the trapeze after many failed attempts.

Except she shouldn't be feeling this way...not about a lesson. She was here to do a job. And that job was to find Dalrymple's will.

Chapter Eight

JEREMY SAT AT HIS DESK, staring at the small pocket watch next to a stack of neatly folded letters he'd spent the better part of the day answering. It had been approximately fifty-one hours since Miss Kurt had coaxed Ivy down from her tree and taken up her post as governess. It had been eight hours since he'd left home for the day, leaving strict orders with Babcock, who was without question the most reliable man God ever created, to send word if anything was going awry.

Blessedly there had been no harried notes from Babcock. Perhaps Miss Kurt, despite her suspect upbringing under a circus tent was, in fact, exactly the right person to manage Ivy. Or perhaps not.

He'd learned the hard way that the adage about no news being good news was generally a crock of shit. No news simply meant that life was going on without him, and the life he'd thought he'd had was crumbling to pieces around him. News meant there were details he could manage. Problems that could be solved before they got out of hand. But as Jeremy sat in his office reviewing a speech he was writing for one of the Lieutenant Governor's upcoming appearances, it finally occurred to Jeremy that he'd had no news from Hastings House in the fifty-one hours and twenty-six minutes since Gemma Kurt arrived.

A moment later, Jeremy found himself dashing out the door of Government House in a driving rain, so single minded in the urgency of his errand that he narrowly avoided tripping over a mound of horse droppings in the middle of the road. It was an urgency driven by a sensation that he would acknowledge only to himself when sober, and perhaps to Babcock when drunk—that somehow, something was falling to pieces right under his nose.

He was absolutely *not* running across Bishop Street in the rain because he was thinking about Gemma Kurt. The way she tapped her fingers on her lips when she was thinking had somehow gotten stuck in his brain alongside oyster bouchées, which yielded all sorts of unholy thoughts. It should have been all the more reason to keep his backside in his office, immersing himself in a mountain of mundane tasks that would keep him occupied by anything except Miss Kurt's lips.

But he would never allow himself to think that. He had no depth of feeling for Miss Kurt and he was bloody well certain he would never have any. He'd experienced love once and had thought it perfect. But perfect things never lasted. And the pain of losing it was too much to consider ever having it again. Especially for a tiny, dark-haired pixie that was Miss Gemma Kurt.

Unlike any of the other proper misses that had been sent to him by the good women of the New Women's League, Miss Kurt was, in fact a woman. She clearly had the confidence and experience of a woman who'd seen something of life and knew how to apply it to the challenge ahead. Not that Jeremy had been completely absent, and his brother Alexander had without question welcomed Ivy into his home. But Ivy was like Isla—a strong-willed dreamer. And society didn't seem to know what to do with a girl who was either of those.

Neither did he.

Perhaps that was why he relented and allowed Miss Kurt to try.

He dashed inside, eager to escape the pounding rain, and was greeted with the scent of warm molasses and butter. He brushed the water from his wool coat and looked up to see Harold Babcock coming up from the hall with a tray of biscuits. It was so inviting that Jeremy almost missed the fact that his soldier-valet was playing at housemaid instead of sentry duty.

"What the devil, Babcock?" Jeremy said. "Why aren't you in the schoolroom?"

Surprise crossed Babcock's brow.

"Colonel! It's good to see you sir, if unexpected." He straightened, and nodded in greeting. "Would you like a report?"

"Is there anything to report?" Jeremy asked. "Has all been quiet, or am I off to find another governess?"

Babcock smiled and shook his head. "No, sir. There was a bit of a mishap earlier with a bit of spilled ink, but that's been managed. No harm done, aside from one of Miss Ivy's pinafores, but I've got it and Miss Kurt's skirt soaking downstairs. I'm just going up with a bit of refreshment. They've been at their lessons now for a couple of hours."

"Mishap?" Jeremy pursed his lips. "What happened to Miss Kurt's skirt?"

And why in hell was he suddenly preoccupied with the notion of Babcock being in possession of it? He should have turned around, right there, and marched back to his office slowly, going the long way, to let the cold rain soak through his clothes and set his head to rights.

"I'm not sure what happened, but Miss Kurt assured me it was an accident. Miss Kurt's skirt is soaking in the kitchen, and I've put some vinegar to it to get out the stain. And they cleaned the floor."

"They?" Jeremy asked, uncertain of his hearing. "Ivy was cleaning?"

Ivy was not exactly a spoiled child, but she had been born into a rarified strata of privilege, and dealing with the consequences of her own actions had not been something any governess had been able to manage thus far.

Babcock nodded, apparently nonplussed by the entire battle report. "It's all back to rights up there, and as I said, they've been busy with their studies ever since. I thought they deserved a bit of a treat."

Jeremy started. "Did you bake those?"

"Cook did," he said. "I'm just the delivery mechanism."

"Colonel!" Mrs. Whitehead appeared from the top of the next stair. "Thank goodness you are home."

"I heard about the ink spill, Mrs. Whitehead." Jeremy pursed his lips. One minor mishap with a bit of ink? Seemed too good to be true. "I am going to see to it now."

"It's not the ink. They two of them have been locked in the nursery for hours. There is an unnatural amount of laughter coming from behind the door."

Something unexpected in Jeremy's chest squeezed. "Laughter? Well, I suppose that's better than tears."

"I was cleaning Miss Ivy's room sir," she said. "And there was a dreadful amount of clunking coming from above. I went to the room, to see if there was any trouble, and was told all was well. But the door was locked."

"Lead the way, Babcock," he said, and followed his trusted sergeant up the stairs. "Thank you, Mrs. Whitehead. I'll take it from here."

He could tell the woman wanted to protest, but he gave her that well-practiced look that would tell anyone with eyes that any discussion was over, then proceeded to the top floor. He was concerned, a little, about the locked door. Was Miss Kurt concerned that Ivy would dash?

When he arrived at the nursery, Jeremy paused and put an ear to the door. He could hear some hushed whispers, and a bit of giggling, and squeal of laughter that sounded like it was coming from Ivy. It hardly sounded like learning at all.

Jeremy nodded to Babcock, who unlocked the door and stepped aside for Jeremy to enter.

It was empty.

Or at least, there were no people.

It took him a moment to register what he was seeing. The desks had been moved to one side. On the floor, there was a blanket, a couple of books, and an assortment of cutlery and cups and apples that hinted at...a picnic? Was the afternoon segment of the schedule reserved for reading and quizzes? Were they done early? Impossible. There were two sets of boots on the floor.

"You're doing it!"

The encouraging tone of Miss Kurt's voice rose about the hush, catching every fibre of his being and pulling at it with an inexplicable sense of longing. It came from behind the door.

Jeremy took a step in and was confronted by—*legs*? Four legs in fact - Ivy's shorter ones, all drawers and stockings, and Miss Kurt's beside hers. Her legs were together, straight, her toes pointing to the ceiling. Her calves were elegant, but strong, and she held herself there perfectly balanced. He spied a flash of her inner thigh where the slit in her drawers gaped. It should have been so insignificant to see amongst the volume of fabric that fell around a woman's legs, but the effect on his body was instant.

Christ almighty.

"Stay where you are, Babcock," he said, holding out his arm.

The sound of his voice brought the giggling and encouraging words to a standstill. In a fluid motion, Miss Kurt somehow folded in two, and then right up again, her form perfect. She then helped Ivy gently come to rights herself. His daughter's cheeks were ruddy from a combination of exertion and the position in which she was holding herself, but her eyes were wide and he was taken aback by something he'd not seen on Ivy since—well, he couldn't quite remember.

Joy.

"Did you see what I did?" she exclaimed, her expression

bursting with pride. "I did a handstand. It took me an hour to do it by myself, but I did it."

Jeremy knew what he should say. He should tell her how fine young ladies did not display their bodies in such a scandalous fashion. He should tell her that she was never to do it again. Instead, greedy for another second of that joy he hadn't seen in her eyes before, he smiled at his daughter, then spoke firmly.

"Ivy, will you go with Babcock down to the kitchen? He has a plate of biscuits that Cook has made for you."

"But what about our lessons?"

"I think you've learned quite enough for today." God, he felt like such a bastard. But he was her father, and if he wanted her to make her way in the world, she needed the education of young lady, not some free-spirited vaudeville act.

"But—"

"Ivy," Miss Kurt said, her voice steady and bright, "why don't you go with Sergeant Babcock, and I'll show your father what you've accomplished this afternoon?"

Ivy looked from Miss Kurt to Jeremy, the joy fading from her eyes.

When he heard the door click behind them, he turned to Miss Kurt.

"What in the devil was that?"

Jeremy had inspected thousands of soldiers in his career. While he was hardly a harsh commander, he'd come to except a certain kind of deportment from his men. Backs straight, chest proud, hands at their sides. They needed to be able to listen and to trust, because at some point, they were going to have to something unpleasant because he'd ordered them to.

Miss Kurt, however, was not one of his soldiers—not that he needed much reminding. That hint of flesh at her inner thigh and the solid, shapely curve of her calves was a memory that might carry him through until the end of his days. She stood, lips pressed firmly together, watching him with those dark brown eyes of hers, her stance guarded but confident.

"It was a handstand."

"That is not an answer."

"It is the only answer to that question," she replied with an edge of impatience. "I taught her how to do a handstand. You should be proud of her. She picked it up quite quickly. Her upper body is quite strong."

Jeremy paused, his brain muddled perhaps by the way the hem of her skirts moved over the top of her feet, exposing her stockings. Or it could have been that she was talking about his daughter the way someone might talk about a workhorse, or a stevedore.

"My daughter has no plans to be a circus clown, Miss Kurt. She is to grow in to a fine English gentlewoman, and marry," he said. "I'm afraid this arrangement, made against my better judgment, must come to an end."

"Very well then," she said, her voice clipped as she turned away from him, plucking her boots from the floor. "I trust you will convey to Miss Webber that I am not abandoning her."

Jeremy stilled, her choice of works catching in his chest.

"What did you say?"

She stopped, clutching her boots to her middle, and swallowed. "I trust you will make it clear that I am not leaving her."

"I hardly see why that matters. I don't need to explain myself to my daughter."

Her mouth fell into a frown as she gazed up at him from across the suddenly too small room. Her hair was mussed from her activities, leaving a few wayward strands of hair teasing at her neck. Awareness of her rippled through his body as he flexed his fingers, fighting the urge to reach out and touch her.

"It matters to me. I have never given up on a student," she said. "No matter how difficult they have been to teach. We don't give up on people at Everwell, Colonel Webber. We help. But clearly my help is not wanted."

"If your help involves teaching my daughter to display herself in such an unladylike manner—"

"Oh for heaven's sakes," she said, letting out an exasperated sigh. "Ivy needs an education. She needs to learn to do math, so she can manage a household and not fear for being cheated. She may need to learn to read a contract. She needs to learn about the ways of the world, so she can move through it, not hide from it. I assume you want your daughter to be able to protect herself, when you are gone?"

"Of course I do," Jeremy said, his heart lurching at the very idea. "I love her more than life itself."

"Then allow her to learn in a way that makes sense to her."

She walked toward the chalkboard, her steps light and effortlessly graceful. On the board was a full row of verses, done in a steady hand. Ivy's hand. Since they'd arrived, it was the first evidence he'd seen of her progress.

"We have a bit of a deal worked out, you know," she continued. "I will teach her to juggle, and she will learn her multiplication tables. For verses, she gets a handstand."

As if to prove her point, she flipped the chalkboard over to the other side, where there multiplication tables. Again, the hand was Ivy's.

"Colonel Webber," she continued, her tone shifting, her stance less protective than it had been a moment ago. "Ivy needs exercise built into her routine. What happens to your men if you keep them cooped up all day?"

"We try not to. It makes them restless. Prone to fights or other mischief. So we do drills, or put them to work." He looked up at her, swallowing a smile at the hint of smug satisfaction in her face. "I see what you are doing Miss Kurt, but those are men."

"I hate to inform you, but women are no different. Except in the expectations, perhaps," she said. "Women are people. While some have temperaments that are given to sitting alone and being quite happy to do so, many are not. We just aren't perceived as requiring it."

"But a handstand?" he asked. "Couldn't you take a turn about the room?"

"Pacing in a circle in such a small space is hardly conducive to clearing the mind and making it ready to learn," she said. "In Ivy's case, I think it might make it worse. More restless. Your daughter is very bright. And she is very talented."

She went to the floor, where they evidence of the picnic they'd concocted still lay. It looked like a merry scene—a counterpoint to the blustery day out the window. She picked up a small piece of paper and put it in his hands.

It was a drawing done in charcoal—a castle sitting on the edge of a cliff overlooking a stormy sea.

"She drew this for me, after a little coaxing," she said. "She told me that the words in her head come too quickly for her hands to write, so I asked her to draw instead."

"Ivy did this?" Jeremy studied the drawing. He'd known that his brother had provided for a tutor for her in England, but he had never commented on her work. Maybe he never thought to ask. The drawing was still obviously a child's hand, but it showed a remarkable appreciation for perspective and shadow.

"She did," she replied. "And without my help. I have no talent for the graphic arts whatsoever. Or any art, truthfully. But Ivy clearly has a gift for it. Did your wife draw?"

"No." He did. But he was not about to share that with her. "She appreciated art—we both did. But she did not draw."

She nodded, a delightfully thoughtful look furrowing her brow. "You should find a tutor for her. Phillipa is quite good—she is one of the teachers at the school. She would not have time for private tutoring, but you might consider bringing Ivy to Everwell for a class with some of the other students. It would do her well to have some friends."

"I'll take that on advisement," he said.

"I would like to speak to you about one other matter," she began, then went to her desk where she picked up a neatly folded piece of paper. It was Ivy's schedule that Jeremy had laboured over before her arrival. "We must address Ivy's itinerary. I cannot see the advantage to having her time fully accounted for in this way."

Jeremy was certain he blinked, confused by Miss Kurt's impertinent question. Surely a teacher at a girl's school would understand the value of a schedule. Jeremy had kept regiments going with schedules—supply lines and road building and every manner of modern logistical miracle came as a result of a well-orchestrated schedule.

"A lady must be punctual," he said. "They must meet the expectations of her station and society, manage guests and household and whatever else it is that women do."

There was a little fire that came alive in her impossibly dark brown eyes and somehow, quite miraculously it shot through Jeremy's chest. He nearly flinched with awareness from the sensation.

"Providing Miss Webber with no chance for exercise or social activity or allowing her the choice, however brief, to determine how she might spend her time will not prepare your daughter for managing a household, or whatever else it is that women do." She paused, her eyes locking on him. "Which, I would add, is generally far more than most men realize."

There was a lock of her black hair trailing along her cheek, wavy and yet ethereal, almost like the diminutive woman standing before him. And like Miss Kurt, it was bewitching, this little lock of hair, tempting him to toss aside any sense of deportment, good sense or manners and reach out to touch it. He flexed his hands behind his back as he willed himself not to satisfy his need to feel what he was certain as soft as silk.

Her lips parted and they stood silent a moment, unwilling to acknowledge this delicious tension in the room.

"I understand that, with your career, you would see orderly conduct as important. And it is," she said, brushing the hair aside as if it were nothing. She had no idea, he realized, just how lovely she was. "Society would not function if there were not some rules that we can all agree upon."

Jeremy cleared his throat.

"In a battle, it can be the difference between defeat or victory, life or death. A soldier's life is a hard one. Especially an enlisted man. A bit of order and dependability isn't a bad thing. Knowing there are regular meals and a place to lay your head and expectations of conduct can help a man cope with all the chaos in between."

"I grew up in a circus," she said, nodding. "Always moving. Always beginning your day in one place and finishing it in another. To an outsider, it probably looked like chaos. Believe me when I say I understand the need for some touchstones in a nomadic life. And when you are flying forty feet in the air, or trying to keep an elephant calm in an unruly crowd, that sense of order and calm can be a matter of life or death."

She faltered ever so slightly, and though she smiled, he could see it was forced. She continued.

"But there is a difference between the dependability of the schedule and being a slave to one. Your daughter is young and active, with a lively imagination and a will of iron."

Like her mother, he couldn't help but think.

"A schedule provides comfort," he said. "At any given time, I can take comfort that she is where she is supposed to be, and not up a tree somewhere."

He needed to know. Know that she was safe. Secure. Because for six months, he was in Egypt, blithely unaware Ivy was watching her mother slowly—and sometimes painfully—dying. And he didn't know. His heart couldn't survive another blow like that.

It was that simple, really. And that complicated.

Miss Kurt, for her part, stood silent, watching him with an intense curiosity.

"The schedule is for you then," she said with a bit of a nod, as if she understood something she had no business understanding. "For your comfort."

"I didn't say that."

"But you did," she said. "A schedule provides comfort. You literally just said it."

Did she not understand that he was the ranking officer here?

"Perhaps I did. But that is not what I meant." Which was a bloody lie. It was exactly what he meant. He just hadn't meant for *her* to know that's what he meant. "I am her father. It is my duty to ensure my daughter's care and security."

She paused, pursing her lips ever so slightly—the smallest betrayal that she was planning some kind of counter attack.

"Could we not find a middle ground? All the same lessons, the same timetable, but we could add another column, here," she set the schedule on his desk, rotating it until it faced him, pointing a margin on the page. "Geography in your study, where there is a large globe, and no doubt an atlas or two. Arithmetic in the kitchen, where we might discuss measurements."

It did make sense, he wanted to concede, but he was temporarily distracted by the rush of colour pouring into her cheeks and the subtle scent of her perfume. Orange blossoms and vanilla. It was unexpected and alluring.

"At Everwell, we move the children about from the library to the schoolroom and out of doors," she continued, blithely unaware of his distraction. "It provides the girls a respite from sitting all day, keeping their minds active and their attention engaged on the lesson, rather than on the hardness of the chair they've been forced to sit on for hours at a time."

"The schedule I set her for created on advice of the tutors hired by my brother. It would be for a life she is expected to lead. And my brother would only hire the best." Jeremy could only imagine what Alexander would think of a woman like Miss Kurt.

"You will excuse me, but didn't your brother also hire the woman who abandoned Ivy the moment she arrived?"

She raised one eyebrow and a smile teased the side of her mouth. A mouth that was inexplicably tempting. He wondered what it would be like to taste that mouth, run his tongue along her lips, along her neck to the crook where it met her body. Would she sigh, or give a moan of pleasure from those lips as he kissed her senseless?

Christ, every second he spent alone with this woman was having questionable effects on his good sense.

Miss Kurt did have a point, however. Two, actually. Jeremy enjoyed a certain order to his day, but that order still included variation in task, location, and company. If Ivy were to have a future running a large household, learning the necessary skills and applying them did make sense. And, the sooner this was settled, the faster he could himself from this curious effect Miss Kurt had on him.

"Very well," he said, careful to keep his tone business like. "Create a new lesson plan. I will review when it's complete."

"Of course, Colonel," she said with a look of triumph he found inexplicably intoxicating.

"Excuse me, Colonel Webber." The polite but firm interruption came from Mrs. Whitehead, who was standing in the door, a tray in her hand. "Cook is preparing dinner. Where would you like to take it?"

Relief and regret warred in him as Miss Kurt stepped away, the exchanging the smallest of polite nods with the housekeeper before disappearing from view. He would have to be careful. She was an employee and had no right to be subjected to whatever madness overtook him when she was in his presence.

"In my study, Mrs. Whitehead, thank you," he said, "I have a few hours work ahead of me yet."

He would go speak with Ivy first, of course. She'd been disappointed by his dismissal. In truth, part of him was amazed at her accomplishment—or accomplishments. There had been many. Who knew what talents his daughter had? His brother had hired the best tutors for her, but in none of his letters did he mention Ivy's artistic skills. And Jeremy doubted very much that anyone had taught her to do a handstand.

His brother Alexander could be an insufferable know-it-all, Jeremy knew. It couldn't be helped, he supposed, when one was a

Viscount, surrounded by those who reinforced the apparent correctness of every thought that came into his head. Alexander had clearly indulged Ivy, out of a misguided attempt to make up for the time she'd spent alone with Isla. Maybe he'd been soothing his own guilt at not being aware of Isla's illness before it was too late. And Jeremy could hardly blame him for that. Isla had managed to shut out everyone save her physician about her condition. Her physician, and Ivy.

And he would never understand why. He was her husband and he'd loved Isla more than he could have thought possible. And when he returned—she was already in the ground by the time he'd arrived—the hole that opened up in his heart, the one that had filled with grief, had started to turn to something darker. Resentment. He'd tried to push past it, to understand that maybe, somehow, she thought she'd done the right thing, shutting him out. But, in the quiet moments between meetings and schedules and speeches and answering correspondence…it was still there.

He'd put it on the top of his own agenda to stop thinking about the state of his heart.

Chapter Nine

AFTER SHE'D PUT Ivy to bed for the evening, Gemma began a thorough search of her own room. According to Sergeant Babcock, it had been a guest room, an as such, rarely. It gave Gemma the faint hope that the eccentric Mr. Dalrymple would have somehow surmised Gemma's current predicament and put the document right under her nose, thereby shielding her from the necessity to be under Colonel Webber's keen eye for much longer.

But after an hour of turning out the drawers in the small dresser, under the bed, and knocking on every floorboard, she'd come up with nothing but the extra work putting her room back to rights as a reward. It seemed Mr. Dalrymple cared not an ounce for Gemma's hopes of an early exit from Hastings House.

One plan scuppered, she turned to her governess duties. Lighting a taper, she returned to schoolroom on the third floor, being careful—but not too careful—about being quiet. Already she'd learned that the third and seventh stair had a loose nail, squeaking under foot, which she would avoid when she didn't want to be heard. But she had no particular need to be quiet, and Gemma didn't want to give the appearance of sneaking about when she didn't have to.

She set the taper down at her desk and unfolded the schedule, smoothing the paper flat. She then pulled out a pen and ink and started making notes in the margins. Gemma's tutelage of Ivy Webber was not the primary reason for being at Hastings House, but she did represent the Everwell Society. If Gemma could secure a good reference with the colonel for her services as a governess, it could open the door for other such opportunities for their older girls. The good word of a man like Colonel Webber would be a boon.

She sat back in the chair, her gaze trailing out the window. The last of the twilight highlighted the silhouettes of masts and smoke stacks from vessels docked in the harbour half a mile away.

Ironically, for all her time travelling in her youth, the only time Gemma had ever been on a ship was when she'd arrived in Halifax. She'd run and jumped on a steamer in Montreal, stowing away in the cargo hold. She'd been caught by one of the deckhands and dragged to the deck where Phillipa Hartley had, without ever having been aware of Gemma's existence before that moment, claimed her as a cousin to the confused deckhand who'd been about to throw her overboard, and invited her to stay in her cabin. After two days of quiet conversation, Gemma found herself invited to stay at Everwell, just until she knew what she would do next.

In truth, Gemma had had no intention of staying. Her first plan was to return to Italy, to the village where her mother's family was from, and join a convent. A life shut away from the world where she could live in a state of penitence for her horrible mistake that had ultimately cost her friend Penny Adamos her life. Somehow, she never made the journey. After nearly four years, Gemma was still here. It was the longest she'd ever been anywhere in one place.

She remembered the day Phillipa discovered her doing sleight of hand tricks to amuse the daughter of a newly arrived family who'd come in search of temporary shelter. Everwell was full of amazing women with amazing talents. Phillipa's gift was her ability to see the possibility in everyone, no matter how broken they appeared to be to the rest of the world. And so, that fateful night, she asked Gemma if she would do a very special favour and relieve a well-to-do merchant of the key to a safety deposit box that contained evidence he'd been overcharging for fraudulent work. It was that night she became a Scandalous Spinster.

She usually worked with Elouise Charming. Elouise in front, being diverting and demanding attention, while Gemma stayed in the shadows. She'd been nervous, but Elouise was an expert at reading people and keeping Gemma out of the spotlight. Rimple had made Gemma a special set of dark clothing, and Maddie had been waiting at the exit, ready to swoop in if anyone dared to harm her. Phillipa and the others had given her this magical gift of trust, and Gemma honoured them by trusting herself. The job had been a success, because they somehow knew what she needed to be successful.

Did the colonel know what Ivy needed to be successful? Gemma guessed he was still struggling to know his daughter. Still struggling with his own fears.

It seemed at odds with how he showed himself to the rest of the world. He walked around with a quiet confidence that was not showy, though Gemma found it impossible not to watch him. His presence was some kind of irresistible magnetic force, drawing her gaze to his strong, clean-shaven jaw.

When had a man ever made her knees weak? Never. She had, for a time, been quite taken with Luis Ortega, who'd joined the circus and had a talent for swallowing and spitting fire—and capturing the eye of every red-blooded woman and man within twenty feet of him. Even Penny had an eye for him, before her heart had been stolen by Gemma's brother Nico.

Her heart squeezed as that old pain came roaring back, as fresh as the moment Nico had crouched over Penny, her legs broken. He'd looked up at her with an expression that danced between fury and heartbreak. He wouldn't let her near Penny. Never let her say she was sorry.

She blew out a low, shaky breath, forcing herself to focus on her task. She had to be methodical. Logical. If she was going to search the house, she needed to do it room by room. She needed a map and a timetable. She already had a reasonably good idea of the colonel's schedule. And she had an excellent idea of Ivy's. She needed to find a way to use it to her advantage.

She sat back in her chair, stretching out her back, and closed her eyes.

"Miss Kurt, if you need a more comfortable chair or more lamp oil, all you need to do is ask."

Gemma started, chiding herself for allowing herself to be taken by surprise. The rich tones of Colonel Webber's voice spilled into her veins, her body coming alive with that tingling awareness that happened whenever he was near. Which, thankfully, hadn't been that often.

She put her pen down and quickly pulled herself to her feet, the hem of her nightgown skimming the tops of her feet. Heat poured into her cheeks as she realized she was standing in front of him in little more than her dressing gown. Fighting the impulse to back into the safety of the shadows, she crossed her arms in front of her in a vain attempt to hide her state of undress. He, of course, was still fully dressed, still impeccable, save for a hint of fatigue at the corners of his eyes and the faint shadow of a growing beard on his chin. There was something about that less-than-perfect edge about him that she felt right in the back of her knees. Like Tilda's spiced rum punch.

"Please," he said, gesturing to her chair as he took a few steps into the room. "I didn't mean to disturb you."

"Not at all," she replied, forcing a smile on her face. "Sitting for too long never suited me. I should retire to my room."

"Of course."

There was an awkward pause. Gemma knew she should go, and he was not blocking her exit. Still, she found herself hesitating.

"Preparing your lessons?" The question seemed almost forced, as if he couldn't think of something to say. Gemma couldn't help but wonder if he too felt this inexplicable need to linger.

"I was working on the schedule, as promised," she answered, looking down at her notation, because she needed to look someplace else or her gaze would stray to that place at his collar where he'd unbuttoned it. "I was wondering about your daughter's interests. They might help with my lesson planning."

"She's ten," he said tightly. "Do ten year olds even have interests besides play?"

"I'm sure I did." By ten, she'd already learned some sleight of hand magic tricks, though her primary interest was learning how to climb the ropes in the big tent. "Play is preparation. What does Ivy like to play? Besides scouting for invading armies, that is."

He paused, and for a moment a shadow passed over his face, causing Gemma to wince inside. He hadn't seen his daughter in nearly two years, she remembered.

"I'm not sure how her interests have any bearing on her lessons," he replied, and for the first time Gemma heard the shift in his voice. The hint of warm and conviviality had been replaced by a more military bearing, clearly intended to increase the distance between them, even though they were only a few feet apart. "Ivy's requirements are reading, practicing her letters, and basic arithmetic, as well as the more feminine arts."

Gemma stopped before she rolled her eyes. "Feminine arts?"

"You saw the schedule," he said, motioning to the desk.

"Yes. I was making adjustments to it," she replied. "I was at a loss for what 'feminine arts' might be for a ten-year-old."

"Sewing. Painting. Needlework. You are female." He nodded in her direction, as if that was explanation enough.

Gemma wanted to laugh. Her talents with a needle were passable. When she was younger, she helped her mother with their costumes and she could do basic needlework to hem a petticoat. But the finer needle arts were lost on her. And her skills with a paintbrush or charcoal were nonexistent. She could sing tolerably well, and she could dance, though her experience in that regard were far too limited to tutor anyone.

"If you are amenable, I will consult with my colleagues. We train girls for many opportunities," she continued. "But knowing Ivy's natural interests will help me teach her in a way that engages her mind and may serve to keep her focused on her work, rather than climbing trees. Not that there is anything wrong with climbing trees."

His mouth twisted, as if she'd just declared that that tomorrow was Christmas.

"A young lady is meant to have her feet on the ground," he replied, then cocked an eyebrow, an affectation Gemma found somehow both intimidating and enticing. "Ivy has been tutored in England to the expectations of her class. I do not expect to have that undone, Miss Kurt."

To the expectations of her class. Gemma wanted to roll her eyes. Instead, she pressed her lips together then forced a smile.

"I see. Well, the three of us shall discover it together."

At her declaration, his eyelashes fluttered—not the verb she would have expected to use to describe any part of a man as solid and impervious as Colonel Webber. And solid did seem to be the word for him. His chest was like a wall of red across her vision, and even though this was the closest to a state of undress as she'd ever seen him, she was absolutely certain that the man underneath the coat was solid as well.

For heaven's sake, Gemma...stop imagining him without his coat.

Why did she say the three of them, as if she, Ivy, and the colonel were some kind of trio? She had no intention of doing anything except the bare minimum with the colonel. Her body seemed unnaturally aware of him, commanding her attention. And she very well couldn't sneak around his house if she was preoccupied the broadness of his shoulders or the small patch of skin at this throat where he'd loosened his collar.

"No matter," he said, an unmistakable clip in his voice. He

smiled, but it was a tight smile of suppressed unease. "May I see what you've arrived at?"

Gemma picked up the page and handed it to him, trying to ignore the heat that passed between them as his fingers brushed up against hers. He eyed the page, his gaze hard, and Gemma wondered if he was hoping to find fault with it. She stood opposite him, his form a towering presence and he seemed determined to look anywhere but at her, which suited her perfectly well. They were close enough she felt the heat from his body. Breathe in his scent.

"There is a lesson in the cemetery," he said, pulling Gemma out her thoughts and looking at her as if she'd lost every ounce of good sense. "What practical lesson do you wish to impart in a boneyard? She attended her mother's funeral. I assure you she has learned that lesson well enough."

"There are oak trees, which I will ensure she does not climb." Gemma answered quickly. "But I thought we might do a study of them. There is a fence so she can run, and still be safe from the road. I have planned for a portion of every day to be spent out of doors, if possible. A little exercise and fresh air is good for her, and there are many opportunities for all subjects to be taught with practical applications. Your daughter has a keen mind, Colonel, and a strong spirit. But locked in this room all day, both will wither."

He looked at it again, and Gemma fought the urge to step away. There was a stillness to him that felt almost dangerous.

"One week, Miss Kurt," he said at last. "We can try this for one week."

One week should be enough to search the house. It was far too much time to spend under Mrs. Whitehead's scrutiny. It might even have been too long to spend trying to convince herself that this unnamable sensation she had whenever Colonel Webber was near was nothing more than nerves.

He looked at the schedule once more, his eyes narrowing.

"What's this?" he asked, pointing to an item toward the bottom of the page and grimacing, as if he'd swallowed a bit of sour milk.

She took the page from him, scanning it for whatever had caught his attention. It only took a moment.

"Bedtime?" she asked.

"Story time," he replied.

"You do not wish to read your daughter a story before bed?" Gemma took the page from him, reviewing it. She'd added his name purposefully, so he could see that she'd considered the colonel's role in his daughter's life. As man who clearly appreciated routine, she'd assumed, incorrectly it appeared, that he'd appreciate the explicit direction.

"I may not have the time," he replied.

Gemma tried to school her features, but the burning in her cheeks had already betrayed her feelings. Story time was a quarter of an hour. Fifteen minutes in a schedule had accounted for at least twelve hours of the day.

"If you don't have the time, why is she here?"

Jeremy drew back at her question, his heart stinging. A heart he'd thought he'd quite securely protected under many plates of armor. Who was this woman and who did she think she was, questioning him? He was a colonel in the British Army for heaven's sake. He let out a bitter laugh.

"What exactly is the mission of this Everwell Society for the Benefit of Woebegone Widows or whatever you call yourselves?" he asked, his tone deliberately dripping with condescension. It was a weapon, he knew, but if this Miss Kurt was as plainly adroit with her opinions of him, he could parry. "To issue judgment on family function? I thought you were here to see over my daughter."

She walked to the small desk, picked up the pen, dipped it in the ink, then watched her make a couple of marks on the paper with an efficiency that would make his clerks envious. She blew on the page to help dry the ink, then pushed the page at him.

"Someone has to, since it appears you will not."

Jeremy was stunned to silence as he watched turn on her heel and walk toward the door. On the page in his hands, she saw his name scratched out.

How dare she? How dare she leave him alone after throwing that shattering bit of truth at his feet and leaving him to pick up the pieces himself.

Before he understood what he was doing, he'd crossed the room, putting himself between her and an escape.

"If you hurt me," she said with a voice that was so calm it was unnerving, "please know you will have to do deal with my fellow Spinsters, and I don't think you want that."

Her simple declaration blew away his anger in a heartbeat. He stepped back, too late aware of size, how he towered over her, and the threat she would perceive from his action.

"I apologize." he said. "I would never hurt you."

He pressed his lips together as a fury of emotion slammed in his chest—fear, regret, and fierce protectiveness that threatened to tear him to pieces if he didn't somehow grab hold of it. It was the same conviction that had made him bring Ivy to Canada. He needed to have the people who mattered most to him close. Even if he was clumsy about it. Even if he didn't know what to do with them when they were close. He just needed to know they were safe.

"I love my daughter," he continued, even as the words felt inadequate for the depth of his feeling. Why he felt the need to have Miss Kurt know this didn't make sense.

"I know."

His spiral of thought was halted by the shock of tenderness in her voice.

Instead of running away—running right out the door, like she had every right to do—she came toward him, closing the distance he'd put between them.

"If you wish to quit this post," he heard himself saying, "I understand. My behaviour has been unconscionable. I will write you a letter of recommendation to ensure there is no stain on your reputation."

She didn't respond, merely continued to regard him, so continued to blather on, because he had no bloody idea what else to do.

"If you wish to stay, I would be inordinately grateful. You have my daughter's best interests at heart, and I cannot fault you for fighting for her. Indeed, you have my gratitude."

Her gaze lingered over him, and he wondered if he was alone in noticing a tendril of delicious tension swirling between them. The distance between them had closed further, so that he could feel the heat from her body. It would be nothing at all to reach out and touch her skin.

"It's late," she said, and, reaching out in a move that shocked them both, ran her fingers along his jaw. She pulled her fingers back, too late aware of what she'd done.

In response, he took her hand, rested it back on his skin, and watched her respond. Her eyes closed slightly at his touch, and he heard the gentle exhale of her breath. A wave of desire rippled through his body, going straight to his loins. He gently cupped her face, and brought his mouth to hers. The smallest moan escaped her parting lips, and he responded by pouring a need he couldn't name into this kiss.

And she accepted it. Somewhere amidst the white blazing sear of his own lust, channeled into every tantalizing taste of her mouth, he felt her need, her tongue stroking his lips, her hands around his waist, pulling his body close. He savoured her curves through that thin nightgown, and in return it would have been impossible for her not to know how absolutely aroused he was.

It was that very thought that pulled him back. He had to break this kiss even if it killed him, and as he gently pulled away, he very well wondered if it might. The hitch of complaint in Gemma Kurt's throat as he did so nearly ended his resolve. They stood silent for a moment, each averting their gaze as if both of them instantly wished themselves somewhere else.

"It's late," he said, mimicking her words only a moment ago.

"I should go," she said, and Jeremy nodded in agreement. Without another word, she left, leaving Jeremy to wonder what the hell had just happened. He waited a moment, out of some nameless obligation to rules of propriety, even though he'd just broken every one.

Chapter Ten

THE NEXT MORNING, Jeremy stood at his bedroom window. Barrington Street which had come alive with carts and carriages trundling along on their early morning runs, but his attention was drawn to the stillness of the burying ground across the street, where tall oak trees stood amongst the stones. Only a few days ago, Ivy had managed to climb one of those trees. Part of him wanted marvel at the accomplishment, but one slip, one misstep, and that could have been the end of her. Jeremy closed his eyes and tried to shake off the image of his daughter falling in slow motion to the ground. It was a fiction, but in that moment, it felt absolutely real.

Part of the reason why it remained a figment of Jeremy's over-cautious imagination was no doubt due to the woman who'd managed to coax Ivy out of that tree. The very same woman who was somehow managing to coax some complicated feelings in Jeremy.

It was because of Miss Kurt's innate abilities with Ivy—and her insistence on fighting for what was best for his daughter—that made Jeremy box up those unwise and most unwanted feelings and throw away the key. After their encounter last evening, he'd gone to bed as stiff as a fucking board. His hands had itched to touch the gentle curves only hinted at by the lose robe she'd cinched at her waist.

Perhaps he should have taken his brother's advice and found a mistress.

He hadn't been able to lay with another woman since Isla. It had only been two years and he'd been encouraged to move on, marry and procreate sons, and logically, he supposed, it made sense. He wasn't getting any younger, and a young wife would be good for Ivy.

He'd loved Isla so deeply. Their life had been a happy one. As the wife of an officer, she'd been privileged to travel the world with him and she often did, even after Ivy was born. He remembered the excitement he'd felt when he'd learned of the posting to Egypt. They'd talked about seeing the pyramids and shopping at the spice bazaars. And then, just as they'd begun to pack, she insisted her place was at home, with Ivy. He would decline the posting, he'd said. She told him not to jeopardize his career. In hindsight, she must have known she was ill, and she'd sent him off without a word.

He'd been in Egypt when she died. And in his darkest moments, he admitted to himself that her silence felt like a betrayal.

Anger tightened his throat, followed by a wave of guilt for feeling it. A knock interrupting the darkness that had settled on him, pulling him away from window. Without waiting for a reply, Babcock opened the door and walked in, ready to help Jeremy get on with his day.

"'Morning, sir," Babcock said, entering with a small tray that carried a cup and a carafe of coffee, which he set down on a nearby table. He poured out a stream of the hot, aromatic brew, its steam reaching up into the cool morning air. After a fortifying sip, Jeremy and Babcock began the morning ritual, which had begun between them over a decade earlier. Babcock prepared Jeremy's face with a hot towel and a fresh lather of shaving soap.

"Am I on guard duty again today sir?" Babcock asked.

Jeremy had his eyes closed as his soldier-valet expertly negotiated the razor along his throat and chin, but he swore he could hear a smile in the man's tone.

"I will need you at Government House today," he said, taking in a deep breath. "Just be on guard, in case of emergencies."

"Of course, sir." Babcock said. "If I may, I think Miss Ivy seems to be getting on with Miss Kurt."

"Her new governess has suggested some improvements to her curriculum," he replied at last. "I was skeptical, but given she's the first to last more than a day, I'll allow it."

The only sound in the room was the gentle pull of the razor against Jeremy's skin and the rinsing of the blade in the washbowl.

"With Miss Ivy here, and Miss Kurt settling in," Babcock said, applying a warm, moist towel to Jeremy's face, "it seems like a whole new start. Just want you need."

Babcock's words landed like a stone in Jeremy's gut for reasons he couldn't comprehend. A perfect new start. Could he give Ivy a new start? And was Miss Kurt to be a part of that?

He'd had perfect, and it had broken his heart.

After a moment, the towel came off and Jeremy was handed a mirror to inspect Babcock's handy work, which was, as usual, flawless.

Jeremy dressed in silence, his mind turning over the plans for the day, which he'd created the day before. A meeting with the Lieutenant Governor, to discuss an upcoming soiree to mark the tenth anniversary of the founding of the Halifax Merchant's Association and the opening of the club that bore its name.

He liked this sense of order. Routine kept chaos at bay. In the days and months' after Isla's death, it had kept him sane. He'd finished his coffee, then took a light breakfast in his study before meeting with his staff precisely at a quarter past eight. His duties ranged from the mundane to vaguely ridiculous, but his primary role was to ensure that Government House and the Lieutenant Governor's schedule ran like a ticking clock.

Speaking of ticking clocks, the clock on his mantlepiece struck eight. He took one last swallow of his coffee, reviewed the day's agenda, and prepared to take his leave. Since Ivy's arrival, he'd taken a few minutes to check on her before leaving for the day. He paused outside his study door, prepared to climb up the stairs to the nursery, when the faint sound of female voices wafted up from below. Following the sound, he opened the door to the dining room to find Ivy and Miss Kurt hunched over a rather large tome laid out on the table. On one end was the remnants of breakfast.

Jeremy paused.

"Miss Kurt."

Two faces looked up at him, and Ivy broke into a wide smile.

"Papa!" Ivy hopped off her chair where she'd been standing, and ran over to him. "Must you go already?"

"I'm afraid so," he said.

He glanced at Miss Kurt, who'd somehow appeared next to Ivy without capturing his notice. How was this even possible? After spending most of his adult life with heavily booted men who made every sort of noise, perhaps his ears had become insensitive. Still, his body was increasingly aware of her presence.

"Good morning, Colonel."

"Miss Kurt," he said. "I did not realize we would be implementing the new curriculum at breakfast."

Her smile tightened somewhat. "It was on the schedule."

Right. The bloody schedule. He'd made a good show of examining it, when he was far more preoccupied with other, more forbidden thoughts. Christ.

"The light in this room is so welcoming in the morning, and it has such a wonderfully large table," she said, and Jeremy was struck by the thought, which thankfully he kept to himself, that the light in the room had nothing at all to do with the sun, but the woman who occupied it. "We thought we would take advantage of both amenities to study the position of Scandinavia."

"Papa," Ivy asked, her face turned up with anticipation that squeezed in Jeremy's chest. "Will you be home for dinner tonight?"

"Six thirty on the nose," he said. "I believe that is on the itinerary, unless it has been changed?"

He cast a side glance at Miss Kurt, whose cheeks turned a delicious shade of pink. She gave the smallest shake of her head.

"Ivy, my dear," he said, "please return to your studies. I look forward hearing all about it at dinner tonight. But I would like a moment with Miss Kurt."

Ivy nodded, then resumed her place at the table. He walked to the door, stepped outside, and waited for Miss Kurt who stood before him, hands clasped in front of her.

"Miss Kurt, I am not accustomed to having my orders disobeyed."

Her eyelashes fluttered, and she was clearly taken aback by his declaration. She flushed further, then swallowed and though Jeremy had not raised his voice nor, he thought, used a particularly harsh tone, he suddenly felt, quite inexplicably, like the worst cad in the world.

"I do not recall you ordering me to do anything," she said at last, her voice low but bright and firm. "I showed you the schedule, explained my rationale, and you gave me a single answer."

"Indeed," he said.

"Exactly," she said.

Jeremy was tempted to roll his eyes. Insufferable woman with lips that were soft and full and made for kissing and Christ, was he about to do this to himself again?

"I didn't think it was necessary to point this out, Miss Kurt," he said, "but 'indeed' is not the same as 'yes'."

"It isn't? Because you *just* used it to imply the affirmative."

"I did."

Did she have to be so bloody quick? A good quality in a governess for certain, but Jeremy wasn't accustomed to explaining himself to someone who questioned every word he uttered except to say 'yes, sir,' 'no sir,' or better yet, simply nod and get on their way.

"You said it in exactly the same tone last night," she replied, her hands suddenly becoming animated. "You said it with an air of finality and then left. With such a reply, I could only assume that the matter was concluded."

He'd left because he'd been stiff as a goddamn flagpole and he had to remove himself before things became even more wildly inappropriate than speaking to his daughter's governess had already been. 'Indeed' was Jeremy's all-purpose word—it sometimes meant agreement, sometimes not, sometimes he said it when someone seemed to want a verbal response. Of course, Miss Kurt didn't know that. She simply did what any good soldier would do upon discovering a weakness in the enemy's barricade-- use it to their advantage to turn the tide of a battle.

Gemma Kurt was terribly good at maneuvering past many of his defences, and she seemed blissfully unaware she was doing it.

"My mistake, then," he said. "I should have been more clear. I would have liked to review it more thoroughly and give it my approval. Put it on my desk and I will do so this evening."

"And what about today?"

"You seem to have taken over the dining room. Just have it clear before Mrs. Whitehead and the kitchen staff need to prepare it for dinner. You and Ivy may join me."

She blinked. "Me?"

"Why ever not? We can conduct our business together and I can quiz Ivy on the day. I have no other engagements, and I actually do enjoy spending time with my child."

Her face lit up in what appeared to be a genuine smile of approval, which had a remarkable effect on Jeremy's insides. It made *him* want to smile because, for some unnamable reason, her approval meant something to him. And it shouldn't. After all, she was his employee.

"Of course sir," she said, blissfully unaware of this bedeviling affect she was having on him.

"However," he continued, "I do expect Ivy to be able to sit on the chair for dinner, Miss Kurt, not stand on it like a doomsayer on a soap box in Grand Parade," he said, referring to the city square where he'd found local preachers and doomsday men. "Is that understood?"

She clasped her hands in front of her, her teeth grazing her bottom lip, as if she was actually considering her answer. After a moment, she spoke.

"Perfectly."

A strange sensation, something like an awakening, appeared in Jeremy's chest. He couldn't name it—or perhaps didn't want to —but there it was, uncoiling itself like a daffodil, as if sensing warm and light after a prolonged period of winter. He regarded her and her smile and forced himself to walk away and out the door before he found a reason to linger. A reason to allow himself another moment to stay with this new-found lightness.

But the conversation had nearly made him late for his own start of the day. So he dashed out the door, and back to the routine of his work day and the steady thrum of comfortable problems to untangle that would tamp out this bewildering sensation. He met with his staff, reviewed the latest pile of correspondence and invitations sent to the Lieutenant Governor, and at precisely nine o'clock, walked into the Lieutenant Governor's office to drink coffee, talk politics, and endure the pungent smell of Tupper's favourite pipe tobacco.

Lieutenant Governor George Tupper brought his own set of challenges, though his were of a more familiar sort. Tupper was an excellent man who took his duties with a vigour that led him to rearrange an entire day on extremely short notice, leaving Jeremy to pick up the pieces and try to sort them into a new semblance of order on the spot. Like a juggler, perhaps. Miss Kurt would probably know a thing or two about that.

"Good morning, Colonel," Tupper said, peering over a stack of papers with all the enthusiasm of a man looking over a plate of spoiled food. "Tell me there is some good news in that stack of correspondence."

"The Royal Engineers new Commanding Officer is expected to arrive next month, with a swearing in ceremony not long after," Jeremy said. "And you have been invited by the president of the Halifax Merchant Association to their club for a special dinner to mark the tenth year of their establishment." He paused, and frowned as he read the note over several times, then mentally did a review of the week ahead. "It's next Tuesday evening."

"Timothy Beveridge wants to have a party, does he?" Tupper asked, not bothering to contain his enthusiasm. He sat back and puffed on his pipe. Tupper was as naturally inclined to social gatherings as Jeremy was not. "I suppose I'll have to say some-thing about gracious about the bastard and his humble beginnings."

"I didn't realize Mr. Beveridge came from humble circum-stances," Jeremy replied. Timothy Beveridge was the head of the New Empire Insurance Company. They'd met once before, at a dinner party hosted by one of Beveridge's business associates, George Coughlin. It had been Jeremy's first introduction to Halifax society, which had been followed by a blur of invitations.

"His beginnings are the only thing humble about him," Tupper replied. "Still, it's a fine price to pay for what I'm certain will be a cracking good evening. You may send him my confirmation."

"Don't you wish to consult your schedule? I believe you are due to review a proposal from The Horticultural Society regarding a parcel of land," he said.

The Lieutenant Governor shrugged his shoulders. "I'm certain you can move it, Webber. In fact, some of the members will be in attendance at the Halifax Merchant's Club. They can assail me there with their garden plans."

Jeremy smiled through gritted teeth. He could move it...the same way a bricklayer might have to move a brick from one part of a nearly finished wall.

"You are going to accompany me, of course," Tupper contin-ued, taking a sip of his coffee and pointing his pipe in Jeremy's direction. "You need a good night out in the company of men, away from dinner parties involving matchmaking matrons."

"Mrs. Turnbull in particular has been quite persistent in her invitations to card parties and the like," Jeremy acknowledged, referring to the wife of Archibald Turnbull, a brewing magnate who'd made his fortune supplying beer to a thirsty populace. "I appreciate their intentions are good."

"You're still in your prime, you have a young daughter, and probably a few boys in you," Tupper said, pausing to take a puff on his pipe. "You should let them find you a wife."

"With respect, I've had a wife," Jeremy replied, perhaps more curtly than he intended. Since his arrival four months ago, he'd been singled out as a possible match for every niece, cousin and daughter of every well-to-do family within a hundred miles of Halifax.

Tupper's right brow perked up, "What about your daughter?"

"Ivy will do just fine," he said, desperate to change the subject. "Especially since I've finally secured a governess who seems up to the job."

"Excellent," Tupper said, leaning back in his leather chair, and handed the invitation to Jeremy. "See to the reply."

Jeremy rose and bowed, gripping the invitation in his hand. Moving one appointment was never about moving one appoint-ment. It often meant moving half a dozen. Inquiries needed to be sent, as well as apologetic letters to decline or rearrange previous commitments. He would have to research a little about the Halifax Merchant's Association and write a speech for Tupper. And then, most egregious of all, he had to stuff himself in his best uniform and sit in a smoke-filled room and listen to others drone on about their virtues, when he'd much rather be home reading, painting, or spending time with Ivy.

Guilt pricked at the edge of his consciousness. If he bothered to dwell on it, Jeremy knew he was lying to himself. He was often contained to his study at night, working. He'd neglected his painting since Isla died, not having the heart for it. And the only thing he'd read was newspapers and correspondence. And then he'd retire to bed, and sometimes notice a faint hint of light coming from under Miss Kurt's door as he walked past. Sometimes he would pause, overcome by an intense curiosity to ask her why she was up so late.

The sounds of shouting from the other side of his office door caught Jeremy's attention. Aside from bombastic meetings with Tupper and some of his political cronies, Government House was relatively quiet. He rose, about to see what the hubbub was about, when his door opened, and a young housemaid rushed inside.

"My apologies sir," she said, her cheeks ruddy, "but you must come. A pipe's burst down in the kitchen."

Christ almighty, of course it did.

He was up, and out the door in seconds, leaving what turned out to be the first, but now less immediate of his problems, to the wayside. He'd have to leave the Halifax Merchant Association plans until tonight.

Maybe a night out was exactly what he needed.

Chapter Eleven

"JUST FIVE MORE MINUTES?"

Ivy Webber glowered at Gemma from under her thick lashes as she clung to one of the bedposts. Six thirty had come and gone, and since dinner, which they'd eaten alone, Ivy's mood had gone from disgruntled to outright frustration. Gemma had managed to convince Ivy to get her nightdress on at least, but getting her to sleep was another matter altogether.

Downstairs, the large grandfather clock chimed nine times. Eight o'clock was Ivy's bed time. It was the one point of Colonel Webber's schedule for his daughter that he and Gemma had absolute agreement on. That and dinner, which had come and gone without him present.

"The colonel is quite insistent on your bedtime," Gemma said, biting back her own frustration. Colonel Webber might have been preoccupied with punctuality and timetables, but he alone seemed exempt from the tyranny from the blasted daily schedule. The irony that he'd missed his promised appointment to review her changes to it was not lost on her.

"I wanted to show him my multiplication tables," Ivy pleaded, her lower lip quivering. "I worked very hard on them."

Gemma forced a smile. "He can see them in the morning, at breakfast."

"But he said sixty thirty on the nose!" Ivy said, her cheeks getting puffy from disappointment that was becoming dangerously mixed with fatigue.

Gemma prepared herself for another volley of protests when the sound of a door opening below caught both their attention. Ivy was soon off like a shot, out the door and running to the top of the stairs.

"Papa!"

Gemma nearly jumped at Ivy's cry. The child bounded down the stairs, her braids bouncing off her shoulders.

"Good evening!" Colonel Webber replied, catching his daughter's embrace. He gave her a small kiss on her forehead, glanced up at Gemma with an arched brow that somehow managed to communicate an entire lecture about his expectations about his daughter's bedtime. Gemma rankled at the silent inspection, merely tilting her head toward the clock.

"My, you are full of energy for so late an hour," he continued to Ivy. "I would have thought you worn out from all your lessons."

"I am exhausted father," she said with a hint of dramatic flair.

Funny, Gemma thought. She'd been up half the night searching her room for the will, only to be up near the crack of dawn to start her day with Ivy, and ignoring every sidelong glance from Mrs. Whitehead, who just happened to be walking by or taking it upon herself to be cleaning a random shelf in the same location Gemma chose to be teaching a lesson. If anyone should be exhausted, it should have been her.

"Exhausted," Colonel Webber replied, casting his glance up at Gemma who started down the stairs. If she didn't know better, it almost seemed like he was sharing a silent joke with her. He returned his attention to Ivy. "It seems to me you have bundles of energy now."

"I thought you were to dine with me," Ivy complained, her

bottom lip coming out in a pretty little pout. "You said you would be home by half past six."

"I am sorry," he said, crouching down to look her in the eye. "My duties kept me waylaid. I will try to do better tomorrow."

He'd made that same promise the day before, Gemma couldn't help but note.

"Colonel Webber," Mrs. Whitehead said, appearing from the hall. "Shall I see to your dinner?"

"That would be appreciated," he said, dismissing his house-keeper before turning to Ivy. "Now, why are you not in bed?"

"I wanted to wait to see you," she protested. "Only little girls get ready for bed so early."

"It is nine o'clock. Not that early at all. Off to bed with you."

"My apologies Colonel," Gemma said. "She was very eager to show you what she accomplished today."

"Can you not come see my multiplication tables?" she asked.

"I would love to my dear, but I have a few letters I need to see to first," he said. "But I'll be up bright and early and you can show me in the morning."

The smile on Ivy's face froze, and she looked at Gemma in defeat. Hadn't she said just the same thing? But Gemma took no triumph in it. She looked up at the colonel, the hint of a shadow on his jaw, his eyes tired. Of the two, he looked far more ready for bed than his daughter.

She took Ivy back upstairs, and tucked the girl into bed.

"I'm sorry." Gemma smoothed the covers over Ivy, tucking them in around her sides. "I'm sure he will be happy to look at your work in the morning. He's a very busy man."

The girl's cheeks were flushed, and she closed her eyes, clearly trying not show the disappointment that was bringing to the edge of tears. She turned over on her side, burying her head in her pillow.

"He's not too busy for everyone else," she said.

"Perhaps we can practice some more juggling tomorrow," Gemma said, brightening, trying to give Ivy something to look forward to that she could depend on. "You did so well with your multiplication tables today, I think we can try two practice balls. I bet you'd be ready for three in no time."

"Maybe," she said, her voice low, as if she was hiding a tiny sob.

Gemma gave Ivy's shoulders a little squeeze, then turned down the lamp. She left the room, about to disappear into her own, when the sound of Sergeant Babcock's voice caught her attention. He was speaking to the colonel.

She needed to go to her room and plan where she would search next. She thought she'd try the room on the third floor by the nursery—the one Mrs. Whitehead had insisted was off limits. Gemma needed the time. With him distracted downstairs, this was the ideal moment.

A low, masculine rumble of laughter came from below. There was something about it that caught in Gemma's belly and soured.

He's not too busy for everyone else.

Before she could think twice, she found herself treading *down* the stairs, toward the laughter, allowing her anger to propel her toward the colonel, rather than where she should have been going, which was away from him. She walked into his study and found him standing over his desk, a tray of food untouched nearby. His jacket was off, no doubt taken away by Babcock to be hung up. The top button of his shirt, undone. If she wasn't so irate, she would have taken more of an opportunity to savour his relative state of undress.

"What are you doing?"

He looked up at her, his eyes narrowing at her intrusion.

"Excuse me?"

Gemma paused, her heart thrashing in her chest.

"The only way I managed to get Ivy to focus on her studies at all today was with the promise that you would join us for dinner," she began. "She waited all evening."

"Miss Kurt, not that you deserve an explanation, but I have

several hours of undoing the mess of a rash decision ahead of me. It's not work I wish to do. But it is mine to do."

"What about the work of being a father?"

"Take care, Miss Kurt," he said, his voice lowering, his gaze steel. "You are on tricky ground."

Tricky ground. Gemma paused, the phrase rolling around in her mind. She'd been on highwires fifty feet or more above the ground. She hated that darned wire. But no one was better at navigating tricky places than her. This felt dangerously like that highwire act she hated so much. All eyes on her, waiting for her next move. Waiting for her to fall.

She found herself standing mere inches away from him, breathing in a heady mix of pipe smoke and his own tantalizing scent from the exposed patch of skin from his unbuttoned shirt. The sharp heat of his stare was like an intoxicant, making her brave, or foolish, or both. She itched to graze her fingers over the light sprinkling of chest hair, a hint of the man under the normally tightly buttoned-up officer.

His gaze swept over her, pausing at her mouth. Her breath caught in her throat, and she realized at that moment that she wanted—no, needed him to kiss her. Somehow the world was tilting, her balance shaky, and she was looking for something to hold onto.

And it was him.

Panic—her cold, prickly, but strangely reliable companion—found her at last, making her realize she'd gripped his arm. She withdrew it quickly, then stepped back and clasped her hands together, ignoring the pounding in her chest.

She'd slipped, but hadn't fallen. Not this time.

"Five minutes," she blurted out, attempting to recover her self-composure. "I promise you. Sit with Ivy for five minutes. Ask her what she's learned today. Tell her one thing you did. Have one moment with her. That's all I ask. It may not seem like much to you, but it would be the world to her."

He tilted his head, and for a moment she wondered if what

she'd said had come out as something completely nonsensical. If instead of speaking about Ivy, maybe she'd muttered something about the little lines at the corner of his eyes, perhaps. Or that small curl of thick dark hair that fell onto his forehead.

"Very well," he said after what felt to Gemma like a very long pause, then gestured to the door. "Lead the way."

She was about to walk out with him, recovering her senses at last, inspiration hit. If he had five minutes with Ivy, she'd have five minutes in his study, alone.

"I think you two can spend some time alone," she answered, pasting on a smile and hoping she didn't sound as nervous as she felt. "I think she would prefer it. She's had to look at me all day."

"Then I am quite envious," he said. "Her view has been far superior to mine."

Gemma felt blood rush into her cheeks "I—"

"Do not get missish, Miss Kurt. I spent my morning in a den of pipe smoke with Lieutenant Governor Tupper and then spent the afternoon looking at a broken drainage pipe. It was an objective observation."

He nodded, then brushed past her out the door, leaving Gemma flabbergasted.

She listened for his steps as he climbed the stairs, then looked at a nearby clock perched over the hearth. Five minutes. Knowing Colonel Webber, it was probably exactly four minutes and twenty-two seconds and counting.

She started with the desk. It was the one piece of furniture she recalled being in place when she'd arrived, and so she'd assumed it had belong to Dalrymple. Carefully she started to knock along the hulking piece of furniture, looking for a hidden door or panel.

"Can I help you, miss?"

The sound of Harold Babcock's voice made her jump and brought her straight to her feet, her sleeve catching a few of the carefully stacked letters to the ground. She smiled, not bothering to try to hide her fluster as she scooped up papers. One of the names on the top of a neatly folded note caught her eye: Mr. W.

Hatchett—the new owner of Hastings House. Thankful she was hidden by a large piece of furniture, but keenly aware of Sergeant Babcock's presence, she stood, placed them back on the desk, then placed herself in front of it.

"Sergeant," she exclaimed, trying to keep her voice light. "Good evening. No. I had just come in to speak to the colonel about Ivy. I was about to leave and I knocked a letter opener off his desk. I was just trying to find it so I could put it back before he discovered it. I am rather clumsy at times."

How on earth did Elouise do this? Gemma thought. Elouise was always so quick-witted, always able to act the part, whatever the part was that needed to be played. Gemma had no capacity for pretend. She relied on stealth, on darkness, and being alone.

"Can I give you a hand?" he asked.

"Perhaps I should ask the same," she said, hands behind her, nimbly reaching for a small letter opener and slipping it up her sleeve, then reached out to him. "You look like you have your hands full."

"Just the evening's work," he said, walking past her, laying them down on his desk and arranging them in a way that no doubt made sense to him. It was the first time she noticed that the sergeant favoured his right leg ever so slightly.

"He made mention that he had a mess to clean up," she said. "He must have had a trying day."

The sergeant nodded, but there was something in his expression that made her wonder.

"No more or less than the rest, as far as I can tell, though I think that burst pipe didn't help," he said. "His employer is a bit of a free spirit. Makes him hard to pin down. And that's the colonel's job, see. Making sure he's in the place he's supposed to be. Because generally, he's got to be there with him."

"I see," she said. "We have that problem with some of our students. Not used to structure. And of course, some people crave more or less."

"Yes, the colonel likes his bits and bobs all in the right place."

As if to illustrate his point, he carefully set down the portfolio of work, and arranged it on the desk.

"And do you know where they all are?" she asked, genuinely interested. "The right places, that is."

"Pen, always to his upper right," the sergeant said, motioning to the desk top. "Correspondence and other matters to be dealt with here, marked by priority by notes clipped to the side. Present work in the centre, and that to be actioned immediately, upper left; that which he wants to think on a bit, or he needs more information, here."

Gemma studied the desktop carefully, getting a picture of it in her mind in case she needed to return to it later. "My, that's quite the system."

"It is. But it works for him. Everything in its place. That way he can see it all and manage it," he said. "He's been doing it that way ever since I met him."

"You've been working for him a long time then?"

"For near fifteen years," he said. "Since were both little more than lads, really. I'm a bit older than him, mind you. But he's a good one. Plenty of these officers aren't people you'd want to spend five minutes with. But Mr. Webber is a gentleman, in the best sense."

There was no affectation in Sergeant Babcock's voice as he spoke. He clearly liked the man.

"He must keep you very busy," she said. "His duties seem to keep him well occupied."

The sergeant's smile tightened, and he shook his head.

"I think he likes to keep himself occupied," he said. "Ever since he lost Mrs. Webber. Shame, that. She was a lovely woman."

"How long?"

"More than two years I'd say. He was in Egypt when it happened."

"Everything in order, Babcock?"

Gemma was not given jumpiness, but the suddenness of Colonel Webber's re-appearance startled her.

"Indeed, sir," Sergeant Babcock answered. "Just setting out your things. Shall I bring round some tea?"

"No need tonight, thank you." He said with a crisp politeness, before turning his attention to Gemma. "Miss Kurt."

"Colonel, sir," she began. "How was Ivy?"

"Better." He softened ever so slightly. "Thank you, for your advice."

"I should go," she replied, and then, remembering the story she'd told the sergeant about knocking over the letter opener, let go a little sigh of relief. "Ah!"

Carefully she angled her body away from the colonel, and popping the letter opener out of her sleeve and on to the floor, then picking it up as if it had been there all along.

"I'd knocked this off the desk earlier," she said, holding it up then placing it on the desk. "I was looking for it when Sergeant Babcock came along. I'm sure he'll tell me if it's in the right spot."

"Very near," he said, angling it.

"Well, I will tend to Ivy," she said. She turned to the sergeant, who nodded with a smile, and then turned and escaped—for now. She'd be back for that letter.

Chapter Twelve

SEVERAL HOURS and three pen nibs later, Jeremy sat back in his chair and rubbed his eyes. After editing one of the speeches Tupper would have to give this week, Jeremy had reviewed the list of tradesmen he needed to meet in the morning to discuss the repairs to Government House as a result of the burst pipe. His mind was racing in a thousand different directions even as his body wanted nothing more than to crawl in bed.

He stared up at the plaster ceiling in his study, bathed in shadow, and stifled a yawn. He'd spent far too many evenings staring up at that ceiling, instead of being with his daughter. That's why he'd brought her here, was it not? To start a new life with her. Perhaps he'd indulged himself too readily in the fantasy that he could somehow compartmentalize the old hurts, smothering them with busyness. Instead, it just seemed to cause more pain.

After Gemma Kurt's dressing down, he'd been almost sheepish going to see his daughter. But Ivy had greeted him open arms, and the way she'd dug her face into his wool coat and squeezed him tight had buoyed him through the following hours of tedium. It had been a mere five-minute detour from his schedule, but the sensation had propelled him through the rest of the evening.

What would he give to spend five more minutes with Isla? At one time he would have burned the world down for that chance— a chance he'd missed. That she hadn't given him. A chance she'd only shared with Ivy.

Bitterness, familiar and unwelcome, tightened his throat. He sat forward and reached for the small glass of brandy Babcock had poured for him, drinking it down in a single swallow, and forced himself to focus on the present. That moment when Miss Kurt, standing opposite him in this very room, dared to challenge the lie that his work was more important than his daughter.

She'd been right, of course. But what also felt inexplicably right, but had to be absolutely wrong, was the moment she'd stood in front of him, her hands resting on his arms, holding him fast with a look he recognized as desire.

He'd damn near kissed Gemma Kurt so hard he would have made them both forget their own names.

Another reason to get back to work.

Jeremy stretched before he cramped up completely, then surveyed the last bit of paper demanding his attention. It was a letter from William Hatchett, Jeremy's landlord. Hatchett was former fellow officer, who, through his wife's family, had come into possession of Hastings House. Jeremy scanned the first few lines, which were full of the customary bombast he'd expected from a man like Hatchett.

Shifting his weight in his chair, he was about to go over the letter's contents in more detail when he heard a noise, like scratching, coming from overhead.

Odd.

He dismissed the noise as an errant rodent, and was making a mental note to alert Mrs. Whitehead in the morning, when the distinct sound of approaching footsteps made him pause and listen further.

It was well past midnight, and no one should be awake at this hour.

He should have ignored it, but it had been a long enough bloody day, and sapped of his discipline, he set the letter aside and went to the stairs to listen. He stood there for a moment but hearing nothing more, returned to his office, the only light in the room coming from the tapers on his desk. He rubbed his eyes, about to take his seat which, after several hours, had stopped being comfortable.

Was it his imagination, or did the faint scent of orange blossoms hit his nose? He paused, his body on alert, but not at the thought of an intruder.

Perhaps it was Miss Kurt, up for a glass of warm milk or some other elixir to help her find some sleep. Perhaps she'd padded down the stairs, her hair down like ribbons of dark brown satin, her shoulders draped in a thin white chemise and a dressing gown.

Arousal, unanticipated and certainly most unwelcome, shot through his body. He wanted to put it down to being celibate for two years, despite the insistence of his brother and well-meaning officers that he simply take a mistress. But this wasn't simple carnality, and somewhere deep inside, he knew it.

Footsteps broke through his woolgathering, different from those he'd thought he'd heard before. Jeremy turned, went to the door once again, and peered down the hall, stretching every one of his senses to detect the source of the noise. The sound kept getting louder, and joining it was the creeping warmth of a taper. Recognizing that no intruder would be so foolish as to alert the world to their presence with a light, he relaxed slightly.

"Ho there," he said in a tone barely above a whisper, lest he wake the rest of the house.

The light grew brighter, temporarily blinding him, then lowered, revealing his solider valet wielding an iron poker.

"Christ, Babcock," Jeremy said. "At ease."

"Sir," he said, letting go an audible sigh of relief as he lowered the poker in his hand. "I thought you were an intruder."

"If it's any consolation, I thought the same of you," he said, which was a lie given that he'd made himself stiff as a bloody board even imagining he'd caught the scent of Gemma Kurt.

"I thought after Miss Ivy had seen that person scaling down the drain pipe, that maybe we should be more careful," he said.

"It was probably just her imagination, you realize," Jeremy replied. "She does have a very active one."

"Perhaps," Babcock shrugged. "But that morning, when we were moving in, I thought I saw someone upstairs, in one of the front windows."

Jeremy paused. He thought he had too, but it had been so brief, more like a shadow, he'd dismissed it as a trick of the light. A ghost. A smile crept across his face.

"Harold Babcock," he said, "Do not tell me you believe in ghosts."

"I don't not believe in them," Babcock replied with a shrug.

Jeremy gestured to the poker in his sergeant's grip. "I think any ghost is not going to be bothered by a poker."

"Well, you never know," Babcock replied with a smile. "Can I get a brandy or anything, sir?"

Jeremy shook his head. "Go on to bed. I have one more letter to finish."

Gemma forced herself to focus. Whether Harold Babcock had realized it or not, she owed him a boon—not once, but twice. The first was giving her the key to Colonel Webber's work habits that would help her navigate the four stacks of papers on his desk. The second was drawing Colonel Webber out of his study, engaging him in conversation. His timely arrival gave her a few more precious moments to slip into the study and nab the letter from Mr. Hatchett.

The gleaming brass lamp at the corner of his desk cast a warm glow across the neat piles of paper on the colonel's desk. There, set to one side, was the letter. She held in a sigh of relief as she snatched it, folded it up and shoved it into the pocket of her dark breeches.

"—just wanted to review one last item." It was Colonel Webber's voice, low and rich, coming from outside the office. And it was getting louder.

Her only exit blocked by the colonel and his soldier-valet, Gemma uttered a silent curse and scrambled for a place to hide. She slipped behind a chair at the far side of the room, praying that stillness and shadow, along with her dark clothing, would shield her from notice.

"With all due respect, sir," came a second voice she recognized as Babcock, "I think you should turn in. You've got a long day ahead of you and you want to be sharp."

Listen to the sergeant, she thought. *Get to bed.*

"You've always been a mother hen," the colonel replied. "And you're getting worse with age."

"You need a woman to hound you so I don't have to," Babcock said.

"Don't you start," he said. "I don't need a woman if I have you."

"With all due respect sir, as much as I'd love to hear those words spoken to me, you're not my cup of tea," Babcock replied, and though she couldn't see the smile, she was struck the sense of friendship between the two.

"What about Miss Kurt?" she heard Babcock say, causing her to fight the urge to strain forward at the sound of her name. "She seems like a sensible woman."

Sensible. She'd been so utterly gobsmacked by Jeremy Webber that she'd nearly kissed him. She was hardly sensible.

"She was raised in a circus," the colonel replied, the disbelief in his voice plain. "And teaching my daughter how to do a handstand."

Babcock laughed, causing Gemma to smile.

"Then she's used to being around animals that need taming," he said. "And she juggles. No wonder she fits in here. She'd be good for you."

For the briefest moment, she was tempted to step out from her hiding place and have words with Sergeant Babcock. If they knew she'd become a capable safe cracker and thief on behalf of the Scandalous Spinsters, she was quite certain that being raised in a circus would have been the very least of the colonel's concerns.

So much for sensible.

"Christ, Babcock, it's bad enough I have to fend off the match-makers at these dinner parties George Tupper insists I attend," the colonel replied with a frustrated sigh. "Foisting their daughters and nieces and female relations in front of me to choose as if they're dessert."

Gemma wasn't sure why the idea of someone matchmaking Colonel Webber made her mood darken.

"Besides," she heard him say, "she's not my type."

Not his type?

Well, of course he wasn't her type, either. Not that she knew what her type was. But she knew it couldn't be someone as intractable and stodgy as a British officer. So why on earth did those words sting?

"Her eyes...are too big," he continued. "Like big, dark pools. It's like she's always watching everything."

A grunt came from Babcock, who was clearly not having it, and put him solidly in first place as her favourite red-coated Englishmen in the house.

"All the better to keep an eye on you," he said. "So I don't have to."

"And her mouth," the colonel continued. Gemma rolled her eyes, which were apparently too big and dark. "She's always making suggestions, or improvements or giving orders. Doesn't she know I'm the ranking officer in the house?"

"Do you mean she doesn't put up with your guff?" Babcock replied. "Well, I think I'm liking her more and more. I suppose you're going to tell me there's something wrong with her hands. Too big perhaps?"

The colonel chuckled, and she heard the gentle motion of a chair being pulled back along the floor.

"Enough. Go on to bed, why don't you? I've got one more bloody thing do deal with and then I'll—"

Gemma tensed, listening she heard the shuffling of paper. He was looking for the document in her hands.

"What is it sir?" Babcock asked.

"I was about read through that bit of correspondence from Will Hatchett," Colonel Webber replied, distraction evident in his tone. "I could have sworn I put it right here."

"Maybe it's a sign you need to go to bed."

"Or a sign that there is a ghost in the house."

"Now don't start talk like that in the middle of the night," Babcock said, a hint of unease under his jovial tone. "Come now, whatever it is can wait until morning."

Perhaps it could, but Gemma had already come to appreciate that the colonel was a very insistent man. She heard more shifting and then he spoke again.

"Maybe it fell under the desk, or slipped onto the floor."

Gemma's blood froze as she saw a bit of light moving in the distance and the movement of furniture. Was there a more persistent man ever made than Jeremy Webber?

"Sir," Sergeant Babcock said, his tone sharpening. Was he daring to give the colonel an order? "You have a long day ahead of you, and it's closer than you want it to be. I'll look for it in the morning, right?"

Gemma sat, crouched, absolutely breathless, waiting for signs of Colonel Webber moving toward her. Her muscles were starting to ache and her own fatigue made concentrating even harder. She wasn't particularly religious, but she uttered a little silent prayer to Saint Genesius, which seemed to work.

Colonel Webber let out a sigh, and his movement stopped.

"You're right, Babcock," he said. "Brew the coffee extra

strength tomorrow, will you? And remind me to put the completion of inventory of the Lieutenant Governor's office on tomorrow's list. The man is convinced that there are a couple of volumes are missing from his library…"

Gemma waited, then nearly collapsed with relief as the colonel's voice trailed off into the distance as the door closed behind them. Just to be certain, she stayed in the study for a short while, then crept back upstairs to her room, lit a small taper, and read the letter, her heart sinking with every word. The Hatchetts were coming to discuss the Dalrymple properties and the final disposition of the will with their lawyer, and according to this, they would arrive within the week.

Every day she was still here was yet another day she'd failed. Another day that she'd missed the mark, and that someone else would pay for her error. She would have to try harder tomorrow. Try a more daring trick.

In the morning, she'd send word to Phillipa. She'd know what to do.

Despite Gemma's fatigue, worry robbed her of sleep. This was the longest Gemma had spent on a job. The longest she'd felt on the highwire. And there was something about sneaking around Colonel Webber that didn't sit well with her. Here was a man who was trying—and failing—to keep his work commitments and his personal ones in balance.

Maybe he wasn't the only one.

Chapter Thirteen

THE FOLLOWING morning Gemma took Ivy on a small excursion to the Public Gardens to do a small study of the plant life and allow both of them a small respite from Mrs. Whitehead's pinched expressions. They arrived home with a small basket of leaves, two pebbles Ivy had taken a particular liking to, and—much to Gemma's surprise—a small frog, which Ivy promised she would look after.

"You're going to have to ask the colonel if you can keep it," Gemma said as they concocted a makeshift terrarium from a large jar she'd found in the kitchen. "And we'll have to get this poor fellow a proper house."

"I will," Ivy replied, smiling at the creature they'd nested in a bed of leaves at the bottom. "I'm sure Papa will like Henry. He will eat all the flies."

Gemma was far less certain about that, but Ivy was so engaged with the creature at the moment, she let it be for now. Anything that captured the child's imagination seemed to be a good thing. They put the jar in the nursery, and Gemma turned her attention to the next room to search—the colonel's study.

A fresh sense of urgency brought on by the news of the Hatchetts' impending arrival emboldened Gemma to become more daring. Ivy sat crossed legged on the floor, accepting books that Gemma pulled off the shelves under the guise of a reading lesson. Ivy carefully sounded out the title, flipped through the book and found an interesting fact or two, then carefully placed it in a new pile for Gemma to re-shelve. Meanwhile, Gemma searched the emptied shelves for a false panel or a compartment of some kind where Mr. Dalrymple might have stored his will.

Earlier that morning, Gemma had dashed off a quick note to Phillipa. Back in the colonel's study, Gemma slid the letter she'd taken last night in a spot under the desk where it might be 'found' by Colonel Webber or Sergeant Babcock.

Gemma let go a sigh as she handed Ivy another small handful of books. Normally she had the freedom to focus on her part of a job—picking a pocket, planting a document, or ensuring a door was left unlocked. But never was she truly alone, as she was now. Occasionally it was more complicated, but never did she have maneuver her way around a steely-eyed mountain of a man who made her warm and soft at all the wrong moments. It made her feel...something. Something good. It was a feeling she didn't deserve to have. Once upon a time, her brother and her best friend were in love. And because of Gemma, they would never have a future together. Because once upon a time, Gemma had convinced Penny to do a trick they weren't ready for. Maybe this job was part of her punishment, because she hadn't felt ready for this.

"Papa's books are very boring."

Ivy's disgruntled observation broke through the painful bout of memory. Gemma opened her eyes, the wave of panic that had gripped her stomach passing away as she scooped up another small pile of books and carefully placed them back on the shelf.

"They must be interesting to him," Gemma answered as her fingers ran over the spines. She couldn't exactly disagree with the child's observation. This particular shelf of texts was dedicated to military subjects such as *The Life and Campaigns of Napoleon Bonaparte, The Operations of War,* and general knowledge, like *Tomlin-*

son's Cyclopaedia of Useful Arts. But scattered amongst those were also books of poetry, philosophy, and even a book about birds in Australia. "Your father is a very learned man who must turn his mind to a host of complicated problems. Let's see if this shelf is a bit more interesting."

The next two shelves of books were far outside her reach. The ceilings on this floor were easily ten feet high, and the books went right to the top. Perhaps this was the spot where Mr. Dalrymple hid his will. It was too high to be within casual reach of anyone, even the colonel, who was at least six feet tall. Without giving it much thought, Gemma climbed up the bookshelves, which were as sturdy as any ladder, and started to pile a few books on one hand before coming down and placing them beside Ivy.

"Uncle says he just orders people about and writes down the words of people more important than him," Ivy said.

Gemma tried not to frown. "That does not seem like a very charitable thing to say."

"Uncle Alexander is a Viscount," Ivy said, as if that both explained and excused the comment.

"And what do Viscounts do?" Gemma said. "I thought they just owned land they did nothing in particular to earn."

Ivy paused at that.

"He says he's very important," Ivy said. "He said I'm going to be a lady and need to marry very well."

"What do you want to do?" she asked.

The girl paused. "What else is there?"

"Join the circus?" Gemma asked, trying to bring levity as she grabbed another handful of books.

"Could I?" the girl asked, her expression telling Gemma this seemed like a marvellous idea. And it was, in a way. Gemma had loved the circus once. She loved the frenetic energy of it, always moving from place to place. "Do you get to climb in the circus, like that?"

"It depends, I guess," Gemma said, balancing a small stack of books on her head as she deftly climbed back down the shelves, landing lightly on her feet. "If you are an acrobat, yes, you definitely do climb. But there are other things—being a clown, for example. Some do magic tricks, or juggle with fire. And some ride elephants, or work with the tigers."

"Can you teach me to climb those bookcases?"

"I think your father and your uncle would be in agreement that I shouldn't do that," Gemma said, as she scaled up again the shelves and started pulling more books off the shelf. "I think we'll continue with juggling for now. I did promise you an extra ball to practice with today."

Each time she removed a few books, she ran her hand along the wood panels at the back, feeling for any imperfection that would suggest a hidden panel. The wall behind it seemed solid enough, though she noticed a peculiar knot in the wood. She ran her fingers over it and...was that a small seam?

Gemma's heart started to race, even as she listened to Ivy below, talking about the circus. Gently she pushed on the knot, and like magic (or like physics, Rimple would have said), a small panel popped open. This is it, she thought, unable to contain her triumph.

She reaching inside but there was—nothing. Expectation soured into disappointment as she felt around every corner. Just in case. But—

"What the devil?"

Gemma froze. She always froze when she heard someone coming into a room. Movement caught the eye. She'd freeze, assess the situation, and move out of sight if possible.

But he was right there. Standing, no doubt looking god-like and impervious, looking right at her. She couldn't see him of course. Her back was to him. But she could feel his gaze as if he were touching her.

Grasping the sturdy wooden shelf, she turned slightly, forcing a smile on her face to distract him from the movement of her other hand as she closed the hidden compartment. She saw his face, wearing an expression that she couldn't quite make out but it seemed a mix of fascination and disgust.

The old fear crept up inside her. Nausea gripped at her insides and she swallowed, trying to catch the breath that was stuck in her throat. She should look away, focus on climbing down from the shelf, but her body was unable to work to her command. Instead of doing what she wanted it to—which was very carefully and deftly climb down the shelves and land on the floor like she had half a dozen times already—her limbs were shaky and unsure.

She was on the high wire. She'd pushed too hard, taken too big a risk.

Books slipped from her head, tumbling to the floor, and soon Gemma realized she was falling, too.

Jeremy had arrived home early, prepared for a quiet afternoon in his study. It was partially penitence for his missed dinner engagements with Ivy, and partially because clean up from the burst pipe had made it impossible to concentrate at his office. He'd been looking forward to some peace and quiet, and maybe peeking in on Ivy's lessons and catching a glimpse of Gemma Kurt's radiance in the light of day. The last thing he'd expected, however, was to come home and find his daughter's governess climbing his book shelves as effortlessly as he would cross a room.

The moment he made his presence known, however, he'd seen the terror—and it was terror—in her eyes. The change had been as unexpected as it had been dramatic. Only a moment ago he'd been watching her from just outside the door jamb as she'd practically floated up and down those shelves, stacks of books in her hands and more resting on her head. Her body had moved with fluidity and confidence that had him spellbound. And then she crumpled.

He dashed across the room, his heart leaping from his chest into his throat, as if his heart had anything at all to do with this situation. Jeremy was vaguely aware of Ivy's scream as Miss Kurt started to tumble.

He caught her just before she hit the floor. He ran his hand along her hairline, then patted her cheeks, trying to bring her back to her senses. After a terrifying moment of stillness, she sucked in a large breath, and her colour, which had gone almost ashen, returned, blood rushing to her cheeks.

They remained there, somehow suspended in time, as she opened her eyes and started regaining her senses.

"I'm fine."

It took Jeremy a moment to realize she'd spoken. His heart thumped in his chest, the rush of panic replaced with something else...this unwelcome fury of need to keep this woman from harm. To never let her go.

He pushed back that inconvenient thought, locking it away somewhere inside him with a mental note that he would find longest pier on Halifax's waterfront and pitch the key into the harbour. He lifted her up and settled her into a nearby chair, then fetched a glass of brandy from the sideboard, all the while ignoring the rush of heat thrumming through his body as he took her hands and wrapped them around the glass.

"Drink," he ordered.

She gave her head a small shake. "I don't—"

"If you don't, I bloody well will." Damnation, he needed something to dull his senses, which crackled with awareness of her.

She took a small sip, as if to satisfy him.

"Thank you," she said, refusing to meet his gaze. "I don't know what came over me."

Somehow, he knew that she was lying. But he let it go.

"I don't know what would possess you to be climbing up the walls like some kind of jaguar climbing a tree," he said.

Ivy rushed to her side. "Are you hurt, Miss Kurt?"

"I am fine, Ivy," she replied with a warm smile. "I'm sorry I scared you."

"Ivy," he said, "can you help pick these books off the floor?"

His daughter nodded and turned toward her task, while, to his dismay, Miss Kurt was pulling herself to her feet.

"Don't you think you should rest?" he asked. "You may have injured yourself."

"I appreciate your concern," she replied as she rose, like a flower recovering in the sun after a heavy rain, "but aside from my ego, which will be bruised for a little while, I am quite recovered. And I should be cleaning up the mess I made."

He watched her carefully, telling himself the sole purpose for doing so was to ensure there was no evidence of injury, which, given she was clad neck to floor in a rich, plum-coloured fabric was objectively impossible. Or maybe she was hurt, and she just hid it. Like Isla.

He pushed the thought aside. This softening. This unwanted concern.

"What was the purpose of this?" He plucked one of the texts that Ivy had set in a pile on a small table. Some of them he hadn't opened in years.

"Ivy was having a reading lesson," Miss Kurt replied, bending down to pick up the last errant book as if that actually answered his question. "I decided I would take advantage of this library to do it."

"You were climbing the shelves like some kind of—" He searched his vocabulary for a noun, an adjective, or even a metaphor that would adequately describe a smallish woman adept at climbing bookshelves, but there was none at hand.

"—a lemur!" Ivy offered helpfully. "We learned about those today. They are mammals from the west coast of Africa that scale trees."

Jeremy turned to Ivy, who's eyes were bright and wide and clearly proud of her new knowledge.

"Excellent, Ivy," Miss Kurt replied, her attention fixed on Ivy, which Jeremy guessed was a tactic for her to avoid eye contact with him. "You have an excellent memory. I don't have a tail, though I do enjoy fruit."

"Ivy," Jeremy cut in. "Would you ask Mrs. Whitehead to bring around some tea?"

Ivy looked at Jeremy and then to Miss Kurt, then ran out of the study, leaving the two adults alone. They stood in silence, unnamed tension swirling around them, like a force pulling them closer. Jeremy could practically see it, blurring out the image of everything around Miss Kurt, leaving only her. He wanted to close his eyes, capture this feeling and pour it out on a canvas or in a sketchbook. His hands itched with the need to paint. To run his fingers along the curve of her lips.

Whether she was aware of it, he couldn't say. But Jeremy admitted to himself that there something about the way she moved that was utterly bewitching.

"I'm quite recovered," Miss Kurt said at last. "I don't know what came over me."

Jeremy wondered what in the hell was coming over him. Lust, no doubt. And that was fine. Or at least, more understandable than this other, deeper sensation that had nothing to do with Miss Kurt's undeniable beauty.

"I am similarly in the dark," Jeremy said, shaking off the madness that was threatening to overtake him. "Why on earth would you think it was a good idea to use my bookshelves as a climbing apparatus?"

"We were looking for some books on topics that might interest her," she said. "We made a little game of it, going through the texts. Your daughter has a very keen mind. And an interest in animals. Did you know there is a zoo in town?"

"Please do not try to charm your way out of answering my question."

The vixen actually had the gall to look bewildered.

"Charming?" she narrowed her eyes, as if disbelieving. "I'm not the charming one. I'm merely giving you an honest answer to your question."

What she was giving him was all sorts of complicated sensations that were going straight to his loins. This had to stop.

"Miss Kurt," he began, pacing the room, back straight, hands clasped being his back, "your job is to teach my daughter the skills she needs to be a proper young lady. Not to literally climb the walls."

"If Ivy doesn't have her natural curiosity sated one way or another, she will find herself figuratively climbing the walls," she said, standing straighter, her passion evident. "Don't you want that for her?"

Jeremy swallowed, taken aback by the question.

"I would move the world for her."

"A woman should be able to have the education to be able to live something of a life on her own terms," she replied. "With respect, Colonel, give her the tools so she can move the world on her own."

The idea of Ivy moving through life on her own, unprotected, created a pit in Jeremy's stomach.

"I couldn't protect Ivy's mother," he said, wondering why the hell he was making this admission. Gemma Kurt was just so damn easy to talk to. And he needed to make her understand. "I can't make the same mistake with Ivy. I know it's not traditional for fathers to want to raise their daughters, but I can take care of her."

"I know you can."

The conviction in her reply shocked Jeremy. Possibly because it was the first time he'd heard it from anyone, most especially himself. Alexander had questioned Jeremy's decision to send for Ivy, and as for his fellow officers in the garrison, he'd been the subject of endless questions and jokes about his wits. Who thought that a man who could organize the repair of roads, move supplies over deserts and move troops thousands of miles could see to the care and feeding of a ten-year-old child? No one, apparently, except Gemma Kurt.

"Miss Kurt, my daughter's education and wellbeing are very

important to me," he said, honouring her trust in him with an honest reply. "Her conduct in society, fairly or unfairly, is something she will be judged for. Your conduct must be a guide for her. And it cannot involve scooting up bookcases like you are under the big top."

She opened her mouth, but before she could say anything, the door to his study opened, and in came Mrs. Whitehead and Ivy with a tray laden with the trappings for tea, along with a few sweets. Jeremy needed brandy. And probably an ice bath.

"My apologies, Colonel," Mrs. Whitehead said as she poured a cup of tea, sweetened it, and added a drop of milk, then handed the cup to Miss Kurt, her disapproval evident. "I should have been more attentive."

Miss Kurt said nothing, turning her attention to the cup in her hand. She was still a little shaky, and Jeremy worked very hard to overcome the intense need to hold her until her nerves were calmed. All the while, the housekeeper watched Miss Kurt with thinly veiled distain. Was there something going on between these two he was unaware of?

"Papa, there is a letter under your desk," Ivy said, dragging his attention away from the governess. He turned to see Ivy holding up an envelope. He held out his hand, and she brought it to him. The return address was from the Hatchetts.

"Where did you find this?" he asked, curious. He'd searched all around his desk last night, and did a quick second look this morning, and had found nothing.

Ivy pointed to a corner of the floor. Jeremy placed it back on the desk, back in the spot where he'd last seen it. He must have been too tired for his own good to spot it last night.

"Well, Ivy," Miss Kurt said, setting the cup down, her expression brighter. "You and I should see to our next lesson."

"I thought you said we could play a game of hide and seek?" Ivy proclaimed.

"Maybe tomorrow, if the weather is fine," she said, then turned to Jeremy. "I promised her we might play the game if she had done particularly well with her lessons today. Some fresh air and exercise, as we discussed earlier."

He remembered their discussion. Her impassioned argument on his daughter's behalf. Whatever her quirks, Miss Kurt's undeniable concern for Ivy's wellbeing and education could not be dismissed. And despite every rational thought demanding that she should be dismissed for breaking rules he hadn't even dreamed needed to be an actual rule, there was something necessary about Miss Kurt in his life.

Christ. *In Ivy's life, you idiot. She is not necessary to you.*

"Of course," he replied, feeling his back straighten as he reminded himself of his place in the world, which was as commanding officer of his own household, if nowhere else. "Now, be off with you. I have work to do."

He watched the two leave the room, Ivy's hand in Miss Kurt's, when something squeezed in his chest.

Something like yearning.

Chapter Fourteen

❧

GEMMA SAT IN HER BED, knees pulled up, idly tapping a pencil as she reviewed the small list she'd made. Starting from the ground floor, Gemma created a list of every room, hallway, and feature of Hastings House. The dining room had been thoroughly searched and could be crossed off the list. So could her room, the nursery, and Colonel Webber's study. The discovery of the panel had provided some encouragement, despite her rather spectacular fall. She could barely recall the event without her cheeks burning with embarrassment. But after that sensation faded, what she was left with was something far more pleasurable and dangerous—the absolute security she'd felt in Jeremy Webber's arms.

Her fall in the study went beyond simple wounded pride. He'd seen her weakness, this nearly uncontrollable force that stole her otherwise exceptional control over her body, her ability to see and even to catch her breath. They'd begun not long after Penny's accident—a price, Gemma supposed, she was destined to pay in exchange for walking away from an act when Penny did not.

The one upside, if she could dare admit it to herself, was the sensation of being cradled Jeremy's powerful yet tender embrace afterward. She'd felt utterly safe there, when she should not. Jeremy Webber was a man she was supposed to be tiptoeing around, not falling straight into his arms. She remembered the concern that had creased the corners of his eyes as her gaze met his. And there was *something*, before he recovered his mask of propriety and imperiousness, that had struck her. He'd been worried. Afraid for her. And it made her feel...something.

The bells of the grandfather clock downstairs chimed ten times, a stark reminder that the Hatchetts would soon be arriving and Mrs. Lynde was one day closer to losing the security Mr. Dalrymple had promised her.

Gemma took stock of her list, focusing on the third floor. Sergeant Babcock had a very small room there, though there was something about moving through the sergeant's room that instilled a feeling of unease. And then there was the matter of the other space—the one that Mrs. Whitehead had made quite clear Gemma was forbidden to enter. Not that a lock made much difference to her. She just needed the opportunity.

She closed the notebook and shoved it under her mattress, then lay awake, listening to the sounds of movement in the house. Colonel Webber hadn't gone to bed yet—and with only one way in or out, searching his bedchamber would be too risky.

Didn't the man have any evening engagements? She knew from the papers he was considered one of the most eligible bachelors in town. She would have thought he'd been off to some dinner or another—just like the one where she'd first seen him, months ago, while she and her other Scandalous Spinsters were helping their last client. Still, as useful as it would have been for the colonel to spend his evenings in the company of Halifax society, the idea of him being served up to their daughters and nieces as a potential husband soured her stomach.

Urgency tangled with a feeling of helplessness. Letting out a breath of exasperation, Gemma pulled herself out of bed. She'd considered going upstairs to check on Henry, Ivy's frog, but decided to leave him until the morning. Ivy still hadn't confessed the animal's presence to the colonel, though in truth she'd had little opportunity.

Perhaps a glass of warm milk and a ginger cookie would help induce Gemma to sleep. Of course, she'd have to walk by the colonel's study, where he was no doubt up working late, but she would not—absolutely not—slow down nor even steal a glance his way. She had a job to do.

Still, as she passed the study and saw it unoccupied, she tried to ignore that twinge of disappointment as she continued down to the kitchen, wondering how she missed the sound of his bedroom door when he'd retired for the night. Just as she was entering the kitchen she saw movement, but it was only Sergeant Babcock, standing over the stove.

"Sergeant Babcock," she said, keeping her voice low so as not to disturb Mrs. Whitehead, whose room was close by. "I wasn't expecting you."

The big man turned to her, his head capped by a linen nightcap, solid form wrapped a robe. It was then she noticed his slippered feet—or rather, slippered foot. What she could see of his left leg appeared to be made of wood.

"Miss Kurt," he said, his mouth turning up into warm smile. "I wasn't expecting company at this hour."

"I couldn't sleep," she said. "I thought some warm milk might help, and maybe a cookie, if there were any left."

He gestured toward the tin sitting on the kitchen table.

"I'm just warming up some milk now to make a cup of scatlin for the colonel. Would you like some?"

"I've not heard of it," Gemma said, sitting herself down.

"A little warm milk, some whisky, a little honey and a bit of spice," he said. "Perfect for a cool damp evening like this one."

"It does indeed," she said, and watched as he took a third cup off a peg and poured out a serving of the steaming liquid into each. As the steam rose, he took a nutmeg and grated it on top each one. One cup he gave to her, and Gemma inhaled the warm, spiced drink, then took a sip. "I didn't see the colonel in his study."

"That's because I finally coaxed him out of it," he said,

beaming with accomplishment. "It's only taken me a fortnight. We set up that studio for him, and he hasn't visited it once."

"Studio?"

"For his painting." The sergeant took a sip of his own drink, then carefully placed two cookies on a small plate.

"Painting?" The very idea of Colonel Webber applying himself to anything remotely artistic was tantalizing. Was this where Ivy's affinity for drawing had come from? "I had no idea."

"As he prefers it," the sergeant replied, taking a sip of his own drink and sitting down at the table next to her, shifting to adjust his prosthetic limb. "I'm probably risking my life and yet another limb mentioning it." He gave her a wink.

"I suspect you're too valuable to spare. He's very lucky to have you," she said, and she meant it. Harold Babcock seemed like the one person with whom Colonel Webber could be himself. She'd thought she'd gotten a glimpse of it herself, once or twice. Each time, it was a surprise to them both, but for Gemma at least, she felt like she'd been treated to a rare gift.

"That he is," the sergeant agreed with a soft laugh. "He's a good man, the colonel. A very good man. I realize he can be a bit stodgy at times, but his heart is as soft as they come when he dares to show it. I've been trying to get him to pick up his brush since we landed here. He hasn't had the heart to do it since Mrs. Webber passed."

Gemma forced a smile. She knew what it was like to lose someone she loved dearly. Pushing back a lump in her throat, she turned her attention to Sergeant Babcock who pulled a tray off a shelf, onto which he placed the plate of cookies, along with a napkin and a cup for the colonel.

"Well, I should deliver this before it gets cold."

If Gemma had been tempted to stay behind and make a more careful mental map of the kitchen, her resolve weakened as she watched Sergeant Babcock pick up the tray. When she was at Everwell, she enjoyed the kitchen table chats with her fellow Spinsters. Sitting here only reinforced the fact she was here alone.

She walked along with the sergeant in companionable silence, but when they reached the top of the first flight of stairs, he paused.

"Oh dear," he said, looking over his shoulder. "I've forgotten my keys in the kitchen."

"I can run and get them for you," Gemma whispered, already turning around. "It's no trouble."

"Actually," he replied in an equally hushed voice, his eyes brightening as if he'd just discovered the answer to some long unsolved mathematical problem, "if you could take this to Colonel Webber before his drink gets cold, then I'll go fetch my keys. You'll be there and back before I get back down the stairs, I reckon."

He held the tray out to her, hopeful expectation in his smile. Or was that...mischief?

Of course it wasn't. Gemma's stomach was just so twisted she was no doubt seeing things. It would be all sorts of trouble for her to interrupt the colonel in the one part of the house that was forbidden to her. Where he would be alone, expecting a broad, red-haired, moustached sergeant in a night cap and slippers.

But what kind of opportunity was she throwing away if she didn't? That door was always locked and even Ivy seemed to understand it was a place they shouldn't go. She could plan no lessons there. But if she could get a look—well, maybe she'd get a little closer to finding that document and leaving Hastings House forever.

Jeremy stood, hands on his hips, looking inside a trunk that held a half dozen unfinished paintings. Each one he'd started and stopped in the past decade. They were primarily landscapes—Egyptian deserts and oases, the reds and greens stunning against a blazing blue sky. There were English pastures, and from his youth, a remarkable visit to Shanghai with his father. Photography had made more realistic images of these landscapes now, but they still could not capture the vivid colour, or even the feel of a place, like a painting. A little part of his soul had gone into each one. Since his arrival in Nova Scotia, he'd promised himself he'd start painting again. Like the one he'd done of Ivy and Isla on his brother's estate. Maybe Ivy would be part of the painting, if he could get her to sit still long enough to capture her. She'd be reading, or working on one of her embroideries, or on her own drawing.

Or he might sketch Gemma Kurt, looking up at him with a knowing smile, her long lashes kissing her cheeks, her hair down, falling over one shoulder. Arousal rippled through his body at the very thought of it.

Time to stop thinking about it.

"Colonel, sir?"

Jeremy was used to cannon fire and gunshot, but the sound of a female voice from behind him nearly caused him to jump out of his skin. He spun on his heel to see Gemma Kurt standing where Harold Babcock should have been.

"Where's Babcock?"

"My apologies, Colonel," she said, her voice calm, but looking as uncomfortable as Jeremy felt. "I offered to take this for Sergeant Babcock, as a favour."

She was wrapped in her dressing gown, her hair loosely pulled back, her brown eyes looked like dark pools in the lamp light. And if he looked down, which he definitely shouldn't have done but Christ, he couldn't help it—there were her bare feet.

And just as suddenly as she'd arrived, so had the thought of lavishing her with every possible bodily pleasure. Starting with kissing those toes.

He put a halt to those thoughts immediately, lest he find himself in deep water. He'd asked Babcock to send up a nightcap, which he realized was the height of laziness on his part, but Babcock had spent the fifteen years being both valet and mother hen to the Jeremy. He'd learned that refusing Babcock's mothering made his sergeant rather grumpy. But having Babcock badger

Jeremy into accepting a cup of punch and then sending this creature up to surprise him like this when he was already distracted? Surely this was breaking some kind of sacred contract between them.

"Babcock doesn't get to have personal business," he said, sounding every bit a privileged sop. "He was the one who insisted I have it."

What was Harold thinking? Jeremy was in his shirtsleeves, eschewing the red wool coat and even his waistcoat for far more casual dress. But when he caught Miss Kurt's gaze roaming over him, lingering on his arms and his hips, realization dawned.

Babcock, you sly bastard. Halifax's matchmaking mavens had nothing on his sergeant.

"Well, I'm here now," she said at last, as if that wasn't the most complicated thing ever to come out of a woman's mouth. She held out the tray in her hands. "Shall I put this down?"

Right. That flash of desire or something he thought he saw may have simply been the disgruntlement of a woman who had other things to do. It was also a cue that Jeremy had spent far too much time standing there, staring at her like a complete idiot.

"Of course," he said, gesturing to a small table he'd just set up nearby. It was a simple platform, stained with pigments of all kinds.

He turned his head to where she was looking—the open trunk, a host of half-painted canvases on display, his bag of brushes in his hands.

She walked past him, seemingly not interested in his reply, gravitating to one of the smaller canvases, a small study he'd done of a small desert village while he was in Egypt. Not only did she study it, but she set down the tray and picked up the canvas, holding it to the lamplight. She turned to him, her smile bright and encouraging, releasing some of the tension in his chest.

"It's very good."

He was so tempted to say something to deflect her praise, but it turned out that Jeremy did in fact have an ego, and like most men, he enjoyed it being fluffed up now and again.

"I'm not an expert by any means, but I think it would give other people joy to look at them," she continued then set the painting down. "I bet you would take the art world by storm."

"Thank you," he said. "But I don't think I am ready for that sort of public display yet. Every time I look at them all I can see is what I'd do differently."

Gemma nodded, wearing an encouraging smile.

"That's natural, I think," she said. "Every year, Maddy is looking to improve her gardens. Elouise decides that our annual Christmas pageant is perfect, but could be even more perfect, if we just tweaked 'something.' Rimple is always perfecting her machines and designs even if the rest of us think they are already perfection. We are all our harshest critics."

"You are a most unusual woman, Miss Kurt."

"I will take that as a compliment," she said, then gestured to the door. "But I should go. It's late and I've broken I don't know how many of your rules just standing here."

An unexpected panic rose in Jeremy's chest. As if her leaving would make him feel more alone than he had before she'd arrived, which made no sense at all. But he found himself compelled to keep her here just a few minutes longer. To stave off the shadows.

"At least five," he blurted out, unable to stop smiling as this unnamable feeling bubbled inside him. "Possibly six."

She blinked and let out a gentle laugh. "Five? How?"

He started holding up fingers.

"No whistling before eight in the morning."

"What?" she said. "You can't be serious."

"Perfectly serious," he said, then continued. "No adjusting of schedules without permission of the commanding officer."

She raised her brows. "You are not my commanding officer."

"I am the ranking officer in the house," he said, then held up another finger. "No use of milk or sugar in tea."

"That's not a rule, that's a preference."

"It should be a rule. It's awful."

He watched her roll her eyes, an utterly artless gesture that made him feel inexplicably light and aroused at the same time. Talking to her like this was definitely against the rules, but, he reasoned, despite that rather spectacular transgression when they'd kissed in the nursery, he wasn't a lout who wasn't in charge of his bodily impulses. If a little bit of discomfort in his nether regions was the price he had to pay to have this spellbinding conversation with her, so be it.

"I've lost track already," she continued, crossing her arms. "Perhaps I can get Ivy to scribe them as writing practice."

"Excellent idea," he said, then continued, holding up his thumb. "No scaring the wits out of your employer by climbing up the bookcases."

Even in the lamplight he saw the pink rise into her cheeks.

"On that we can agree," she replied, her tone more subdued. "Thank you for being there."

"Not at all. Perhaps if I hadn't startled you, you wouldn't have fallen."

Gemma stilled, and something shifted. She'd become...brittle. Fragile. Her eyes widened, though he could see she wasn't looking at him.

"She fell."

The phrase came out as a terrified hush.

"Excuse me?"

He regretted his question the moment he'd uttered it. Something was wrong. Her chest rose and fell as if she fought for each breath. There was a fragility to her that was new.

"Miss Kurt? Gemma?"

Chapter Fifteen

"Gemma?"

He may have said something after that, but she didn't hear it. All she knew is that in the next moment, she was being swept up in his arms and placed on a chair. He knelt in front of her, his large masculine form a comfort, his eyes soft and protective, his fingers tracing a delicate line around the edges of her face.

"Look at me," he said, his voice a soft command. "Look at me and just focus on my face."

He saw her panic, she realized, and was helping her to manage it.

After the panic finally subsided, embarrassment flooded her. She wanted to get away, but Jeremy's arms rested on the sides of the chair, forming a protective wall between Gemma and the rest of the world. Which right now seemed only to be the two of them.

"Just breathe," he said. "One low breath in." He demonstrated, pulling breath in through his nose, and the blowing it out again slowly. "And out. Can you do that with me?"

His voice was so gentle, his smile so earnest that it reached past her humiliation, past the shock of painful memory, and she found herself mimicking him. After a moment, she started to feel a little more human.

"That's better," he said, a relieved smile on his face. "Just give yourself a moment."

"Thank you," she said, wiping a tear from the corner of her eye.

"I've seen many people in shock on the battlefield, and then later," he said. "It's not often talked about, but it is not uncommon."

Gemma blinked.

"I don't know what happened."

"I was asking you about the time you fell from the bookshelf," he said, pushing a stray lock of her hair off her cheek. "You scared the hell out of me."

More tears started to well. He wiped them from her eyes and held on to her hands.

"But at least I got to play a hero for once," he said, with mock bravado. "Very dashing if I say so myself."

Gemma smiled through her tears. "Very dashing."

She tried to smile, but all she did was choke back a sob.

"Or not at all," he said with a smile. "Come Gemma, this is not good for my brittle male ego."

"You were very dashing," she said through a blubbering smile. "There are times I just..." She paused, searching for the words. "I just disappear into myself."

"I see," he said, and she had the very real sense that he did, in fact, see. "Is this why you left the circus?"

She shook her head and let out a low, shaky breath. "I left because I killed my best friend by encouraging her to do a trick she wasn't ready for."

The phrase came out in a rush, Gemma daring look Jeremy in the eye only briefly before looking away as she waited for the rebuke. But none came. There was only patient silence, and somehow, she found it necessary to continue.

"It was always natural to me, the acrobatics—and I loved it. I did my first matinee when I was eight. My brother Nico was ten, and Penny was nine. We had a little act together." Even after all these years, she smiled at the memory of she and Nico doing tumbling and juggling and jumps to roaring applause. She swallowed, a fresh stab of pain pulling at her heart. "As we got older we did more daring tricks. Always pushing the limits. The crowd loved it, and so did I. Our parents were so proud of us." She could see her parents now, in her mind's eye. "They were certain the three of us were destined for a big show, like Cushing's. Until the accident."

Emotion bubbled in her throat, but she forced herself to keep it in check as she shook her head.

"You don't have to tell me," he said.

"Yes, I do," she replied, forcing herself to look him in the eye. There were so many things she should tell him, but they were not entirely hers to tell. This one was hers alone. The fault was with her. And maybe when this was all over, he would think less of her, and that would make the parting easier.

"We had just arrived for a show just outside Montreal. We had been practicing some new tricks, and I'd become far too confident for my own good," Gemma continued, allowing herself to be transported back to that fateful afternoon. "She wanted to do the tightrope, which I disliked, so I talked her out of it. Instead, I pushed Penny to do something on the trapeze she clearly wasn't ready for."

She paused, every muscle stretched so taut with shame she feared she might break. Jeremy sat with her, his body providing a comforting warmth as he gently stroked the inside of her wrist with his thumb. The soothing motion siphoned away the suffocating guilt and emotion that had been trapped inside her for so long.

Gemma closed her eyes, trying to pull out the memory and cast it aside, but she couldn't do it. A tidal wave of hurt came crashing down, and there was no way for her to stop it.

"We'd practiced and practiced, but Penny wasn't certain. I should have listened to her, but I didn't. I was so fixated on what I wanted—" She stopped and sucked in a ragged breath. "She slipped through my fingers and fell. We were thirty feet in the air."

"You don't use a net?"

"Always. I was confident, but not foolish. But when she fell, one of the corners of the net gave way—either it wasn't secured properly or it snapped—I don't know. They called a surgeon and took Penny to the hospital. But she never healed. She couldn't walk. And she just wasn't the same. She passed away this past summer."

"That wasn't your fault, Gemma. It was an accident."

"But it wouldn't have happened at all if it wasn't for me," she replied. "Because of what I did."

She thought she would crumble then, but she found herself folded into his arms and for the first time she could recall, let herself fall. She held on to him and cried until she had nothing left.

When she found her strength, she pulled back and he pressed a handkerchief into her hands. She wiped her nose and looked up at him through bleary eyes. Part of her was expecting censure or judgment, but there was only patience.

"Nico left the circus to be with her. She had to go to a convalescent home near Montreal, where her parents lived."

"Were you ever able to see her?"

A fresh wave of guilt passed over her. "No."

She dabbed her eyes and tried to withhold a fresh wave of tears when she felt Jeremy's touch, smoothing her hair, calming her heart.

"My poor darling. It's amazing to me at all you can stand with all that on your shoulders."

"That's what everyone says," she said. "But I can't help how I feel. If I hadn't pushed her, none of this would have happened."

He silenced her rambling with the most tender of kisses to her cheek.

"Gemma, I have sent men to their deaths." he said. "I nearly had Babcock killed, in fact, all those years ago. I was young and out of my depth."

"But that was war," she protested.

"It doesn't lessen the guilt. If you could replay it again, it would have worked out differently. Maybe something else might have happened to your friend. Fate has its own agenda—it is neither good nor bad. It just is." he said. "Sometimes it's cruel, taking something away someone you loved so much that the idea of living another day without them seems impossible. And sometimes it's merciful and brings something so good into your life you can scarcely believe you are worthy of it."

"I don't know if I'm worthy," she said.

"I'm definitely not," he said. "And yet, here you are."

Whether it was impulse, hunger, or a simple need to drown her memories in pleasurable oblivion, Gemma didn't know. She sat up, holding his face in her hands, savouring the roughness of whiskers on his skin, pushing back the lock of his hair that had fallen onto his forehead. She pulled him toward her and pressed her lips against the hard line of his brow. She heard the sharp intake his breath and it roused her blood. She moved her mouth to his ear, brushing the tender skin of his earlobes with her mouth.

"Here I am."

Arousal shot through Jeremy, flooding him with need. A need to worship this woman. Prove she was worthy of every ounce of pleasure he could lavish.

He was on his knees before her, and she offered her mouth for the taking, bestowing herself to him like a benevolent goddess. And he would offer himself up as a sacrifice to her need. Her kisses were urgent, hungry, her lips open for him to explore while her hands ran along his chest, brushing through the linen of his shirt, running along his nipples, sending a bolt of heat straight to his cock. In response, he peppered kisses along her jaw, then ran them along her neck to her collar, allowing him to taste the tender flesh along the top of her breasts. He was rewarded for his efforts with a soft moan.

"I want to pleasure you," he managed to get out between breathy kisses. "To worship you."

She answered him by pulling his hand out of her hair and placing it over her breast, rising to meet his touch. As his skin grazed her nipple through the thin fabric of her nightgown, she gave a little gasp of pleasure, her kisses more urgent. She protested as he pulled away. He lifted up her nightgown, turning his attention to her breasts, gently palming one while running his tongue over the other, the nipple at a fine point. She responded by digging her fingers into his hair, releasing the most luxurious sigh of pleasure.

"Christ Gemma, you are perfect," he whispered. "So perfect."

He ran his hands along her calves and upward to her thighs, where he was gifted with soft, sensitive flesh. He hadn't even reached her delicate core and already she shivered with pleasure from his touch.

"Open for me," he pleaded. "I need to taste you."

She seemed confused by his request, but granted it, and he rewarded her trust with the smallest brush of his thumb against her sex. She gasped, and he grinned as his thumb slid easily over her damp folds. He teased her with long, soft strokes, watching her breath deepen and her chest move as she lost herself to her desire.

He found her opening and gently he pushed his finger inside her. She accepted his offering, moving back and forth to his gentle strokes, until she loosened enough for a second finger. She was a vision, his Aphrodite, bathed in lamplight, scented of orange blossoms, her golden skin on fire. She could be his.

Madness, lust, or something else gripped Jeremy—a fierce need to have Gemma, to be able to worship her every night, to make her his. As she lifted her hips to meet his rhythm, his own need throbbed, wanting nothing more to be buried in her soft, tight heat. He lowered his face to her sex, lapping her lushness.

She writhed under his touch, and Jeremy exalted as she arched off the chair and cried out his name as waves of pleasurably oblivion overtook her.

As her orgasm subsided, he pulled down her skirts, and she leaned forward kiss him when he caught her by the hands, bringing them to his mouth and giving them a hard, but very chaste kiss.

He looked up at her, seeing the confusion in her eyes. She opened her mouth to speak, but before she could say anything, he put finger to her lips. The feel of her plump lips against his flesh damn near caused him to spill his seed in his pants. He was so hard, so aroused, he feared that even the smallest touch from her would have him lose control.

He held her tight for a moment before she rose, leaving him alone once more, somehow more alone than he'd been before she'd come. As for Jeremy's so-called rules, what they'd just done shattered them all.

Jeremy rose to his feet, discounting the very idea even as it popped into his head. He wasn't in love with Gemma Kurt. That was impossible, wasn't it? This nameless sensation—this yearning, this need to be with her, to right the world for her, had to be *something*. If it wasn't so bloody late, he'd have gone and searched in a dictionary.

He might have been captivated, he supposed. That felt, if not safe, at least not quite so treacherous. The treacherous feelings he could bury in work. In rules. In agendas. In neat little piles on his desk that he would work through until he could barely stay awake, until fatigue somehow bested the emptiness.

Chapter Sixteen

GEMMA LAY IN HER BED, hands gripping her coverlet as the sound of birdsong announced morning's arrival. Sunrise came a little later with every passing day, a small but persistent reminder that she was running out of time. And with the news that the Hatchetts were on their way to Halifax from Upper Canada to finalize the disposition of the estate, she knew she'd have to press on.

Last night in Jeremy's makeshift studio, there had been no mask of propriety. There was just the man and a private passion. He hadn't meant to share it with her. But he did anyway.

And she shared everything with him. Things she hadn't shared even with Elouise, who'd taken Gemma under her wing almost immediately when she'd landed on the doorstep of Everwell Manor. He could have seen her for what she was—self-serving, thoughtless, and entirely too reckless to look after Ivy. He could have turned her out on the spot, and this entire job would have been over.

Instead, he held her close, bearing some of the weight of her sorrow and guilt. Even the memory of his touch brought a fresh ripple of yearning through her body. But it had been more than a carnal affair. He'd made her feel less alone in the world. He'd made her feel...worthy of a good person's love.

Which suddenly made everything she was doing at Hastings House feel wrong.

It was impossible to tell him why she was here. The Hatchetts were acquaintances with distant, but no doubt important, family to Colonel Webber. He wore a red coat that stood for upholding the social order, and that order didn't include disenfranchised housekeepers who were getting in the way of a tidy inheritance to someone several rungs up the societal pecking order. And she definitely couldn't let down her fellow Scandalous Spinsters the way she'd let down Penny. If Everwell's special activities were uncovered, she would ruin more lives, and she'd already ruined enough.

There was too much at stake.

Gemma was never the Spinster to play the long game—that was Elouise and Phillipa's specialty. Gemma, Maddy, and even Rimple were always part of a job for very specific, very targeted purposes. Maddy, Everwell's Librarian, often did the research and provided an extra measure of security for times when precaution was needed. Rimple, too, was behind the scenes—providing some of the special gadgets the team needed. She helped Gemma with her lock picking tools, or, her true passion, creating the specialized clothing needed by the crew to do the work. She'd made Gemma's darks—the shirts and trousers that would accommodate her small frame and allow her to move and hide away whatever valuables she was liberating in a series of pockets. She'd spent considerable time with Gemma to find the right sort of material for gloves and shoe coverings to give her extra grip so she could climb with confidence.

And Gemma—her job was not to be seen. When she'd fallen into the colonel's arms, she'd felt absolutely naked. Last night, she'd felt his desire.

Gemma closed her eyes as an unwelcome sensation, pleasurable as it was, ran over her body. Heat prickled under her skin, her body remembering now with utter clarity the pleasure of his touch she should never have experienced in the first place.

That was another reason she was running out of time. This inconvenient and captivating feeling growing inside her for a man she had no business feeling anything for. Not fascination, not fondness, not whatever this unholy feeling that was making her body tingle with the same exhilaration she used to feel flying through the air under the big top.

Even if it felt wonderful. She didn't deserve that feeling.

Focus, Gemma. Focus on the job.

After her morning ablutions, she dressed and went down to the kitchen for breakfast. Ivy would be having breakfast with her father, and Gemma would collect her precisely at seven thirty. That gave her fifteen minutes to have a strong cup of coffee and some of the cook's eggs.

As she walked down the stairs, the low tones of Jeremy's voice caught her attention. She wasn't ready to face him after last night. She paused, gripping the second floor newel post so tightly that it twisted. The swift motion came with a definite clicking sound. She looked down to see a hidden panel that had swung out at her feet, depositing a small, folded piece of paper. She swooped down in elation, plucking it from the carpet and unfolding it. She sucked in a breath as she scanned the neat handwriting.

Oatcakes as made by Aunt Edwina
3 handfuls oats
Salt --

A recipe? She stifled a moan as she shoved the paper in her apron pocket. After a few steps however, found her disappointment giving way to something far more attractive. Hope.

If this has escaped her notice, there was more to discover.

"Good morning," she said as she walked past the housekeeper's office into the kitchen, seating herself at the small table, taking in tantalizing aroma of coffee. To her surprise, Sergeant Babcock was by the stove tending to small copper vessel. A pang of nostalgia and excitement made her smile.

"Is that a *cezve*?" she asked, standing next to him. The little Turkish pot was steaming, but not quite come to the boil.

The sergeant turned to her, beaming.

"It is!" He regarding her an expression that seemed like curiosity. "Would you like to have some?"

"Mr. Babcock," the cook said, the woman looking over at the sergeant with amusement. "That will go straight through a wee thing like that. It's strong stuff."

"I haven't had coffee prepared like this in a long time," Gemma said, her heart squeezing a bit. "My father always had it this way."

"I don't believe Colonel Webber would approve of his daughter's governess consuming coffee prepared in a *foreign* fashion." Mrs. Whitehead's sharp gaze sliced though Gemma just as the housekeeper spooned a bit of sugar into her tea. "That does not look like a beverage a woman of good breeding would consume."

Gemma felt the woman's barb, which touched a rare but raw flashpoint.

"Breeding has nothing to do with taste, Mrs. Whitehead, unless you're the animal being bred for the table," she said as she took a seat at the table. "Good taste is honed through experience, an open mind to try something new, and building your palate."

The housekeeper let out a huff, like air being forced from an overstretched bellows, and she opened her mouth to speak before Sergeant Babcock let out a laugh.

"All coffee comes from the tropics, Mrs. Whitehead, or did you not know that?" Sergeant Babcock said, then gestured to her cup. "Having tea from Ceylon sweetened with sugar from the Caribbean is the very definition of foreign."

Mrs. Whitehead's lips pulled together in a tight line, before taking what she no doubt felt to be a very dignified sip of tea and fixating on her breakfast.

Once the coffee had boiled to his satisfaction, he poured out the dark velvety liquid into a beautiful demitasse and set it before Gemma, giving her a mischievous wink.

"Tell me what you think."

As she took a sip of the steaming hot, strong coffee, a thousand pleasant memories flooded her. Sitting on her father's lap, laughing with her brother Nico, and the conversations that happened in an endless number of languages, dialects, and accents that made up the world of the circus she'd grown up in.

"You've been missing that," Sergeant Babcock said. "Nothing like a taste of home."

She looked up at him and smiled, and it occurred to her that Sergeant Babcock and probably the colonel too were not dissimilar in some ways. A lifetime spent in other places, a kinship built from never being in one place too long. Place became the people you were with. Everwell had become that for her.

"Are you well after your little tumble, Miss Kurt?" Sergeant Babcock asked, concern furrowing his brow.

"Yes, thank you," Gemma replied with a fresh rush of embarrassment. "Not one of my finer moments."

"You need to be careful, a wee thing like you climbing heights like that," he said.

"Not to mention it's highly improper," Mrs. Whitehead said dismissively. "If you were mine to deal with, you have been dismissed immediately."

"But she is not, Mrs. Whitehead. Miss Kurt is mine."

The rich sound of Jeremy Webber's voice brought the table to attention, and gave Gemma a small rush of panic. She wanted to put her hands to her cheeks because she was certain she blushing. Before she could spend too long worrying about that, however, she was distracted by his words.

Miss Kurt is mine.

Now she was really going to blush.

"Well, it appears I just startled you all again," he said, his gaze pausing on Gemma for the smallest of moments before taking in the scene in front of him.

Did he notice that her cheeks were becoming as red as his coat? Of course, he did. This man noticed everything about her.

"Babcock," he said, using the name as a command that was

neither loud nor aggressive, but had the sergeant on his feet at the door in seconds.

"Sorry sir," he said, pulling himself to his feet. "I lost track of the time."

"Miss Kurt," Jeremy's eyes slid past his sergeant to Gemma, who wanted to slide under the table and disappear. "Your charge awaits your instruction. And a reminder, Mrs. Whitehead, that Babcock and I will not be dining at Hastings House tonight."

"Of course sir," Mrs. Whitehead replied.

Gemma stilled, the implications settling on her. If the colonel wasn't dining at home, the chances were excellent she'd have the opportunity to search his rooms at last.

Without further ado, he turned on his heel and left, Babcock behind him. Gemma released a silent breath.

"I should go," she said, taking the last of her coffee, her nerves settling on her. She rose, reminded of the recipe she'd found. She pulled it out of her pocket and pushed it across the table at Mrs. Whitehead. "I found this in the newel post this morning, quite by accident."

The housekeeper's eyes narrowed as she examined it. "I shall put it away for when the Hatchetts arrive."

"Miss Ivy's room was the old housekeeper's room," the cook offered in a cheerful, but slightly conspiratorial tone. "It was considered scandalous, considering it is on the same floor as Mr. Dalrymple's bedchamber. That's where the colonel sleeps now. And who knows what he stuffed into the floor board there. You might find an entire cookbook."

The cook's offhanded joke settled in Gemma's thoughts as she climbed the steps to the second floor to collect Ivy, when she was greeted by Sergeant Babcock.

"This just came to the door this morning for you Miss Kurt," he said.

"Thank you." Gemma reached out, swallowing her excitement as she accepted the envelope. An elegant 'E', pressed into wax, emblazoned the envelope, and the script she instantly recognized as Phillipa's. She would have preferred to read it in private, but given Mrs. Whitehead's ill will, Gemma had no desire to further excite any suspicions the woman had. Gemma slid her finger under the end of the envelope, breaking the seal, and pulled out the note, holding her breath. It was short, but as she read it, a small weight lifted off her shoulders. Phillipa and Rimple would visit and see about her progress. The note was written to imply her progress with Ivy, but Gemma knew it was more than that.

"Mrs. Hartley and Miss Jones from Everwell School would like to call upon me," she said. "To check on my progress and to see if my work is up to standard."

"I'll pass it on to the colonel, but I know he will have no complaints. He has far too busy a day today, getting ready for the event at the Halifax Merchant's Club this evening."

"Will it be an especially late night?" she asked, hoping her question sounded like pleasant conversation, instead of a clumsy attempt to fumble for information.

"I believe so," the sergeant said, then rolled his eyes. "I don't expect to be home much before two, the way these things tend to go on. He'll be a bear in the morning."

Two? Gemma did a silent calculation. If she snuck in his room at ten, which was after the general hour Mrs. Whitehead retired for the night, she'd have four hours to search. Jeremy might be a bear in the morning, but she'd have the will in her hands. It would all be worth it.

Between the anticipation of Colonel Webber's outing, the imminent arrival of visitors from Everwell, and a frantic search for Henry, who'd hopped out of his jar sometime overnight, the morning flew by. Ivy had been upset by the amphibian's disappearance, and worried that Mrs. Whitehead might decide to bash him with a pot. After a frantic hour of searching with no luck at all, they were interrupted by the doorbell that signaled Phillipa's arrival.

Gemma let out a breath and rushed to the door where Mrs. Whitehead stood, clearly disapproving but no doubt wise enough to keep her opinions to herself. After a polite and restrained greeting at the door, hats and coats taken away by Mrs. Whitehead, the Scandalous Spinsters retreated to the parlour.

"It's so good to see you," Gemma exclaimed as she took Rimple by the hands and gave them a squeeze, then pulled Phillipa in small embrace.

"You are looking well, Gemma," Phillipa said, looking her up and down, before her eye strayed past her. "And who is this?"

Gemma looked over her shoulder where Ivy Webber stood, watching the older women with undisguised curiosity.

"Phillipa, Rimple, allow me to introduce Miss Ivy Webber," she said, gesturing to her pupil. "Ivy, this is Mrs. Phillipa Hartley and Miss Rimple Jones."

"What kind of a name is Rimple?" the girl asked. "It sounds strange."

"I suppose it is if you aren't used to it," Rimple answered. "It was given to me by my father. His mother was born in India."

Ivy's head cocked to one side, her eyes narrowed, as if she was being presented with a puzzle. "You sound Welsh."

"I am. I am part Welsh, and part Indian," she answered with a shrug. "But I'm all me."

"My mother was Portuguese," Ivy said. "She died."

There was something so remarkably matter-of-fact about Ivy's statement that saddened Gemma. So much sorrow borne by two short words.

"If you like, I would be very pleased to hear about her," Rimple said. "Wouldn't you, Phillipa?"

"We would indeed," Phillipa answered, as they took their seats around an elegant tea service. Gemma poured the tea while Phillipa and Rimple asked Ivy about her parents, about England, and her schooling.

"Is this a picture of your mother?" Phillipa asked, gesturing to a small portrait on the wall of a woman with proud, comely features, many of which lived on in her daughter.

"She was very pretty, don't you think?" Ivy asked.

"Very," Phillipa said. "That is a lovely picture of her."

"She didn't want anyone to know she was sick. But I knew." She said it clearly enough, but at the end, Gemma detected the smallest hitch of pain in her voice. It was the first time Ivy had spoken so freely about her mother and the load the child had to bear alone. Gemma's heart broke for her.

"I lost my parents too, when I was your age," Rimple said. "I am sorry, Ivy."

"I am here with Papa now, and with Miss Kurt, and she is teaching me how to juggle," she said, then turned to Gemma. "Do you think you could always be my governess? You are not going to go?"

Gemma opened her mouth just as her heart jumped in her throat.

"Miss Kurt isn't going anywhere for the time being," Phillipa said warmly, intervening with that gift of hers to say something that was absolutely true, but somehow meant entirely different things depending on who was listening. "We are so thrilled you are getting along. It makes up for the fact that we are missing her at Everwell."

"Ivy," Gemma said, "I have some private matters to discuss with Mrs. Hartley and Miss Jones. Did you want to continue looking for poor Henry? After that, I've promised you another juggling lesson."

"Henry?" Phillipa asked, her brow dipping in concern.

"My pet frog," Ivy said, her lips pursing in a worried pout. "We went to feed him this morning and he hopped away."

"Frogs have a tendency to do that," Phillipa replied in that no-nonsense way of hers. "I do hope you find him."

The girl nodded, then flew up the steps in search of the elusive amphibian.

Phillipa started talking about Everwell, which always began with a list of all the texts that the children were studying, while Gemma went to the door, putting her ear to it, listening for the subtle scuff of a shoe, the heaviness of a breath, or the rustle on of her skirts against a freshly starched apron. She heard nothing. She turned to Phillipa, nodded, then returned to her seat.

"You are doing well, Gemma," Phillipa said, a knowing smile on her face. "Very well, actually."

Gemma shook her head. "I'm not sure how, given that I've nearly botched this job since the moment I've started."

"It doesn't look that way. You've done wonders with Ivy Webber," she countered. "According to gossip, she was practically unmanageable."

"She needs some attention, from her father especially," Gemma said. "She has a keen mind and a lot on it that needs to be expressed."

"And someone to express it to," Rimple said. "Clearly you're that person."

"Until I find the will," Gemma replied, thinking about this evening. "But I might be close."

"The governess job doesn't have to be," Phillipa said. "If Ivy needs you, surely we can extend your post here, at least for a while."

Gemma took a long sip of her tea. Could she spend more time under the same roof as Jeremy Webber? Every time he entered the room, her body responded to him almost against her will. And while the sensible part of her would note that it was preferable to the panic she normally felt under the gaze of strangers, the not-so-sensible parts of her wanted his touch. Besides, he wasn't exactly a stranger anymore.

But she didn't deserve that pleasure. Not after she'd robbed her best friend of the chance to feel those things.

"What about the Hatchetts?" Gemma asked, needing to change the subject. "Have you learned anything more about their arrival?"

"We still have a week, possibly less," Phillipa said. "How are you making progress?"

"It's frustratingly slow," she said. "During the day is difficult, as I have Ivy's studies to attend to. But the colonel will be out this evening, which gives me hope of success. But if not...is there any way you could stall them, Phillipa?"

"I'll see what I can do," Phillipa replied, "but we must continue with our existing plan. We had a new family arrive last night, and they are taking shelter with us until we can properly assess their situation. That is taking up some of our immediate energy at the moment."

"Maddy is seeing to them, and Lady Em and Tilda are there to help," Rimple added. "Elouise and Dominic are also able to provide some assistance."

"Do not trouble yourself, Gemma. After all it was my idea to put you here," Phillipa said.

"Tell me about Colonel Webber," Rimple asked, her eyes twinkling in that way they did when she was about to get up to mischief. "Is he as handsome as everyone says he is?"

"I don't know who 'everyone' is," Gemma said, trying to pretend that Jeremy Webber wasn't actually a specimen of a man who threatened to make her weak in the knees every time he walked past. "He is handsome, but generally isn't here during the day."

"All the better for your search, then," Phillipa said.

"Mrs. Whitehead watches me like a hawk," Gemma replied, unable to hide her distaste for the woman. "She doesn't trust me, my association with Everwell, or anyone in general."

"And Colonel Webber," Phillipa continued, being the mother hen that she was. "He has been treating you well?"

"Colonel Webber has been a gentleman the entire time," she replied, which was not entirely untrue, but wasn't exactly true, either. Of course, she hadn't exactly been a paragon of virtue. "Even when we've had disagreements, they have been quite civil."

"Quite civil?" Rimple parroted, cocking her head and giving her a mischievous grin. You've had disagreements? With the colonel?"

"Disagreements are perhaps too strong a word," Gemma

began, trying to ignore the sly glance Rimple gave Phillipa. Gemma wanted to hide under the chair even as a rush of heat rushed into her face. "We have had conversations about our differing views on the education of young women."

"They must have been very invigorating ones," Rimple replied. "Your cheeks are the same colour as Maddie's hair."

Gemma opened her mouth to reply when a knock on the door interrupted her. Seeing her chance to end Rimple's teasing, she went to the door, expecting to see Mrs. Whitehead or even Sergeant Babcock.

Instead, it was the devil himself.

"Colonel Webber," she said, somehow becoming breathless and cursing herself for it. "This is an unexpected pleasure."

"My apologies for the intrusion. My duties take me away this evening, so I came home to spend a little time with Ivy beforehand," he said, his tone formal but with a noticeable warmth. "Mrs. Whitehead informed me you were having guests, and I wanted the opportunity to introduce myself."

"Not at all," she replied, cursing herself for sounding breathless. "It is your house, after all."

"For the time being, at least," he added with a smile, and something in Gemma's stomach lurched at the reminder that all of this—whatever this was—was temporary. "I won't disturb you for very long."

Gemma was certain she blinked. "You are—disrupting your schedule?"

"It occurred to me today that if I can perform miracles with his Honour's schedule, I should be able to perform some lesser ones with my own," he replied. "Which I realize means I could be interrupting yours."

An inexplicable lightness bubbled up in Gemma's chest at the warmth in his voice and the way little creases formed at the corners of his eyes. He was smiling, and she stood in an absolute daze, realizing that he was waiting for her consent.

"You are the ranking officer," she said. "You will make her incredibly happy."

You are making me incredibly happy, too.

She turned, lest she stand there longer, lost in whatever euphoric sensation was grabbing hold of her. She needed to stay grounded.

"Colonel Webber," she began, leading him into the parlour. "May I introduce you to Mrs. Phillipa Hartley and Miss Rimple Jones? They are fellow teachers with me at the Everwell School."

He nodded to both of them, then turned to Phillipa. "Mrs. Hartley, I believe I have you to thank for sending Miss Kurt to me."

Phillipa nodded. Her manner was as straight forward as Jeremy's in her own way, and she ran both the Everwell Society and the exploits of the Scandalous Spinsters with an efficiency that would no doubt impress him if he wouldn't be equally horrified by their activities.

"Thank you, yes," she replied. "I trust she is serving you and your daughter well?"

"She is." He paused, then somehow managed to look a bit sheepish in Phillipa's presence. "I admit her background had made me a little suspect of her abilities. But she has proven her talent to me and made good strides with my daughter."

"She is in her study room at the moment, working on some sketches," Gemma said.

"Ivy is a delightful, bright girl," Rimple said. "Is she adjusting well to being here?"

The colonel's face lit up, and Gemma smiled. "Having a regular routine and Miss Kurt's steady hand has done much to ease her adjustment to life at Hastings House," he said, his gaze straying to Gemma who tried to ignore this giddy warmth winding its way through her body. Funny how grey eyes could create such heat.

"If I may," Phillipa said, "Miss Webber is always invited to visit Everwell. We have a small number of students who board with us. They would be pleased to welcome her, and she would have some girls her own age, or close enough, to have some companionship."

"Papa!"

Ivy's gleeful cry drew everyone's attention as she rushed into the room, her cheeks red, her eyes beaming, clearly excited at seeing her father. The colonel smiled and Gemma saw his joy at his daughter's presence. He held out his arms, and she walked over to him, every inch a young lady.

"Can I go to Everwell, Papa?"

"We can discuss it with Miss Kurt at a later time," he said, throwing Gemma a quick smile that threatened to flip her heart over in her chest. He turned his attention straight back to his daughter. "In the meantime, I understand you have been sketching."

Ivy nodded. "Miss Kurt has been teaching me."

"Which is to say, I have been encouraging her," Gemma said, then turned to Phillipa. "Ivy is quite naturally gifted."

"Ivy, why don't you and I go look at your sketches," he said. "Perhaps we can persuade Cook to bring us some biscuits and relax in my study, and leave Miss Kurt to her visitors."

Gemma's heart squeezed as she watched Jeremy hold out his hand, which Ivy took. He paused briefly at the door, nodded his farewell, and left the room with Ivy.

"Well," Phillipa said, "I think you are making more progress than you think."

"What do you mean?"

Phillipa set down her cup and smoothed her skirt. "Does the colonel often leave his duties behind to turn his attention to his young daughter?"

"Absolutely not." Gemma replied, not bothering to hide her surprise. This was completely unexpected. "He loves Ivy dearly, of that I have no doubt. But his first priority has always been to the Lieutenant Governor. I didn't expect to see him back in the middle of the day." Just the thought that he'd rearranged everything to make some time for Ivy brought a surge of warmth that made her smile.

"I think that's not all he's focused on," Rimple said, giving Gemma a smile that made her want to slide under her chair. Normally Gemma loved Rimple's natural good humour, but not when it came to the colonel. "He practically lit up when he saw you."

"He did no such thing," Gemma protested with far more vigour than required. "He was merely being polite."

"He was merely being captivated," Rimple said. "And why shouldn't he be?"

There were a hundred reasons why Jeremy Webber shouldn't be captivated by Gemma. First, he hopelessly outclassed her in every possible social scale that mattered. And there was the small matter that she was snooping around under his nose. He'd put a great deal of trust in her, and if he discovered the truth, that trust would be shattered into a thousand pieces.

But most importantly of all, even if by some miracle all of that could be overcome, which seemed impossible enough, there was the simple fact that she did not deserve him. Did not deserve happiness—not after what she'd done. When she'd made that mistake, she'd robbed Penny of a happy, loving future. Nothing she'd ever stolen since had been more valuable. And Gemma could never give herself what she'd taken away from someone else.

Chapter Seventeen

❦

It was nearly midnight when Gemma stood outside the door to Jeremy's bedroom, lock picking tools in her hands. She let out a long, quiet breath and reminded herself that she'd picked more locks that she could remember, and that Jeremy Webber's door was no different than any of the others. Indeed, while she'd been waiting for Mrs. Whitehead to retire for the night, Gemma had paced the floor of her room, reminding herself of this fact until she'd nearly had herself convinced.

With a few deft movements, the lock yielded to Gemma's touch and as she turned the knob, she uttered a silent prayer of thanks for the well-oiled hinges that assisted her silent entry. Shutting the door behind her, she paused to calm her racing nerves. The thrill of working with the Scandalous Spinsters had often provided Gemma with a rush of excitement like she'd once gotten from swinging on the trapeze. But tonight, the thrill had given way to unease. It was the highwire. A host of people, watching her, waiting for her to fall. Which was utterly ridiculous, because there was no tent, no audience, and most especially, no wire.

The scent of sandalwood and shaving soap filled the air, and Gemma breathed it in. She closed her eyes and an image of

Jeremy appeared, standing god-like in his shirtsleeves, running his fingers through her hair, a shiver of pleasure rippling through her. She opened her eyes, forcing aside the memory that tugged at her concentration, because she needed every drop of it. If she was successful tonight, tomorrow she could be sleeping in her own bed. Back to her own routine. Out of the spotlight. Down from the highwire.

Focus, Gemma.

She lit the Davy lamp she'd brought with her, its gentle glow lighting up the space. The modest-sized room was furnished in the typical fashion, with a large four-poster bed taking up most of the space. Most of the furniture belonged to the former owner, and each piece provided an opportunity for a hiding place.

She started by searching the hearth, drawn by the discovery of a hidden compartment in the mantlepiece in Ivy's room earlier that evening. Sitting smartly in the centre of the mantle was a simple but elegant clock, which read nearly three minutes past the hour. Above it was a beautiful painting of what Gemma assumed to be the English countryside, a woman, and a small child picking flowers. Gemma stared at the painting, understanding its subject, the paradox of wistfulness happiness and melancholy laid bare before her. She knew, somehow, without looking for the artist's signature that Jeremy had painted it, and something tugged at her heart.

She studied the image for some time, getting caught in her own memory—a memory of Penny Adamos. On instinct, her hand went to the locket around her neck, a locket that contained the smallest lock of Penny's hair. It was the only thing she had left of her friend. A symbol of pain and penitence.

The sound of a late night cab rumbling along Barrington Street roused Gemma from her memory. She turned her attention to the mantle, searching for small hidden compartments in the wood panels that surrounded the small hearth. Finding nothing, she moved on to the armoire. Inside were a collection of uniform jackets and perfectly starched white shirts. Drawn to it, she allowed her fingers to graze over the fine linen.

Unease prickled at the back of her neck, causing her to pull her hand away and quickly shut the door. She stood, looking at the dark walnut door, the warm glow reflecting in its richly polished grain, and tried to rationalize away this sense of violation. Jeremy wasn't the target in this job...he was merely in the way. It wasn't personal, she reminded herself.

But it was feeling very, very personal.

She turned away from his clothes and was confronted by large four-poster bed that commanded the room. Gemma was suddenly consumed by an image of the colonel laying there, wearing—what exactly? A nightshirt? Her father and Nico had slept in a simple nightshirt. Their living quarters had been small and modesty was required, even in a circus where the many of the costumes would be considered risqué in the extreme. But Jeremy was quite alone. Did he wear a nightshirt? Or nothing at all??

The sensation of his body—the firm planes of his chest and torso, the long, solid muscles of his arms, came roaring back from their encounter in his studio. She'd felt every hard plane of his chest through his linen shirt last evening. The tautness of it. Of all of him. She'd been pressed up right against him and even now, the memory of it sent a fresh river of heat settling between her thighs.

"Hold on there, Colonel," came the motherly but firm voice of Harold Babcock from somewhere in the darkness on the other side of the door. "Let me get your head dress."

Gemma's heart leapt into her throat. What on earth was he doing home already? Everything she knew about these fancy club get togethers amongst wealthy men is that they lasted well into the night, and involved many, many bottles of brandy.

She went to the door, but the sound of footsteps—something akin to a small pound of elephants—was rapidly approaching.

"Harry, I am perfectly sober," came Jeremy's voice with the protest from someone who was, in fact, not perfectly sober. He wasn't completely pissed, Gemma guessed, but certainly there was a tone in his voice that was something other than the carefully measured words she normally heard. And she'd never heard him refer to his soldier-valet as anything but 'Babcock'.

Their muted conversation was getting louder by the second. She opened the door, ready to slip out, when the glow of her lamp sitting on the mantle caught her attention. By the time she'd gone to extinguish it and returned to the door, the men had just landed at the top of the steps.

Uttering a silent curse, she closed the door again, enveloped in near total darkness, and with nowhere else to go, she dove under the bed.

"Here we are," she heard Sergeant Babcock say, and two sets of footsteps, one clearly steadier than the other, entered the room. "Home sweet home at last."

A gentle glow from a taper cast a thin line of light where the hem of the dust skirt skimmed the carpeted floor. Gemma had been forced to dive under a few beds in her day, some saggy and riddled with dust bunnies, chamber pots, and the occasional stray slipper, so she'd come to have an appreciation for a tightly pulled bed frame and a swept floor. While she could see very little at the moment, the mattress didn't feel claustrophobically close to her face. Mr. Dalrymple clearly enjoyed a high bed, and there was, thankfully, more than enough room under it for her as Jeremy sat down.

"What a complete waste of an evening," she heard him say, his voice a clumsy hush that wasn't particularly quiet.

"I'm sure you had a fine evening," Babcock said. "You got the Lieutenant Governor there on time, he said his piece, and everyone was happy. And the brandy couldn't have been too horrible, by the looks of things."

"I just want an evening at home. With Ivy," Jeremy said, his weight shifting above her. "That was the reason I brought her here, you know. So I could spend time with her."

"And you are," Babcock replied with a note of gentle encouragement. "Miss Webber is a sharp thing. She understands you have an important job."

The colonel didn't respond, but Gemma heard the gentle groan from the ropes above her as he bent forward, as if to unlace his boots. She held a breath. Even though the chances of him spying her under the bed were slim, they weren't nonexistent.

"Let me help you with that," Babcock said, and Jeremy seemed to listen as the movement stopped.

"I miss seeing her," Jeremy continued. "Miss Kurt, too."

Gemma stilled even further at the sound of her name on his tongue.

Miss Kurt is mine.

Honestly, if she left here tomorrow, she would hold on to the memory of him uttering that into her next life.

After more shuffling around, she saw Jeremy's bare feet alongside the sergeant's booted ones, followed by the sound of linens being turned down. Gemma realized to her horror that Jeremy was probably in nothing but his nightshirt as he slid into bed.

"Perhaps you could take Miss Webber to the zoo," Babcock said. "A special day for you both. No doubt Miss Kurt can turn it into something educational."

There was a beat of silence, and Gemma wondered if the colonel, overcome by brandy, had drifted off. But any relief Gemma felt at the anticipation of her escape evaporated at the colonel's next words.

"She has very pretty eyes, don't you think? Gemma, that is."

Gemma fought the instinct to bury her face in her hands as a swirl of conflicting emotions—surprise, shock and, dare she think it, excitement, sent a veritable torrent of butterflies lose in her belly. How could she be both flattered and terrified that he'd not only noticed her eyes, but thought they were worth remarking on?

"Gemma?" The amusement in the sergeant's voice was unmistakable, and Gemma winced. "I suppose she does."

"I'm not supposed to notice," Jeremy replied. "I'm married."

"You're widowed," his sergeant replied softly. "And I don't think Mrs. Webber would have wanted you stop living when she did. You don't need to forget her. You shouldn't forget her. But I'm pretty certain that heart of yours is big enough to make room for someone else."

A beat of silence passed between them before Jeremy answered.

"You're a good man, Harry."

Gemma closed her eyes to stifle the tears that had welled up. Harold Babcock was a good man. And so was Jeremy. A man afraid to love again, but a man so deserving of it. From a deserving woman.

Something Gemma was not. How could a woman who'd done the things she'd done be deserving?

The door closed, and Gemma laid there, waiting for Jeremy to extinguish his lamp and nod off. Instead, he shuffled above her and once the creaking of the bed stopped, the gentle turning of pages.

Was he *reading?* Didn't he know he was supposed to go to bed? Wasn't that what most people did, after having a few glasses too many? They were supposed to get tired and fall asleep.

If she could have let out a sigh of exasperation she would have. She was tired and wanted nothing but to crawl into her own bed, which wasn't her own bed, and forget that Jeremy thought she had pretty eyes. Her eyes were brown. There was nothing particularly special about them.

She lay still, waiting for the sound of a gentle snore or something to let her know he'd dropped off to sleep. The gentle glow of lamplight remained however, and soon she heard the sound of him turning another page in his book.

This was going to be a long night.

Jeremy woke with a start, his face covered with a book he'd apparently thought would make excellent reading after a night at a gentleman's club. He blinked, plucked the volume from his nose, and set it aside, pausing only to read the title imprinted on the spine. Tacitus' *Histories* did not make for riveting bedtime reading.

It was still night, though how much was left of it, he was uncertain; there was just enough oil in the lamp to bathe the space near him in a soft glow, but not enough to be able to read the clock on the other side of the room. He'd brought it with him from place to place, a singular and consistent piece to help him sleep wherever he'd called home.

The fuzziness from the brandy had cleared, an indication that it might be closer to dawn than he wanted it to be. He rarely took too much—not for any particularly virtuous reason, but it didn't agreed with him, and as he got older, the effects became harder to shake off.

In the morning he'd have another fresh set of problems to solve, and among them would not be his increasingly complicated feelings about Miss Gemma Kurt. Those feelings should be blazingly simple—nonexistent, in fact—except in matters related to his daughter. He scraped up some conviction. No more inconvenient thoughts about the way Gemma Kurt's skin looked in candlelight, or how the thought of her made him smile when he should have been working through correspondence.

By a sheer act of will, he forced his thoughts back to matters of horticultural societies and exactly who should be on the guest list for a dinner with the Earl of Newport. That would be the social affair of the season, and as soon as word reached the gossip circles, he would be inundated with requests to ensure this gentleman or that was invited. It would turn his office into a veritable zoo.

Zoo... Jeremy closed his eyes, reaching back into the haze of memory from a few hours ago. Hadn't Babcock mentioned something about a zoo? Something about a day with Ivy, which suddenly seemed like the most pressing event to be put into his social calendar. And of course Gemma Kurt would have to come and make it an educational outing, and regale them both with a story about tigers or peacocks. A picture of the three of them, laughing and enjoying each other's company emerged in Jeremy's consciousness—a forbidden and tantalizing sense of happiness and Christ, he had to go to sleep before he tortured himself further.

He reached over to turn down the lamp when he paused, his attention caught by a soft gentle hush in a steady, slow rhythm. It sounded like...breathing.

He stilled, forcing his senses to sharpen through the dullness of fatigue and the lingering effects of his imbibing. He'd been in this house for nearly three weeks and had yet to learn all of its noises, or the regular rhythm that rose from the street below. But it was still the middle of the night, and this wasn't the noise of scratching of a rodent that had somehow found its way into the house, or the clopping of horse hooves from a distant cart. It was steady, gentle breaths—deep, contented breaths of slumber.

Was that coming from *beneath* him?

His muscles tensed, his body on alert.

Gingerly he pulled back the covers and swung his feet over the edge of the bed, ignoring the chill as they touched the floor. If the creaking of the ropes from the movement had alerted the intruder to Jeremy's presence, he gave no sign. He crouched down and flipped up the bed skirt, ready to grab the intruder and pull them out from underneath the bed.

He'd expected to see a hulking brute, or even a street urchin that had wandered in looking for a bit of warmth and something to sell for food.

Who he had not expected was his daughter's governess snoring under this bed.

He watched her for a moment, which upon retrospect was probably not the most polite thing he could have done. Given she had snuck into his room and fallen asleep under his bed however, Jeremy reasoned he could be forgiven. She was utterly still, except for the gentle rhythm of her breath, her hands clasped lightly across her middle.

After some deliberation, he reached out to rouse her with a gentle shake of her shoulder. Her eyes opened and her head turned toward him, blinking adorably as she woke.

As she came to her senses, she let out the most adorable yelp that threatened to make him laugh even when he knew he should be angry with her. A second later she scrambled out from under the bed on the opposite side of him, a petite, beautiful fury.

"What are you doing here?" she asked in a frantic whisper.

Jeremy was certain he blinked at the audacity of her question. "Given you are in my room, I might ask the same."

Her eyes widened as her mouth fell open, as if she was absolutely gobsmacked. Then, apparently unable to speak, Gemma clapped her hands over her eyes and turned away.

"What?" he asked, his patience wearing thin.

"You…you have no clothes on," she whispered. Jeremy couldn't decide if her tone was stifled laughter or indignation.

Oh Christ. He really had lived on his own for far too long. He pulled his robe from a hook on the back of the door and pulled it around himself.

"You can turn around now," he said. "I'm covered."

He could tell from the way she spoke she had buried her face in her hands, as if looking in the completely opposite direction was not enough to protect her from the sight of him.

"If you're going to snoop around a grown man's room, you should expect such a thing," he grumbled, if only to cover his own embarrassment.

He saw her body hitch as she sighed, then turned on her heel to face him. Her hair was down, tied back in a loose braid that trailed over one of her shoulders, leading his eyes down along her body, which was clad in a simple white nightdress and a dressing gown. There was a vee of exposed skin where the rich, deep-patterned silk of her robe crossed across her chest, highlighting the form of her body. Her skin glowed in the lamp light, and his fingers suddenly itched to touch it.

"I—" she began, then faltered, as if distracted. Was Jeremy

deceiving himself, or was she looking at him? She stood, nearly motionless, a curious tension and awareness crackling in the room as surely as the dying embers in the hearth. At last she spoke. "You weren't supposed to be home until much later."

Jeremy took a few steps toward her. "I don't exactly see how that answers my question." He paused, as her response settling on him. "Did you plan to invade my room?"

"Of course not. You've flustered me with your—" She gestured toward his middle, then crossed her arms in front of her, looking up from under her long thick lashes. "That's not what I meant."

Jeremy smiled in triumph at her discomfort. She'd done this to herself, the minx.

"What did you mean?" He challenged, trying to shore up his rapidly eroding resolve to be upset. "And don't give me that doe-eyed look."

"You said you liked my eyes." Before he had a chance to register that, she put her hands over her mouth, those eyes getting even wider. "I need to go. You are flustering me."

She'd heard that? What else had he confessed to Babcock that she'd been privy to?

"How long have you been under there?" he snapped.

She made her way around the bed, trying to avoid him as she made for the door, but he caught her by the arm. Instead of pulling away, she stilled, her gaze lingering over his form. His body responded as surely as if it had been her fingers running over his flesh.

"Since before you came home," she answered at last. "I didn't intend to still be here."

"What did you intend? To sneak into my bedchamber, root through it, and then leave before I noticed you?" he said, indignation pushing aside his arousal. He trusted his daughter with this woman. "Is this your normal routine when you go on your charity work to teach school children?"

"I-I was looking for something," she said. "It's not what you think."

"You do not want to know what I am thinking," he replied, his voice low as he attempted to keep his lust in check. "I'm tempted to believe you're trying to distract me with your beauty so you can make your escape."

She gifted his question—and somehow flustered him—with a small burst of laughter.

"It's not my job to be the beauty," she said with far too much conviction for Jeremy's liking. "But I am definitely trying to escape."

He let go of her arm, reaching out and toying with the edge of her braid, tracing the twists and turns of it until he came to her ear. Despite her declaration, she made no move to escape. Encouraged, he leaned in and nuzzled her ear with his lips and tongue, stroking the tender flesh of her ear lobe, then trailed down her neck.

"I'm not going to let you go until you tell me," he whispered between kisses.

She let go the smallest of sighs and a hushed phrase in Italian that he didn't understand but made his knees go weak. Encouraged by her response, his mouth found hers. She'd parted her lips for him, accepting him, and while he ravished her mouth, her hands greedily explored his body. The sensation of her hands around his waist, as her fingers tracing the curve of his back drove him wild. He was as hard as a rock, and it would take so little to undo the tie on his robe, lift her on top of him and feel what he knew had to be the most perfect, lush sex. And somewhere in the haze of this carnal need came this other sensation, this sense that being with Gemma Kurt was *right*.

Jeremy had just forced that notion aside, content for the moment to savour the delectable softness of Gemma's body, when the gentle but insistent chime of a nearby clock pulled at his attention. A chime that probably meant something, though for the life of him he couldn't recall what. But somewhere in the deep recesses of his brain that still had a fibre of rational thought left, he knew he should be paying attention. But to what?

A sharp knock at the door reminded him.

Christ.

They both froze, breaking the kiss, their breath ragged.

"Ready for me, sir?" came a low and damnably chipper Harold Babcock from the other side of the door.

She stepped away from him as if he was on fire—which was not an inaccurate description—her eyes wide with panic, her mouth delightfully full from their kiss.

"Give me a minute, Babcock," he said, trying not to sound too awake. He looked at Gemma who dove back under the bed as he climbed back into it.

The door opened and his trusty sergeant poked his head in with his traditional pot of coffee. "Feeling a little under the weather, sir?"

"I'm not as young as I used to be," Jeremy said, dragging his fingers through his hair. "You wouldn't be so good as to fetch me one of your special tonics, would you?"

"Of course," Babcock answered dutifully, without asking another question. The two men been through battles and skirmishes together. Twice Harold had saved Jeremy's life, and the two shared secrets that each of them would protect to the grave. If Harold suspected anything, Jeremy knew his sergeant would never breath a word of it. Still, he wanted to protect Gemma from even the smallest hint of impropriety. Even if Jeremy still had his own questions.

After waiting a moment, Gemma popped back out from under the bed, and without looking back, silently slid out the door. Jeremy watched her go, then rested his head back against his pillow, his body still alive with the sensation of her. Touching her like that broke every one of his rules. And how she was making him feel broke a few more he didn't even realize he had. It was almost enough to distract him from the fact that she'd been in his room.

Almost.

Chapter Eighteen

GEMMA FLOPPED down on her bed just as she heard Sergeant Babcock coming back up the stairs. Her body ached in a thousand pleasurable and forbidden ways, while her insides roiled with an unsettling mix of giddiness and guilt. She'd been on flying on the trapeze, distracted by the thrill, and she'd stumbled. Badly.

She was his daughter's governess, for heaven's sake. The Everwell Society for the Benefit of Sorrowful Spinsters and Woeful Widows had always struggled, particularly amongst parts of Halifax society, to be considered "worthy" of their financial consideration. It was the Everwell name and Lady Em's aristocratic pedigree that had given the society the credibility it had, no matter how small. If word got out that Gemma had allowed herself to be in the company of a respectable man, the damage would be considerable. More importantly, the young girls they educated and trained would be viewed as tainted or worse, targets to be hired by unscrupulous employers.

Aside from that misstep, there was a deeper, older hurt that had weighed her down. Her fingers found their way to her neck, and she idly played with her locket. The locket that reminded her that she'd had a friend. A friend she loved. A friend she lost. How could she take such pleasure for herself when she'd robbed Penny so cruelly of her own?

Gemma blinked back the tears that pricked at the back of her eyes, and pushed herself off the bed, determined to put aside any ridiculous feelings she had and get on with this job. Last night was a stark reminder that the sooner she found what she'd come for, the better it would be for everyone. She went to the window and pulled up the sash, allowing the morning air to drive the lingering heat from her body, then she quickly washed and dressed before going to see Ivy.

She opened the door to see Jeremy coming out of his bed chamber, all spit and polished. For the first time, however, she was beginning to see the man normally restrained by brass buttons and a military bearing. It was there in the flash of his piercing grey eyes.

"Good morning," he said, as crisply as if he hadn't made her burn with passion just moments before. It was detached, businesslike, just as it had been every day before.

"Good morning, Colonel Webber," she said. "Did you sleep well?"

"I might have slept better, but there was a mouse under the bed," he said, an eyebrow lifting.

"A mouse?" she said. "I would have thought you weren't afraid of mice."

"Perhaps it was a little larger than a mouse," he said, cocking his head. "Why were you there, Miss Kurt?"

Gemma pulled back her lips into a tight smile. Somehow, she'd managed to duck out of the room before they'd got to that part. And somehow, she hadn't managed to think of an excuse. She still didn't have one.

Her mind raced, groping for some half-truth or passable lie that might satisfy his question, when her attention was drawn by a curious sound, almost like a low, short quack coming from her...feet? Gemma looked down to find Henry bleating at her feet.

"There you are," she said, bending over to scoop him up,

when inspiration struck. She held up the creature. "I was looking for him."

Jeremy blinked. "A frog?"

Gemma nodded, so pleased with her plan. "We found a frog, two days ago, when we were out on our nature study. Ivy insisted on bringing it home. I relented, and I absolutely should not have. I promised her I would keep it in the nursery until she'd asked permission. But the thing escaped."

"And so your logical conclusion to this caper of a missing frog was to come into my bed chamber?"

"Ivy was worried," Gemma insisted. "We'd searched all the other rooms on this floor, and yours was the last." Well, that was almost the truth. "Mrs. Whitehead didn't know, and we didn't wish to involve her," she continued. "We were trying to keep it our little secret."

He blinked and something about him cooled, but he seemed to have accepted her explanation at least. It should have been a relief.

"I should tell her I found him," she said, her smile faltering at his changing demeanor. "We'll take him back to the park today. The poor thing doesn't belong here."

Eager for escape, she darted toward Ivy's room. The girl was already up, dressed, and waiting for Gemma to braid her hair. Gemma found she was coming to adore their little morning ritual.

"Good morning," Ivy said brightly as she sat at the edge of her bed. "You found Henry!"

A knock at the door interrupted their conversation, and Gemma was surprised to see Jeremy standing there. He typically dined with Ivy at breakfast.

"Good morning, ladies," he said, a strained smile on his face. "How are we this morning?"

"Good morning, Papa," she said, beaming.

"I heard that we might have a visitor in the house," he said, his gaze brushing over Gemma to the amphibian.

"It was my pet frog," Ivy said. "His name is Henry."

"Why didn't you tell me about Henry, Ivy? You know how I feel about secrets," he said. There was an unmistakable edge to his voice that shocked Gemma.

"I'm sorry," Ivy said, her voice edged with sadness that broke Gemma's heart. "I would have told you. But you were gone."

He remained still, even cold. "We will discuss it at breakfast."

He closed the door, leaving the Gemma and Ivy alone. Gemma prickled with unsettled energy. Ivy was absolutely still, the air around her almost brittle.

"He's angry," she said, and Gemma's heart broke at the hitch in her voice.

"This is my fault," Gemma folded the girl into her arms, giving her a hug.

"He doesn't like secrets," Ivy said, burying her face in Gemma's chest. "Mama and I had a secret. But she asked me not to tell anyone," Ivy said. "I think Papa is still mad at me."

We were trying to keep it our little secret.

Gemma winced. She'd inadvertently found a wound and thrown salt in it. *Oh Gemma, you idiot.*

"Oh no, Ivy," she said. "I can't imagine it. Your father loves you very much. And you were little, even littler then you are now."

She smiled, but Gemma could see the pain and doubt in her eyes. Gemma folded her into her arms and gave the girl a hug.

"Go have breakfast with your papa while I return Henry to his jar. I will speak with him after," she said, straightening a pretty red ribbon in Ivy's hair. "Maybe he was just tired. Adults can be pretty grumpy when they haven't had enough sleep. Just like babies."

Ivy gave her a cheerless smile, then went to the dining room. After returning Henry to the nursery and washing her hands, Gemma went back to collect her pupil. She watched quietly just outside the door as father and daughter ate in a strained silence, before Ivy was excused. Her eyes were bright, as if she was keeping tears at bay. Gemma gave her a kiss and sent her to the schoolroom with the promise of a third juggling ball and a walk to the park where they would return Henry to his natural habitat. Then, allowing anger and indignation to fuel her steps, she smoothed her skirts and marched into the dining room and closed the door behind her.

"What on earth was that about?" Gemma said.

He put down his paper. "Excuse me?"

"You are punishing that child for not communicating with you by sitting in stony silence with her when you have the opportunity to talk to her."

He looked up at her, his expression maddeningly neutral. "I do not have to explain myself to you, Miss Kurt."

"You demand explanations from everyone else," she said. "And you have been given one that was more than adequate."

"She could have told me she wanted a frog," he said.

"When exactly?" Gemma challenged. "Should I have sent a message to you at Government House? Or would you rather that I walked her down to the Halifax Merchant's Club and waited for your answer there?"

"I was thinking in general, not specific terms," he said.

"Well you seem to be very specifically angry about this specific thing. And I hardly think she wanted it as a pet—she just wanted to look at it for a while," she said. "It was a spur of the moment bit of fun. I am sorry that wasn't written into your schedule."

His eyes fluttered for the briefest of moments before recovered. He folded up the paper.

"I have to go."

Gemma put her arm on the back of his chair, as if she could somehow keep a man his size from moving exactly how he pleased.

"You are not leaving until you tell her you love her," she said. "Right now she thinks the man she loves more than anyone else despises her because she'd hadn't told him about a frog."

"Secrets are not always harmless."

Gemma shook her head in frustration. "Of course not. But do

you not trust her to know the difference? She's not eight years old anymore."

"She told you?"

For the first time, the veneer of indifference cracked. She'd caught the quiver in his voice. Saw the hurt creasing the corner of his eyes.

"She told me about her mother's illness," she said, softening her tone as she moved her hand from the chair to his shoulder. "And she believes you are still angry with her."

He turned away from her, his motion swift. And though she couldn't see his face, she could somehow feel his anger.

Gemma stepped forward, awareness settling on her shoulders. "You *are* angry with her."

He turned his face away, but she saw his cheeks flush and the muscles around his jaw tighten as if he was using every bit of his energy to stay in control and failing. He was angry. But not at Ivy.

"You're angry at yourself."

"And Isla."

Jeremy looked straight ahead, somehow trapped in a moment he'd thought he conquered. But as the lump formed in this throat, all the hurt came roaring back.

"How could the woman I loved more than my own life decide she couldn't tell me a secret like that? How could she not trust me?"

She reached out and took one of his hands, offering a small but wonderful comfort.

"Perhaps she didn't wish to hold you back from whatever choices she thought you'd make," she said, compassion in her smile. "Chances she didn't want you to miss out on."

"Perhaps," he said. "But I felt like an idiot. Here I was, blissfully ignorant, going on with my life, setting up our apartments in Cairo. She'd always wanted to see Egypt. She was adventurous— more so than me. That's where Ivy gets it from you know—her penchant for adventure, climbing trees, all of that. It's not me. I just get to, because I'm a man. But Isla was so excited. She asked me to write every week, asked me to paint little postcards with tiny vignettes. She wanted to see it, and I have no gift for descriptive prose. I sent her a new one a couple of times a week."

"That is an astounding act of love," Gemma said, her face breaking into a smile. Her eyes were bright, and Jeremy realized those unshed tears were for him. "Perhaps she needed you to go on that adventure for her—one last adventure. And you wouldn't have done that if you had known the truth."

Jeremy blinked, pushing back the telltale pricking of tears, concentrated on the sensation of Gemma's fingers grazing over skin.

"Sometimes you have a secret—a fear—and it's so terrifying to you that you need to pretend it's not there. It's not real," she said, giving him a sad smile. "And you don't know why you don't share it, even with the people you love the most. Maybe because they are counting on you, and you don't want to disappoint them. Maybe it's because you're too afraid to admit it to yourself."

"I wasn't there when Isla died," he said. "My brother contacted me two days before she passed, urging me to return. It was only then I learned the truth. We wrote constantly, but in all that time, she never gave any indication she was actually ill."

He could still recall the disbelief when he received his brother's telegram. He'd gone numb.

"When I got home, she'd already been gone for a week," he said. "Alexander discovered Ivy had always known about Isla's sickness. Known before I even went to Egypt. I would never have gone if I'd known the truth. But Isla had forbidden her."

"Oh, Jeremy," she said, pulling him close to her chest, taking the weight of his sorrow. He let himself rest there a moment, breathing in her scent, her compassion, her strength until he'd recovered some of his own.

"It wasn't Ivy's fault," he continued. "But part of me was so envious. Why had Isla shared this with her child, and not her husband? I could have cared for her—I should have been there for her. And not just at the end. It makes me wonder...did she not love me enough to think me worthy of this precious truth?"

"Jeremy, I am certain she loved you."

Jeremy looked down at Gemma, taken by the conviction in her statement. Confusion reigned. Gemma didn't know Isla. Until a week ago, she hadn't known Jeremy.

"How can you say that?" he challenged.

She tilted her head, looking down at him with a warm smile that cut through the haze of hurt and memory. She stood straight, stepped back, and held out her hand.

"Come with me."

She led him to his study, then walked to one of the several book cases in the room, running her fingers along the edge of the shelf. He would have been mesmerized by the graceful dance of her fingers if he hadn't been utterly consumed by the comfort he'd found in simply being with her. He was still holding her hand.

"Here," she said, then looked at him with playful eyes. "I will need my other hand back for just a moment."

He let go, already sensing the loss of her touch, and somehow consumed by a sense of happiness that he couldn't explain.

She plucked the volume off the shelf and Jeremy recognized it instantly—it had been one in their home, back in England.

"I sent this to Isla," he said as she handed him the volume titled *A Hand-book for Travellers in Egypt*. "I thought she might enjoy it."

She cocked her head to one side. "You haven't looked in this, have you?"

The question startled him. "No. I've just been carrying it around from house to house. I'm not sure why. I was going to leave it behind, but I couldn't quite do it."

"Well, you need to trust your heart more often," she said. "Look inside."

She pressed the book in his hands, and Jeremy accepted it, his heart pounding in his chest. The warm gravitas in her voice, the gentle urging, caught him off guard.

He looked at the cover, which had gentle wear along its edges. He hadn't seen it since the day he sent it to Isla. He opened the cover, his gaze moving over the simple inscription he'd put in the cover.

"To Isla, to prepare you for our next adventure—Jeremy"

Below it, however, was something else—different words, words he didn't write. He recognized Isla's elegant script.

"Jeremy, thank you for taking me to Egypt—Love, Isla"

Inside were tiny inscriptions in the margins done in pencil, with little numbers—dates, he realized, and sometimes tiny two line descriptors.

He flipped through the pages, which became more and more difficult with each passing moment, his eyes blurring from the tears he was fighting.

"She loved you Jeremy, and perhaps she was a little selfish because she knew that the only way you would give her this gift was for you to go and give it freely," Gemma said. "But it wasn't because she didn't love you."

Jeremy looked over at her with a new-found wonder. "How did you find this?"

"Ivy and I were talking about your trip to Egypt because we were going to pick another country to study, and I let her pick," she answered, motioning toward the book. "Egypt was it. She said you never talk about it."

He never talked about it. For years he'd wanted nothing more than to excise it from his memory. It was the time he'd been off blithely working while his wife was dying.

"We were looking at your book shelves and the title immediately caught my eye," she continued. "I pulled it off the shelf and was amazed by what I saw. And I was certain, by the stiffness of the binding, that it hadn't been opened in a long time."

"I'd wanted to throw this out," he confessed. "Leave it behind. Burn it. But something told me to hold on to it."

"Well, I'm glad for once that you actually listened to some sensible advice."

He laughed, the outburst surprising them both. It came straight from his middle. Where had it come from, this lightness? It felt so strange, after so long, even as his laughter channeled tears, as if his body was excising a wound from deep inside him. He was a storm of emotion, all of it raw, and for once, he allowed himself feel it. And Gemma was there with him, reaching out, holding his hands, laughing and crying with him.

"You should talk to Ivy," she said, gently wiping the tears from his cheeks. "She's older now, but the two of you are still clearly bearing the wounds of that time."

"I wouldn't know what to say," he said. "And I'm not good with conversation. Not like you."

"You brought her all the way to Canada," she said. "Why did you do that?"

"To be with her," he said. "We've spent too much time apart."

"Then be with her," Gemma said. "Just start by being with her."

Chapter Nineteen

GEMMA FOLLOWED Jeremy upstairs to the nursery. He'd taken the steps two at a time. She would have had to run to catch up with him, but she decided against it, leaving the two with some much-needed time to decompress together. By the time she'd reached the nursery door, which was wide open, she saw Jeremy standing with Ivy, her arms around Jeremy's waist. Jeremy held her tightly, joy flowing from them both.

There was something else too—an aching sensation coming from deep inside her. Was it longing? Envy? It had been four years since she'd run away. Four years since she'd embraced either of her parents. Laughed with Nico.

She stood quietly, but they must have sensed her presence. Jeremy's gaze met Gemma's with an expression of such joy and contentment and gratitude that Gemma had to force herself not to look away.

He released Ivy, then bent down to her level.

"I have to go to work now, but when I come home, we will have a lovely dinner together. We haven't had that in a long time," he said. "And that's my fault."

"You're a very important man, Papa," Ivy said, repeating a

phrase Gemma knew the child used as a shield against her own heart.

"And yet somehow I've forgotten that you are the most important person to me," he said. "I needed Miss Kurt to remind me."

He stood, then pressed his timepiece into Ivy's hands.

"I will be home promptly at six," he said, kissing her on the head then walking to the door. "Ensure I keep to my schedule."

"I'll have her ready," Gemma said.

"You can join us as well," he said.

Gemma blinked. "But I don't have anything appropriate for dinner."

"It's a family dinner," he said. "You're perfect the way you are."

He disappeared, and Gemma felt the blood flush into her cheeks. Perfect. For years, all she could think about was her mistake. Her error. And while she knew no one was perfect, for just a moment Jeremy made her fell that way.

After a non-eventful day, Jeremy arrived home at a quarter to the hour. He'd been determined to keep his promise to Ivy and to himself. Ivy had been in the parlour with Gemma, both of them working on needlework when he'd surprised them. The look of disbelief in Ivy's wide-eyed expression had both charmed and saddened him. After all, he'd made many such promises to her, and this was the first time he'd truly honoured her trust. He resolved it would not be the last.

After leaving the ladies to get ready for dinner, he'd gone up to his painting studio, hunting for a very particular cherrywood box he'd buried, along with so many memories, in one of the trunks he'd brought from England. His hands shook a little as he opened the lid; the last time he'd shut it was when he'd shoved it in this chest after Isla's death.

Inside was a stack of small drawings and watercolours he'd

sent home to her when he was in Egypt. Some were landscapes that had captured scenes that were becoming famous now in Europe and North America—the famous pyramids, and the mighty Sphinx at Giza. Others were more humble—the bright colours of the spice bazaar, with bags of nutmeg and cardamon pods, or the profile of a young boy he'd seen in the door way of a shop where he'd stopped to take a cool drink.

Every week, and sometimes twice, he'd sent home a little scene. Something to get Isla ready for a future, it turned out, she was never going to see.

When he'd discovered them a week after the funeral, he'd been tempted to cast them into the fire. His brother had stopped him. And while he and Alexander had a sometimes fractious relationship over the years, Jeremy had been grateful for his intervention.

He flipped over one of the drawings. In light pencil was a note or two, in Isla's hand, with annotations. Some included numbers, which he realized referred to pages from the book that Gemma Kurt had found on his bookcase.

Hastily he took the small chest with him to his bedchamber, where he shrugged off his red coat and changed into a less formal waistcoat and jacket for dinner. A family dinner. Something he hadn't had in a long time.

As he exited his room, cherrywood box under one arm, he was greeted by Ivy, whose smile reminded him so much of Isla it sometimes pained him, though today it was less. She'd changed for dinner, he realized, no doubt with Miss Kurt's help.

"Ivy," he said. "You look lovely."

"Thank you, Papa," she replied. "As do you."

"Where is Miss Kurt?"

"She said she would be down in a moment."

He took Ivy's hand, and the two went to the dining room, which had been beautifully lit. He pulled out a seat for Ivy before seating himself.

The dinner was a simple weekday meal, but sitting at his own table felt like a novelty. It shouldn't have been. Ivy sat to his left, looking just a little more grown up than he probably wanted her to. She was losing her little girl looks, he realized, and the last thing he wanted to do was miss what she had left.

While waiting for Gemma, he put the box on the table in front of Ivy.

"I wanted to show you these," he said, gesturing for her to open the box.

She looked inside, pulling out a few cards, carefully studying one before moving onto the next. Her eyes lit up with a sense of excitement that made Jeremy's heart jump and instantly brought a smile to his face. "You sent these to Mama."

"I did," he said, swallowing the melancholy.

"I remember," she said. "Mama used to take her book, and we would find a page that described part of what we thought was on the card."

Jeremy's heart should have twisted bitterly at that memory. A moment Ivy had shared with Isla. Another moment he wasn't there, blithely unaware of what was happening back home. But how many moments since had he lost to grief? To misplaced anger? And in his own way, he was coming to realize he'd been there all along, through those drawings.

"Papa, did you draw these?" Ivy asked, as she carefully examined each piece.

"I did," he said, and she looked at him with such admiration and wonder he nearly blushed.

"You should have an exhibit," she said in a terribly grown-up sounding voice. She turned to the entry. "Don't you think so, Miss Kurt? Papa should exhibit his paintings."

A hint of orange blossoms hit his nose, and anticipation crackled in the air. He followed Ivy's gaze to the door, where Gemma Kurt appeared like a vision.

He opened his mouth to speak, but his voice temporarily abandoned him as he drank her in.

Her hair was simply dressed but she adorned it with a pretty clip that sparkled as the light caught it. Her dress was simple, a deep blue that complemented her warm colouring. The neckline was square, and while it was hardly risqué, it teased at the promise of what he was certain were a pair of two perfectly formed breasts beneath. The sleeves were three quarter length, showing her wrists, which he decided then and there were in need of kissing, just to verify that the skin was as soft as he imagined, and then, by means of comparison, he would have to taste the skin at the spot where the gentle curve of her neck met her shoulders, just to make sure.

She looked over at him, her blush apparent, as she took a tentative step into the room.

"I think I need to see them for myself," she said, throwing him a cheeky look.

Jeremy rose to his feet, and gestured for her to enter, pulling out the chair opposite Ivy and seating her. Small tendrils of raven hair fell along her neck, tempting him to touch it.

Ivy reached across the table with a small handful of drawings, thrusting them at Gemma, and now it was Jeremy's turn to be shy. He'd rarely shown his work to anyone. He watched as she carefully studied one, then moved to the next.

"You did all of these?" she asked as Jeremy poured himself and Gemma a glass of wine. "Why, there must be dozens!"

She looked at him with wonder, which did peculiar things to his insides, like make him feel special. People over the years had told him he was talented, organized—even punctual. But no one managed to make him feel like more than what they'd expected to see. The colonel. The officer. Never the man.

"I did," he said. "Two every week."

"They are remarkable. Drawing and watercolour?" she asked. "Your sense of line and proportion are excellent. Phillipa and Lady Em would be very impressed with you."

"Excuse me?" he asked.

"Miss Emmaline Everwell," she said. "She is one of the co-founders of the Everwell Society for the Benefit of Sorrowful Spinsters and Woeful Widows."

Ivy giggled. "That is a very long name for a society," she said. "Are you a sorrowful spinster?"

"A spinster?" She paused. "Yes. Sorrowful? No more or less than your average person, I suspect. But I do know that Miss Everwell does has a certain affinity for alliterations."

"I thought you called her Lady Em," Jeremy said.

"Her father was made a Baronet, owing to some act of bravery," she said. "General Everwell became Lord Everwell, and though she doesn't actually carry a title, people insisted upon calling Miss Everwell 'Lady Emmaline," and I think she just got tired of correcting them."

Everwell. For some reason, the name twigged in Jeremy's memory.

"Lord Everwell," he said. "That names rings a bell."

"I'm afraid that's all I know of him," she said. "Lady Em doesn't talk about him much, and when she does it is not in the most complimentary way." She paused. "But Lady Em has a very good eye for art. And to be able to capture the nature of the place so faithfully, with both charcoal and colour is remarkable. Ivy is right—you should exhibit them."

Jeremy turned that over in his head. Was that even possible? A salon perhaps, to break up the monotony of those long dark winter evenings.

Ivy's high-spirited laugh broke interrupted him thoughts. Her laugh was warm, light and made him smile. He wondered why he hadn't done this sooner. And why he couldn't do this every evening.

"Papa, I love this little monkey you've drawn," Ivy said, holding up one of his pencil drawings of a street performer with his pet capuchin monkey. "I wish I could have seen it."

"Me too," he said. "Perhaps we could visit the zoo when we go to visit your uncle in London."

"We do have a zoo in town," Gemma said. "Down's Zoological Gardens. It's quite lovely. I can't recall if there are monkeys or not, but it would make for a pleasant visit, and you two could make an artist's event out of it."

The words were barely out of Gemma's mouth when Ivy's eyes widened, and she broke out her widest smile.

"Oh, could we visit, Papa? On Saturday," Ivy exclaimed, practically bouncing out of her chair. "Miss Kurt could come with us, and she could visit the animals and remember when she was at the circus."

Jeremy looked to Gemma, who's smile momentarily dimmed.

"I think that would be a lovely idea," he said, reaching out and playfully tapping Ivy on her nose. "Though I wonder if Miss Kurt hasn't had her full of monkeys right here. Perhaps she would like a respite from us."

He turned to her, struck by just how much that last statement bothered him. That she might prefer to be away from him. It was ridiculous, of course. He had the benefit of interacting with new faces in different places daily. He should have every expectation that she might prefer a day to herself. Along with Ivy, Gemma Kurt was rapidly become his respite from the world. She was becoming...necessary. He found himself holding his breath, trying not to look as if he cared if Gemma Kurt chose a day without him. Even though he couldn't imagine his heart wanting anything more. Wanting came with a cost—a cost he'd paid once that left him bankrupt for so long. But at this moment, it seemed worth the risk to try again.

In a heartbeat, shadow faded from Gemma's face, replaced with a smile.

"Of course, I would love to come," she said. "Thank you for inviting me."

Ivy's response to this news was instant and joyous, and distracting enough to allow Jeremy to let out a breath of relief. With the decision made, Ivy sat down in her seat, speaking with great animation about monkeys and frogs.

Jeremy had no doubt made several dozen decisions today, and none he realized were as satisfying or as meaningful as the one to take Ivy to the zoo. Was there anything more important to be accomplished than making Ivy laugh, and Gemma Kurt smile?

He couldn't think of a single one.

Chapter Twenty

SATURDAY MORNING BROUGHT a cloudless blue sky and the promise of a lovely day at Down's Zoological Pleasure Gardens. Ivy could barely keep still as Gemma brushed then braided her hair into a single plait down the back of her head, a task made harder by the swinging motion of her legs in the chair. Not since Gemma had arrived had she seen Ivy so full of energy. For her part, Gemma had spent a restless night. Her decision to accompany Jeremy and Ivy had been ill considered. With Mrs. Whitehead off for the day, she would have the entire house to herself, including the kitchens and Mrs. Whitehead's room. She was quickly coming to the conclusion that the housekeeper, who was in the employ of the Hatchett family, had already secured the will if it existed. This would be a rare opportunity to discover the truth. Certainly, Jeremy and Ivy could use the time together, without her, couldn't they?

"Ivy, I need you to keep still for a just a moment longer," Gemma said. "You are as jumpy as a monkey yourself!"

"I cannot wait to see the monkeys!" Ivy replied, her face breaking out into an animated smile in the mirror. "And tigers, too. Do you think they have tigers?"

"I believe they do," Gemma replied as she bound the girl's thick braid with a blue ribbon.

"I went to a circus once," Ivy said. "In England, when I was little. There were monkeys there, too. And people who flew through the sky, like birds. Why did you leave?"

Gemma smiled even as a ball of emotion formed in her chest. She'd once flown through the sky like a bird. And she loved the thrill of it. The sensation that the only thing keeping her in the air was her own body, her skill, her sense of timing. She would work harder and harder, doing riskier tricks because for her, it was easy. Like breathing. And that rush—that thrill—had become as necessary to her as breathing as well. She didn't love the crowd. But she could always block them out...except perhaps when she was on the highwire. She'd always had Penny with her on the highwire, giving her confidence to get through the trick. Always encouraging, never pushing.

Gemma had pushed.

"I—" She swallowed, her voice trembling. How could she tell a ten-year-old that she'd hurt her best friend so badly she would never recover? That her brother would never forgive her? That she would never forgive herself?

"Good morning!"

Jeremy's warm greeting commanded Gemma's attention. She looked to where he stood in the doorway. Gone was his brushed red coat, and in its place was a fine, dark brown woolen suit with a matching waistcoat and cravat. She'd heard people say that a uniform improved the look of any man, but Jeremy was the exception. Then again, he was exceptional in so many ways.

His face lit up with a smile, his gaze fixed on Gemma, her joy marred by guilt. Here she was, rummaging through his house. He might have encouraged her to forgive herself, but if he found out why she was truly here, she wondered if he would be so charitable. She was keeping a horrible secret from him.

"Good morning, Papa!" Ivy said, turning her head, as Gemma fiddled with the ribbon on her braid.

"The carriage is ready," he said. "Are you ladies?"

"I am," Ivy said, bounding out of her chair.

"And you Miss Kurt?"

It was so tempting to tell him she had a headache, or that she simply wished to spend the day alone. Neither were true.

"If you would rather have the day to yourself, Miss Kurt..." he said. Did he sense her wavering? "Ivy and I can leave you. But it's not every day I get to go out with a pair of beautiful ladies and treat them to ices."

Was it her imagination, or did he look disappointed at the idea she might stay behind?

"Ices!" Ivy spun around, taking both of Gemma's hands in hers, a pleading expression on her face. "Oh, please Miss Kurt, do come with us. It wouldn't be nearly as special without you there."

"Ivy," Jeremy said, his voice soothing, as if he sensed Gemma's unease. "Miss Kurt might like a day to rest. She can come with us another day."

Except there would be no other days, would there? She'd find the will, or she'd fail again, but either way, this little caper could conclude. And even though that should have been a relief, the idea of leaving Jeremy and Ivy squeezed in her chest. She'd already left one family behind in disgrace. Gemma had stolen so many things over the years. Important papers, fancy vases, keys and corporate seals. Could she not steal a few hours for herself?

She was guilty of so many things. But as she looked into Ivy's pleading eyes, she knew she'd be guilty of so much more if she'd deprived herself of this one simple pleasure...a day with a family who wanted her.

"Actually," she found herself saying, "I would like to come. Thank you."

His face brightened at her answer, warming her like wine on a cold, winter evening. A small rush rippled through her, light and dizzy and perfectly happy—a feeling she hadn't had since she'd flown on the trapeze.

Soon they'd piled into the hired cab and headed off to Dutch

Village just off the peninsula of the city, which was full of small cottages and a few farms, and amongst it, Down's Zoological Pleasure Gardens. The Gardens were a prized local attraction featuring a menagerie of mammals, birds, and plants from around the world. On a brisk but fine Saturday like this one, the park was humming with people.

They strolled the winding gravelled paths from paddock to paddock, where a large array of animals were on display. Ivy skipped along a few feet ahead, stopping at one set of enclosures or another, while Gemma walked along with Jeremy in companionable silence for a time. Gemma drank in the pleasant fall breeze that brought with it the scent of Jeremy's cologne.

"They have two tigers!" Ivy said, clearly excited, running ahead to a large paddock where two big cats were lounging in the grass. "Look Papa!"

"They are happier when they are a pair," Gemma said.

"Sensible animals," Jeremy said, and somehow that offhanded comment gave Gemma a little thrill.

"Were you a lion tamer, Miss Kurt?" Ivy asked.

"No," she said. "Though my brother sometimes worked with the big cats."

"I didn't know you had a brother," Jeremy said, tilting his head thoughtfully. "But then I suppose I know nothing about you."

"There's nothing to tell really," she said, pasting a smile over her nerves. There was actually so much to tell. "I'm a governess now—a teacher at Everwell. And before that I worked in the circus."

Jeremy looked at her with incredulity. "Come Miss Kurt," he said. "Not every little girl grows up with tigers and elephants and acrobats."

"Miss Kurt was an acrobat," Ivy said. "She taught me a handstand."

"I do recall that," he said, one eyebrow curving up to a perfect arch, which was no surprise, given that the rest of him was perfect. "Let me guess—you were a member of The Flying Kurts?"

She rolled her eyes. "Fabrizi, actually. That was my mother's name before she married my father. They decided it sounded better—more fantastical. The circus is about pageantry."

"That would have been an interesting childhood," Jeremy said. "Certainly a much more colourful one than mine. I was sent off to Eton, then Sandhurst. I think my parents had my life planned out from the moment I was born."

"My life was actually remarkably routine," she said. "We would set up, put on a show, tear down, and move on. I didn't know exactly where, but it didn't matter really. The inside of the tent was the same, and the crowds were remarkably similar, no matter where we went. It just seems unusual."

"Having a tiger to play with when you were eleven would be unusual to most people," he said, his lips tipping up into a devilish smile before turning contrite and lowering his voice. "I apologize. If you don't wish to discuss your time in the circus, I completely understand. I suppose I spent far too much of my time with men who are far too eager to talk about themselves and their accomplishments," he said. "Asking questions of bombastic men is part of my job."

Gemma smiled as she realized he was making fun of himself to deflect any sense of obligation to him. He was trying to make her feel safe, and he was succeeding. Why was he being so good to her? So forgiving? Maybe she should have stayed back and kept up her search. Finish the job.

"Gemma?"

He looked down at her with such concern, nearly broke her heart. And he shouldn't be breaking her heart. He shouldn't be doing anything to it. But she was, too late, realizing she was falling in love with this man. A man who would despise her if he discovered her little secret.

. . .

He'd touched something raw and hidden, like those drawings he'd sent home to Isla then scooped up and hid away in a box. He wanted to do nothing more that wrap his arms around Gemma and tell her everything would be better. But aside from the fact that he was her employer, such an open display of affection to a woman to whom he was not married would be scandalous in the extreme. Unless he planned to become engaged to her, he had to keep his hands exactly where they were—at his sides. And the very notion of becoming engaged to Miss Gemma Kurt should have been outright preposterous.

Except it wasn't.

It was captivating.

It was also a bloody warning sign to talk about something else.

"Shall we get some ices?" he asked.

"That would be lovely," she said, relief evident in her eyes.

They walked to a small confectionary where Jeremy bought them all a small dish of shaved ice, and they sat on a nearby bench, the three of them, Gemma with her lemon ice, Jeremy and Ivy with their cherry. It was, like the last day or so had been, perfectly enjoyable.

Contented.

After finishing their ices, they continued along when the sound of a gaggle of children caught Jeremy's attention. Ahead was a group of perhaps seven girls of various ages, along with three women, two of whom he recognized from their visit last week. The third was an older black woman in an elegant, light blue dress.

"It's Miss Jones and Mrs. Hartley," Ivy said, looking to Gemma.

"I believe it is!" Gemma replied, and Jeremy felt a small stab of envy at how her face lit up at seeing them. "And Mrs. Gilman is with them. She is one of the co-founders of the Everwell Society. May I introduce you?"

"I would be honoured," he said.

Gemma raised a hand, waiving warmly to get their attention.

Her gesture was returned with a trio of smiles. Jeremy and Ivy followed as Gemma led them toward her friends.

"This is a pleasant surprise," Gemma said. "I didn't think a trip to the zoo was in the plans for this weekend."

"It wasn't," Mrs. Hartley answered. "But we'd had an especially busy week with you gone and the last of the repairs complete at the school. We decided we all needed a bit of a treat."

Instantly Gemma was crowded by the small gaggle of girls, who clearly missed her.

"Colonel Webber," she said. "These are some of my students. Girls, this is Ivy Webber. She is new to the city, and I am betting she would love to know some of you better."

Jeremy watched his daughter, clearly excited by the possibility of being with a group of girls her own age.

"Ivy," he said, before she even had the opportunity to ask. "Would you like to look at the monkeys with these girls?"

She nodded.

"Off with you then. Just take care not to stray too far, and listen to Miss Jones."

"Colonel Webber," Gemma continued, "may I introduce Mrs. Clotilda Gilman."

Jeremy started at the name.

"Excuse me," he said, nodding to her. "I once knew a nurse by the name of Clotilda Gilman. She practiced in the Persia, many years ago."

The woman, who was easily thirty years his senior, smiled, and Jeremy was struck again but the familiarity.

"I was in indeed in Persia, Colonel Webber," she said, her eyes narrowing. "I have met many soldiers, and I am afraid I cannot place you."

On impulse, Jeremy held out his hand to shake hers, which she accepted.

"You saved the life of my sergeant. Harold Babcock is his name," he said, excited beyond measure at the coincidence. "Truly, I am in your debt."

"Was the battle at Khushab? I can't say I recall your sergeant. There have been so many over the years."

Jeremy reeled at her quiet modesty. The hospital staff had saved the lives of hundreds of soldiers, plus the local population. He'd been absolutely green, and it had been one of their first missions together as a young officer and foot soldier. A bullet had pierced Babcock's leg, shattering the bone, and it had to be removed. The surgery that saved his life also threatened it. It was the tending at her hospital that kept the infection at bay. The wound, which had cost Babcock part of his leg, kept him out of the service. It was the only time Jeremy had used his name—or more to the point, his brother's influence—to pressure London to allow Jeremy to retain Harold in his current position.

"I never had the pleasure of thanking you in person, but without fail the sergeant and I have toasted to your health annually on the seventh of February." Jeremy doffed his hat and bowed. "This is truly an honour, ma'am."

Mrs. Gilman nodded.

"The world is indeed a smaller one than we imagine it," Mrs. Hartley said. "You and your daughter should come to Everwell for a visit, Colonel. It might be nice for her to play with girls her age, and you and Mrs. Gilman could speak further."

"I wouldn't want to impose," Jeremy said, gesturing toward the students. The peal of laughter arose from yards away, where Ivy was playing with the other children, and he realized it was the first time he'd seen her play with other children. "You appear to have your hands full."

"If it were an imposition," Mrs. Hartley said, "we wouldn't invite you. Sergeant Babcock is also welcome."

He looked to Gemma, who had stepped aside to speak with Miss Jones. They were deep in conversation of an almost conspiratorial nature, but every once in a while, he felt the heat of her stolen glances.

"Thank you—we would be honoured."

"Excellent. We rarely have guests for dinner, but hosting you and Ivy would be a pleasure," Mrs. Hartley said. "We shall see you tomorrow."

After the exchange of pleasantries, the Everwell contingent continued on, leaving Ivy and Jeremy with Gemma once more. The promise of dinner and the opportunity to meet with the girls tomorrow had made the parting bearable for Ivy. By the time they'd arrived home, the lull of the carriage ride coupled with a full day with fresh air and exercise had Ivy nodding off, her head resting against Gemma's shoulder.

"This has been a remarkable day," Jeremy said. "And I owe it all to you. But then, you are a remarkable woman."

Pink crept into Gemma's cheeks.

"It was Ivy's idea," Gemma said. "You have a remarkable daughter."

"I'm glad she's sleeping now. I expect her to be up at the crack of dawn, raring to go to Everwell," he said. "I suppose you will, too. It is your home, after all."

"I will be excited to see the others, certainly," Gemma said, then let go a little sigh. "Everwell does have an air about it. But there is a rhythm to it, as chaotic as it can appear to those outside it."

Did she miss it? He wanted to ask, afraid of the answer even though it was completely illogical for her to give any other question but yes. He'd been so pleased to have a governess in place that he'd hadn't given any thought to how long the arrangement might last. But the idea of letting Gemma Kurt out of his life was unimaginable.

Chapter Twenty-One

❧

WITH MRS. WHITEHEAD STILL OUT, Jeremy had given the cook the day off, so a pleasant informal meal capped off the day. Ivy had found a second wind, regaling Sergeant Babcock with the highlights of the afternoon, including meeting Tilda and the invitation to Everwell. By the time supper was over, however, Ivy was already fading, and Gemma offered to put her to bed, leaving Jeremy and the sergeant to talk.

Gemma tucked Ivy into bed and started reading from a book of fairytales she'd found in Jeremy's library, but she'd hardly made it past the first page before Ivy's eyes grew heavy. Gemma closed the book, slid a bit of ribbon between the page to mark the spot, and turned down the lamp. She rose and went to the door, surprised to see Jeremy leaning against the door frame.

"I think that's the first time Ivy has fallen asleep before I had a chance to finish a story," she said in a low voice as she went into the hall, Jeremy closing the door behind them. "Normally she's begging for more."

"Well, I was riveted," Jeremy said, his mouth inching up into a smile Gemma was coming to love. "I think we should go into the study and you can finish it for me. I don't think I can wait another night to find out how it ends."

That might have been an innocent, playful, offhand remark, but there was something in the low timber of his voice that made the idea absolutely enthralling. And yet, she knew how this had to end.

"It's Jack and the Beanstalk," Gemma said, ignoring the pang of melancholy in her chest. "Jack steals the harp and scampers away. Haven't you heard that one?"

"Perhaps," he said. "Truthfully I always felt bad for the poor giant."

"Well naturally," she said, gesturing to him. "Look at you. You are a giant."

"In my family? Hardly. My brother is a full two inches taller," he said with a self-deprecating smile. "But this poor man is in his own house, not bothering anyone, when a little scamp climbs up a beanstalk and takes his goods and his harp? I'm not sure what he did to deserve such an invasion."

"He's a giant," she repeated. "And poor Jack was starving."

"Poor Jack sold the cow for some beans," he insisted. "I am tempted to think Jack's faculty for good judgment is very small."

He was teasing her, she realized. And she liked being teased by him. Except this particular subject was a little too close to the bone.

"We should move away from Ivy's door and debate this elsewhere," Gemma said. "Or she's going to wake up I'm going to have to find a new set of stories."

"I'm sure I have a book on military tactics that might put Ivy to sleep quite easily," he said.

"Why don't you tell her a story?"

"I have no stories to tell," he said.

"Surely that's not true," she said. "You've been in Egypt, and to Persia, and probably ten other places equally interesting."

"What they don't tell you about military life is that it is quite monotonous most of the time," he said. "It's either boring, or it's terrifying and horrible, and I'd like to spare her the latter."

She poked a finger at his chest, overcome by a fit of playfulness. "You have a box of nearly one hundred little postcard drawings from Egypt. I bet there is a little story attached to each one of those, or you wouldn't have drawn them. And most importantly, those stories are about you. And she loves you more than anything."

He smiled at that.

"Besides, I'm not going to be here forever," she said, trying to keep the smile on her face even as his faltered. "You will no doubt want a more suitable governess."

"I think you are perfectly suitable," he said. "Perfect."

She blinked, swallowing back the welling of an unbearable lightness and joy that she didn't deserve. She clasped her hands together even as they itched to reach out to him, pull his mouth down to hers, and kiss him.

The chiming of a clock roused her from her thoughts, reminding her she was running out of time. She had exactly one hour before Mrs. Whitehead would return. One hour to search her room. Gemma stepped away from Jeremy, even as her body craved his.

"Would you like some warm milk?" she asked, cursing herself for the unnatural pitch in her voice.

His brow furrowed, clearly confused by her question. "Excuse me?"

"I'm going to the kitchen to make a little warm milk, to help me sleep," she said, far too cheerful for the topic at hand. "I thought you might like some as well."

"My dear Miss Kurt," he said, cocking an eyebrow that threatened her resolve to walk away. "That is why some smart Frenchmen invented brandy."

"Governesses aren't supposed to take brandy," she said. "It's against the rules."

"Those rules are ridiculous," he said, his voice low, moving through her veins and threatening to weaken her at the knees. "What if we don't tell your employer? He doesn't need to know everything, does he?"

Jeremy's offhand and entirely innocent remark was the shock Gemma needed to bring her to her senses.

No, he doesn't. Because if he did, she'd be on the street at best, and at worst, at the provincial penitentiary.

"What if I join my employer with a little warm milk while he sips his brandy?"

She turned away and padded down the stairs, not bothering to wait for his response. She needed to put some distance between them. She'd allowed the enjoyment of the moment to get away from her, put herself before the job at hand. She couldn't fail the Spinsters the way she'd failed Penny.

She stood in front of Mrs. Whitehead's door, just outside the kitchen, and knocked to be certain that the housekeeper hadn't returned early. To Gemma's relief, there was no answer. The housekeeper had said she'd return by eight, and according to the clock she'd passed in the main hall, Gemma had a little less than an hour. It should be plenty of time, but she wasn't about to waste another moment.

She pulled out her tools and made quick work of the lock. She snuck in, put her taper on the chest of drawers, which she searched, before turning her attention to a small truck near the foot of the housekeeper's bed.

Mrs. Whitehead, as one would expect, kept a tidy room. There were a few books, a small pile of temperance literature, and a pamphlet from the New Women's League, the homegrown improvement society founded by Mrs. Emily Coughlin and several other of Halifax's elite women. If Gemma had not been inclined to think well of Mrs. Whitehead since arriving at Hastings House, the housekeeper's association with the NWL, which had in the past actively spoken out against the Everwell Society, did not improve Gemma's opinion.

She kept searching, careful not to disturb the contents of the room, as the eagle-eyed Mrs. Whitehead would no doubt notice things out of place. She looked for correspondence from the Hatchetts, but there was nothing.

The sound of keys in the rear door caught her attention. In a moment, she exited the door, locking it behind her, and walked into the kitchen, just as Mrs. Whitehead entered the kitchen.

"Good evening," Gemma said brightly.

"Good evening," she said, nodding with that cool politeness Gemma had become accustomed to.

"I was just making myself some warm milk," Gemma offered. "Would you like some?"

"Yes, thank you," she replied, unbuttoning her coat and walking toward her room. "I'll be but a moment."

Gemma busied herself in the kitchen, lighting the stove and pulling a small container of left-over milk from the icebox.

"Did you have to find a cow to milk?"

The sound of Jeremy's pulled at Gemma's tense nerves, and she jumped.

"It took me a bit to light the stove," she said, which was a convenient, but clumsy fib. "I didn't realize you were waiting for me. I assumed after a full day at the zoo you would be eager to have a little time to yourself."

"This may surprise you," he said, "but I can become quite bored with my own company. And if you hadn't noticed, that is how I spend nearly all my evenings."

"A good thing then that you'll have all that company at Ever-well tomorrow," she said.

Mrs. Whitehead returned, and Gemma could see she was surprised by Jeremy's presence in the kitchen.

"Good evening, Colonel," she said. "Can I help you with something?"

"Nothing at all, Mrs. Whitehead," he said. "I trust your visit to your family went well?"

"Indeed it did sir," she replied. "But I would have returned earlier if I had known I was needed."

"Be at ease," he said, raising a hand. "I merely came down to see if Miss Kurt had been swallowed by the stove. She came down here some time ago to make herself a cup of warm milk and disappeared."

Gemma flashed a tight smile. "I had trouble lighting the stove," she said by way of explanation. "But I seem to have that in order. There was no need to check on my welfare."

"Cook had a lovely meal for us," Jeremy continued, "so we were well taken care of."

Gemma picked two mugs from a peg on the other side of the kitchen, poured a drizzle honey into the bottom of each, followed by the steaming milk. She picked up the mugs and handed one to Mrs. Whitehead.

"I'm going to retire for the night," she said with a smile. "I believe the fresh air has tired me out. Good evening to you both."

Jeremy watched her leave. The tension between the two women was unmistakable. Mrs. Whitehead had never bothered to hide her issues with Gemma Kurt, but Jeremy had dismissed it as some kind of rivalry that he had no desire to get into the middle of. Politics of the upstairs variety had been enough for him. But he found himself put out on Gemma's behalf. He prepared himself to leave, eager to follow and be in her presence.

"Is there something I can do for you?" Mrs. Whitehead asked.

"Not at all," he replied, then remembered his plans for Sunday. "Please let Cook know that Ivy and I have plans tomorrow for dinner at and so will not be dining at Hastings House."

"Of course," she said. "Miss Webber will be delighted to receive her first dinner invitation."

"Indeed. We received an invitation to dine at Everwell Manor."

"Everwell?" she said, her lips so tight that Jeremy nearly feared she might swallow them.

"Is there a problem?"

"I just believe that a man of your reputation might want to be extra careful about where he is seen and the company he keeps," she said. "There are rumours about what goes on there."

Jeremy started. "What kind of rumours?"

Her lips tightened and she lowered her voice even though they were quite alone.

"They educate all the children there together," she said.

"As in boys and girls?" Jeremy asked, perplexed. "Mrs. Whitehead—"

"As in white and black and brown," she said, looking at him as if he were dull.

"I see," Jeremy said, not the slightest bit amused. "And you feel I should be disturbed by this?"

His offhanded remark made her step back.

"My dear colonel, it's against the natural order," she said, not bothering to hide her incredulity.

"If you ever stand in the wake of a structure that was perfectly engineered pyramid, or the Great Wall, or witnessed the ferocity with which men in red coats like mine have butchered others, you might find yourself questioning 'natural order'," he said, not bothering to hide his disgust. "Now, aside from the crime of educating children, what else is the Everwell Society up to?"

"They say one of their so-called teachers is an escaped murderess," she said with a low whisper.

Jeremy forced himself not to roll his eyes. He had little patience for this sort of hush hush business. Clearly the gossip mills must have the Everwell Society hiding a monster in the cellar, and a magician who turned straw into gold as well. Either way, he had no time for such nonsense.

"Mrs. Whitehead, do not be missish. If you are making an accusation, have the courage of your convictions and just say it."

She pursed her lips, her eyes sliding to the hall where Gemma had gone a moment ago.

"There is a belief, amongst a certain well informed and excellent ladies, that the Everwell Society is little more than a front for a gang of thieves."

Jeremy couldn't help it. He laughed. And then some part of him hardened with anger at her implication toward Gemma.

"Thieves?" He recalled both Mrs. Hartley and Miss Jones and could hardly imagine it. They were both pleasant, amiable women who took a great interest in Ivy and their students' welfare. Students, he noted, that were from the less privileged parts of society. "And where are you hearing these rumours? I've spent far too many hours in the company of people who seem to know all the comings and goings of this city and never once have seen fit to utter a word about them."

"With respect sir, the society you are dealing with do not pay charities of the kind such as Everwell any attention. But I have worked with groups similarly focused on improving the character of this province, and this city, which has fallen in the past years into degradation and ill morals," she said. "Those associations are in contact with many people across the area. People who have been touched by Everwell. People who have claimed they've been" —she paused, and Jeremy could tell she was choosing her words carefully — "helped by the Everwell Society. And the nature of that 'help' is most disconcerting."

Jeremy had always known Mrs. Whitehead didn't approve of Miss Kurt. Was this the reason?

"Isn't that what a charitable organization should be doing? Helping?"

Mrs. Whitehead released a breath that could have been a huff but for her own self-restraint.

"I am merely stating that the society may not actually be what it appears, and they are teaching young women ideas that are not fit for them to have," Mrs. Whitehead said. "And having Miss Webber under the influence of one of them is less than ideal, never mind the entire lot."

"Mrs. Whitehead," he said, his voice stern, his impatience growing. "I know my daughter. She has blossomed under Miss Kurt's tutelage. I fail to see what an afternoon and a supper would do to her development other than allow her to play with children her own age."

"Those children are not Miss Webber's equal," she said. "They will grow up to be servants at best, and if the rumours are true, thieves at worst."

"The Everwell Society is run by two women—one, the daughter of an English Colonel, and the other, a heroine of the British Army."

"They live together in an unnatural fashion," she said in whisper.

"I think we've spoken enough on this subject," he said. "I understand that the Hatchetts recommended you, but take care that while it is your duty to look after the house, that I am the master of it while I am here. And you will not speak ill of Miss Kurt or the Everwell Society while I am here."

She nodded, her eyes hard, but lowered.

He turned away, and she spoke again.

"Before you go sir," she said, "this telegram arrived for you this morning, after you left."

She held out an envelope. Inside was a note from William Hatchett, announcing their plan had changed, and they would be arriving in Halifax early.

He let out a breath.

"Order a joint of meat, will you Mrs. Whitehead?" he said as he left. "It seems we'll be having company for dinner on Monday."

Chapter Twenty-Two

A STIR of feelings knotted in Gemma's belly as she returned to Everwell with Jeremy, Ivy, and Harold Babcock. She was arriving without the will. Failure and remorse had been a familiar, if unwanted companion in her life. But as she turned watched Jeremy and Ivy sitting beside each other chatting merrily about a drawing that Jeremy had done, the knot loosened a bit. Maybe she'd accomplished something. And every once in a while, that warmth grew hot, and she'd look over to see Jeremy gazing at her, as if she were the only person in the world that mattered.

She'd overheard him last night, defending Everwell from Mrs. Whitehead's accusations. Everwell, in the eyes of finer Halifax society, was guilty of a countless number of sins. Over the years she'd overheard stories of secret brothels, the active promotion of non-Christian faiths, and more commonly, promoting ideals that were merely out of line with the status quo. Most were plainly untrue or rooted in ignorance. But never had they been accused of thievery.

That one was harder to laugh off. She had to tell Phillipa.

They were greeted at the door by the full contingent from Everwell Manor. Ivy was quickly scooped up by the other children, disappearing in a joyous gaggle to go play in the gardens,

Maddy keeping a watchful eye. And there was not a dry tear in the place when Jeremy introduced Harold Babcock to Tilda.

Tea, pastries, and other delights were brought into the front parlour, where Jeremy and Sergeant Babcock sat with Tilda and Lady Em. Gemma went to the kitchen to help Phillipa and Rimple with dinner preparations, and shared the rumours she'd overheard the night before.

"I hope I made enough," Rimple said as she pulled a fresh batch of her famous biscuits out of the oven. "Elouise and Dominic will be joining us, and the last time I made these, I think he ate nearly a half dozen on his own." Dominic Ashe was a former Boston police detective who had just started his own business as a private consulting detective. He'd also been one of Everwell's recent clients, and he and Elouise had an unlikely romance that ended in their engagement.

"Are you certain that's a good idea?" Gemma asked in a low whisper, fearful of being overheard. "Jeremy has met both Dominic and Elouise."

Dominic and Elouise had become unwitting partners in a scheme on their last job, which involved them posing as a socialite couple from Boston at a well-attended dinner party held by one of Halifax's most elite families. A dinner party that Jeremy had also attended.

"Elouise was in disguise, and Dominic has a good over story if Colonel Webber does recognize them." Phillipa said as she sliced up potatoes and onions and neatly arranged them in a roasting pan. "I am choosing not to worry about that."

Phillipa's answer gave Gemma pause. When Phillipa *chose* not to worry about something, Gemma was never entirely certain what that meant. How could she not be concerned about the Scandalous Spinsters being unmasked?

"I think we need to worry," Gemma said, focusing her nervous energy on chopping carrots. "I think the Hatchetts might suspect something."

Phillipa looked up from her task. "What makes you say that?"

"I overheard Jeremy's housekeeper talking to him about me," Gemma replied. "About us. About how Mr. Dalrymple's house-keeper had employed us."

"And what did the colonel say?"

"He brushed it off as nonsense," she said. "But what if he hadn't? Jeremy isn't a fool. The Hatchetts are due to arrive tomorrow."

"Jeremy?" Rimple smiled, unable to contain the mischief in her dark eyes.

"Stop it, Rimple," Gemma said, tossing a slice of carrot at her friend. "This is serious. I meant the colonel."

"No," Phillipa said, arching her eyebrow, watching Gemma with concern. "You meant Jeremy. Is all well at Hastings House?"

"Do you mean aside from the fact that I've searched every nook, cranny floor board and drawer in that house and come up completely empty?" Gemma said, allowing the frustration to be here. "A woman is going to lose her roof because of me."

"Not because of you," Rimple protested. "Because of her well-meaning, too-clever-for-his-own-good employer who made promises and then hid them so thoroughly no one could find it."

"Don't forget the miserable new owners," Gemma said, then turned her gaze to Phillipa. "Who are coming to meet with their solicitors tomorrow."

"Gemma," Phillipa said, putting on that voice of hers that was at once comforting and yet could be mildly irritating. "What do we say at Everwell?"

"We help."

"Well, yes, but what else?"

"We never let someone else's version of the truth get in the way of the facts."

Gemma had not been raised with sisters. But here, each of the teachers had become like a sister to her. And while Gemma was the youngest at twenty-nine, and far from being a baby, Phillipa was well over a decade older and, whether she realized it or not, seemed to embody the role of the somewhat bossy oldest sister.

"All we can do is the best that we can do," Phillipa continued in that no-nonsense way of hers, "and Gemma, you have never failed to do your best."

That should have made her feel better. Had she done her best? Or had she been too busy being captivated by Jeremy Webber's touch?

"What about that rumour?" Rimple asked, wiping her fingers on her apron. "You have to admit that it's a bit troubling."

"There are plenty of stories in town," Phillipa said. "Witchcraft may our last hold out, I believe. They make for good gossip and that is all. Besides, having Colonel Webber here as an invited guest, with a most remarkable connection to us, does boost our reputation favourably."

Gemma piled the last of the carrots into a pot, filled it with water, and placed it on the stove.

"Is there anything else I can do?" she said, trying to make herself feel better. Phillipa was always so confident, and if there were something truly amiss, surely she would share it.

"I think that's it for now, Gemma," Phillipa replied, wiping her hands on her apron. "Why don't you go join our guests?"

Jeremy sat in the parlour with Harold Babcock and the two matrons of Everwell Manor. The reunion of Babcock with Mrs. Gilman was as every bit as satisfying and he'd hoped. It had been nearly two decades since he'd been a much younger, inexperienced Second Lieutenant, fresh out of Sandhurst, and facing his first armed encounter that nearly cost him his life, and Harold Babcock his leg.

The afternoon passed with easy and pleasant conversation, but occasionally Jeremy found his attention straying out the window looking for signs of Ivy, and to the parlour door, wondering if Gemma might return. Of course, this was Gemma's home, and there was little wonder why she loved it so. Everwell seemed to be a place where people were free not only to be themselves, but valued for being themselves.

The clock struck the half hour, and as if by some miracle, Gemma, Mrs. Hartley, and Miss Jones appeared in the door.

"Here they are at last," Mrs. Gilman said. "We wondered where you had gotten to. I'm afraid the poor colonel was a little lost without you, Miss Kurt."

Jeremy didn't flush normally, but be damned if he didn't feel called out by her observation. Was he so bloody obvious?

At least he wasn't the only one. Gemma bit back a smile.

"I'm certain Colonel Webber is looking for a reprieve from the interrogation," she said, smoothing her skirts.

"Would you like a tour of the property, Colonel? I'm sure Miss Kurt would be happy to take you," Lady Em said, and if Jeremy didn't know better, he would have thought her eyes were twinkling as she said it. "Perhaps you can catch up with your daughter. And by the time you return, dinner will be ready."

He looked over at Gemma, and though he shouldn't have been happy for the obvious bait of her company, he was thrilled to have it.

"I do not want to trouble you, Miss Kurt," he said.

"It's no trouble at all," she said. "I can show you the gardens and the improvements that have been happening. And perhaps you will see some prospects here you might like to draw."

"You are an artist, sir?" Mrs. Hartley asked. "What medium?"

"Artist is too generous a word for my talents," he said. "I enjoy ink and watercolours primarily."

"He's being modest," the sergeant offered. "He's very talented. Isn't he, Miss Kurt?"

"Yes," she said, catching his eye and giving him a generous smile. "Very talented. And suddenly very modest, too."

"Next time you come to dine with us, you must bring a portfolio of your work," Lady Em said, her tone more of an order than a request.

"Supper will be in about one hour," Phillipa said. "Plenty of time for you to have a tour of the place, and perhaps do us a favour and round up the children as well."

Jeremy rose to his feet. "You're sure, Babcock, you don't mind being left to fend for yourself amongst all these women?" he said, feeling a certain responsibility to his sergeant.

"I'll be fine. These ladies are fine company indeed," he said, gesturing to Gemma and giving him a not-so-subtle wink. "You should be off now."

A moment later, she led him out the front door, stopping to grab a small shawl to throw around her shoulders. The air was growing a little crisp as the sun descended.

"What would you like to see?" she asked. "I'm not certain what a man who's traveled like you have would like."

The breeze caught a few stray locks of her hair, catching and teasing them as the sun caught fire in her dark hair, and answer was as plain as the nose on her adorable face. What he wanted to look at most was right in front of him. What he wanted to touch and hold.

"I'm happy for you to lead the way." He offered his arm, which she took. Contentment washed over him—a sense that this was how things were supposed to be. It was as real as the scent of Gemma's perfume in the crisp fall air, or the leaves gently rustling in the trees overhead. He offered his arm, and she took it, satisfaction settling on him as she rested her arm on his. Even though they'd touched in far more intimate ways than this, finding comfort in each other's presence felt just as vulnerable. They walked along, talking about nothing in particular, sometimes enjoying the silence, and savouring each other's company.

She led him past the kitchen gardens. The greens looked to be past their peak, though there were pumpkins and squash sprawling along the ground, and hardier herbs, like rosemary, sage and thyme still in full glory. The gardens gave way to a small orchard, still laden with apples that needed to be picked and stored for the winter.

"These gardens are truly spectacular," he said, marveling at the bounty in the rather modest space.

"You should see them at their peak," Gemma replied. "Maddie's fixation on them is an obsession. But surely this must be nothing compared to your family estate."

Jeremy considered that. Grenfell, settled into the rolling hills of Kent, was a sizable estate and, thanks to the careful management of it by his father and his brother, had managed to remain prosperous not only for itself, but the families the area supported.

"My own family home is quite grand, to be sure. But it doesn't take away my awe of the place," he said, breathing in the stillness like a balm before his gaze rested on Gemma. Because as grand or as luxurious as Grenfell was, it was missing something. "Maybe it's the company."

The comment put a smile on her face so genuine that he thought his heart might burst.

"I would agree."

She led him to a carriage house which looked to have been freshly painted and edged with charming gingerbread trim on the gables. It stood apart from a modest barn and several other small outbuildings. Gemma pulled open a door and beckoned him to come inside. Immediately in front of him was a cart that looked to be in regular use, and tucked in one corner, a smaller carriage of an older style. But it was a structure on the other side of the building that caught his eye.

Jeremy walked toward a roped off area that looked something like a cross between his training facilities at Eton and an underground boxing ring he'd bet and lost an entire month's worth of earnings when he was young and stupid.

To one side stood a tall bag, hung on a hook by chains. On the other, there was a small pile of what looked to be straw mattresses, neatly stacked along the wall. Above them was a block of wood painted like a target, its colour faded with time and its surface marred by the puncture of what appeared to be blades.

"What is this?" he asked with undisguised curiosity.

"This is where Maddy and I practice," she said. "Miss Murray is an accomplished fighter and familiar with several different martial arts. She teaches the rest of us some methods of self-defence."

He looked at her, not bothering to hide his surprise. "Are you concerned about a mutiny amongst the children?"

Gemma's lips curled up in a smile.

"Hardly. But we do take in women who often suffer violence at the hands of their partners," she said so matter of factly it made Jeremy start. "While we rarely need to use these skills, it is useful for us to have them."

Jeremy frowned. While he knew quite rationally it made sense for women to be able to defend themselves, particularly from violent men, the fact Gemma and the other women had Everwell considered this necessary horrified him.

"You said rarely." Jeremy paused, inspecting a notch that had been made from what appeared to be an exceptionally large blade. "That's not never."

"Maddy is exceptionally good at what she does."

That answer did not mollify him, but he left it when she walked toward a corner where a net was stretched between four pillars, a rope dangling in the middle.

Gemma ran her hands along the rope. "But here, this is where I practice."

Jeremy put his hands on his hips and looked up to a sturdy beam a story up where the line was secured. He knew she was an acrobat. She'd told him as much. But aside from the day he'd watched her dangling from the bookshelves or when she'd taught Ivy a handstand, he'd never seen her perform.

"Do you climb it?"

She wrapped her arm around the rope, then looked over at him.

"I could show you," she said.

Jeremy held up his hands, ready to protest. "I thought you didn't perform anymore."

She cocked her head, looked up at the ceiling, then back to him. "I don't perform for strangers."

Her phrase settled on him, the meaning of it unfolding in his chest, filling it until he thought he would burst with happiness. She was offering him a gift.

Her trust.

"I would love to watch," he said. "As long as you're certain."

"I am," she said. "Can you wait a moment?"

He nodded, and she disappeared behind a screen. When she emerged, Jeremy thought he'd died and gone to heaven. Dressed in a simple type of maillot that covered her torso but little else, her strong, shapely legs were on full display. She spent a moment winding tape around her hands, no doubt to protect them from the burn across the fibres of the rope, then stuck her fingers into a bag of chalk that hung in on a nearby nail.

She ran over, kissed him on the cheek, then pulled herself up the cable a series of powerful, purposeful movements. There was something about the way she walked that exuded confidence. Like she was exactly where she should be. She climbed the rope as easily as he might walk across a room, and then she started to fly, swinging from side to side, supporting herself with only her knees wrapped around the bottom of the swing. A couple of times he held his breath, his heart in this throat. But most of the time he was simply transfixed.

Soon the performance was over. She climbed down, her breathing heavy, and her cheeks flushed from the exercise. Jeremy clapped, quickly wiping his eyes with the back of his hands.

"That was the most breathtaking thing I have ever seen," he said.

She approached, his chest rising and falling with deep breaths from her exertion, the tops of her breasts just visible above her garment's bodice.

"Come now," she said. "You've seen the great pyramids and many other wonders, I bet."

"I remain fixed in my opinion," he said, looking into her eyes, bright and warm. "Breathtaking."

She shivered, and it occurred to Jeremy she was standing here, mostly naked while he was still in his full dress uniform while the temperature outside was starting to fall. He took off his red coat and draped it over her shoulders, then pulled her into his arms, savouring heat of her body, nuzzling his nose in her hair.

"I would love nothing more than to peel this costume from your body and kiss every square inch of you," he said, running his lips along her hairline, peppering her with kisses. "I'm not sure how so little clothing feels like too much, but apparently I'm a greedy bastard when it comes to you."

He felt her smile against his cheek and her breathy laugh sent a thrill straight to his core.

She looked at him with an unmistakable hunger in her eyes.

"It turns out that I can be greedy, too."

Jeremy stilled as her hand gently stroked him through the fabric of his trousers. He was hard and aching.

"Gemma," he said, his voice low with need, his hands wrapped around the firm curves of her backside.

She silenced him with a deep kiss, her tongue exploring his mouth, one hand behind his neck. The other had somehow already unfastened the buttons on his trousers, because—*bloody hell*—she was using it to explore the length of his shaft in firm strokes.

Goddamn it. He was about to spill his seed all over the front of his best dress uniform.

"Let me pleasure you," she said, looking up at him, he realized, looking for his consent. "I want to make you feel as wonderful as you've made me."

He paused, a moment of clarity peeking through the haze of lust that threatened to overtake him. She was asking him to trust her. To give himself to her, the way she had given herself to him. Watching her on the trapeze was as much a pleasure for her as it was for him.

He nodded, and a second later she crouched down, and in the most indescribable feeling of pure carnal bliss, took him into her mouth. Lost to sensation, to pleasure, to his own need, he buried his hands in her hair, aware of nothing but the sensation of her hands and her tongue, stroking and kissing him straight to the precipice.

Somewhere in the recesses of rational thought, he would have found and itemized at least fifty reasons why this was wrong. In a neat, orderly list.

In the end, there was only one reason—and one person—that made this right. That made the list meaningless. There was something else. A kind of certainty, that maybe fate had intervened for a good purpose. Falling in love with another woman had never been part of the plan.

Maybe it was time to make new plans.

Chapter Twenty-Three

✦✦✦

JEREMY HELPED Gemma out of her maillot and back into her dress. It was an exercise that should only have taken a couple of minutes, but owing to his intoxicating, tantalizing strokes between her legs paired with hungry kisses along her neck and shoulders, a full half hour had gone by. Gemma wanted to savour every minute of her time with him. It had been selfish but Gemma decided to indulge herself in this fleeting illusion of contentment she had when Jeremy held her. He looked at her as if she were worthy of affection. And it was affection she saw there, wasn't it?

She would enjoy the illusion that she could be loved by a worthy man. That illusion would disappear soon enough. And even if, by some miracle, he never discovered why she was at Hastings House, why she'd inserted herself into his beloved daughter's life, she would know. And she couldn't bear the weight of another secret. It would smother her.

And yet, the Spinsters' work had to remain secret. The damage from having that secret revealed was more than she was willing to bear. Dominic Ashe knew of course, but Elouise's fiancé had discovered it almost by accident, and they'd worked together on a job of mutual interest. Dominic's strong sense of justice and his equally fierce love of Elouise made him a powerful ally to Everwell's mission.

Jeremy wasn't like Dominic. He was without question Dominic's equal in terms of his goodness and fierce love for those close to him, but Jeremy also had an affinity for rules and order that didn't trouble Dominic. Dominic had come from the fringes of society; Jeremy been born into the pinnacle of it, and benefited from the series of rules—written and unwritten—that governed it.

At last they left the carriage house, Gemma determined to soak up the bittersweet emotions and then push them aside. The two continued in companionable silence. Jeremy offered his arm, which she took, leading them along one of the paths that brought them to the edge of the property.

"You have neighbours," Jeremy said as they came around a bend where a new and handsome house was being built. When it was finished, it would be a lovely, stately home.

"Everwell's properties are quite extensive," Gemma said. "More than we need. We recently sold a parcel to a buyer."

Dominic had bought a couple of acres of land to build a house after the successful completion of their last job had netted him a substantial cash reward from a Bostonian benefactor.

"Lucky man, whoever he is," Jeremy said, then took out his watch and checked the time, a flicker of concern crossing his brow. "We should return before I am accused of impropriety with one of Everwell's educators and late for dinner. Heaven knows I've gotten quite the reputation for the latter. I'd like to preserve yours, at least."

Gemma smiled at his self-depreciation, her heart doing a little flip as he looked down at her with what she could only describe as affection.

"Gemma!"

The sound of her name pulled Gemma out of her thoughts. She recognized the voice at once. Elouise Charming, Everwell's teacher of manners, deportment, and resident actress, was calling out to her from the road. She looked positively radiant as she stepped out of a cab, her short, dark blond curls capped by a light blue directoire that matched her dress. Beside her was Dominic, regarding Elouise with unabashed adoration.

She was happy to see them, but as far as reunions went, Gemma was nervous. Jeremy had met them the very night Gemma had first laid eyes on him. It was the night of the Boston Job, as the ruse had since been dubbed, when Dominic and Elouise, posing as husband and wife, stole a vase from one of Halifax's finest families. A vase that had already been stolen and used at the centre of an art fraud ring that had killed Dominic's brother. Dominic had gone to retrieve it but needed the help of the Scandalous Spinsters. And, in the most unlikely of scenarios, Elouise, who had decided that a man was never worth her trust, fell in love.

Jeremy had been there. And while Elouise had been in disguise, Gemma wasn't entirely certain it would be enough. Jeremy had an artist's eye. An eye for detail. And he noticed Gemma in a way no one else ever had.

"Here are the owners of the house now," Gemma said, determined to be nonchalant. Elouise was used to these situations after all, and could concoct a believable story on the spot. Dampening down her concern, Gemma ran toward her friend, arms wide, and Elouise returned the gesture, the two wrapping each other in a warm embrace.

"Gemma, how are you?" Elouise asked, as Gemma drank in the sisterly embrace.

"Very well," she said as she released her friend, and accepting a kiss on the cheek from Dominic. Dominic gave her a warm smile, which she returned. "How is your sister-in-law and young nieces? Are they joining us for dinner tonight?"

"They are," he replied. "In fact, they are continuing on in the cab. We just wanted to take a moment to survey the work."

"He's been here nearly every day," Elouise said. "In fact, I think he'd prefer to be here, swinging a hammer than back in his office."

"There is something straight forward about building a house," he said, then looked past her to Jeremy. Gemma could tell he recognized Dominic.

"Does he know?" Dominic asked in a low voice.

She shook her head. Why did she feel so horrible about lying to Jeremy? He wasn't part of the job. But he was. And she could not risk any more exposure.

"Don't worry," Dominic said with a wink.

Gemma turned back to Jeremy, gentleman that he was, who waited to be introduced. He was English, and he played by a certain set of rules.

"Colonel Webber," she said, walking back to him, "I would like to introduce you to my friends. This is Mr. Dominic Ashe, from Boston, and this is my dear friend, Miss Elouise Charming. Mr. Ashe is a consulting detective who has recently opened a business in town."

Dominic extended his hand. "A pleasure to meet you."

"Have we met?" Jeremy asked, and Gemma held her breath.

"We have, in fact," Dominic replied, in that smooth way of his. "At the Coughlin's dinner party this past summer."

Gemma smiled inwardly, her gaze sliding to Elouise, who, if she was concerned, gave no evidence of it.

Jeremy's eyes narrowed. "You were looking at the vase," he said. "The one that was a counterfeit."

Dominic nodded. "I was working a case at the time. About that very piece. You turned out to be very helpful to me that night. I should buy you a drink sometime, to thank you."

"I would enjoy that," he said. "It is a pleasure to meet you both. And I suppose congratulations are in order. I understand from Miss Kurt this is to be your new home?"

"It is," Elouise said, turning to the building site. "Everwell is the dearest place in the world to me, and I couldn't bear to be far from it. But tell me about yourself, Colonel. I understand you have a daughter, and I've heard reports from Gemma that she is a bright, talented girl."

And just like that, Elouise had him charmed. It wasn't preda-tory. And in this case, it was completely earnest. It came naturally to her, this gift she had of making whomever she was speaking to seem like the most important person in the world. When harnessed, it allowed the Spinsters to carry out no end of jobs. Elouise used her talent for disguise, along with her natural beauty and warmth to divert the attention of their mark so that the others —normally Gemma—could sneak in and do her part unseen. And that balance had always worked, until now.

The four of them walked back in good company, Jeremy falling back to talk to Dominic, giving Gemma the chance to speak with Elouise. Elouise took Gemma by the arm and the two walked along at easy pace. If Jeremy had any sense at all that anything was amiss, he didn't seem to indicate it. Gemma swallowed the cold comfort.

"I'm eager for news. Do you finally have a date for the wedding?" Gemma asked, desperate to distract herself with more pleasant thoughts.

"We expect the house to be done just before Christmas, so we've just decided. We're going to announce it at dinner tonight."

Gemma stopped and squeezed her friend tight. "Congratula-tions! I'm so happy for you."

"Thank you," she said. "This is of no bigger a surprise than to myself. We just need to find someone who is willing to do the ceremony."

Gemma shared the troubling rumour she'd heard last night while eavesdropping on Mrs. Whitehead. Elouise had always been a confidant of sorts to Gemma, and it felt good to discuss it with her.

"Are you certain?" Elouise asked, her brow furrowed.

Gemma shrugged. "Phillipa said she was choosing not to be concerned about it, but perhaps you and Dominic could investi-gate it? Maybe it is nothing."

"I'll speak with Dom about it tonight," her friend answered. "Hopefully your Colonel Webber can stay in the dark about this caper. Though I suspect he would be understanding and discreet. He has an air about him I find inherently trustworthy."

Gemma paused. Elouise's statement was no small judgment of Jeremy's character. He'd certainly met Gemma's confessions about her involvement in Penny's fall with compassion and understanding. But this job...she come to him under false pretenses, and she'd become so entwined in his life and Ivy's that she had no reason not to think he'd see it as some sort of betrayal. After all, it had been years since the accident with Penny, and Nico had never forgiven her. Why should Jeremy be any different?

"It's hardly a proper caper, Lou," Gemma replied at last. "And it doesn't matter what we call it, because the will isn't there. I'm starting to wonder if Mrs. Lynde was mistaken."

"It's entirely possible," Elouise said, patting Gemma's hand. "They don't all work out, remember. Don't you remember the job with the Swinehard brothers?"

"I do," she replied. It was a building scheme that trapped poor unsuspecting people into buying homes of poor construction. Gemma barely escaped capture—and worse—from that job. Unfortunately, they were never able to find the evidence they required.

"You have the most difficult part of any job, Gemma. You're the pointed edge of the knife. You go where the rest of us can't. Or at least, not as well," Elouise said, then paused, as if struck by inspiration. "Heavens, if you had gone to the charity event the night I met Dominic, you would have picked his pocket so well he never would have noticed. And he wouldn't be here right now."

"But that was different," Gemma protested. "Normally I'm in and out. I can't do the long game. It's getting..." She trailed off, her eyes trailing to Jeremy, who was deep in conversation with Dominic. He looked up then, as if sensing her attentions, and returning them with a smile. A rush of giddy pleasure flooded her, a welcome bit of warmth against the cool autumn breeze. She continued on with Elouise. "...complicated."

"You have feelings for him," Elouise said.

Gemma shook her head and let out a small laugh.

"Oh Elouise, I have many, many feelings for him. Feelings I shouldn't be having."

Elouise's brow furrowed. "Why ever not?"

Gemma sighed. She and Elouise had had this conversation more times that she could count. Elouise hadn't been there that night Penny slipped from Gemma's grasp. She wasn't there to see Penny's broken body, or be refused entry to her room, unable to apologize, to beg for her forgiveness. And in the end, Gemma wasn't even permitted to say goodbye.

"You know why."

Elouise came to a stop, facing Gemma.

"Gemma Miray Kurt," Elouise said, evoking her most stern voice even as she smiled. "You cannot deny yourself a lifetime of happiness because of one single mistake."

"Elouise, you remind me of Jeremy," Gemma protested.

It was Elouise's turn to pause, not bothering to hide her surprise. "You told him about that?"

Gemma nodded, and she could still recall the moment she felt the weight of that secret fall from her shoulders.

"Well then, Colonel Webber is an excellent man indeed," her friend replied, pressing a soft kiss to Gemma's forehead. "We love you, Gemma. You are a good person, if you care to remember it. You must forgive yourself."

And then she remembered what Jeremy had said to her about forgiveness. About fate. He was still learning to forgive himself for being in Egypt when his wife passed away. And Gemma had urged him to do it. For Ivy's sake. For his own.

Could she do the same?

Of course, she'd been lying to him about her real purpose at Hastings House. And she wasn't so certain he would be willing to forgive her for that. But she'd told him about Penny, and he hadn't judged her. If she could find a way to tell him about the will and his friends the Hatchetts without betraying Everwell, she would. It would be easy enough to do, surely.

Except it didn't feel easy. She was on the highwire, heart in her hand. Too terrified to keep going, too far along to turn back.

They returned to the house just in time for supper. The dining room was stuffed to the gills; adults and the children all ate together at tables that had been pushed together to accommodate everyone. The food seemed boundless and of excellent quality and reflected not only European sensibilities but a taste of Caribbean spices, no doubt courtesy of Mrs. Gilman's influence. It was as close to a holiday celebration as Jeremy had encountered since he'd arrived, and certainly the most agreeable he'd had in memory. There was a riotous joy to the place he found unexpectedly intoxicating. It was not disorderly, but neither was it regimented. It just...worked somehow.

He sat next to Dominic Ashe, who proved to be an affable sort with a warm sense of humour the students of Everwell clearly appreciated. They discussed the case he'd been working on when the two met, and Dominic talked with great affection for the women of Everwell, who welcomed his sister-in-law and two nieces into their fold with open arms. Indeed, the eldest of the two was sitting by Ivy, chatting merrily, as if they'd been lifelong friends.

When the last of the pie had been eaten and the tea cups drained, he and Babcock were escorted to a room that could only be described as a book lover's sanctuary. A fire crackled in the hearth, chasing off the chill that had settled in as the sun set. Two walls were dedicated solely to books, and several chairs and a small chesterfield made it the very place to sit on a cool autumn evening to read. The shelves contained an eclectic mix of texts from philosophy to poetry, natural sciences and works of fiction.

"This is an impressive collection," Jeremy said to Mrs. Hartley, who was sitting with Lady Em by the fire. With them were Rimple Jones and Mrs. Gilman.

"Miss Murray is quite proud of it," Lady Em answered, referring to Madeline Murray, whom he met at dinner and was now in the kitchen with Gemma. "Many belonged to Lord Everwell, but we do manage to acquire the odd volume from time to time. My father was not a great reader, though he did enjoy collecting books."

Jeremy was about to respond when a larger blue volume with gold lettering caught his eye. *Redoute.* He paused, the title rousing his memory, though he couldn't place why. It sat on an oversized shelf next to a fine piece of Italian pottery.

"Something catch your eye, Colonel?" Mrs. Gilman asked.

"This volume," he said, picking the book off the shelf. It was a beautifully bound volume, full of remarkable drawings of roses of every imaginable variety. "It's quite remarkable."

"Lord Everwell had appalling tastes in many things," Lady Em said, "But he was quite fond of roses. Indeed, he originally had many varieties planted here, but alas, the weather is not conducive to those we might find in England. Miss Murray, however, has done a spectacular job breeding a few varieties that seem to be quite at home here."

Jeremy turned the pages. On either side of the folio was the identical image—one in ink, the other a full colour print of the highest quality. In a recent inventory of the Lieutenant Governor's Office, several volumes had been unaccounted for. The gardener in particular had mentioned a volume about rose varieties brought by Lady Wentworth during Governor Wentworth's term. The man might be pleased to learn there was a copy here, if for some reason he needed to refer to it.

"Are you quite well, Colonel Webber?" Lady Em asked him. "Should I get Tilda to examine you?"

"For heaven's sake, Emmie," he heard Mrs. Gilman say with a playful chuckle. "He's not sick, just literate."

"Excuse me ma'am." He placed the book back on the shelf where he'd found it and gave his hostess his full attention. "I am quite well. Just engrossed in my own thoughts."

"Young Miss Ivy is remarkably well adjusted," Lady Em

continued. "She seems to be enjoying the company of the other girls."

"That she is. My brother was seeing to her education while I was abroad, but I cannot say her company was particularly varied," Jeremy said. "I have not devoted myself to her as I should have."

"Do not berate yourself on that score," Lady Em said. "Many daughters are of little use to their fathers, particularly of our class, unless it is to secure an alliance through marriage. That you are willing to dote on her is a credit to you."

Jeremy nodded, gratified by her kind words.

"My daughter's happiness means everything to me," he said.

"Ivy would be welcome here any time, perhaps even as a day student. She could have friends her own age," Mrs. Hartley said. "There are, of course, more established schools for girls in town. But for someone of Ivy's temperament, she might do very well here. Our curriculum is well established on the basics—literature, writing, mathematics, science, and the social sciences. But we also put an emphasis on other skills, like deportment, gardening, learning about animals, managing finances, and even art, drama, needle work, and some sport."

"All of this?" Jeremy marvelled. "How many of you are there?"

"Just the five of us," Phillipa said. "And Lady Em and Tilda occasionally lead a special lesson or two. Occasionally Mrs. Ashe, Dominic's sister-in-law, will assist, but she is busy helping Dominic with his consulting business. We all teach several different subjects or specialties. Gemma, for example, teaches languages."

"Don't forget dance," Mrs. Tilman added. "She floats like a bird, that one."

"And handstands," Jeremy said, remembering that first shocking sight.

A curious silence fell over the room as all attention fell on Jeremy.

Miss Jones put a hand to her mouth as if to stifle a laugh. "She taught you how to do a handstand?"

"Heavens no," he replied. "Ivy."

"Well now I'm feeling quite jealous," Mrs. Hartley said, with a warm smile. "I don't think I've ever seen her do a handstand. Perhaps that is something Ivy could teach the other girls."

In truth, Jeremy had given little thought to Ivy's education. He'd expected her to have a governess, as was common with girls of her class. His gaze strayed out a nearby window, where he saw Ivy sitting under a tree with another child who appeared to be the same age. They were talking to each other, pointing up at wonders he couldn't see, sharing a moment of joy. And something in Jeremy's heart broke open. Something fierce. His daughter had made a friend. She hadn't had a friend in so long.

At least he had Babcock. Ivy, he hadn't truly realized until now, had no one. Even her relationship with Gemma wasn't quite friendship. It was mentorship, of a fashion. Even motherly.

Could Everwell provide her with friends and an education? It would have been unusual, but that didn't make it a bad idea. Bringing Ivy to Canada in some small way freed her from the more regimented expectations of class in England. And while the new nation was hardly a bastion of true social equality, it was still much easier for Ivy to have real friends whose parents weren't members of the peerage.

"Colonel Webber," Mrs. Hartley said, breaking through Jeremy's woolgathering. "How do you find Hastings House? I understand the new owners are acquaintances. It is a very small world indeed if that is so."

"We are acquaintances, but only through the most circuitous of routes," he said. "Mr. Hatchett and I attended Sandhurst. He left the army some time ago. However, they were highly interested to learn I was coming to the area. There was some advantage to having someone familiar that could occupy the house while they were focused on settling of the estate."

"I see," Mrs. Hartley continued. "And did you know the late owner?"

"Not at all. I understand he was a bit of an eccentric man," he replied. Hatchett had given him only the briefest of histories of the place. "I took it primarily for its proximity to Government House. They are apparently arriving tomorrow to meet with their solicitor."

The conversation continued on merrily when two children arrived at the doorway. It was Ivy and a girl Jeremy recognized as the girl she'd been speaking with outside.

"May I speak with you, Papa?"

He excused himself and went into the hallway, where Ivy was waiting.

"Papa, this is Sylvie."

"I am very pleased to meet you," he said, bowing to her.

"Colonel Webber, would it be all right if Ivy plays charades with us in the parlour?"

"I think that is very kind of you to invite her," he said. "Of course she can."

Ivy broke into a wide smile then took the hand of her new friend and disappeared into the parlour with an explosion of giggles. The joy in his daughter's eyes as she entered the room allowed Jeremy to hope that his shortcomings as a father had been lessened by this single act of allowing Ivy the chance to play.

The sounds of laughter from the kitchen, which he recognized as Babcock and Miss Jones, alternated with the quiet clinking of plates and cutlery from the dining room. He found himself moving in that direction, with the idea that he could make himself useful to the women of Everwell by moving tables and putting the room back to rights. At least that's what he told himself as he knew, somehow, that it was Gemma's presence drawing him there. Did he really need to lie to himself on that score?

He stood silently in the doorway, his presence masked by the din of the charades in the parlour across the hall, where Elouise

Charming and Dominic Ashe were clearly presiding as the masters of ceremonies. He saw Gemma, stacking some of the larger display pieces and folding linens. She worked alongside Miss Murray, the tall, red-haired woman he'd been introduced to upon his arrival. Of all the people at Everwell, she was by far the most restrained in her manner. She wasn't dour, but it was clear that if there was a subject matter expert on the art of small talk, Miss Murray was not it.

As he stood, he was struck by the most remarkable sensation. Somehow, he'd been in this position before, with these two women, cleaning up dishes at a dinner party. He tried to shake off the feeling—he'd been to so many dinner engagements since he'd arrived that it was hard to remember which. But as Gemma straightened and looked at him, her eyes wide and searching, the sensation had grown even more powerful.

And then he saw the panic take her.

Gemma froze, her body locking her inside herself. It was like the day Jeremy saw her climbing the bookshelf. She was on the trapeze again, watching Penny fall. Watching the net catch her, then collapse, dropping her to the ground like a stone.

She'd ruined everything again. He was going to figure this out —this lie—and this time she wouldn't just lose Penny. She'd lose them all.

Gemma wasn't entirely certain of what came next, except that she felt the steady hand of Maddy Murray on her arm.

"Gemma." Gemma heard Maddy's no-nonsense voice like a beacon in the darkness, pulling her up from the place about to swallow her.

"Will she be all right?" Gemma heard a second voice say. Jeremy's voice.

"She will, in a moment."

Gemma was vaguely aware of the two of them talking. Of motion happening in front of her. It felt like everyone was under water and she was struggling to breathe. Like that night Penny fell.

And then she was aware of a flash of red and smelled Jeremy's scent, and she found herself coming back. Back to herself.

"There you are."

She looked up, and there he was, looking at her with those soft, expressive blue eyes, and a smile that allowed her to breathe once again.

"Here I am," she said, before putting her hands to her face, embarrassment making her cheeks burn. "I don't know what came over me."

Maddy looked at Jeremy and then back at Gemma.

"I have an idea," Maddy answered, but gave no further explanation.

She didn't need to give any. Once upon a time, Jeremy had first laid eyes on Gemma at a dinner party, where she and Maddy were posing as hired staff, cleaning up the dishes in the dining room. They'd been waiting to pass on a message to Dominic, when Jeremy had come upon them. His presence then had left her unnaturally flustered. That he might recall it now left her terrified she'd inadvertently ruined the job. She wanted to say something —anything to distract Jeremy long enough that any sense of déjà vu that had troubled him would pass. Instead, Maddy spoke.

"Thank you, Colonel, for your calm assistance. It appeared you arrived just in time."

Gemma tried not to gape. First, because Maddy was chatting, unprompted, with Jeremy. Secondly, it had been...complimentary. Not that Maddy was necessarily rude, but she wasn't exactly bothered by social graces.

"Not at all," replied, his tone businesslike, and it occurred to Gemma at that moment that Jeremy was much like Madeline in some ways, at least when they first met. Not unpleasant, and not unkind, but not exactly warm, like Dominic, or exuberant, like Nico. But it calmed her.

Jeremy's feelings were often buried deep inside him, but like

Maddy, Gemma knew he cared deeply. He just let those feelings come out differently. Through his art, just the way Maddy brought hers out in her gardens. Or the boxing ring.

And like Maddy, Gemma was coming to realize, that protective streak—that caring, that wanting to protect her from all harm —was strong. It just didn't come out the way it might with someone like Dominic, who wore his heart on his sleeve.

"Ivy has gone to play charades," he said. "And given Babcock is making himself useful in the kitchen, I thought to see if there was something here you would have me do."

"That's hardly necessary," Gemma said.

"It's a little-known fact that early in my career I was given the duty of overseeing some improvements to the Wellington Barracks in Hong Kong, and I was particularly adept at it," he said, the edge of his mouth lifting into a smile. "I am not completely incapable of cleaning up after myself or other people, whatever Babcock might say to the contrary."

He was trying to get her to smile, she realized. And that made her smile.

"Perhaps you should sit in the library and recover," Maddy said, her tone attempting brightness that seemed almost out of character. Gemma knew exactly what she was doing—pulling Gemma out of the dining room would lessen the chance Jeremy might recall their presence at the Coughlins during the Boston Job. "And Colonel, if you could assist here, I would appreciate it."

"That sounds like an excellent suggestion," Gemma said, rising to her feet. Sitting with Phillipa and the others might do her a world of good. She'd been a bundle of nerves since they'd arrived here. It made her clumsy and prone to mistakes. Though she was beginning to wonder if everything she was feeling about Jeremy was a mistake.

Maybe the mistake was getting too wrapped up in how appreciated and wonderful he made her feel. She walked to the door when Jeremy spoke.

"After I am done here," he began, his hands resting on the back of chair, "it will be time for us to take our leave. If you are not well, Miss Kurt, and would prefer an evening or even a day home, with your friends, it is completely understandable. You have not had a day of rest in over a week. We can make do."

Jeremy's offer both tempted and perplexed her. Tempted because leaving Hastings House was exactly what she'd wanted. To stop pretending her only purpose in being there was for Ivy's schooling and Jeremy's piece of mind. What could be better than to sit in the parlour at Everwell after a long day, pick up her wretched needlework, and listen Rimple and Phillipa banter on? To crawl into bed and allow herself to disappear into the comfort of the dark silence of night?

Except that was a lie, too. Gemma didn't love the silence. She didn't love the dark. She'd just become afraid of the spotlight.

"Not at all," she heard herself say. "Your guests are coming tomorrow, and it would be good for Ivy to have someone help prepare her for the occasion."

With the Hatchett's arrival, the disposition of the Dalrymple estate would be complete. There was no need for this curious arrangement to continue. She didn't know if she could make do without Jeremy, and all too soon she would have to learn how.

Chapter Twenty-Four

THE DAY at Everwell had been perhaps one of the most enchanting Jeremy had ever spent in recent memory, for more reasons than he had fingers on which to count them. But it had to come to an end at last, and by the time he, Ivy, Babcock, and Gemma returned to Hastings House, it was dark.

That Gemma had chosen to return with them eased the pain of their departure and set in motion a whirlwind of emotion in Jeremy's chest. He'd tried desperately hard not to read too much into her decision. It might have been duty to Ivy, or even to Everwell, that encouraged her decision return to Hastings House that evening. But it felt like there was something more.

Something that lingered between them, enticing but unsettled.

"That was the best day," Ivy said, breaking Jeremy out of his thoughts. Ivy has been practically bouncing all the way back from Everwell, full of the joyous energy of youth.

"It's a good thing this carriage is well sprung," Jeremy said, giving Gemma a warm sideways glance. "Otherwise, we'd have gone right over at that last turn."

The two had tried very hard not to glance at each other like doe-eyed youth from the moment they'd left the carriage house and returned to the manor. He was thankful for the low light in the carriage, which allowed him to ignore Babcock's sly looks.

"Can we go back tomorrow?" Ivy asked. "I could see Miss Kurt every day, and Miss Jones. She's very smart. She said she would teach me about telescopes."

"My heavens," Gemma interjected, lacing her fingers in Ivy's, which gave Jeremy's heart a squeeze. "I would have thought all that activity would have worn you out, not wound you up."

"It was only a few hours," Ivy said. "I could stay during the week, Papa, and be no trouble to you at all."

Jeremy stilled and he leaned forward, taking Ivy's hand in his.

"Ivy, you have not, nor will you ever be, trouble to me, do you understand?" he said, using all his strength to keep his voice steady. "And if I have made you feel that way, then I must beg your forgiveness, because it is I who have been the trouble."

Ivy squeezed his fingers and gave him a look of indulged tenderness—an expression that reminded him so much of Isla his heart lurched. Instead of drawing away, he allowed the feeling to wash over him, recognizing it for the gift that it was.

"I love you, Papa," she said, planting a small kiss on his cheek. "I was just excited to have new friends. I miss them already."

"Well, I for one am very happy for you to have good friends," he said, settling back in his seat. "But I am not sure there is room at Everwell for a new student. They need the room for the little girls who are not as fortunate as you to have a safe place to sleep at night."

Ivy quieted, considering Jeremy's observation.

"Perhaps you could ask the Lieutenant Governor to give them some money, so they could build more beds," she suggested.

Jeremy paused. It was not a bad idea. Why couldn't he use his influence to gain more patrons for Everwell? Perhaps they wanted their patronage to be quiet. They'd just received a substantial donation from George Coughlin to refurbish the roof, and except for the announcement about the commencement of the project, and a second one at its completion, Jeremy had noticed little fanfare about it. It should have been something they could have used to gain more support. Expand their services. Help others.

Then again, delivering a service that also temporarily sheltered women in need might be part of the reason for the secrecy around the place. Still, there had to be a way. Even if the Society was not always viewed as a cause righteous enough by the standards of polite society, it did actually do good work. Jeremy had much privilege in his position—perhaps there was a way for him to use it.

"But in the meantime, I could speak to Mrs. Hartley about the possibility of you attending during the day," he added. "Though I'm not sure what Miss Kurt would do during the day."

"She could come to Everwell with me, and then we could return home at night," she said, looking at the both of them as if the solution was so obvious it was hardly worth mentioning. And there was something about that arrangement that did seem...natural. Desirable. Having Gemma at home with them in the evening. In his bed at night. Waking up next to her in the morning.

Almost against his will, his gaze slipped to Gemma who seemed to be deliberately focused on Ivy.

"It's late," Gemma said, taking Ivy's hand in hers. "I'd wager that once we're home, and we're back in our own beds, all of this energy will settle back down, and you'll be asleep in no time." She stifled a yawn herself. "We can talk about Everwell in the morning."

Home. There was something about how she said the word that settled in him. It felt so right. So natural. But not Hastings House. The house itself was fine, but Ivy needed a place to run. Jeremy wanted a garden. A place to paint.

When they arrived at Hastings House, there was already a carriage waiting outside. They reached the door just in time to see a very harried Mrs. Whitehead coming to the door.

"Colonel Webber," she said. "We expected you home an hour ago."

"Our departure was waylaid," he replied, piqued by her tone. "Mr. Hatchett has been waiting."

"Hatchett?" he replied. "Wasn't he supposed to arrive tomorrow?"

"He arrived a day earlier than intended," the housekeeper answered. "I told them you'd planned to be home by seven o'clock."

Jeremy took off his hat, and put it in Babcock's hands, and checked his watch. It was nearly a quarter to eight.

"Ivy," Gemma said, her voice low, carefully avoiding eye contact with Jeremy. "Why don't we go upstairs and prepare for bed?"

Ivy nodded, and the two raced up the stairs, while Jeremy walked into his study where his landlord was waiting.

They'd last spoken at Isla's funeral, though there was little Jeremy could recall with clarity. He'd been so overwhelmed with grief and had directed every ounce of his energy toward putting one foot in front of the other. He'd had little time for polite conversation. The two had been school mates at Sandhurst and had stayed in touch over the years, their relationship further solidified when Hatchett's cousin had married into Jeremy's family. Still, it had been a shock when William had offered Jeremy the lease to Hastings House. Their interests were largely split between Toronto and London, the Halifax connection coming via Mrs. Hatchett's relation.

"Hatchett," Jeremy said, extending his hand. "My apologies for keeping you waiting. I had no idea of your arrival."

"So I was informed," he said, looking vaguely put out.

"Well, you are here now, and I trust that Mrs. Whitehead has made you comfortable," Jeremy replied, offering the man a glass of brandy, which he accepted. "What brings you to town?"

"Cleaning up the last of the estate." Hatchett took a sip of his brandy. He shook his head and sat back in his chair. "There has been some nasty business afoot, I'm afraid. And I fear you may have been unwittingly drawn into it."

Jeremy paused, taken aback by Hatchett's declaration. "What business is this?"

"Dalrymple's former housekeeper is contesting the will. She said it's counterfeit."

"That's a serious charge."

"It's slander, is what it is," he said, setting his glass down on a nearby table. "Why on earth would we do such a thing?"

"It is curious," Jeremy concurred, trying to keep his tone neutral. He knew almost nothing of Hatchett's business interests, but Jeremy had seen enough of the world to know men of his class would never consider the interests of the servant class to be anything other than a nuisance. "Why does she suggest the will is counterfeit?"

"She was his caretaker when he was ill. Claimed he wrote up a will that left a chunk of property to her, and the rest of his fortune to an engineering school in New Brunswick, leaving his own family out of it all together." He let go a disdainful snicker.

"And there were no witnesses to this will?" Jeremy said. "That should clarify everything shouldn't it?"

"She claims one of his solicitors notarized it, but he left the city shortly after Edgar's death, which I should add seems highly convenient," Hatchett said. "Perhaps the woman had him killed."

Jeremy couldn't help but laugh at Hatchett's curious leap of logic. "That is highly incredulous, don't you think?"

"If one were going to go to the lengths she has to pursue this ridiculous claim, I am prepared to consider all possibilities. And so should you."

Hatchett's insinuation made Jeremy sit up a little straighter.

"I don't understand."

"There is a rumour that a will, penned by Dalrymple is hidden somewhere in the house," Hatchett said. "And I have it on good authority that the housekeeper's relations have hired a rather notorious thief to retrieve it."

Jeremy paused, recalling that movement in the window he'd seen the morning they moved in. The same one Babcock had admitted to. Ivy's cries of the man scooting down the drain pipe.

"I think we may have encountered them and disrupted their plans the day we moved in, so you should have no concerns on that score," Jeremy said, raising to pour himself a glass of brandy. "Hatchett, if you are certain the will is counterfeit, why are you concerned about it?"

"Because if the signature is genuine, it could tie up the estate in the courts," he said. "We want this settled quickly and quietly. My wife's family has been through enough with her uncle's death. To have his name brought up in such a salacious way is something we are trying to avoid."

"Are you suggesting that Mr. Dalrymple was having an affair with his housekeeper?"

It wouldn't have been the first time such an event would have happened.

"It's entirely possible—you know how women can be. But unfortunately, Dalrymple was a rather unusual man with unorthodox beliefs. Anything was possible," he replied. "I am to see my solicitor tomorrow at two o'clock. He will confirm that all properties owned by Mr. Dalrymple will fall as is natural, into the hands of family. I just pray we are quick enough to see the business done. That's why I came here to warn you."

Jeremy took a sip of his brandy, trying to swallow his impatience at the same time. He was tired, he had an early start in the morning, and clearly there was no more to discuss this evening.

"Warn me? Come now, Hatchett. We interrupted your thief."

Hatchett shook his head, his voice lowering, taking a cautious look at the door.

"I'm not so certain. How much do you know about your so-called governess?"

Anger prickled under Jeremy's flesh. "I don't know what you mean."

"The woman you hired to look after your daughter," Hatchett said, leaning forward. "She's from that Everwell School."

"She is," Jeremy said, trying to remain calm even as every nerve threatened to put him on edge. "Ivy is quite taken with her, as am I. She had done Ivy a world of good."

Hatchett gave a bitter chuckle. "Teaching her the fine art of thievery, no doubt."

Jeremy was certain he flinched. "I beg your pardon?"

Hatchett sat back in his chair but kept his voice low. "There is a rumour that the Everwell Society is run by a former convict. And that she employs women to do her thieving for her."

If Jeremy hadn't just swallowed his brandy, he would have choked on it.

"Your teacher is not some fresh-faced young miss here to teach your daughter, I'd wager," Hatchett continued.

Jeremy was not normally given to outbursts of anger, but he found himself struggling to keeping his temper in check.

"That is the most preposterous thing I'd ever heard," he replied.

"Then why was she snooping around in Mrs. Whitehead's room the other night?" Hatchett challenged.

He had enough of this. Without a word, Jeremy rose and without another word, rang the bell for his housekeeper, summoning Mrs. Whitehead to the study.

"You rang, Colonel?" she said, standing in the door, hands clasped at her front.

"Mrs. Whitehead, my friend tells me you discovered someone in your rooms," he said.

The housekeeper straightened, her mouth in a tight line, and nodded.

Jeremy blinked, a sour note opening in his gut. "And how do you know this?"

"I suspected my rooms would be searched," she said. "She's been going through this house, room by room. She went through mine last night."

Jeremy recalled the night he'd woken, finding her under his bed, and his heart thudded hard in his chest.

"I announced I was going to my ladies' association and left," she continued, "but I didn't go far. I came back and watched her go into my room."

"You locked your door?"

"She picked it," she said. "A lock wouldn't stop her, sir. It hasn't yet."

He'd locked the door to his bedchamber, he recalled. And last night, when she'd gone to make some milk, she'd been there far longer than she probably should have been. The scent of orange blossoms in his study.

Resolve hardened in his gut, wrapping around that niggle of doubt, as if his heart was trying to protect itself from this torrent of inconvenient pieces evidence being laid before him. That the woman he'd trusted with his daughter—and with his heart—was a sham artist? Mrs. Whitehead clearly had William Hatchett's interests at heart, and for that matter, she could have been paid to make these serious accusations against Gemma. Over and over again, Gemma had demonstrated how much she cared about Ivy's wellbeing.

He turned to Hatchett. "All I have are words. I need proof."

Hatchett reached into a jacket pocket, pulled out an envelope and pushed it across the table. Jeremy accepted it. He pulled out a folded newspaper article. The text was in French, and though his grasp of the language was mediocre, he'd decoded enough to read about a young woman who'd been caught after breaking into a small convalescent hospital by crawling through a second story window. Alongside it was the image of the perpetrator. It was unmistakably Gemma Kurt.

Pain, like a shard of ice into his chest, robbed Jeremy of his voice. He swallowed down the rest of his brandy in a single gulp, hoping the fire going down his throat might soothe it. Taking a moment to collect himself, he turned to Hatchett.

"You will excuse me, William," he said. "As you can imagine I have some private business to attend to. I trust you will see yourself out."

He brushed past Mrs. Whitehead and took the stairs two at a time toward Gemma's room. Babcock, who'd been waiting outside the study door, was at his heels.

"I can't believe it," Jeremy heard Harold say through the fog of anger and hurt. "Perhaps there has been some mistake, sir."

There had been a mistake all right. And Jeremy had made it.

"Only in my judgment."

"Sir," he said. "There might be a reasonable explanation for that mugshot. People get caught up in trouble all the time. I mean, back home my cousin was put in irons for spitting on a street corner."

"I know what you're trying to do, Harold, but you and I both know she's been up to something," he said.

"But is it what they say?" Harold asked. "It seems a little fishy to me, Colonel."

"It all seems a little convenient to me," he said. "Do you remember, the first day we moved in? Ivy claimed she saw a man climbing down the drain pipe. I dismissed it as a raccoon, or even a cat. But I thought I saw someone in the window that morning. It was dark."

"It could have been a trick of the light," Babcock said.

"And it could have been Gemma Kurt." He'd watched her balance neatly on the end of a chair. Scale a length of rope as easily as he was climbing these stairs.

There had been a thousand clues. He didn't need to see the picture of her to confirm it.

The night she was caught under his bed. Climbing bookshelves. Isla's book. She'd probably found it going through his things. His life.

He marched to her door, a mix of anger, grief, and betrayal swirling in him. He swallowed hard, buckling down those emotions that she'd teased from him, opening his heart. It had been a mistake to let her do that to him. A mistake to allow her into his life.

He opened the door, the scent of orange blossoms in the air.

And he remembered smelling that, too. That day he was in his office, working on his nightly correspondence. Looking for a letter that had somehow gone missing. A letter from William Hatchett, no doubt warning him that his governess was a thief.

The air was cool, the evening breeze catching the drapes from the open window.

He tore past Babcock, down the stairs, and out the front door, jumping over the iron guardrail. Darkness made it difficult for him to see, but a flash of movement caught his eye, and he ran after it. She might be trying to escape, but he wasn't going to let her. Not this time.

She'd almost made it. Almost.

Her breath was ragged from the pain in her ankle. She'd sprained it several months ago, and in the flurry to escape, she'd landed on it badly. This time there was no carriage waiting for her, so she'd tried to run.

From almost the moment they'd arrived back at Hastings House—the place she'd so foolishly alluded to as home but thirty minutes ago, she'd known something was amiss. As soon as she'd seen Mrs. Whitehead speak to the colonel in hushed tones, and watched him disappear into the study, she knew. The Hatchetts had arrived, and with them, news about the Scandalous Spinsters.

She probably should have run right then, but she couldn't leave Ivy. Summoning her last scrap of resolve, Gemma got the child dressed, and listened to her talk with great animation about her day at Everwell, and how she wanted to go visit again, and her friend Sylvie. She wanted to invite Sylvie for tea. And she also talked about three new places they thought she could search for the will.

Gemma wasn't a crier by nature. But tonight, it was all she could do to keep the tears from falling.

She barely had time to throw her few belongings in her bag before tearing open the window. She didn't even have time to change into her darks, and navigating the descent in a heap of skirts had been treacherous. On the last hop, her foot caught in her petticoat, causing her to miss her footing. She fell, and hard, but there was no time to tend to it.

She'd managed to pick herself, grab her bag, and hobble away. But any exhilaration she'd felt was fleeting. She'd barely made it twenty feet when she felt herself being pulled by a powerful hand on her shoulder, stopping her mid-step, and spinning her around.

"Where do you think you're going?" Jeremy's voice nearly unrecognizable. Cold and hard. Harder even than that day he'd dismissed her from his study.

"I—"

"Don't. Don't play this game with me."

Gemma swallowed, ignoring the ache in her ankle. "Jeremy—"

"Don't call me that."

Though he wasn't hurting her, he had her pinned, his massive frame keeping her in place. Even in the darkness, she sensed the hurt in his eyes, and she forced herself not to look away. There was nowhere for her to go.

"It's not what you think," she said, her heart pounding in her chest. "I was here to recover Edgar Dalrymple's will. And to help you with Ivy."

His throat tightened at the mention of his daughter. "Don't ever say her name again. How dare you come into my home and threaten my family?"

"I never threatened your family," she said. "My job was to help a poor woman to get what was promised to her. This had nothing to do with you. You weren't even supposed to be there."

"I didn't want to believe it," he said, a ragged edge to his otherwise clipped tone. "Hatchett showed me the mugshot."

"I was arrested, in Montreal," she said. "Not long after I ran away."

"For thievery, no doubt."

"I was trying to see Penny."

"Don't bring up that sob story with me," he said. "You were in my home. I trusted you with my daughter. I left you alone with her."

"What did you think I was going to do to her? Murder her in her sleep? That child is dear to me." Gemma straightened, allowing her own indignation to give her strength. "The very last thing I would want is to put Ivy in harm's way."

"And here I thought I was being the ogre, seeing to my daughter's safety and security," he replied, not bothering to hide his bitterness. "My insistence on structured learning. And all the while you were subverting her wellbeing for your own ends."

"I was doing nothing of the sort," she said. "I have been teaching for four years and have taught many dozens of students. I've been taught how by some of the best in the business. How many children have you educated, Colonel Webber?"

"Do you mean the women at that so-called charity of yours?" he replied. "I should report you to the authorities."

She swallowed then.

"Fine. Report me. And then maybe I shall report to the papers about how the Governor General's so-called Private Secretary cannot manage the care of a ten-year-old girl under his own roof. Or should I focus on your landlord's insistence on leaving a woman penniless so he can scrape up every last coin to fuel his gambling coffers?"

He blinked then, apparently not used to the threat. Then again, Gemma was not used to being so threatening. But he had her cornered, and more to the point, he'd cornered the Spinsters.

"Jeremy," she said, daring to say his name. "Do you think a woman of Mrs. Clotilda Gilman's integrity would assist someone to dupe them out of their rightful inheritance? Do you believe, just for a moment, that we would risk so much if we didn't believe with utter certainty that what we were doing was the right thing? I beg you, we can prove the veracity of the story."

He paused, and she realized she might have struck a chord with him, but it was fleeting.

"Even if there is an ounce of truth to any of this, what you did is illegal."

"I didn't break into your house," she said. "You hired me."

"Not the first time," he said. "I knew I saw something in the window that first morning. A shadow. A ghost. I brushed it off as a trick of the light. But it was you. And you were at the dinner party that night. With Miss Murray. I saw you. Christ, were you robbing Coughlin too? The man just made a mighty donation to Everwell. Or did you blackmail him? Is that Boston detective even a detective?"

"Dominic Ashe is an honourable man," she said, anger flaring. "Why don't you ask him about poor George Coughlin and all his money? Do you know what else is illegal? It's illegal for Mrs. Gilman to nurse. It's illegal for me to wear trousers. What is legal is not necessarily what is just, Colonel. Just because you carry a rank doesn't mean you have a monopoly on honour," she said.

"Why didn't you just come to me?"

His voice shook, just a little, his hurt seeping through a crack in the armour he'd put back in place. Why hadn't she come to him?

"You have connections to the Hatchetts," she said with more insistence, as if somehow that past two weeks they had spent together, growing together, hadn't happened. "When you hired me, you gave me a long list of rules to follow. What was I supposed to think?"

"That after fifteen years in military service, I know how to keep a schedule and an orderly home."

"And then there was that letter from the Hatchetts—"

"The one you snuck into my study to steal—"

"I was in your study looking for the will," she insisted. "I saw the letter, and I panicked. You don't understand what it would mean if we were discovered."

He looked away, as if struggling to compose himself, before turning back to Gemma, his eyes narrowed.

"So you admit that Everwell is just a cover for something more nefarious?"

Gemma closed her eyes. God, she was making a mash of this. This wasn't her job—to bat her eyes and lie like Elouise, or even confidently pull on a thread of secrets, like Phillipa. He was right. She had been there to steal things. So she did the only thing she could—tell him the truth.

"Everwell helps people who can't help themselves," she said. "The only thing nefarious about it is how badly these people are treated before they resort to our help. And that happens in plain sight. No one cares. Not really. But we do."

"Don't," he protested, his voice thickening with emotion. "Don't try and turn whatever this is into something noble. You came into my home and played me for a fool. Were you thinking about that when we made love?" he asked. "Or was getting me to fall in love with you part of the plan?"

Gemma paused, as if she'd been struck. That was impossible. She didn't deserve love, ever. She'd hurt the two people she loved the most, depriving them of it. And yet here was Jeremy Webber declaring his love for her.

"You" —disbelief flooded her words— "love me?"

He looked away for a second, and on impulse she reached out to him, but he caught her hand in his.

"You're bleeding," he said.

"It's just a cut. I told you that climbing in skirts is dangerous," she said, attempting a bit of levity. Anything. In that moment she felt like she was up on the trapeze again, Penny's hand in hers, about to lose her grip. "What are you going to do with me?"

In the distance, she heard the sound of oncoming footsteps and the sound of an unfamiliar voice.

"Webber!" she heard. "Did you find the criminal? Does she have the will?"

Gemma held her breath. If she were caught, it would be the end. The end for all of them. She'd ruin it for Everwell even worse than she had for Nico and Penny.

She steeled herself, already making escape plans. She couldn't run with her ankle like this, but she could try.

"She's gone," he said, yelling up the road. He released his grip and started walking up the road. "I ran after her, but the minx was too quick."

Gemma watched, dumbfounded, as Jeremy walked up the road toward a small group of figures coming after him in the dark. She wanted to take some small pleasure in the fact he hadn't turned her over. But there was no time for that.

She had to run.

Chapter Twenty-Five

JEREMY ROSE AFTER A SLEEPLESS NIGHT. Babcock knocked on his door precisely at a quarter to six with a fresh cup of coffee and the morning paper folded and presented to him. They dressed in silence, and Jeremy tried to take solace in his routine. He went through the motions like a pantomime. And truth be told, he felt hollow.

He went down to his study, sat at this desk, and stared at the pile of papers his sergeant had laid out for him. Jeremy picked up the first one from the stack, his gaze unfocused. Several times he found himself staring off into nothing, awash in a rushing tide of his own thoughts and emotions.

It occurred to him, somewhere on the edge of his thoughts, that he hadn't felt this way since Isla died. The grief wasn't quite as profound, but the sense of disconnection and a boundless, godawful ache in his chest was a reminder of his loss. Hadn't he promised himself he wouldn't give his heart again? That no woman would be worth the pain?

Apparently, he'd been wrong. He'd been wrong about many things.

"Where is she?"

Ivy's voice in the distance pierced through the haze of

muddled emotion and lack of sleep, pulling Jeremy out of his slouch. Normally, Gemma would have been helping Ivy get dressed, and the two of them would be heading to the dining room, where the three of them would take their breakfast before the day's business began. With Gemma gone, it was Mrs. Whitehead's job to help her get on with her day. And since he had no idea of who would see to Ivy now, exactly how Ivy would get on with her day had not occurred to Jeremy until this very moment. And maybe it didn't matter. He would put out another advert, find another governess, and this time when they arrived all pretty with a recommendation letter full of unusual experiences that included the trapeze and handstands, he would send her on her way. And he wouldn't care if she coaxed Ivy or the Queen herself from a damn tree.

Better for everyone that way.

Or, at least, that was the lie he preferred to tell himself.

In the background he heard the patter of Ivy's steps as she raced toward the stairs, Mrs. Whitehead trailing behind her. While he couldn't hear the words, the harshness of Mrs. Whitehead's tone was clear. And it wasn't working.

A moment later, the cacophony burst through his door.

"Where is she, Papa?" Ivy asked, running to his desk and placing her hands on the top. The force of her fury made a mess of his desk, which didn't seem to trouble his daughter in the least. "Where is she? Did that mean man get rid of her?"

"Ivy," he said, "you will clean up this mess at once."

Ivy looked at him with a mix of defiance, and, to Jeremy's surprise, panic. "Where is Miss Kurt? She can't go."

Mrs. Whitehead put her hands on Ivy's shoulders.

"You heard your father, girl. Clean up this mess and leave him alone."

Ivy whipped around. "No. You hated her. You helped make her go."

Mrs. Whitehead put her hands on Ivy's shoulders, giving her a violent shake. "You will not speak to adults like this," she said, her voice imperious. "And you will apologize to your father for your vile behaviour."

"Mrs. Whitehead," he said, his voice sharp. "You do not touch, nor parent my child. That is not your job. Do you understand?"

"But sir," she said. "You asked me to tend to your daughter this morning."

"I did," he said. "And I recognize that you are not up to the task. So I will parent my daughter, and you can return to your regular duties."

"I can manage one ill-tempered child," she said. "If that miscreant of a woman had not spoiled her so and introduced what is clearly a horrible example—"

"Mrs. Whitehead, you are dismissed."

She looked as though she was going to say something more but thought the better of it. And while Jeremy couldn't technically dismiss her—she was part of the lease agreement—he could dismiss her from his sight.

When she was safely gone, Ivy gathered up the stack of papers, and put them neatly back on the desk.

"Sorry Papa," she said. "I just got excited. But not good excited."

"I understand you are upset," he said. "But that is no excuse for this behaviour."

"Yes, it is," she said, her voice quivering and her face reddening. "She's gone and it's all my fault."

"The reasons Miss Kurt had to leave are not your concern."

"Yes, they are," she said. "I miss her. Can I not go to Everwell? And see her there?"

"Absolutely not," he said.

"Is it because they are trying to help Mr. Dalrymple's housekeeper? The Hatchetts didn't like her."

Jeremy's gut twisted, anger and confusion waring with something else. A niggling sense of doubt.

"How do you know all this? Did Miss Kurt tell you?" he said. "This is exactly the reason—"

"No. She didn't tell me. I listened, at the door, when Miss Jones and Mrs. Hartley came to visit. And I overheard Mrs. Whitehead talking to Cook."

Jeremy sat forward. "When?"

"The day before Miss Kurt came," Ivy said. "I heard her complaining about some piece of paper, and if they found it, the Hatchetts would be cross."

"Why didn't you tell me about this?"

"Because Miss Kurt would go when she found it," she said. "And I didn't want her to go away. I like her, and she likes me." She put in head in her hands. "And now she's gone, and it's all my fault."

"How is this your fault?"

"I found them. The papers she was looking for," she said, her voice partially muffled. "They were hidden behind a brick in the fireplace in my room."

Jeremy blanched. "What?"

Ivy raised her head, tears streaming down her cheeks. "I found them a few days ago. I should have told her, but I wanted her to stay with us. I didn't want her to leave, like Mama did."

Jeremy's heart cracked right in two. He'd been so concerned with his own welfare, with his own grief, that he'd forgotten somehow, that Ivy had her own. She'd kept her mother's secret, out of fear that if she told everyone she was dying, it would be so. And she'd done the same thing with Gemma.

He got up and pulled his daughter into his arms.

"Here's my secret," Jeremy said, bending down to brush the hair out of his daughter's eyes. "I didn't want her to go either."

"But why did you let her leave?"

Why did he let her leave? Because she'd lied to him. Because she had left him out of her life, a life he had no business inviting himself into. It dredged up an old hurt, opened the wound, and on reflex, he pushed away the very person who'd help to heal it in the first place.

"I don't know," he said. "Come, show me the papers you found."

❀

Jeremy walked up Spring Garden Road, Babcock at his heels, the sun stretching over the tree-lined lanes of Spring Garden Road. Ivy was holding his hand, clutching a piece of paper he'd torn from the Halifax Chronicle that morning.

"Papa," she said, "you're walking too fast. I can't keep up."

He looked down at his daughter, her braids swinging wildly as she practically ran to catch up with him.

"Sorry my pet," he said, modulating his strides. "I was a little too focused on getting to our destination. What street does the advertisement say?"

"Eleven Birmingham Street," she read off carefully. "Are we hiring a detective?"

"Possibly," he said. "Mr. Ashe was at dinner, don't you remember?"

After the occasional stop to ask for directions, they made their way to Birmingham Street. On the corner stood a square, flat-roofed wooden house painted a rather remarkable shade of blue with clean white trim. A sign to one side of the door read "Dominic Ashe & Associates, Consulting Detective." Satisfied he was in the right place, Jeremy rang the buzzer. He didn't wait long before he let in by a young woman, perhaps the same age as Gemma, with light brown hair, fair skin, and a sprinkling of freckles across her nose. He recognized her as Clarice Ashe, Dominic's sister-in-law, who had been at dinner yesterday with her daughters.

"Good morning," he said. "I am hoping to speak to Mr. Dominic Ashe, if he is about. I sent a message up here earlier this morning. Jeremy Webber is calling."

"Colonel Webber." Jeremy's attention was immediately caught by the sound of his name. Behind Mrs. Ashe was the man himself.

"Mr. Ashe," he said. "Thank you for seeing me on such short notice."

Dominic beckoned them inside.

"I suspected it was urgent. Good day to you, Sergeant," he said, shaking Babcock's hand, then turned his attention to Ivy. "Miss Webber, it's good to meet you again."

Ivy offered her hand, and he shook it.

"You have to help us," she said. "We have to help Miss Kurt."

If Mr. Ashe had a reaction to Ivy's plea, he hid it well.

"Do you mind if I speak with your father and Sergeant Babcock privately?" he said. "Unfortunately, my nieces are at school right now, but Mrs. Ashe could take notes from your findings and we could compare them?"

Mrs. Ashe held out her hand. "Why don't you come with me and tell me about Miss Kurt?"

Ivy seemed to be placated by that and left with Dominic's sister-in-law.

"Come this way," Dominic said, leading Jeremy and Babcock into his office where he sat at his desk and offered them a seat. Jeremy declined—he was too bloody anxious to sit. Babcock looked at the chair, then to Jeremy, and continued to stand.

"Sit, Babcock," Jeremy said.

"I can't sit," the man protested with all the indignation of a gentleman being forced into a morning suit at afternoon tea. "A sergeant doesn't sit when his colonel stands. It's not done, sir."

"Gentlemen," Dominic began, a bemused expression on his face, then turned to Jeremy. "I would ask what brings you here, but I suspect one of two things. And it's not the first that has you looking like you want to crawl out of your out skin."

"I didn't realize I was so bloody obvious," Jeremy grumbled.

"Once a woman pulls on you like that, I don't know if it's possible not to be," Dominic replied with a grin. "You look like you need a drink, but the sun's not quite over the yard arm."

Jeremy looked past him to a bottle of whiskey that sat on a

shelf. It looked far too tempting and, he reasoned, it was probably not quite noon in London. Did that count?

"I need answers, Ashe," he said, pacing the floor in front of his desk because he had to do something to keep himself from crawling out of his skin. "How good are you at looking at fake documents?"

"Not bad," Dominic answered. "I do know someone who is an expert, though, if I can't tell. Is this about the will?"

Jeremy shouldn't have been taken off guard by Dominic's casual knowledge about Dalrymple's will, but it stung. He shook his head.

"I think I'm the last person living at Hastings House to know anything about it," he said. "Maybe the entire city."

"Don't be so hard on yourself, Colonel," Babcock said with a warm smile. "You were still in a relatively new position in a city you didn't know, moving into a new house, trying to raise Miss Ivy whom you hadn't see in an age."

"Your sergeant's right," Dominic said giving Babcock a nod before turning his attention back to Jeremy. "When I first arrived, I didn't even have a decent pair of shoes on my feet. You're miles ahead."

If he hadn't been absolutely certain he appreciated the American detective before, Jeremy was rapidly changing his mind.

Jeremy nodded to Babcock, who pulled an envelope out of the portfolio he'd brought. It was made of fine paper and had a red seal on back. Babcock pushed it across the table to Dominic, who instantly sat up with interest.

"She found it," Dominic said.

Jeremy shook his head.

"Ivy did." He swallowed his mixed emotions about the discovery. "In her room."

"She's quite clever, Miss Ivy," Babcock added, beaming like a proud parent. And in some ways, Babcock had been just as much of a parental figure for Ivy as Jeremy.

"Well then," Dominic replied as he carefully unfolded the small packet of papers. "Maybe she does have a future with Everwell. Unless she wants to work for me."

Jeremy pulled his lips into a tight smile. He could imagine Ivy being a part of a group of smart, strong-spirited women. Hell, he could imagine her leading one.

He watched Dominic pore over the papers, written in a neat but very tight hand. However, it was clear that the will was very thoughtful in nature, and that the majority of his properties, including a tract of farm land to the north, were bequeathed to those other than his own relations, whom he clearly had significant distain for.

"Is it genuine?" Jeremy asked.

"His law firm would know," Dominic said. "His own lawyer, Jennings, has been out of town for months, but they would have other records there."

"I also have this," Jeremy nodded to Babcock, who produced another piece of paper and placed it on the desk. "Gemma found it."

Dominic studied the writing, which was a recipe for oatcakes that Edgar Dalrymple had transcribed. To Jeremy's unpracticed eye, handwriting matched.

"No wonder the Hatchetts were happy to you have you let the place," Dominic said. "They expected you to unwittingly protect their claim simply by having you occupy the house. They probably expected you to be their ace in the hole, as it were—guard the place before the wolves could come and sniff it out."

"I'd wondered about the arrangement with Mrs. Whitehead," Jeremy said. "And her aversion to Gemma's presence."

"Yes," Dominic said, then sat back in his chair, eyeing Jeremy with undisguised mischief. "So, what is the situation with you two?"

Jeremy wanted to roll his eyes. Trust an American to get straight to the bloody point. Except he was, quite uncharacteristically, aching to talk about Gemma with someone. If only to make sense of it all.

Babcock, bless him, being the model of discretion, took his leave under the guise of wishing to speak with Ivy. But not before giving Dominic a wink.

"She left." Jeremy sunk down into the chair at last, overwhelmed by his grief and self-loathing over his missteps. "William Hatchett was waiting for me when we returned from Everwell and wasted no time with their accusations. She probably overheard—the woman moves like a cat on the prowl. She tried to escape, but I caught her and she told me everything. I felt like a fool. This entire thing happened under my nose. She couldn't trust me enough to tell me, and I know that's not her fault. I understand what this red coat means to some people. I know I have a certain way that does not invite people to share their secrets with me. I've been—"

"Alone."

Jeremy nodded, allowing Dominic's observation to settle. "And I'm bloody tired it."

There. He'd said it.

"I thought it would be easier, after my wife died. I loved her," Jeremy continued, then paused, thinking of Isla. "I still do—the memory of her."

Dominic shuffled in his chair.

"Look," the detective said. "Far be it from me to tell you how to live, but I know my brother loved Clarice more than anyone or anything else except his girls. But he'd be damned if he didn't want to see her be happy after he was gone. You're a big man. There's got to be room in that heart of yours for someone else without squeezing out the space you have for the woman you happened to love first."

Jeremy nodded, then gestured to the documents on the desk.

"The Hatchetts have a two o'clock meeting with their solicitors. We must get this to a probate court first, before the assets are further dealt with. I need to take the will to Everwell. They will know what to do with it. And I need to talk to Gemma."

"Gemma. What did you do to her?"

Jeremy rose to his feet and turned around to see Elouise Charming. The calm, relaxed manner she wore yesterday had been replaced with a tension that furrowed her brow creased the skin around her eyes. In a flash, Dominic was on his feet and crossing the room, his focus on the woman he clearly loved.

"Nothing," Jeremy said, "except go out of my mind with worry. What's happened? Is she safe?"

Elouise turned from Jeremy to Dominic. "I got a panicked message from Maddy and Phillipa. Gemma came back to Everwell last night."

"How is she?" Jeremy asked, recalling the cut on her hand. "I shouldn't have let her go, but I was more afraid she'd be caught."

"In body, well enough," she replied, her gaze hard on Jeremy. "But her heart was a different matter. She told us about the Hatchetts. She was so upset. Inconsolable in a way I've never seen. Phillipa tried to make her seen reason, and we thought by nightfall she'd be settled. But when we woke this morning, she was gone."

Jeremy's heart thudded.

"Where?" Dominic asked, looking from Elouise to Jeremy. "Would she go back to her family?"

"Possibly," Elouise said. "But I have no idea where they are. Gemma said they were always travelling."

"I will find her," Jeremy walked over to Elouise and looked her in the eye. "I swear on my life. I made this mistake, and by Christ I will fix it."

She looked from Jeremy to Dominic, who nodded.

"Right, we need a plan." Jeremy rubbed his hands together, turned to Dominic, and pointed at his desk. "Ashe, I need your desk for two minutes."

Jeremy sat, was given a pen and paper, and scrawled a hasty, but he hoped sufficiently detailed message to the Lieutenant Governor. It was, no doubt, a highly inappropriate use of his access to the man, but Tupper was a lawyer and he had power. It was time for him to use it in a way that mattered to Jeremy for a change.

"Babcock," he said, "take this packet, along with this letter to the Lieutenant Governor. Tell him he needs to look at it directly and explain the circumstances. Take this second letter to the offices of Chapman and Kent. Tell them that the Hatchetts are about to involve them in a case of fraud, and that it has been reported to the highest of authorities."

He scrawled out another note, looking up at Dominic. "Do you have any reliable contacts in the press?"

"Reliable?" Dominic scratched his chin, then looked to Elouise. "Ben Miller at the Halifax Herald, perhaps."

Elouise considered the suggestion. "He's definitely not afraid to take on a challenging story, though he's probably not our favourite."

"Is he not reliable?" Jeremy asked.

"He's not afraid to publish stories that put the paper's owner in a less than complimentary light," she said, "which I suppose is something positive about his character. He did a feature on Everwell a few years ago which was not the most flattering, though I think that was simply a case of putting on what he considered a 'puff piece' rather than 'serious journalism'. But I'd wager he's reliable enough."

"Excellent," Jeremy said. "Babcock, if you do not get anywhere with Tupper or the lawyers, send this to Mr. Miller at the Herald. And let them know your intent to carry out my orders."

Babcock straightened, saluted smartly, and walked out the door. "Miss Charming, I believe your client's property will be secured before the sounding of the noon gun."

"Thank you," she said, though it was clear that Gemma's whereabouts were the far greater worry. "We should regroup at Everwell. I am certain Phillipa has a plan—she always does. But dear heaven, Gemma could be already stowed on a ship somewhere and there are hundreds in the harbour. You know Gemma."

Jeremy paused. He did know her. He knew every curve in her

body, every detail of her face. He knew she liked black coffee and disliked clear tea, and that she'd never had the opportunity to apologize to Penny Adamos before she died.

"Where is Penny Adamos buried?" he asked.

His question clearly shocked Elouise and Dominic.

"I'm not sure," she said, her demeanor less guarded. "Somewhere in Montreal, I believe. That's where the letter was postmarked when she received the news of her death."

"With respect," Jeremy said, "I think I know where she might be headed. But there are probably half a dozen ships in port right now that would be heading up the Gulf of St. Lawrence."

"The Harbour Master should have that information," Dominic said, looking at Elouise. "With any luck, we'll find her."

After ensuring that Mrs. Ashe was able to watch Ivy until their return, the three were out the door, in a cab and driving toward the waterfront. Halifax was a remarkably busy port, and Jeremy forced himself not to lose hope that searching for Gemma would be like finding a needle in a proverbial haystack.

He let out a breath, forcing away the creeping despair. He'd lost love once. He'd be damned if he'd lose it again.

Chapter Twenty-Six

GEMMA WEDGED herself between two large trunks in the cargo hold. She was far slower than she should have been, but her ankle, while now taped thanks to Tilda, still throbbed. After she'd arrived home last night, she'd been fussed over by Rimple, and tended to with great care, which included a stern motherly word or two from Tilda and Lady Em. She was to rest for at least a fortnight. In bed, foot up. No climbing, no balancing off the edge of a piece of furniture, and no dancing.

Gemma had nearly burst into tears at the very thought of dancing. Sometime over the past week or so, some part of her dared to imagine Jeremy taking her in his arms and whirling her around, confidently guiding her around every obstacle, allowing Gemma to bathe in the joy of being in his embrace. A pang of regret caught in her chest. It had been a fantasy, she realized, but it might have been nice for it to be real.

And now it never would be. Jeremy had realized he'd been used, and worse, that Ivy had, even tangentially, been involved. And like Nico, like Penny's parents, he would never forgive her.

But she would find them—her brother, and Mr. and Mrs. Adamos. She was going to tell them what happened. Maybe they wouldn't forgive her, but just maybe she could start to forgive herself and find a little peace. After that, she didn't really know what she would do.

She heard banging from around her, as more cargo was loaded into the hold. The S.S. Sardinian was a brand new ship, and as a passenger ship, would be the perfect place to conceal herself for the four-day trip up the Gulf of St. Lawrence. Soon, they would do an inspection, looking for stowaways. For one last time, she would make herself invisible, as she'd always done.

And then she would be done hiding.

The sound of approaching footsteps caught Gemma's attention. She froze, listening for their cadence. A scuffing might mean that more cargo was being loaded, while the quick click of heels probably meant a final inspection. She waited, holding her breath.

Click, click.

Gemma strained, trying to interpret the sound. Somehow, there was a sharpness to the stride that struck Gemma as familiar. Too familiar.

"Gemma?"

Jeremy. His voice was urgent, with worry, she realized, not anger. But she didn't move. She was frozen even as the war in her heart raged.

"If you're here," he said, "just say so. Everyone's terribly worried about you. All the teachers at the school. Ivy. Babcock. And selfishly, I may be under threat of mortal peril from Elouise Charming if I don't find you."

Gemma swallowed the guilt bubbling up in her throat. She'd left a note—she thought too much of them all to leave without a word. But to hear Jeremy's voice now, on their behalf—

"Everyone at the school wants you to know that you are loved. And wants to know you're safe. They respect that you may wish to move on. But—" His voice faltered there a moment. "I'm not sure I can be that magnanimous."

She put a hand to her out mouth while tears pricked at the corners of her eyes.

"Or at least, I don't know that I can be that stoic about it," he said, his voice thick with emotion. "But no matter. This is not about what Ivy needs, or I need. Gemma, I don't want you to run because you think you've made a mistake. You haven't. But even if you had, the people who love you would forgive you and want you to come home. I want you to come home."

She shuffled, the implication of his words settling on her like the wonder that first snow, making her shiver with delight.

He loved her.

"Well," he said, and somehow, she could hear the smile on his face. "Perhaps I have just confessed my feelings to luggage trunks and mail sacks. Which is fine, because I'm not good at expressing my feelings this way and I probably should have practiced—"

"It was perfect," she said from her hiding place. She pulled herself up over the trunk and emerged, her movements clumsy, her foot throbbing.

She slid out, stumbling, and started to fall.

He caught her.

"It was perfect," she said again, blinking away the tears stinging her eyes. "As is your timing."

He ran a finger along her hairline, his smile warm and comforting.

"I love you," he said. "I know it's sudden for me to say, and it's probably even more foolish to admit it, but I love you. I think I have from the first moment I saw you."

"I love you, too," she replied.

A whistle blew in the background.

"We should go. I asked the captain to hold the departure until I left."

Gemma blinked. "And they agreed?"

He gave her a sheepish smile. "I may have stretched the truth when I said that I was here on official Government House business."

Gemma was certain her mouth fell open. "Colonel Jeremy Webber, did you hold up a passenger ship for me?"

"I would hold up a dozen if it meant finding you."

She reached up and kissed his cheek. Her ankle protested the movement, producing a sharp stab of pain, making her wince.

"Come," he said, scooping her up in his arms. His command was, she had to admit, a little thrilling. "I'm taking you back to Everwell. If I don't produce you—"

"I know," she said. "Mortal peril."

"I would take you back to Hastings House," he said, "but I am busy making other arrangements for where Ivy and I am going to sleep tonight. I may avail myself of the good will of the Navy and apply to stay at Admiralty Hall until I can find a new situation."

"What happened?" Her mouth gaped and she could feel an apology coming, which he silenced with a kiss.

"I'll explain once I get you out of here," he said. "Babcock is waiting and he's going to come after me if I don't produce you soon. And I'm not particularly interested in a trip to Lower Canada in a cargo hold."

He set her down only long enough to retrieve her sack, then swooped her back up and carried her out onto the dock. And even though she probably looked like an absolute crumpled mess, with bleary eyes and a throbbing foot, it all felt terribly romantic.

Amongst the hubbub of the busy wharf, she heard Elouise as they came down the gangway.

"Gemma!"

Gemma raised her head and saw Elouise, her arms flailing madly. Her smile was positively dazzling as usual, and beside her was Dominic and a very relieved Harold Babcock.

When she got to the bottom of the gangway, Jeremy barely had time to put her down before Elouise pulled her into a generous hug.

"You silly, silly girl," Elouise whispered into her ear, before planting a kiss on her cheek. "Don't you dare for a moment think our world is better because you've left it."

Gemma hugged Elouise. "I'm sorry I scared you, Lou."

"Enough apologies," Elouise said. "We're just glad you're safe."

Elouise turned her attention to Jeremy. "Thank you for taking care of things, Colonel Webber."

"It's Jeremy," he said. "There is nothing I wouldn't do for her. And, I hope, in the modest interest of my self-preservation, that presenting her to Everwell may ensure that I can continue to take care of things."

They piled into a cab at the end of the jetty. Jeremy helped Gemma onto the seat, and she savoured the comfort of his body next to hers. They rode in silence for a bit, relief flooding through Gemma, making her drowsy. Still, she had a thousand questions about what had happened with the Hatchetts. As if sensing her thoughts, Jeremy reached into his pocket, producing a packet of papers, and put them in her hands. Gemma's eyes widened.

"Where did you find these?"

"Ivy found it," he said, then looked a little contrite. "And she owes you an apology, because she found them two days ago."

"Where?"

"In her room." Jeremy took her hand and kissed it. "But she held on to them, because she knew you would leave, and she didn't want you to. Neither do I."

Her vision blurred with tears. Tears brought on by exhaustion, relief, and love.

"I don't either," she said, wiping her tears with a handkerchief that Sergeant Babcock produced as if by magic, and pressed into her hand. The carriage headed off toward Everwell, and on the journey, Gemma was filled in what had happened with the Hatchetts. Apparently, it was a lot. And Jeremy took care of it all. Including appealing to the Lieutenant Governor.

"He was going to resign his post if his Honour didn't agree to help him with this business," Babcock said, positively beaming with pride at Jeremy. "Which of course he did."

Gemma sat up, ignoring her ankle against Elouise's protest.

"You blackmailed the Lieutenant Governor?" she blurted out, incredulous.

"It was hardly blackmail, Gemma," Jeremy replied. "It was

merely a negotiation tactic. Besides, George Tupper—his Honour—is a lawyer by trade. He has his eccentricities, but he's generally a decent man. If you read through the will, which Babcock, bless him, did in great detail, my so-called friends the Hatchetts were not just defrauding your poor Mrs. Lynde. Turns out most of his properties and estate had been doled out to other members of his staff, as well as an academic institution in New Brunswick, Mr. Tupper's home province."

Gemma blinked, trying to let it all sink in, including the knowledge that Jeremy risked his position to help them. "What about Hastings House?"

"It turns out it was left to a local engineering society, to be used as a residence for underprivileged students in need of accommodation. I've already sent a note informing them of the situation, and that I intend to quit the place so they can take ownership before the end of the week."

Gemma fell back into her seat. It was all too much.

"But the Hatchetts?" she asked.

"The Hatchetts are sitting at the Duke of Wellington right now, railing about injustice or some such thing. And I assume they have Mrs. Whitehead with them," he replied. "That recipe for oatcakes helped confirm Dalrymple's handwriting. But as an engineer, he would have signed off on countless blue prints across the city. We have plenty of evidence to make any further suit untenable."

Gemma shook her head. "I was so certain I'd failed."

"Quite the opposite," Elouise said, giving her friend a warm smile. "If it weren't for you, none of this would have happened. You were the perfect person for the job."

"So what now?" Gemma asked.

"The Lieutenant Governor agreed at on the spot to be the executor of the will," Jeremy said. "He represents Her Majesty, so he can do that."

Gemma was incredulous. "He has time for that?"

Babcock laughed. "Of course not. Colonel Webber will do it on his behalf."

"More work?" Gemma asked.

Jeremy shrugged. "Composing letters alerting people that they've been granted a bit of wealth they didn't know was coming to them can hardly be considered onerous, don't you think?"

Gemma couldn't help but pull a smile. He was such a good man. And she loved him.

"Poor Mrs. Whitehead. I think she assumed she'd be housekeeper at Hastings House, and now? I shouldn't be happy about that," she said. "She was an employee of theirs. She didn't have power in this situation."

"She had power over her own opinions, and she used them to slander you and Everwell at every opportunity," he said, not bothering to hide his indignance. "You're far more forgiving about it than I am."

Gemma shuffled in her seat. Jeremy gently raised her ankle, supporting it between his knees, rubbing the back of her calf with a soothing touch. Still, she thought about the accusations she'd overheard about Everwell. Was it just the overactive imaginations of a bunch of sanctimonious women caught up in their own virtue? Or had the exploits of the Scandalous Spinsters managed to escape into the society gossips? How had the Hatchetts discovered the rumours? Had they come from Mrs. Whitehead, or through another route?

The conversation turned to more pleasant topics, and Gemma decided she would leave those concerns for later. When they finally arrived back at Everwell, the entire household greeted the carriage.

"Well, Colonel Webber, it turns out you are more than just a handsome face and a fine pair of shoulders stuffed into a red coat," Lady Em said, beaming as the carriage door opened. "Thank you for bringing Gemma back to us."

Jeremy scooped her out of the carriage, following Phillipa upstairs to her room, and laying her gingerly on her bed.

"I have a bit of business to attend to," he said, giving her a kiss on her cheek. Heavens, she could get used to this. He turned to Phillipa and the others. "You will look after her while I'm gone?"

"We'll spoil her rotten, I promise," Elouise said. "Thank you."

Dominic bid his goodbyes, leaving the Spinsters to themselves.

"I like him," Maddy said, completely out of the blue, to the surprise of—well—everyone.

"I do, too," Gemma replied, savouring that warm fuzzy feeling that came from thinking of Jeremy. "I'm sorry I ran away. I just assumed I ruined everything, and I didn't want you to get caught up in my mess."

Phillipa took Gemma's hand and sat down on the edge of her bed. "Gemma, I asked you do to something you were clearly not comfortable doing, and that wasn't fair. If there is any fault, it lies with me."

"And you didn't ruin anything," Rimple said as she handed Gemma a strong cup of tea. "The papers were found, and they will help even more people than we thought. You made the colonel fall in love with you, and he's handling all the nasty legal business. You couldn't have had this work out more perfectly if you tried."

"I didn't make him fall in love with me," Gemma protested as she took a long sip of perfectly brewed tea.

"How could he resist those doe eyes of yours, or that tender heart?" Phillipa said, patting her leg. "I'd have fallen in love with you, too."

Gemma laughed. "This wasn't part of your plan, was it?"

"I would like to take credit for that, but alas, no."

Gemma set down her cup, sobering, and reached out for Phillipa's hand.

"What about those rumours about Everwell?" She paused, the memory of Mrs. Whitehead's accusations infringing on her contentment. "You said you chose not to care about it, but perhaps we should."

"I agree it's concerning," she said. "There is probably little more to it than gossip, but perhaps Dominic could make some discreet inquiries on our behalf."

"I'll talk to him," Elouise said.

A knock at the door interrupted their conversation. There was Tilda, with Ivy.

"Someone wanted to say hello."

Instantly Gemma's chest swelled at the sight of the girl, who ran straight into her arms.

"You're back!" she said.

"I am," Gemma said. "I'm sorry I left without saying goodbye. That was terribly wrong of me."

Ivy nodded through tear brightened eyes. "I'm sorry about the will. If I had given it to you when I found it, you wouldn't have hurt your leg."

Gemma took both her hands into hers and looked her in the eyes. "It's not your fault, Ivy. You were afraid I was going to leave. In the end, the important thing is you found the will and gave it to your father, even when you thought he might be cross with you. That was very brave. You have nothing to be sorry for."

"Papa said we have to get a new house," she said.

"You and your papa could stay with Dominic until you are settled," Elouise offered. "There is plenty of room, and Clarice's two girls would love your company. And then you could come to school here. Gemma would still be your teacher, but you would have me, and Rimple and Maddy as well."

"We will have to talk to Mr. Ashe and your Papa first," Gemma said, then looked up at Elouise. "But that is a lovely offer."

"But what about at night?" Ivy asked. "Who would read me stories at night?"

"Well, your papa would," Gemma answered. "In fact, I know he would love to."

"But I like it when you do it," Ivy said. "He doesn't make the voices like you do."

Gemma's heart squeezed.

"How about we let Gemma have a little rest?" Elouise said, hopping to her feet and holding out her hand to Ivy. "Perhaps we can practice a little dramatic reading downstairs, so that you can read to her sometime, and do all the voices yourself."

"Do you think I can?" Ivy asked, eyes wide.

"Who do you think taught her?" Elouise asked, giving Gemma a wink.

Apparently satisfied, Ivy took Elouise's outstretched hand and left, leaving Rimple and Maddy for company.

"I'm glad you're back," Rimple said, taking Gemma's hand.

"I do need to leave," Gemma said. "Just for a little while."

"What do you mean?" Maddy said, her gaze intense.

"I have to make my peace with Penny's parents. And with Nico," she said. "I was never able to apologize for what happened. I need to do that."

"What if they can't forgive you?" Maddy said.

"I don't expect them to. But I need to start forgiving myself. And the only way I know how is to share what really happened," she said. "I want them to hear the truth. If they can't forgive me, so be it."

Maddy's lips pressed into a thin line, and for a moment Gemma thought she was going to say something. She seemed to be struggling with her emotion, which was so out of character Gemma was tempted to remark on it, but thought better of it.

"If you need someone to accompany you, I'll go," Maddy said. "I wouldn't mind a few days alone to read."

Gemma looked up at Rimple, who merely cocked an eyebrow.

"I'd be careful about your books, Maddy," Rimple said. "Colonel Webber was a little too interested in your new book on roses that you added to your collection recently."

Gemma's eyes widened. Maddy had a passion for collecting books. And the last time she'd 'collected' one, she'd gone on a job with Elouise—at Government House.

"Did he?" Maddy said, then turned on her heel and made for

the door. "Gemma, I like the colonel, but he's not to have my book. Understood?"

"I'm not keeping any more secrets from him," she said. "But I'm certain the two of you can come to some kind of arrangement."

"Very well," she said. "I'll let him have my copy of The Art of War I borrowed from George Coughlin's library during the Boston Job. I'll make it a wedding present."

Gemma gaped, unsure what to react to first—the borrowed book Gemma didn't even realize was stolen, the fact she was gifting any of her treasured tomes, or Maddy's allusion to a wedding. "Who says we're getting married?"

Maddy shrugged and left, leaving Gemma to wonder if the world truly had turned upside down.

Chapter Twenty-Seven

꧁꧂

IT WAS after dinner by the time Jeremy returned. The hours had been spent in a rather uncomfortable visit with Hatchetts, their lawyers, and a judge whom the Lieutenant Governor claimed owed him a favour. The will Ivy had found was the authentic document outlining Dalrymple's dying wishes.

He'd returned to Hastings House to find Mrs. Whitehead had already vacated. The place should have been just as it always was —nothing had ostensibly changed since yesterday, but with both Ivy and Gemma gone, the soul of the house seemed gone as well. He sat down at his desk, making some immediate plans to vacate the premises, to find a suitable home for he and Ivy.

And for Gemma too, if she would have him.

After discharging the first of his duties, he and Babcock took a cab back to Everwell to collect Ivy. Thomas had offered him a guest suite at Government House in the interim, but he'd politely declined. He'd already lived for work. He needed a place to be away from it. To paint. To play with Ivy.

To sit and talk with Gemma, while he painted and she did handstands or whatever it was that made her happy. To make love to her.

"I'm certain you'll find the right spot," Babcock said, interrupting his thoughts. "Who wouldn't want to lease a place to a fine gentleman such as yourself? They always know the place is going to be spic and span with a military man about."

"I won't be an officer for long," Jeremy said. He'd also decided to resign his commission and hang up his red coat. It was a decision he'd mulled over since Isla had passed away, but he was never ready, until now. He'd made the decision with Babcock and offered to hire him as his personal valet and butler.

"Why do you put up with me, after all this time?" Jeremy asked, as they sat in his office. "Heaven knows there must be easier men to work for."

"Perhaps," Babcock said, circumspect. "But I would prefer to work for a good one, sir. And you're a good one. And a safe one, if truth be told. I can be myself around you, and that means something to a man like me."

Jeremy nodded, acknowledging that simple, if ugly truth. If Babcock's inclinations were outed in some way, it would mean the loss of his military pension at the very least, and prison or death at worst.

"And you need lookin' after," Babcock continued. "You're so busy looking after every else's details, you need someone to see to yours. It might as well be me. But it doesn't only need to be me."

"Babcock," Jeremy said. "You're giving me that look."

"Do you mean the one that's telling you something you already know?"

"That's a bit on the nose, isn't it?" Jeremy said. "Honestly, I used to command hundreds of men. Now I can barely command you. I am clearly losing my touch."

"Are you going to ask for her hand?"

Jeremy nodded. "Is this a betrayal, do you think?" he asked, a lump forming in his throat.

"To Mrs. Webber you mean?" Babcock cocked his head to one side, looking at him with all the tenderness of a mother hen. "The woman who hid her illness from you so you wouldn't deprive yourself of a lifelong dream to see Egypt? She loved you, sir.

Loved you enough to make sure your heart was full. I don't think she'd want you to be alone, sir. Let me ask you this. If you and Miss Kurt married, and had a child together, would you love Ivy any less?"

Jeremy looked at his sergeant in wonder. It was a simple, elegant question, but it drew away the last vestiges of doubt—not in his love for Gemma, which was as real as the cab he was sitting in. But about the place Isla had in his past. In a move that no doubt surprised his valet, Jeremy reached over and pulled the man into a warm embrace.

"Of course not," he said, releasing his sergeant. "You, sir, are a prince among men. Thank you."

"Now you're just trying to get into my knickers," Babcock said with a laugh.

"If you weren't my valet, and I wasn't hopelessly attracted to women, I wouldn't have waited this long to try."

Babcock blushed and then left to make arrangements to pack up the house.

The shadows were long by the time Jeremy and Babcock returned to Everwell. The house was bathed in the soft, warm glow of the sun as it was beginning its descent. A feeling of calm settled over Jeremy, even as anticipation reared at seeing Gemma and Ivy.

He barely had his hand to the door when it opened, and they were greeted by the warm presence of Miss Rimple Jones.

"Colonel Webber and Sergeant Babcock!" she said, "Come in. Have you eaten supper?"

The two men stepped inside and removed their headdresses.

"We had a small bite," Jeremy said. "Do not trouble yourself."

"It's no trouble," she said, "and Sergeant Babcock looks in need of refreshment. How about I bring you up a cup of tea and a bowl of something, and you can check on Gemma?"

"How is she?" he asked.

"She's in the library, foot up, telling some of the girls a story,"

Miss Jones said, pointing down the hall, a warm smile on her face. "Including Ivy."

"Thank you," Jeremy said, forcing himself not to run down the hall. There he found her, lounging on a small chaise, several children around her, including his daughter. Sitting next to her, in a corner, was Miss Murray. She had her head down, apparently flipping through pages in a book, but he was aware she was watching Gemma intently. Guarding her.

Her gaze flicked to him, and he acknowledged it with a nod.

"...and he huffed, and he puffed, and he blew the house down!" she said in a dramatic roar, which caused a giggle of excitement around the room. "But the house was made of brick, so nothing happened."

"He should climb up on the roof, and sneak in another way," one of the girls popped up.

"He sneaks in through the chimney," another proclaimed. "And falls into the fire."

"Oh no," the first girl said. "That's sad."

Jeremy raised his eyebrows at that. Normally the wolves weren't the heroes in that, or any story.

"Well, it's not very smart to climb down a chimney," Ivy declared with a level of authority Jeremy recognized. "If it were me, I would have picked the lock on the window."

"I think," Gemma said, her gaze flicking up toward Jeremy, "that perhaps we can finish the story later?"

Ivy followed her gaze and bounced up from her place on the floor.

"Papa!" she said, giving him a bright smile. She ran to him and wrapped her arms around his waist, then looked up at him. "I've been looking after Miss Kurt, just like you said. Did you show the will to the Lieutenant Governor? Is everything going to be better now?"

"Thank you, yes, and I think so," he said, his gaze straying to Gemma, who was watching him intensely. "The document you found will help a lot of people, Ivy. Well done."

She paused. "Does this mean we need to find a new place to live?"

"It does," he said. "But we have a little time to look."

"We could live here, with Miss Kurt. I could go to school, and you can stay in Foster's old room."

Jeremy smiled. Living here at Everwell sounded like a wonderful, and truthfully a slightly terrible idea. Terrible only in that he couldn't imagine being under the same roof as Gemma and not having her in his bed.

"Girls," Miss Murray said. "I do believe it is study time. And since the library is occupied, perhaps we can use back porch for our quiet time."

"Can I go with them, Papa? For just a little while?"

"Of course," he said, then recalled the item he'd stuffed in his jacket pocket. "Miss Murray, a moment."

She turned, possibly taken aback by the sound of her name on his tongue. Her stance was guarded, like a soldier on watch duty assessing if the person uttering words in the dark were friend or foe.

"Yes?"

He produced a small volume and held it out for her inspection. He'd found it at Hastings House amongst his book collection and decided it could be better appreciated elsewhere.

"A thank you, for your assistance. And perhaps, a nice addition to your collection."

She looked down, her brow dipping into a deep vee as she took the book and carefully opened the front cover, then look up at him again, her guarded expression gone, replaced by the smallest hint of a smile.

"Thank you."

Without ceremony she turned, leading the small parade of students out the door, each one of them giving him a look that clearly suggested they were inspecting him. The last to leave was Miss Murray, who walked past him with a quick nod, and shockingly, closed the door behind her.

Gemma looked at him with amazement.

"You have a friend," she said. "Congratulations. That is not easily done."

"Is that what that is?" he said.

"You brought her a book," she said. "Careful, because I'm sure she'd take that as a sign of affection."

"I think she knows where my affection lies," he said. He walked across the room and kneeled down next to her feet.

"Do you mind?" he asked, gesturing to her ankle.

"I've been waiting for your touch," she said, blushing.

A thrill rippled through him at both her words and the flush of modesty in her cheeks as she uttered them. If they were alone, he thought, he would give her everything she was waiting for. With a small pack of girls on the other side of the door, it would have to wait.

He lifted the hem of her skirt, gently feeling around her ankle. It was wrapped by an expert hand—Mrs. Gilman's, he assumed.

"How is that?"

"I doesn't hurt too much, especially if I don't walk on it," she said. "Maddy has become even more of a mother hen than Phillipa."

"Miss Murray is a good friend," he said. "You are lucky to have her."

"We all are," she said, then closed her eyes as he gently massaged her calves. "There are probably a thousand places I want you to touch, but right now this is the most perfect thing and I don't want you to stop."

"I won't, then," he asked. "But truth be told there are about a thousand scandalous things I'd like to do to you."

"Well, I am a Scandalous Spinster, you know," she said with a twinkle in her eye.

Jeremy paused.

"What?" she said, her smile stalling. "Is something wrong?"

Jeremy cleared his throat. "How would you feel about not being a spinster anymore?"

She looked at him, and he watched her eyes grow bright with unshed tears as the meaning of his question took hold.

"I love you, Gemma. And I didn't think I'd be able to love anyone again. But you literally walked into my life and from the first moment I saw you—before I even knew you were you—you captivated me."

"I thought I irritated you."

He laughed. "Irritated, and probably flabbergasted me. But between all of it, you stole my heart. And I've never been happier."

"Well, this is the Everwell Society of Scandalous Spinsters *and* Wayward Women, so I should be able to stay," she replied playfully, before her expression turned more earnest. "Jeremy, I want all of you. The man. The father. I want to marry you."

Jeremy let out a ragged breath, gratified by the implication. Being with Jeremy meant also being with Ivy, and her acceptance of them both meant more than he knew how to say.

He shuffled closer to her, kissing her, and tasting salty tears that had run down her face.

She kissed him back, tender at first, until the passion they'd both been holding back took the reins. He wanted to take her somewhere and make mad love to her, kissing every curve, tasting every inch of her soft, gorgeous flesh until she called out his name and they both collapsed in a haze of spent pleasure. Instead, he broke the kiss, the taste of her lingering on his lips.

"I should do the proper thing and talk to your father, or perhaps Lady Em and Mrs. Gilman," he said, chuckling softly. "I don't even know the rules in a situation like this."

"I don't belong to anyone," she said. "Except you, and Ivy."

"Well, that's a relief, I suppose. I don't have to explain to anyone I'm about to be temporarily homeless. Not a terribly good way to start off a marriage."

"I'm certain a fine upstanding young man with your impeccable references will have no trouble at all finding a suitable place

MICHELLE HELLIWELL

to live," she said. "But Ivy is right...we do have Foster's old room. Dominic stayed in it for a time."

"Maybe I should," he said. "Except I don't think I could keep from wanting to sneak into your room at night like some randy school boy. I'm not nearly as quiet as you are."

They talked and kissed for a little while longer, and Jeremy for once was excited about what the future might hold. There were options, not plans. And whatever plans they made, they would make together.

"I want to go see Penny," she said, out of the blue. "To say goodbye properly. And see my brother."

Jeremy paused, idly stroking the skin on the underside of her wrist.

"I will take you," he said without the blink of an eye.

"You don't have to," she replied. "I'm strong enough to do this alone."

"I have no doubt." He raised her wrist to his mouth and pressed a small kiss to it. "But you don't have to."

"What about your duties to the Lieutenant Governor?" she said. "His schedule? Your dinner with the American Consul General? The Earl of Newport?"

"We have several weeks between those events," he said, appreciating that the timing of those events may have been a blessing in disguise. "The dinner is in a few days. In the meantime, I'll see to the arrangements and we can be off immediately after."

She shifted her weight on the settee and rested her head on his shoulder, a sensation that felt so good Jeremy thought he could stay crouched here beside her forever.

"I just want to say goodbye to her properly," she said. "Speak to her parents. I need to find a way to forgive myself, and this must be part of it."

"Are you certain?"

"I was part of the accident that caused her death. They deserve to hear my apology, even if they cannot forgive me."

"As I said," Jeremy whispered as she pressed another kiss to her temple, "bravest person I know."

"And maybe I can see my parents again," she added.

"We should marry before we go," he said. "And we could have a little honey moon. I could humour you with my horrible French."

It was Gemma's turn to blink. "Are you certain? Isn't that a little spontaneous for you?"

"Not at all," he said. "If you consider that I probably fell in love with you the first day you walked into Hastings House, and since we'd become acquainted months ago at that Coughlin's fellow's house party, I'd say this is terribly well thought out."

"Acquainted?" Gemma let go a laugh that brought a smile to his face. "I think that's overstating it, wouldn't you think?"

"Not at all," he said. "Mere details, my love."

"Well," she replied, a devilish look coming over her that made Jeremy want to whisk her away back to the carriage house and make love to her somewhere wildly inappropriate, "please share your plan, since I'm certain you've formulated six options by now."

"Only one, but it must meet your approval," he said with deadly seriousness. "I met a naval captain earlier this year at one function or another. He could marry us. I'd leave Babcock to find me lodging, and perhaps I could make a request that Ivy stay here for a couple of weeks. I'd pay for her room and board, of course. Then we go to Montreal, you introduce me to your family. We could book a first-class cabin and make love all the way there, and all the way back."

"That is quite the schedule," Gemma said. "An excellent one."

"Do you approve?"

She threw her arms around Jeremy and laughed.

"I do."

THE END

Thanks for reading!

I hope you enjoyed *A Captivating Caper*, Book Two in my *Scandalous Spinsters* Series. If you haven't yet, try *A Dangerous Diversion*, and introduce yourself to the Everwell Society and meet Elouise Charming and Dominic Ashe.

Stay tuned for Maddy's book, *A Tantalizing Treasure*, coming in 2023.

Reviews are welcome - and super important to indie authors, and helpful to readers as well, so you if can leave a review, I'd be super grateful! Feel free to post one where you purchased the book, or on Goodreads.

My website is www.michellehelliwell.com, and you'll find me on Facebook and Instagram as well. Join my mailing list and get a heads up on new releases, and special giveaways that are only for my subscribers.

Read the Scandalous Spinsters...

A Dangerous Diversion

Elouise isn't just Charming by name...being Charming is THE job

When trouble strikes Everwell Manor, headquarters of her fellow Scandalous Spinsters and the only real home she's ever known, being charming isn't enough. Especially when the job calls for her to pick the pocket of a handsome blue-eyed stranger at a high society function.

After a suspicious fire killed his brother, Detective Dominic Ashe pointed the finger at one of Boston's elite and found himself out a job. With his reputation in tatters, he's come north in a last ditch effort to find justice and maybe a little peace...but he's unprepared for the well heeled beauty who seems determined to get in his way.

When Dominic is injured helping Elouise's students, she wonders if she can trust the illusive American with her secrets. But trusting a man has only led Elouise to ruin...and Dominic doesn't know how to deal with a woman who doesn't play by society's rules.

The clock is ticking...will Dominic steal Louisa's heart? Or is Dominic little more than a Dangerous Diversion?

Available at Amazon and select online retailers. Ask your local bookstore or library to order your copy!

Enchanted Tales

All titles are available at Amazon and select online retailers. Ask your local bookstore or library to order your copy!

Not your Average Beauty

When beauty is a curse, only love can break the spell

Stephen Pembroke, the Marquess of Barronsfield, believes that where his love of beauty goes, death follows. Cursed to a loveless existence, and with his legacy at stake, Stephen makes a desperate proposal of marriage to Rosalind Schofield, his steward's new ward - and the plainest girl he has ever met. Rosalind has spent a lifetime being overlooked for prettier faces. When she is singled out for her lack of beauty by the Marquess, she begins to doubt if she is deserving of the love she inwardly craves.

When unusual things start happening around her, Rosalind can't help but wonder if Lord Barronsfield or his curse are who and what they appear to be. When she openly challenges Stephen about the curse, he begins to doubt everything – and comes to realize that this apparently plain, ordinary woman is not as unremarkable as he believed. Strange things *are* happening in Barronsfield. As they move closer to the truth, Rosalind unwittingly finds herself in the sights of the real beast in Barronsfield, and Stephen must decide if his growing love for Rosalind will be his salvation or her doom.

No Prince Charming

Love is the fairest of them all

Dashing off in a daring elopement with a prince handpicked by her mother, Lady Gwyneth Snowdon anticipates a lavish future. But when a mysterious stranger kidnaps her, Gwyneth fears her happy ending is doomed.

Used by his maniacal father, Edmund Pembroke turned his back on society. Seizing the opportunity to say good-bye to his past forever, he makes a deal to separate the pampered countess from a gold-digging imposter. But when Edmund discovers her life is in danger, he is forced to protect the beautiful, well-born Gwyneth Snowdon and to confront his ghosts.

Separated from her plush surroundings, Gwyneth learns she's capable of so much—including love for a man with neither title nor fortune. But she begins to suspects there is more to her rugged, handsome guardian than he's chosen to reveal. After finding herself at the center of a sinister deception, can she dare to trust her heart to a man who's spent years deceiving himself?

Never Trust a Rogue in Wolf's Clothing

A heart all the better to love her with...

After three torturous seasons, Lady Eleanore Pembroke is finished with husband hunting and happy ever after. Following the scandal of a broken engagement, eager to bury herself in her work at the local infirmary, she returns home shocked to discover their trusted physician gone, replaced by a dashing scoundrel. Bastien DuMont is a talented doctor, but Eleanore senses his restless heart. She's no longer prepared to risk hers, nor the trust of the people who've come to depend on him.

Caught up in a revolution that dissolved into terror, Bastien learned that devotion is for fools. On the run from a growing list of men who'd love to see him dead, he's forced out of the shadows and into the shoes of a respectable country physician, putting him under the scrutiny of Lady Eleanore, a local do-gooder immune to his roguish charms. When a mysterious figure emerges, threatening his life and the safety of those around him, can Bastien hunt down his opponent before he becomes the prey? Or is exposing his heart the greater danger?

About the Author

Michelle Helliwell started writing her first novel, a time travel fantasy, when she was 15. She moved on to half-hearted attempts at something more literary, then nearly gave up on the writing all together until one fine day in 2005 a co-worker put a romance novel in her hands and told her to "get over yourself".

She did, and the rest, as they say, is history.

Michelle lives with her husband and two sons in Nova Scotia, Canada where moody weather and bagpipes are plentiful, but alas, guys in puffy shirts are too few.

Find all my books at
www.michellehelliwell.com